WORLD'S END

WRITTEN BY
JAKE HALPERN AND PETER KUJAWINSKI

HOUGHTON MIFFLIN
HOUGHTON MIFFLIN HARCOURT
BOSTON NEW YORK 2011

Houghton Mifflin is an imprint of
Houghton Mifflin Harcourt Publishing Company.

www.hmhbooks.com

The text of this book is set in Aldus Roman.

The illustrations were created digitally.

Library of Congress Cataloging-in-Publication Data
Halpern, Jake.
World's End / written by Jake Halpern and Peter Kujawinski.
p. cm.
Sequel to: Dormia.
Summary: After learning that his presumed-dead father may still be alive, Alfonso
Perplexon, now fifteen years old, takes on the dangerous task of returning to the land
of Dormia to search for him.
ISBN 978-0-547-48037-4
[1. Sleep—Fiction. 2. Adventure and adventurers—Fiction. 3. Fantasy.] I. Kujawinski,
Peter. II. Title.
PZ7.H16656Wo 201 [Fic]—dc22 2010008129

Manufactured in the United States of America
DOC 10 9 8 7 6 5 4 3 2 1
4500263800

To my mother for always,
always believing
—J.H.

To my wife, Nancy Celia Rose,
I love you till the end
—P.K.

CHAPTER 1

BENEATH THE STREETS OF PARIS

THE SOUND OF TEENAGERS giggling and snickering echoed through the well-swept stone passageway. The ruckus grew louder and louder until, finally, the pleading voice of a French tour guide called through the darkness: "Attention, mesdames, monsieurs. Silence! Please, be respectful, we are among the dead!"

The teenagers, however, paid no attention. They all hailed from the same small town in northern Minnesota and none of them had ever been to Europe. Today was their first full day in Paris and they were simultaneously too exhausted and too keyed up to listen.

The tour guide was leading the way down a long passageway

that tunneled deep into the earth, far beneath the Montparnasse neighborhood of Paris. Electric lights shone at regular intervals, bathing the stone walls in a harsh glare. Droplets of cold black water dripped from somewhere overhead. The air smelled dank, musty, and metallic.

The tour guide, a short woman with shoulder-length gray hair, glared at the students.

"If you don't behave," she loudly whispered, "we'll have to leave. These are the catacombs, after all. Have you no respect?"

She was about to continue her lecture when a profound silence came over the entire group. The students had reached the end of the hallway, which opened into a dark vault with an arched, buttressed ceiling and a dirt floor. In the middle of the vault was a stone statue of a woman holding a child. The child appeared either sick or unconscious, or perhaps dead. A sudden uncertainty came over the teenagers. Slowly, they stepped into the darkness of the vault. Several of them gasped as their eyes became accustomed to the gloom. The walls of the vault were piled from floor to ceiling with human skeletons: forearms, tibiae, femurs, clavicles, spines, and skulls.

The French tour guide nodded her head in approval. Now she had their attention. She turned on her flashlight, asked everyone to gather around her, and began talking about the catacombs of Paris. At one point in time during the nineteenth century, the cemeteries of Paris were overflowing, explained the guide. To solve this problem, the city's gravediggers unearthed all the bodies from Paris's three largest cemeteries and placed them here, in a giant hollowed-out mine, below the Place Denfert-Rochereau.

"And now, here we are, in the world of the dead," whispered

the tour guide. "We are standing in this mine, a kilometer underneath the busy streets of Paris, surrounded by millions of lives now many centuries gone. Look around, and think of them. Think of what they saw, who they loved, and what they created."

She looked at the teenagers' awed faces and knew the catacombs were having their intended effect. With a small fling of her head, she led the way deeper into the subterranean vaults, stopping only once to point out a stack of conspicuously tiny skulls of long-dead children. Finally, these American students were quiet! The tour guide tied her scarf a little tighter around her neck and quickened her pace.

Of the two dozen students in the group, one of them lagged behind, walking quietly. This was fifteen-year-old Alfonso Perplexon. Three years had passed since his quest to find Dormia, and now he was back overseas, albeit on a rather tame class trip. Alfonso was very much a teenager these days. Recently, he had gone through a growth spurt, and he was now tall for his age. He was thin, almost gaunt, and he wore his hair long so that it often dangled over his dark green eyes.

One thing had not changed about Alfonso: he was still shy. He had always preferred reading a book or cross-country skiing by himself to playing football or going ice fishing with the other boys his age. It wasn't that he didn't like people. He enjoyed good company when he could get it, but he hadn't found much of it in World's End. The things that interested Alfonso—books, maps, puzzles, and all matters related to sleeping—held no interest for his peers. Alfonso enjoyed some popularity when he did spectacular things in his sleep, like tightrope walking on a set of icy telephone lines, but it had been a long time since he'd done anything like that. In recent years, Alfonso had been sleeping like a normal person, for eight hours a night, in his bed, on his back.

But, suddenly, as he made his way deeper into the catacombs, Alfonso was overcome with an overwhelming urge to fall asleep. Why now? And to what end? He tried to stay awake, but it was no use. Alfonso's eyes rolled back into his head, his eyelids fluttered, and he let out a soft, barely audible snore. And that was that. He was asleep. Well, not quite asleep. He was in a sleeper's trance—the sort that only Dormians entered. His awkward movements instantly turned both delicate and precise, like that of a cat stalking prey. Alfonso slowed his pace, letting the group drift well ahead of him, and then he darted down a side passageway that appeared to be a dead end. But it wasn't. The passageway merely narrowed into a crawl space and then continued deeper into the earth. The passageway intersected with others, but Alfonso navigated his way with great speed and certainty. His sleeping-self knew exactly where to go.

After about ten minutes, the crawl space opened into a large room with a small wooden door that looked as if it led to a utility closet. The door was cracked open, revealing a dim light. At that very moment, Alfonso's eyes opened wide, and he woke up. He glanced around uneasily, trying to get his bearings. *Where am I?* His thoughts were interrupted by the sound of a woman's voice. It was a deep, craggy voice—the voice of a woman who chain-smoked and had damaged her vocal cords with decades of inhaling the hot smoke of tobacco. She spoke to Alfonso in French, which he spoke reasonably well.

"Hello, my young friend," said the woman. "You are a Wanderer, aren't you?"

Alfonso spun around. The woman wore workman's overalls and a helmet with a miner's light. Her face was filthy with dust. She was middle-aged and rail thin. She inhaled the dregs of a cigarette with Chinese lettering around the butt and threw it to the dirt floor.

"What are you talking about?" asked Alfonso.

"I've been following you for the last several minutes," rasped the woman. "You have been sleepwalking with great speed and dexterity. You must be a Wanderer. Do not worry. I am a Wanderer too. There are several of us Dormians who have infiltrated the excavation crew."

Alfonso's mind was racing. This woman was apparently a Dormian—and not just that, she was a Wanderer. Very few Dormians ever left their native land. Every twelve years, however, on an occasion known as Great Wandering Day, a handful of Dormians called Wanderers were sent out into the world. They were an elite band of men and women who agreed never to return home or see their loved ones again, in order to protect the interests of Dormia abroad. He wondered whether he should tell her that he wasn't a Wanderer—he was something even rarer, a Great Sleeper.

"You are awfully young to be a Wanderer," continued the woman. "But, apparently, you have been drawn here like the others. Let me show you what we have found. My name is Sophie, by the way. Stick with me and no one will bother you."

Alfonso nodded appreciatively, but said nothing. Sophie led the way through the small wooden door and Alfonso followed closely behind her. His feet made a noise, as if they were stepping on something metal. He looked down and gasped. He was standing on a metal landing, near the top of a cavernous vaulted room. Several hundred feet below him, accessed by a slender staircase attached to the platform, was a giant hole in the ground. It was a perfect hexagon, lit up on all sides by electric torches. The hexagonal hole dropped into the earth as far as the eye could see.

A great throng of workers, perhaps as many as two hundred in total, were scurrying up and down ladders and working feverishly within the hole itself—stringing up lights, collecting soil samples, taking photographs, and building a makeshift elevator that would descend into the hole.

"Incroyable," said Sophie, "N'est-ce pas?"

"What is it?" asked Alfonso.

"We don't know," replied Sophie. "The catacombs that tourists like you visit were put here only in the last hundred years. Before that, all of Paris lay above a series of honeycombed mines. Perhaps this is part of that same honeycombed system, but I doubt it. The shape—and depth—are so unusual. Other mine shafts go down a few hundred feet. They are also circular. This one is a perfect hexagon. It also goes down three miles, and then veers northeast toward France's border with Germany. Did you know that geologists have discovered other mine shafts just like this one in other cities—Prague, Warsaw, Copenhagen, and Vienna? All of them burrow into the earth and then head in a northeastern direction. Spooky, isn't it?"

Alfonso stared at the hexagon. "All of them are the same shape?" he asked.

"Yes," replied Sophie. "Even stranger, the geologists have used carbon dating to determine that these shafts were all dug around the same time—roughly two and a half thousand years ago. And this, curiously enough, coincides with a period in which a great darkness reigned over most of northern Eurasia."

"A darkness?" inquired Alfonso. There was a slight tremor of fear in his voice.

"Yes," replied Sophie matter-of-factly. "In the history books, apparently, this time is often described as the Cataclysm of Eurasia. They say, several millennia ago, ninety percent of the population of Europe and Asia died rather precipitously. The human race came close to being wiped out entirely in those two continents. The soil went completely barren. All plants withered. Starving men committed great atrocities and depravities. It made the Dark Ages seem positively enlightened. By all accounts, and there aren't many of them, it was an awful time."

Alfonso said nothing for a long while. "So tell me," he said finally. "Why have all these Wanderers from Dormia come here?"

"Ha!" said Sophie with a dry laugh, as she lit a fresh cigarette. "I was hoping you might be able to tell me."

CHAPTER 2

CHILLY WATERS

THANKS TO HIS SLEEPING-SELF, which had apparently done a great deal of hustling, Alfonso had managed to rejoin the group without drawing any suspicion. He and his classmates spent several more days in Paris and then took the *Train à Grande Vitesse*—a high-speed train that averages two hundred miles per hour—south to the port town of Marseilles. As the train sped southward, Alfonso's thoughts remained fixed on the Wanderer named Sophie, and the giant hexagonal hole underneath the catacombs of Paris. What had caused this hole? And why had both Sophie and Alfonso been drawn there?

The first day in Marseilles was uneventful—a museum, a boring history lecture in the hotel lobby, a quick dinner, and then off to bed. The next day, however, the French club had a delicious, three-course lunch in the old city, where crumbling four-story buildings lined narrow, cobblestone streets. After their meal, the students boarded an old, decommissioned tugboat to take a tour of Marseilles' busy harbor. Alfonso felt overly full from lunch. As he sat in the bright sun, it was all too easy to put his head back and close his eyes.

Alfonso woke up from his nap feeling unsteady and vaguely aware that he was balanced precariously on the edge of something.

"Alfonso Perplexon!" shrieked a familiar voice. "Alfonso, have you lost your mind, mon cher? Get down from ze railing at once! Immédiatement, I say!"

Alfonso blinked cautiously and opened his eyes. He was perched on the railing of the tugboat, staring down into the water below, as if he were about to take a dive. Gusts of wind howled across the whitecaps.

"Alfonso!" cried the voice again. "I order you to git off of ze railing—tout de suite!"

Alfonso looked down and saw the French club's chaperone, Madame McKinnon, screaming at him in her French accent. Alfonso found it strange that Madame McKinnon always spoke with a French accent even though she was born and raised in St. Cloud, Minnesota, and had only been to France once before, on her honeymoon. In any case, she looked upset. No, *upset* wasn't the right word. She looked insanely angry.

The old captain of the tugboat didn't look too happy either. "Imbécile!" he snarled. "Idiot!"

At that very moment, Alfonso also noticed an insufferable redheaded boy named Charlie, who was urging him to jump. "Go on, do it, sleeper-boy!" sneered Charlie. "Do it like the old days! Want me to get your pajamas?" A few of Charlie's pals guffawed at this. At one point in time, Charlie and Alfonso had been friends, sort of. Charlie was one of the many kids in World's End who had once been fascinated by the bizarre and amazing things that Alfonso did in his sleep. But ever since Alfonso had started acting like a normal kid, most of Alfonso's so-called friends had abandoned him.

"Alfonso, mon cher, if you don't come down, right zis instant, I am zending you directly home to Minnie-zota!" hissed Madame McKinnon.

"Ce n'est pas drôle!" muttered the old sea captain.

"Okay, okay," said Alfonso drowsily. "I'm getting down right now. I promise. I don't know what..." But he never finished this sentence. Instead, he felt himself being pulled downward into a deep, dank well of utter blackness—a place where lingering thoughts and even dreams dissolved into nothingness. It was a place beyond sleep. He tried to fight it, but it was no use. His breathing slowed, his eyelids closed halfway, and then he leapt headlong into the choppy waters of the Mediterranean. It was a perfect dive and as soon as he surfaced, he began swimming with astounding speed toward a rusty freighter anchored several hundred meters away. The stern of the freighter was emblazoned with a Romanian flag and the name *Somnolenţă*.

"Mon dieu!" gasped Madame McKinnon.

The old ferry boat exploded into pandemonium. Charlie was jumping up and down and screaming that his "friend" was drowning. The other members of the French club began shouting and pointing. Madame McKinnon rushed to the bow and yelled at Alfonso in a voice that—quite suddenly—seemed to have no French accent at all.

The commotion attracted the attention of a motorboat belonging to the Marseilles Harbor Police that was idling nearby. The police gunned over to Alfonso and picked him neatly out of the water. Alfonso's hands and legs still moved in a swimming motion until the police laid him on the floor of the boat. At that point, Alfonso opened his eyes and looked up at the faces of three concerned police officers. He had no idea where he was or how he had gotten there. Despite the fact that he was shivering, he still felt drowsy. Alfonso sensed the pull of sleep, a deep hypnotic draw, like the undertow in the ocean. In the distance he could still see the Romanian freighter *Somnolenţă*, and the mere sight of it filled him with an inexplicable longing. His sleeping-self had risked his life in a feeble attempt to reach that boat. The only question was, *Why?*

That night, Madame McKinnon led her students back to their hotel, a nondescript brick building overlooking the old port. Fittingly, it was named Le Vieux Port. The hotel appeared to be in a bad neighborhood. It sat across the street from a pharmacy that had been robbed the night before and, when Alfonso and the others returned from their boat ride, several police officers were questioning the hotel clerk as to whether he had seen any suspicious activity.

Alfonso didn't pay too much attention to the police because he had other things to worry about. Presently, a red-faced Madame McKinnon was informing him that she had just made arrangements for him to return home to Minnesota—tout de suite! At dinner, Alfonso sat by himself. Charlie and his gang of friends huddled at a nearby table, giggling and talking about Alfonso. In a loud voice, Charlie claimed Alfonso was drunk from French wine when he jumped off the tourist boat.

Alfonso didn't mind them; he was far too preoccupied with what had just happened in the harbor. Why, wondered Alfonso, had he fallen asleep and leapt into the chilly waters of the Mediterranean? Why was his sleeping-self acting up all of a sudden? The previous night, for example, he somehow had managed to gash his right hand in his sleep. The cut required six stitches from a local doctor, at the rate of thirty Euros a stitch.

Alfonso knew intuitively that there must be a reason for his sleeping antics—there was always one. He suspected the reason involved Dormia. Alfonso's sleeping-self was mysteriously and inextricably connected to the Founding Tree in Somnos. Alfonso sensed that the tree was pulling him, beckoning him into slumber. Even now, as he sat in the hotel's dining room, sleep was descending on him.

He finished his food quickly and walked to the fourth floor, where he and Charlie shared a small hotel room. It was a stroke of bad luck for Alfonso that Charlie had been assigned as his roommate for the entire trip. Their room was tiny, with barely enough space for two beds. To make matters worse, the walls were very thin, so thin that Alfonso could hear a young couple next door having a heated disagreement. It didn't matter. Alfonso was tired enough to sleep through nearly anything. He sank into his narrow bed, pressed his face into the sheets—which smelled faintly of cigarettes and cheap cologne—and immediately drifted off to sleep.

By the time Charlie entered the room, Alfonso was out cold, snoring loudly in apparent harmony with the room's hissing radiators. Charlie loudly harrumphed and "accidentally" bumped into Alfonso's bed, but Alfonso did not stir. Charlie gave up and soon fell asleep as well. The rest of the night went by uneventfully, until dawn broke.

It was at that moment that Alfonso got up from bed and began to dress. In less than a minute, he silently packed his backpack and made his bed. He yawned and walked to the door. His eyelids trembled in a half-closed position. Anyone who saw him would have thought that he was sleepwalking. The door creaked open and in the blink of an eye, Alfonso vanished.

Some time later, Charlie woke up and realized Alfonso was gone. For some reason, Charlie was trembling, even though it was quite warm in the room. A whistle blew from a ship in the distance.

"H-Hello?" whispered Charlie. "Alfonso? Are you there?"

No answer. Charlie was spooked. He turned on the light and saw the neatly made bed.

The whistle from the harbor blew again. It was the same Romanian freighter that Alfonso had swum toward the previous day, the *Somnolență*, and it was about to leave port. Charlie looked out toward the noise. He squinted hard. In the distance, he saw Alfonso running squirrel-like across the heavy rope line that lashed the freighter to the port. The rope shone with morning frost, but Alfonso never lost his footing. When he reached the freighter, he dove into an open porthole. Moments later, the rope fell into the water and the freighter pulled out of Marseilles' old harbor into the open seas of the Mediterranean.

CHAPTER 3

STOWAWAY

ALFONSO YAWNED AWAKE in a dim swath of light, rolled over onto his side, and suddenly cried out in pain. Instead of the mattress in Le Vieux Port, he felt coils of coarse rope and various sharp objects underneath him. Confused, Alfonso struggled to his feet. He had been sleeping on a tangle of old fishing nets dotted with hooks. Several feet away, a half-open porthole pitted with rust and salt allowed in weak streams of sun.

He walked over to the window and stared outside at a horizon filled with choppy water. The sun appeared low in the sky. At first he thought it might be dawn, but then he realized that the sun was actually sinking and it was dusk. He had been asleep for at least a full day, maybe more.

Alfonso glanced about and noticed his backpack lying nearby

on the floor. He rummaged through his belongings and quickly found his passport and three hundred U.S. dollars. Alfonso sighed in relief. He then emptied the rest of his backpack and found two books that he had brought with him from Minnesota, a bottle of water, a glass sphere that looked almost like a paperweight, and a few tabs of French chocolate.

Although it appeared empty, his backpack still felt rather clunky. Alfonso examined it at every angle and discovered to his surprise that something was hidden between the coarse exterior fabric and the plastic brace. The outline was hard and rectangular. Alfonso examined the stitching inside the pack and noticed that a row of thread had been cut. The discovery of this mysterious package set his heart thumping. He laid the backpack on his lap and sat perfectly still. He heard only the rhythmic creak of wood planks straining against each other and the droning of the ship's engine. Alfonso took a deep breath and inserted his hand into the small opening in the pack. He pushed his hand downward until he reached the hard rectangular package and slowly withdrew it from its hiding place.

The package was exactly five inches wide by seven inches long and wrapped tightly in gauze. Alfonso unwound the gauze, revealing a metal tin embossed with the following words:

POLYVALENT CROTALID ANTIVENIN

He examined the package carefully and hesitantly popped off the lid to the tin. Inside lay two medical syringes with razor-sharp needles attached, and two small glass bottles of a clear liquid nestled between them.

"What is Polyvalent Crotalid Antivenin and where did this come from?" Alfonso asked himself aloud. He began to put the medicine away when he noticed the gash on his right hand. His mind instantly flashed back to the pharmacy across the street from his hotel in Marseilles. The pharmacy's front window had been smashed. Someone had robbed the place, and suddenly Alfonso knew without a doubt that he was the one who had done it.

Over the next hour, Alfonso investigated the rest of the freighter's hold. It was at least half empty. Aside from the torn fishing nets and rusty hooks, there were a few empty cardboard boxes, some old tools, and in the corner, several dozen crates of dates. Upon seeing the dates, Alfonso realized that he was famished. In fact, he didn't remember ever being so hungry in his life. Alfonso took some dates back to his corner of the hold and sat down to eat. Then, suddenly, the door to the deck opened and a ladder slid down. Alfonso heard voices, and he shrank further into the darkness.

Three sailors clumped heavily down the ladder, carrying boxes. They spoke in French and loudly discussed Marseilles— where they had found the best bouillabaisse, the best cheap hotel, and the best card games. For half an hour, they transferred boxes of dates from the deck to the hold while Alfonso sat in his corner, barely daring to breathe. At one point, Alfonso heard one of the sailors ask when they would arrive in "Alexandre."

"Deux heures," replied another. "C'est bien, l'Alexandre. Tu verras!" Alfonso furrowed his brow. That couldn't be. The freighter would arrive in Alexandria, Egypt, in two hours? His head swam. He must have been asleep for a very long time—

days. Alfonso didn't notice the sailors pulling up the ladder and shutting the door to the hold.

"Alexandria," Alfonso whispered to himself. "Just like the book."

He reached for his backpack and pulled out the two books that he had brought with him. The first was a book that he had originally obtained in Somnos. It was titled *The Basics of Speaking Dormian,* by Dr. Gregor Axel Oxenstjerna. Alfonso had been studying the book for the past several years and now, thanks to his studies, he was reasonably fluent in the Dormian language. Of course, he had no one to converse with, so it was quite possible that his pronunciation was atrocious. Nonetheless, Alfonso was Dormian and he felt that he should know his ancestral language. After all, he wasn't just any Dormian. He was a hero of Somnos—the boy who saved the city and earned the title of Great Sleeper.

The second book, the smaller of the two, was *Architecture of Ancient Alexandria: A Detailed Field Guide* by Dr. Jarislav Lützen. This was a very unlikely book for a fifteen-year-old boy to be reading in his spare time. But there was a reason. Alfonso's father, Leif Perplexon, had actually purchased this book from an online bookseller roughly six years ago. Alfonso still vividly remembered the day the book had arrived. A delivery man brought the book to their house around nine o'clock on a Saturday morning. Leif had read the book carefully for several hours. Finally, he set the book down and went for a swim in Lake Witekkon, near their house. Midway through the swim, storm clouds moved in and the lake was hit with rain and lightning.

Leif Perplexon was never seen again.

Alfonso, who was just nine at the time, waited by the edge of the lake for days, hoping that his father would miraculously reappear. Leif was eventually presumed dead, though his body was never found. In the months and even years after Leif's funeral, Alfonso clung to this strange academic text by Dr. Jarislav Lützen. It was the last thing that Leif Perplexon had ever read, and just by having it nearby Alfonso felt closer to his father.

Alfonso held the architectural field guide in his hands, leaned back against the ship's hull, and thought about his father. Leif and Uncle Hill were both born in Somnos, the last city of Dormia. In the confusion of Great Wandering Day, Leif and Hill, who were both young boys at the time, were pushed through the gates with a group of Wanderers. Miraculously, the boys survived the harsh conditions of the Ural Mountains and were eventually discovered by a sea captain who took them back to North America. Leif ended up in World's End, Minnesota, where he married Alfonso's mom, Judy, and found long-sought domestic happiness.

This was pretty much everything that Alfonso knew about his father's past. It was painfully little. His mother could have probably told him more, but she was the silent type. What's more, it seemed to grieve her to dredge up memories of her deceased husband. Alfonso didn't have the heart to press her on this.

Still, Alfonso did have a few memories of his father. Above all, he remembered the walks that he and his dad used to take in the primeval Forest of the Obitteroos, which surrounded his house in World's End. Many of the trees were centuries old and most were extremely tall. Some of the oldest trees, which had been around since Roman times, stood more than three hundred feet in height. Alfonso and Leif would often walk through the forest at dusk, a magical time when the pine needles glowed like copper shavings and animals came out to drink from the streams. Often fog rolled off the surrounding lakes and settled so thickly that it was impossible to see more than several feet in any one direction.

On one occasion, an especially thick fog rolled in and the two of them were separated. Alfonso had chased after a rabbit and when he finally looked up, his father was gone. Alfonso was reasonably certain that he knew the way home, even in the fog, but he decided instead to search for his father. He searched for hours. It wasn't until midnight drew near that, quite by accident, Alfonso stumbled into his dad. Leif looked terrified. It was the only time that Alfonso could recall seeing fear in his father's eyes.

"If you ever find that I am missing, and you know the way home, you mustn't look for me," Leif had said sternly.

"I'll always look for you," said Alfonso tearfully.

"No," replied Leif with a shake of his head. "Sometimes it's best not to."

Those words echoed in Alfonso's head as he sat in the hull of the Romanian freighter. He sighed and stared at the familiar blue-gray cover of Dr. Lützen's book. Finally, he flipped it open to chapter seventeen, which was titled The Three Sphinxes. The chapter began with a drawing of three sphinxes, each with the trademark head of a woman, body of a lion, and wings of a bird. Beneath the drawing Leif had written the following:

The sphinxes from my dreams . . . Which one of them has the watchful eye?

Leif had written a few other sentences but they were impossible to read because the book had been rained on and the ink had run. Alfonso had found the book lying face-open on the Perplexons' front lawn while Leif was swimming in Lake Witekkon.

Alfonso closed the book and sat silently on the freighter's wooden floor. He felt the churn of its heavy diesel motors. As he stared into the gathering darkness, he thought about his dad—his smile, the roughness of his beard, and how his dark green eyes twinkled as he watched a loon skim the surface of the cold Minnesota water.

An hour or two later, Alfonso leapt to his feet when he heard a great clattering of feet overhead. Then the engines on the boat began to drone more softly and Alfonso could feel the ship slowing down. "Alexandria," he mumbled to himself. At that moment, his eyes drooped heavily with fatigue. Alfonso fought this drowsiness and, as quickly as he could, shoved his belongings into his backpack. He then lay down on the dank floor of the ship and prepared for sleep.

CHAPTER 4

GLIMPSE OF THE LABYRINTH

ALFONSO STARED at the body of a man lying face-down in the snow. He was in the mountains somewhere, perhaps the Urals, but he couldn't be sure. The sky was a dull charcoal color and a heavy snow was falling. He stood in a long corridor of extremely tall hedgerows and shivered violently. He was freezing.

As if obeying an unseen force, he knelt down next to the fallen man and turned him over. The man was dead. More alarming than this, however, was that the man was Leif Perplexon, his father. Alfonso shuddered but, instead of looking away, focused on two small puncture wounds, about an inch apart, located midway down his father's neck. The skin around the punctures was tinged a gray blue, in stark contrast to the grim off-white color of the rest of his neck. Alfonso stared at the image of his father until it disappeared.

It had been a nightmare.

Alfonso blinked furiously as if to ensure that what he was *now* seeing was real. He was standing in a darkened alleyway. The air was warm and balmy. Alfonso spun around and saw a large port, where several dozen freighters were anchored alongside stone jetties. One of these freighters was the *Somnolenţă*, the ship that brought him from Marseilles.

Now what?

The port was deserted and spooky, and Alfonso walked quickly and passed several low-slung warehouses, abandoned forklifts, and fluorescent streetlights that flickered a dull yellow. Every so often he'd hear a *crack* in the distance that sounded like gunfire. The only signs of life were mangy dogs that eyed him warily. The air was filled with a myriad of smells—a mix of spices, seaweed, cigarette smoke, and urine. In the distance, Alfonso could hear the minarets calling worshipers to their prayers.

Eventually, Alfonso came upon a more populated area, a handful of open shops clustered along a crumbling four-lane road. Here he found a taxi driver who said, in very broken English, that he would accept dollars. The man's taxi was an ancient Mercedes, and the painted exterior had long since corroded and flaked off leaving only a coat of rust.

The driver, a wizened old man with white hair coming out of his ears, looked at him through the rearview mirror. "Where to go?" asked the man eagerly.

"The Three Sphinxes," replied Alfonso.

"Three Sphinxes—yes, yes, yes," he said. "I take you there,

finest good sir." Then he smiled, showing two teeth in his mouth, one hanging from the upper jaw and the other from the lower jaw.

Ten minutes later, the taxi pulled up in front of a crumbling brick building; the narrow entranceway was occupied by a very heavyset man smoking a water pipe, called a *nargeelah*. It gave off a smoky, candy apricot smell.

"What's this?" asked Alfonso.

"This is Three Sphinxes," replied the taxi cab driver. He pointed to a sign above the building's entranceway, which read: THREE SPHINXES HOTEL—CHEAP ROOMS & ROOFTOPS AVAILABLE.

Alfonso was about to say he didn't mean for the driver to take him to the Three Sphinxes Hotel, but then he realized it didn't matter. It was a hotel, and he needed a place to sleep. He paid the driver and left the taxi. The man smoking the nargeelah motioned for him to come closer.

"You want a room, fella?" asked the man. He had a bald head and a neck that rippled with at least half a dozen chins. "I am innkeeper."

Alfonso nodded.

The innkeeper showed Alfonso to his room. It was tiny, with enough room for a single bed, a rickety chair, a sink, and a small window near the ceiling that had been painted shut. As the innkeeper was about to leave, Alfonso asked him if he could arrange a visit to the ancient ruins known as the Three Sphinxes.

"Forget the Three Sphinxes," said the innkeeper dismissively. "It is top name for hotel, but not such a good place to visit. You must visit Pompey's Pillar."

"No thanks," said Alfonso politely. "I really want to see the Three Sphinxes."

"As you please," replied the innkeeper. "The sphinxes guard the tomb of the pharaoh Khafra. You know this, eh? One is said to be weeping in grief, another laughing because Khafra took so many riches with him to the afterlife, and a third sleeping because the pharaoh had at last found rest."

"Sleeping?" inquired Alfonso.

"Yes," replied the innkeeper. "The third of the sphinxes is the so-called Sleeping Sphinx."

Alfonso nodded.

"Good night," said the innkeeper.

Once he was alone, Alfonso took a closer look at his surroundings. The dirty yellow walls felt like they were closing in on him. He felt stifled and anxious. Alfonso thought of his mother. By now, certainly, someone had informed her that he had gone missing. He would have to call her first thing in the morning.

Alfonso sat on the bed. It squeaked as a plume of dust rose from the faded green bedspread. He opened his backpack, to distract himself from his fears as much as to make sure that everything was there. One by one, he lifted out his belongings. It was comforting to see these familiar objects in such a foreign place. He paused to examine his blue sphere. It was roughly the size of an orange, but it weighed almost nothing. Alfonso had found it in Straszydlo Forest, on the way to Somnos, three years before. The sphere was a curious thing. It could fly through the air with the force of a cannonball and then return to Alfonso's outstretched hand with the gentleness of a fluttering feather.

But that wasn't all.

Lately, he had discovered a new aspect to the sphere: whenever Alfonso spun it like a top in his hand, images flickered across its round, glassy surface. The images were always of a monk, dressed in a robe, with a single eyeball situated in the middle of his forehead. This was, without a doubt, the same monk whose stone statue Alfonso had come across in the Straszydlo Forest. The images were scattered and usually unrelated. The monk walked, or sat at a desk, or ate. Sometimes more interesting images appeared, such as the monk arguing furiously with several people, their faces hidden in the shadows. There didn't seem to be any obvious meaning behind these scenes or any storyline that might connect them all together. The scenes simply repeated themselves cyclically. However, at that moment, as he held the sphere in the dusty, stifling hotel room, a new image appeared.

The one-eyed monk was walking quickly through a snowy labyrinth of hedges. It was the exact same labyrinth that Alfonso had dreamed about—the one in which he'd seen his father lying dead in the snow.

CHAPTER 5

THE THREE SPHINXES

EARLY THE NEXT MORNING, Alfonso set out from the hotel. The first order of business was to telephone his mother. It was late in the evening in World's End when he called from a pay phone near his hotel. From the sound of her voice, she had been frantic with worry. Alfonso explained that he had simply fallen asleep and committed some "tomfooleries"—this was the word that his family used to describe the crazy things that he occasionally did in his sleep. Alfonso assured his mom, repeatedly, that he was staying at a nice hotel called the Three Sphinxes in Alexandria, Egypt.

"Egypt!" screamed his mother, so loudly that Alfonso nearly dropped the phone. "Are you playing some sort of joke on me?"

"No," said Alfonso as cheerfully as he could. "I'm really in

Egypt. Don't worry, it's nice. Beautiful weather here this time of year."

"Oh my dear, dear, dear boy," said his mother. "Don't move from the hotel and don't go to sleep! I'm calling Mayor Ehrstrom here in World's End. He has a cousin stationed with the Air Force over in Turkey and he'll know what to do. I'll send someone to pick you up just as soon as I can. Someone from the U.S. Embassy most likely. It may take a few hours, dear, so I just want you to stay at that hotel of yours and don't talk to anyone. Okay?"

"Okay," Alfonso replied.

Once this call was completed, Alfonso quickly set out for the local bus station to find the Sleeping Sphinx. The innkeeper had written out directions for him. They involved a bus trip to a place called Al Alamayn, which the innkeeper had written for him in Arabic: العلمين. Of course, this was against his mother's instructions, but he suspected it would take her several hours, if not an entire day, to find someone to pick him up. In the meantime, he had no interest in waiting in the hotel, doing nothing.

After thirty minutes of walking through the streets of dusty, noise-filled downtown Alexandria, Alfonso arrived at the central bus terminal. He expected a large building with many separate terminals, but instead found an enormous parking lot filled with buses belching diesel fumes. There were all types of buses—luxurious tourist cruisers with complimentary snacks and juices, bone-rattling city buses, and small minivans that wheezed and coughed as if diseased. Eventually, Alfonso came upon a minivan with bald tires, a rear bumper attached by several pieces of string, and a roof stacked with no less than two dozen bicycles. In the front windshield there was a placard that read, العلمين. The driver, a teenager who didn't look much older than Alfonso, rolled down the driver's side window.

"Three Sphinxes?" inquired Alfonso.

The driver nodded and Alfonso climbed in. Alfonso still hadn't converted any of his money into Egyptian pounds, so he simply handed the driver a five-dollar bill. The driver looked very pleased.

The minivan lurched through the parking lot and onto the streets of Alexandria. The driver savagely mashed his horn while singing along to the Egyptian pop songs that blared from the radio. In no time, they had exited the city and emerged onto a pothole-ridden desert road. The road offered a wonderful array of sights—a gang of Bedouin children playing soccer with a coconut, four women dressed entirely in black riding a single camel, and a one-armed man sharpening knives in the shade of a broken-down airplane. They drove for about an hour until, quite unexpectedly, the driver slammed the minivan to a halt and motioned for Alfonso to get out.

"Three Sphinxes?" asked Alfonso.

The driver nodded again.

As soon as Alfonso had planted both feet on the ground, the minivan sped away. Alfonso looked around and, at first, saw nothing but brown rocks and dirt that stretched out for miles. The only sign of life was a yellow car with a taxi sign, which lurched into gear and pulled up alongside Alfonso. The driver unrolled the window, letting out a welcome blast of air conditioning.

"Welcome," said the man. He had a full black beard and he wore polarized sunglasses. "You are American, yes?" he asked, in fluent but halting English.

Alfonso nodded.

"You will enjoy the Three Sphinxes," he said. "Not many tourists visit, but those who do enjoy seeing it very much. Please, come inside."

Alfonso hesitated and looked around.

The taxi driver laughed in a friendly manner. "There is no one else," he said. "And why should there be? There is barely enough business for me!"

Another cool air-conditioned breeze reached Alfonso. He stepped into the taxi and let out a sigh of relief as he sank into the spotless leather seats. The driver handed him a bottle of cold water and they sped off into the desert.

"Where are you from?" asked the driver.

"America," replied Alfonso.

"But where exactly? We have tourists coming from all over!"

"World's End," said Alfonso.

The driver quivered, as if a chill had just passed through his body. He stared at Alfonso through the rearview mirror.

"World's End?" he said in a soft but now serious voice. "Is this the World's End in the state of Minnesota or the one in Alaska?"

Alfonso was astounded. Very few people knew that there was a town of this name in either place.

"It's the one in Minnesota," replied Alfonso tentatively. "I'm amazed that you have heard of either of them."

"Don't be amazed," said the driver with a kind smile. "I am a fan of geography—especially of the great northern regions, which are so often blanketed in snow and ice."

After this strange response, the driver said nothing more, and drove deeper into the desert. Alfonso couldn't see any road, but the driver seemed to know every inch of the land. The landscape was dotted with countless boulders and other good-sized rocks that blended into the ground, but the taxi avoided them all.

Several minutes later, the taxi swerved to a stop. Alfonso opened the door and stepped out. Only then did he see that the taxi had stopped about thirty feet away from the edge of a sheer cliff. Far below lay the Mediterranean. It shimmered a deep blue and stretched hundreds of miles to the horizon. To his right, near the cliff's edge, stood three tall sculptures, each about the size of a house.

"This is the place," confirmed the driver, who was still inside the taxi. "Be careful of the cliff, my young friend. The water is quite dangerous. The currents are powerful, and many unfortunate souls have drowned." With that, he settled into the driver's seat and began taking a nap.

Alfonso walked slowly to the edge of the cliff and looked down, several hundred feet below, to the Mediterranean. The water looked cold and inviting after the dusty minivan ride from Alexandria. He looked to his right and stared at the Three Sphinxes. Just as the hotel manager had described, the first sphinx was crying, the second one was laughing, and the third one was sleeping. Alfonso carefully studied the Sleeping Sphinx. It had the muscular body of a lion, two large ears, a small human face, and a set of eyes that appeared to be firmly shut.

Upon closer inspection, Alfonso noticed that the Sleeping Sphinx's left eyelid was cocked open just slightly, as if it were trying to see something out of the corner of its eye. Instantly, Alfonso recalled the words that his father had written in his book: "Which one of them has the watchful eye?"

Alfonso tried to follow the gaze of the watchful eye, which

seemed to be directed toward the edge of the cliff. Alfonso walked along the cliff until, quite by chance, he noticed an unusual-looking flat stone jutting over the edge. Alfonso walked over to examine the stone and discovered that it was actually the top step in a frighteningly narrow and steep staircase that wound its way downward to the crashing waves below. Alfonso was soon trotting down the staircase at a brisk pace, overcome with excitement.

The staircase descended directly into the sea. Alfonso paused just above the crashing waves and looked up at the Sleeping Sphinx. *Success.* The half-open eye was fixed on a spot in the middle of the waves, about twenty-five feet offshore. It looked no different from any other patch of turbulent water, except for one brief moment, in between waves, when Alfonso thought he saw something round and man-made, like a pillar. He stared at the spot for several more minutes as the spray from the waves drenched him.

He saw it again.

It looked like a pillar, but it was difficult to be certain.

Alfonso was not a particularly strong swimmer, and even the strongest of swimmers would not jump into this water. In all likelihood, the waves would drown him before he even reached the pillar.

Alfonso retreated two steps up the staircase and stopped. His mind suddenly felt cloudy and muddled, and his legs became heavy. Sleep was descending on him. Alfonso could almost feel himself being pulled, against his will, toward the water. "Oh boy," he muttered sleepily. "This could end badly . . ." But there was no fighting it. His eyes fluttered drowsily and Alfonso entered a sleeping trance.

"Wait!" cried a voice from up above. It came from the taxi driver. The man looked frantic. But he was too late to stop Alfonso. Alfonso turned back to face the water, waited for an opening between two waves, and then jumped in.

The fierce pull of the sea gripped him immediately and within a matter of seconds, Alfonso was surrounded by whitecaps. The current pulled him out to sea and toward the mysterious pillar. He woke up, gasped, swallowed a mouthful of salty water, and fought desperately to swim back to shore. The current, however, was too strong. It swept him toward the pillar and he lunged for it. Alfonso's fingers scraped at the surface, searching madly for a crevice or handhold of any kind. They slid along the algae-covered pillar, which was about a foot underwater. A vicious wave crashed over him, and he lost his grasp.

Alfonso could feel himself weakening as he fought the current. There was no way he'd be able to return to shore. With all the strength in his body, he lunged again for the pillar, but couldn't find any traction. In desperation, he kicked his legs. They scraped against something hard and sharp and Alfonso's left leg erupted in pain. He swallowed salt water and choked. He was already several feet away. If only he could fall back asleep, perhaps everything would be okay. But that wasn't going to happen. Alfonso had never felt so awake in his life. Gritting his teeth, Alfonso blocked out the pain in his leg, took a deep breath, and dove downward with all of his might.

Underwater, he saw the pillar more clearly. It was perfectly round and about four feet wide. The portion closest to the surface was covered in algae, but below that it was colored a light brown, like limestone. Rusted iron ingots lined the pillar all the way to the ocean floor, which was perhaps thirty feet down. One of those spikes had hit his leg. He swam toward an ingot and grasped hold of it.

Suddenly, a faint light drew his attention. It came from the sea floor. He let go of the pillar and dove down toward the light. It came from an underwater cave that was nestled into a massive pile of rocks on the ocean floor. The opening was small, no more than a few feet wide, and the water there glowed a rich turquoise blue, in contrast to the dark open water where he was swimming. The pressure in Alfonso's lungs grew painful.

He swam as fast as he could into the mouth of the cave. It became a tunnel that burrowed downward and then up toward a bright light. Alfonso kicked ferociously. He burst through the surface and greedily sucked in air. When he finally managed to catch his breath, he discovered that he was floating in a remarkable stone cavern that glittered fluorescent blue. Reflected light shone everywhere, as if the walls were made of stained glass, even though they were clearly made of stone.

Alfonso looked up at the ceiling. It had been shaped into a smooth, round dome. This chamber was obviously man-made; somebody had carved a giant symbol into the ceiling. It looked like this:

Alfonso recognized it at once. It was the symbol of Dormia.

CHAPTER 6

THE CRYPT

ALFONSO PADDLED WEAKLY to the far end of the cavern, where the water ended in a small pebble beach. He slumped to the ground and lay motionless on his back, enormously relieved to be alive. He stared at the walls and ceiling of this underground cavern and marveled at how they glowed from below, as if the ocean floor were pulsing with electric light. His eyes then centered on the symbol of Dormia. *Who had carved this and why?*

Alfonso stood up and double-checked that the sphere was still in his pocket. He glanced around the small cavern and noticed an entranceway nestled in the darkest corner. The stone inlay was covered with intricate geometric carvings, and the entrance opened into a long tunnel that appeared to be lit with a long procession of oil lamps. Alfonso couldn't imagine who had lit these lamps or where the oil had come from, but he was too overwhelmed to think critically about any of this. One thing was clear: he was going to enter the tunnel. There was simply no way that he was going back into the water.

The air in the tunnel was cool and damp, like the basement of a house. Combined with his wet clothes, it made Alfonso shiver. He walked cautiously along the passageway as it angled slightly upward. Once or twice he thought that he might have heard footsteps behind him, and he stopped abruptly in order to listen, but he was repeatedly greeted by silence. His mind undoubtedly was playing tricks on him.

After he'd walked for about ten minutes, the tunnel emerged into a rectangular room with fifty-foot vaulted ceilings. The room was as long as a city block and empty except for a series of twenty stone shelves embedded in a far corner. A few oil lamps illuminated the room, although the floor remained hidden in shadow. The walls of the room were engraved with a large pictograph, which was repeated many times. The pictograph contained three ornately detailed images: a silver pen, a vine containing many clusters of berries, and a bolt of lightning that was striking a tree.

Alfonso walked across the room to the stone shelves. Each shelf was stacked with a dozen or so wooden boxes that were a foot long by a foot wide. The boxes were made of sturdy rosewood that gleamed when Alfonso brushed away the thick layer of dust that covered them. He took one box down from the shelf. It smelled fragrant and vaguely familiar. The top of the box was engraved with the same three images that were on the walls. He tried to open the box, but it was locked, or at least sealed very tightly. "This thing must open," Alfonso muttered to himself, as he tried again. This time he pressed with all his might and the lid sprang open.

Inside the box, nestled securely in a wooden clasp, sat a small glass vial containing a thick, shimmering blue liquid. Two small gold-colored objects that appeared to be seeds were on either side of the vial. Something was weird about the seeds. Alfonso peered closer and let out a small cry of surprise. The seeds were floating about two inches above the floor of the box. They appeared to be completely weightless. He reached into the box and touched one of the seeds with his index finger. It began to vibrate and then spin rapidly. He withdrew his hand, carefully shut the lid, and tucked the box under his arm. "Very cool," murmured Alfonso. "This is coming with me."

He continued to explore the crypt and was relieved to discover a series of solid-bronze handrails leading up one side of the crypt toward a wooden trapdoor. Hopefully this was a way out. Nearby the closest handrail, a massive slab of wood was lying on the floor. It looked like a giant door that had toppled over. Several long knives were scattered across the surface.

Alfonso approached the wood slab and saw that the names of dozens of people were carved on it, along with their ages and places of origin. The writing was in a number of different languages including English, Greek, Russian, Latin, Arabic, Hebrew, and a few others that Alfonso could not recognize. It seemed as if everybody who had passed through this chamber had carved their name into the wood, almost as if it were a guestbook of sorts.

Alfonso quickly scanned the list of names. When he came to the last name, he took a step back. His hands trembled, and he almost dropped the rosewood box. This is what he saw:

His father.

"Th-That's impossible," Alfonso said aloud in disbelief. "Dad drowned when he was forty-four. How could . . ."

At that moment, Alfonso heard behind him a soft, wet noise, like the sound of a mouth opening. He whirled around and saw a man, his face shrouded in darkness, standing only feet away.

"One thing is for certain, my friend," said the man. "Monsieur Perplexon did not die when you say he did, for I saw him well after that with my own eyes." He stepped out of the shadows and revealed himself. It was the taxi driver. He no longer wore his sunglasses and his gleaming eyes were entirely white.

"This man, Monsieur Perplexon, you are his son?" asked the driver.

Alfonso said nothing.

"He was very clever," said the driver. "We tried to follow him, naturally, but he eluded us. That is very rare, very rare indeed."

"Who are you?" asked Alfonso.

"That doesn't matter," replied the man calmly. "What matters is who *you* are. I was hoping that I had found another Great Sleeper like Monsieur Perplexon, but alas, all I have found is a Dormian boy trying to find his father. Quite curious."

Alfonso couldn't contain his shock. "Dad was a Great Sleeper?"

The man smiled in such a way that Alfonso felt a tingle of fear dance across the nape of his neck.

"I don't know what's going on," replied Alfonso shakily. "But I really have to be going." In his left hand, Alfonso clutched the rosewood box. His right hand snaked into the front pocket of his trousers and encircled the sphere. "Please let me pass."

"I am afraid that is not an option, my friend," replied the man. "You see, I am bound by very strict orders."

"Orders?" asked Alfonso.

"Yes," said the driver. "And may God forgive me for killing a boy." He then sprang at Alfonso like a panther. Alfonso turned to run, but his feet came out from under him and he sprawled awkwardly to the stone floor. His leg, which he had injured in the water, throbbed and felt warm. The newly formed scab on the wound had reopened. Alfonso looked up. The man loomed above him, holding two daggers in his hands.

"Such a pity," the man said through gritted teeth. He paused for a second and then brought the dagger down in a smooth motion toward Alfonso's heart. Alfonso had been struggling beneath him, but the instant the dagger began its downward journey, he relaxed. Sleep came milliseconds later and at the moment that the dagger pricked Alfonso's shirt, he moved his torso so forcefully and suddenly that the man fell to the floor, and the dagger fell from his grip. Alfonso sprang to his feet, arms out. He bounced lightly on the balls of his feet, and a second later Alfonso's eyes were back open and he was wide awake.

"Don't make this difficult," snarled the driver as he sprang to his feet. The man then snatched the dagger from the floor and in one fluid motion continued his charge toward Alfonso. Alfonso took the sphere from his pants pocket and threw it at the man's chest. The impact of the sphere lifted the man off the ground and slammed him into the wall twenty feet away.

Meanwhile, the sphere returned to Alfonso's outstretched hands. The instant that it came back, Alfonso threw it again and again. The sphere pummeled the man as he slid down the wall into a crumpled heap.

As soon as Alfonso caught his breath, he felt overcome with nausea. The floor was covered with the man's blood. For a moment, Alfonso feared that he had killed him, but then the man managed to sit up weakly. His eyes looked dull, but vaguely alert. His breathing was labored.

"You won't find Perplexon," gasped the man. "If he's not already dead, he might as well be."

"I'm not afraid of the Dragoonya," replied Alfonso.

The man laughed and then winced in pain. "You're such a foolish child. It's not the Dragoonya who have imprisoned your father. It's the Dormians."

CHAPTER 7

AN UNEXPECTED VISITOR

ALFONSO'S EYES SLAMMED OPEN. For the first few seconds, he had no idea where he was. He lay on a narrow bed, in a small concrete room with a rickety ceiling fan wobbling overhead. *This place seems familiar*, thought Alfonso. Then it came back to him. He was back in his hotel room, at the Three Sphinxes Hotel.

Bang! Bang! Bang!

Someone was knocking on the door—loudly.

Alfonso looked around quickly and, to his great relief, he saw that all of his possessions were in plain sight: his backpack, money, books, passport, and blue sphere. There was also a small rosewood box and, as soon as Alfonso saw this, recent events came back to him: the trip to the cliffs, the Sleeping Sphinx, the dive into the sea, the cave, and then the awful battle with the taxi driver.

But how had he gotten back to his hotel room?

The last thing he recalled was climbing up the bronze hand-rails leading up the side of the crypt. Everything after this was a blank, which meant, of course, that Alfonso must have dozed off and his sleeping-self had taken over.

Alfonso glanced at his watch and, judging by the time and date, he quickly calculated that it had been almost thirty-six hours since he had left the hotel.

Bang! Bang! Bang!

The door to the hallway reverberated under heavy knocking.

"One second!" Alfonso yelled.

"Mr. Perplexon, are you in there?" came a woman's voice from the other side of the door. Her voice had a strange, bird-like sound to it.

Alfonso threw on his clothes and crammed all of his possessions into his backpack. Everything except his sphere. He held this in his right hand, ready for whatever came through the door.

"I have an urgent message for Master Alfonso Perplexon," said the woman. "It is from a friend."

Alfonso walked across the room to the door. He put his hand on the doorknob and hesitated.

"Who are you?" he shouted.

"I am the servant of a friend of yours," said the voice. "Please, we must converse immediately."

"I don't have any friends in Alexandria," said Alfonso.

"This friend is not from Alexandria," replied the voice. "His home is in Barsh-yin-Binder."

This was most unexpected. Barsh-yin-Binder was a city on the edge of the Urals, a dreary place inhabited by Dragoonya, mercenaries, and smugglers. Alfonso and his uncle Hill had passed through there on their way to Somnos.

"Barsh-yin-Binder?" inquired Alfonso.

"That's correct," said the voice. "He has come at the request of Judy, your mother."

Alfonso opened the door. Standing in the doorway was a tall woman with long gray hair, dressed in khaki pants, a tight black shirt, and a snappy Panama hat. She appeared to be middle-aged, but it was hard to know. Her thin, delicate face was deeply tanned. She had a rather long nose and a pointy chin. Alfonso was happy to see that the woman's eyes were not white, but shone a light emerald green.

"Allow me to introduce myself," she said with a slight bow. "My name is Snej Duhamel. I am a pilot by vocation, based out of Persia normally, but in recent time I have been employed by a man who travels quite frequently. You are hereby requested to accompany me to an airship on the outskirts of this town."

"Are you kidding?" Alfonso asked.

"I do not jest," replied Snej.

"But I have to call my mom," Alfonso said.

"Later," replied Snej. "The street is buzzing with the news of an American boy who has killed a local taxi driver and stolen his car. The man's body was found in the desert near the Three Sphinxes and his taxi was found just blocks from here."

"Killed?" replied Alfonso. "Are you sure he's . . ."

"Dead," finished Snej. She nodded.

42

I have killed a man. This thought lodged into Alfonso's brain like a meteor that had just made impact.

"Come," said Snej. "We have no time to waste."

Alfonso grabbed his backpack and quickly followed Snej. Outside, a white Rolls-Royce idled at the curb. It was in pristine condition, without a scratch or even a trace of mud. It had attracted a crowd of amazed Alexandrians, including the innkeeper. At the first sight of Alfonso, the innkeeper pointed his finger accusingly and shouted loudly in Arabic: "That's the American boy! He must have snuck in!" There were several angry shouts from the crowd.

Snej shoved Alfonso into the back seat of the Rolls-Royce. She then reached into the driver's seat, pulled out a rifle, and pointed it directly at the innkeeper. *"Sukat!"* she growled. The innkeeper immediately went quiet. Snej slid into the driver's seat and closed the door. Fists pounded on the windows, but the glass was bulletproof, and hence far too sturdy to buckle under such pressure. Snej pressed her foot on the accelerator and the Rolls-Royce's motor uttered a deep-throated roar. The crowd shrank back. Snej took advantage of their fear, threw the car into gear, and sped away.

After several hairpin turns, the Rolls-Royce left the old city and entered the desert. About thirty minutes later, they arrived at the top of a narrow canyon. Snej threw the Rolls-Royce into its lowest gear and crept down a steep, makeshift road. At the bottom of the canyon they came upon a small airstrip several hundred feet in length. A twin turboprop plane sat on the edge of the runway nearest them. Snej explained that it was a de Havilland Twin Otter, known for its ability to operate in the polar winter as well as take off and land on virtually any surface.

The Twin Otter had no visible markings and was as white as the Rolls-Royce. One of its large propellers turned lazily in the wind.

"If you please, kind sir, my employer waits for you aboard," she said. "After securing the Rolls-Royce under a camouflage tarp, I will join you with all due speed." She pointed at the airplane's stairs. The banisters gleamed with inlaid wood, and the stairs were covered with a thick carpet. One thing was certain. Whoever waited for Alfonso aboard the Twin Otter was wealthy beyond any reasonable measure.

Alfonso grabbed his backpack and walked slowly toward the plane. With some reluctance, he began climbing the stairs. Halfway up he became aware of someone at the doorway of the plane. Alfonso looked up and at first was only aware of the person's massive size.

He was a giant, muscular fellow dressed in a white suit and a sharp red tie. In one hand he held a cane emblazoned with rubies. His long black hair was pulled back in a tight ponytail. He wore dark glasses. After a moment of shock, Alfonso recognized him.

Bilblox.

CHAPTER 8

ABOARD THE TWIN OTTER

BILBLOX ENGULFED HIS OLD FRIEND with a ferocious bear hug.

"I-I don't believe it . . ." stammered Alfonso. He felt elated, and for the first time in days he felt safe. No matter what the situation, he always felt more secure with Bilblox around. "How are you?"

"Not bad," replied Bilblox.

Truth be told, Alfonso was both amazed and relieved to see that his friend was doing so well. Alfonso had first met Bilblox in Fort Krasnik, the windswept, lawless island off the western coast of Canada, which functions as the headquarters for some of the world's top smugglers. The two of them had become fast friends while playing the legendary game of ballast together, and afterward Bilblox had insisted on accompanying Alfonso on his journey to Dormia. But, along the way, Bilblox had gone blind. Alfonso worried that Bilblox would never be able to return to his old way of life. On numerous occasions, Alfonso had written letters to Bilblox to see how he was managing, but Bilblox had never replied. Alfonso had had fears of his friend living on the streets, blind, lonely, and destitute. But clearly these worries were unfounded.

"Come on," said Bilblox. "Let's have some grub! I think you'll dig my plane."

Alfonso followed Bilblox into the Twin Otter and watched as his friend expertly navigated the plane's cabin, which featured plush, oversize leather chairs, Persian carpets, and a gas fireplace. Bilblox led Alfonso to a wooden table bolted into the floor. It was set with fine china, silk napkins, and several different dishes: a savory meatloaf Alfonso remembered from Fort Krasnik, piping hot sourdough bread, a bacon and spinach quiche, rhubarb pie, and tall glasses of lemonade. The sight and smell of the food made Alfonso weak at the knees.

"Dig in," commanded Bilblox. "Your mother's burstin' over with nervousness about you, and it won't do for her to see ya famished."

Through a mouthful of meatloaf, Alfonso managed to respond. "My mom sent you?"

"Who else?" asked Bilblox. "She called ol' Dusty Magrewski in Fort Krasnik and he gave 'er my mobile number. I got the call from Judy last night. She was out of 'er head with worry. She kept sayin', 'Alfonso is a good boy. He always calls. Somethin' terrible has happened.' Lucky fer you, I was just across the way in Athens, on business. I got a gal there who sells me third-century antiquities—real nice vases. They'll fetch top dollar in Hong Kong. It's all strictly hush-hush, of course. Anyway, I flew over right quick on my Twin Otter. Got her secondhand from the Manitoba Forest Service and added a bunch of new goodies." Bilblox smacked the solid steel hull of the plane. "She'll go anywhere, land anywhere, and take off from anywhere!"

"This is yours?" asked Alfonso. "How about the Rolls-Royce? And Snej Duhamel?"

"Snej is a fine woman and an even better pilot," said Bilblox. "She's worth every penny I pay her."

"How can you afford all this?" said Alfonso. "It's incredible!"

"I'm sorry to say that the money comes with sad tidings," said Bilblox with a frown. "I don't suppose ya heard? Nope. I been meanin' to write. Never was good with letter writin'. Vice Admiral Purcheezie, may her soul rest easy, passed away about a year ago. She died the way she would have liked to go—her heart gave way while she was cussin' out a customs official. Since I'd been her right-hand man in the smugglin' business— ever since I returned from Somnos and couldn't find work as a longshoreman—she saw to it that I'd take over her business. I got tired a bouncin' around the *Success Story*. We've upgraded the business with this Twin Otter, and as you can see, I'm doin' very well. Very well indeed. Got offices in Fort Krasnik, Barsh-yin-Binder, and Hong Kong."

Bilblox took off his glasses and seemed to stare at Alfonso. His eyes were still entirely white.

"How is your eyesight?" asked Alfonso. "Are you still blind?"

"Blind as a bat," said Bilblox with a rather sad smile. "But I'm still pretty nimble." He laughed heartily. "I got myself a seein' eye dog of sorts. Her name is Kõrgushüpe, but I call her Kõrgu for short. She's nappin' in 'er kennel now. You'll meet 'er later. Ya know, I don't mind the blindness so much, but once in a while I get these wicked headaches. Sometimes they lay me out for days at a time. I suspect it has somethin' to do with that purple ash I put in my eyes. But I ain't complainin'."

He leaned over and passed his fingers across Alfonso's face, examining the contours of his chin, cheeks, and mouth. He whistled.

"You've grown a lot in the last three years, haven't ya?" asked Bilblox. "You're practically a man by now. Dusty and the other longshoremen would love t'see you now! Maybe you'll stop by for a visit in Fort Krasnik on the way home to Minnesota."

Alfonso looked down at his plate, but said nothing.

"What is it?" asked Bilblox. "Don't get all quiet on a blind man—it makes me jumpy."

"I can't go back to Minnesota," said Alfonso. "At least, not right now."

"Oh fer cryin' out loud," said Bilblox. "Why in the heck not? Is this some sorta teenage rebellion?"

"Nothing like that," replied Alfonso. He paused. "I can't quite believe this, but my dad, Leif, may be alive."

"What!" declared Bilblox incredulously. "Whaddya mean? Where is he?"

"Not sure exactly," said Alfonso. "But I think I know who could help us."

"Who?"

"Josephus."

"Josephus!" said Bilblox with a snort. "The old Dormian historian? He's back in Somnos. You can't just pick up the telephone and call him. You'd have to trek through the Urals and . . . Wait a minute. Are you suggestin' that we . . . No, no way, that's out of the question."

"Look," said Alfonso calmly. "My dad may still be alive, but if he is, I think he's in trouble."

Bilblox stared intently at Alfonso. Snej walked onboard to announce that the Rolls-Royce was hidden and the Twin Otter was ready for takeoff.

"Let's get outta here," Bilblox commanded.

"Very well, sir," replied Snej. "And may I assume the destination is World's End, Minnesota?"

"Just head north," Bilblox growled. "We'll make a decision after I hear what this boy—sorry, teenager—has to say."

The Twin Otter's engines revved up to maximum as Snej settled into the pilot's seat. Soon, the plane took off in a steep ascent out of the desert canyon. Snej set a course due north across the Mediterranean. Meanwhile, Alfonso told Bilblox the whole story, starting in Paris and continuing through the fight with the taxi driver and the discovery that his father was a Great Sleeper.

When Alfonso finished talking, Bilblox sat there in silence. Finally, he spoke. "I remember Leif from the few years that he and your uncle were livin' in Fort Krasnik with me and the other longshoremen," said Bilblox. "He was a few years older than me, but ya could tell he was meant for somethin' special. The way he used to play ballast! Man! I never saw anyone move so quick in my life. A real nice guy he was, too." Bilblox's

49

hand traced the contours of the glass of lemonade and after a moment's pause, he continued.

"But you've gotta realize," said Bilblox, "what yer talkin' about is no small thing. You could be searchin' fer years fer yer old man and, meanwhile, ya got a mom at home who is worried sick about her boy."

"I just want to stop by Somnos," said Alfonso. "That's all."

"That ain't so easy last time I checked," said Bilblox with a snort. "First off, it's winter in the Urals right now and we can't just land anywhere we choose! And even if we found our way back to the entrance, how d'ya suppose we'd get through the mountain gates? They'll never open if we don't have a Dormian bloom with us. And then supposin' we did get in and found a clue in Somnos about where Leif had gone off to, we'd be trampin' around the Urals tryin' to find a needle in a haystack."

Bilblox looked sorrowfully at Alfonso.

"I ain't tryin' to be insensitive here," said Bilblox. "But ya ain't a kid anymore—ya got to think about these things. I mean, let's be honest here, ya really think yer old man is still alive? I mean, I wish to God that he was, but what are the chances?"

"All I know is that I was led to that crypt for a reason," insisted Alfonso. "You remember how it was on the way to Somnos the first time. Everything I did, from raising falcons to growing the Dormian bloom itself, had a reason. It was my sleeping-self preparing me for something. And now it's the same thing. All the things I've been up to—from meeting the Wanderer in Paris to diving into the water in front of the Three Sphinxes—there's something important going on here."

"It doesn't make sense, though," said Bilblox. "Suppose that

50

yer old man is a Great Sleeper, where was he headed? You saved Somnos and that's the only Dormian city left. What was yer dad up to? Where was he headed?"

"I don't know," said Alfonso. "That's why we have to talk with Josephus."

Bilblox sighed heavily.

Neither of them spoke for a while and the only sound in the airplane was the drone of the Otter's engines. Bilblox found himself in a quandary. Of course, the sensible thing to do was to say no. The chances that Leif Perplexon was alive—and that they would find him—were infinitesimally small. Not to mention, it seemed inconceivable that they would even find their way back to Dormia. Then there was the matter of Judy Perplexon. What would she say about all this? Bilblox knew that the whole plan was utterly boneheaded from start to finish.

And yet . . .

And yet Bilblox felt a powerful desire to help his friend. Nothing mattered to Bilblox more in life than loyalty. Riches meant very little. Sure, it was nice to have comforts, but what meaning did they have without companionship, without brotherhood? Truth be told, ever since he had to stop working as a longshoreman because of his blindness, he had been unbearably lonely. He desperately missed being part of the Brotherhood of Magrewski Longshoremen back in Fort Krasnik. He missed the singing, the joking, the rough horseplay, and even the sound of his fellow brothers snoring away in the night. Above all, he missed the feeling of devotion and loyalty that existed among the Magrewski longshoremen. He missed the feeling that if one of them got into a fight, or lost a bet, or suddenly grew ill, that all of them would close ranks and come together. This was the stuff of life—not luxury planes and fancy cars. This was the same feeling that connected him to Alfonso. Again and again, Alfonso had stuck up for him, even when all others believed that Bilblox had become an untrustworthy villain who was addicted to the purple ash of the Dormian bloom.

But there was more to it than just this.

There was Estonia and what had happened there all those years ago, when he was just a boy. This is what really gave Bilblox pause.

Bilblox had grown up in the port town of Väike Kunda. He lived with his mother and older sister, Loviise, in a ramshackle cottage on a cliff overlooking the Gulf of Finland. His father, Hillar, had left them when Bilblox was a baby to seek his fortune in Fort Krasnik. Whatever he earned, he sent back to them, and it was just enough for all three to survive.

Väike Kunda was a poor town and the only real wealth existed in the home of the local sheriff. He was a corrupt and ruthless man, who was known simply as the Käskija, which simply means "lord" when translated directly from Estonian. The Käskija was an older man, in his late sixties, who had been married five times and had outlived all of his wives. Rumor had it that he had beaten several of them to death. The Käskija had an eye for pretty girls, and eventually he set his sights on Loviise, who was a striking beauty. As carefully as she could, Loviise tried to avoid the Käskija, but when it became clear that this would be impossible, her mother made arrangements for her to join a Bridgettine convent in the mountain town of Tamsalu. The convent had been in operation since 1412 and it had a tradition of taking in girls in trouble. The abbess general of the Bridgettine order had taken a special interest in Loviise's situation.

Loviise was to leave by bus in the middle of the night. Bilblox accompanied his sister to the town's small bus station that night and, to their horror, they found the Käskija and several of his goons waiting for them there. They grabbed Loviise roughly and threw her into the back seat of a nearby car. Bilblox tried to intervene, but he was just eight years old, and the goons quickly stuffed his face into the dirt.

As soon as the Käskija's car had motored away, Bilblox began to yell for help. "Appi, appi, appi!" Frantically, he knocked on the door of every house he could find. He explained what had happened and demanded that they help him rescue his sister at once. The neighbors listened patiently, shook their heads sadly, and uttered the same words: "Pole midagi parata." *It cannot be helped.* Bilblox was enraged. This wasn't true, of course. It could be helped. All they needed to do was take action together, as a town, but this required more courage and initiative than any of them had. So Bilblox set out at once on the long winding road that led to the mansion where the Käskija lived. Bilblox arrived at dawn and was greeted at the door by one of the Käskija's thugs, a large oafish man with a pockmarked face.

"Mis see on?" asked the thug. *What is it?*

Bilblox demanded that his sister be let free.

"Tehke, mida iganes vajalikuks peate," said the goon with a laugh. *Take whatever actions you deem necessary.*

Bilblox nodded, reached behind his back, brandished a crowbar, and hit the goon as hard as he could on his right kneecap. The goon wailed out in pain. Bilblox ran past him and into the mansion, calling out frantically, "Loviise, Loviise, Loviise!" She never appeared. Other goons eventually found Bilblox and beat him to within an inch of his life. Bilblox was in the local hospital for three months. When he was released, his mother sent him to live with his father in Fort Krasnik. This was for his own safety. And as for Loviise, she was released only years later, when the Käskija died. She was immediately taken in by the Bridgettine nuns and was never seen again.

This story haunted Bilblox. He still shivered when he pictured the Käskija's face. But he saved his greatest contempt for the townspeople who wouldn't help him. Their words still rang in his ears. "Pole midagi parata." *It cannot be helped.* Bilblox knew that this was the lie that facilitated the greatest evils. It was also the tonic of the spineless wretches who would rather be safe than do what was right.

"Let's just suppose Snej could find a way to land this plane in the Urals—in the height of winter. What's your plan for getting into Somnos?" asked Bilblox finally.

Alfonso smiled.

"Do you remember that the gates to Somnos only open once every twelve years for Great Wandering Day?" he asked.

Bilblox nodded.

"When we left Somnos, Hill told us that the next Great Wandering Day was just three years away. I even remember the exact date because it's nearly two weeks before Christmas—December twelfth. Well, that was three years ago, and it's now December eleventh. The gates should open tomorrow."

Bilblox whistled.

"You think that's a coincidence?" he asked.

"Not a chance," replied Alfonso.

After considering Alfonso's story, Bilblox announced that he would take him to Somnos on one condition: Alfonso needed to tell his mother and receive her blessing. Alfonso used Bilblox's satellite phone to make the call. As he dialed, the Twin Otter headed due north across the Mediterranean, passing above the Greek islands, which appeared as dots of brilliant white against a backdrop of sparkling blue-green waters.

Judy was, of course, incredibly relieved to hear from her son. She had been beside herself with worry. Alfonso assured her that he was okay. Over the static and crackle of the phone, he tried to explain everything that he had learned in the past few days.

"This is madness," said Judy. "Absolute madness!"

"Come on, Mom," said Alfonso. "Didn't the thought ever cross your mind that Dad might be alive?"

"Of course it has," replied Judy. Even across the crackle of the satellite phone, her anguish was apparent. "But that doesn't mean that I want my only child—who's just fifteen years old—to run off on some fool's errand. What if something happens to you? Then I have lost my husband and my son."

"Nothing will happen to me," replied Alfonso. "My sleep-ing-self . . ."

"Your sleeping-self!?" said Judy. "Enough of all that!"

"Mom," Alfonso replied. "I'm begging you—you've got to let me do this."

There was another long, static-filled pause.

"Somehow I have the feeling that I don't have much of a choice about this," said Judy with a sigh. "I really don't know what to tell you. If you're asking me what I want, I want you to come home right this instant."

"What about *Dad*?" asked Alfonso with exasperation. "He may be alive and I'm pretty sure I'm the only one who can help him. We can't just forget about him. *Is that what you want?*"

Alfonso wished he could take back these last words as soon as he had uttered them.

"I can't believe you would even suggest that," said Judy with a choked sob. "Of all the hurtful things you could have said."

"Mom, I'm sorry. I didn't mean . . ."

"I love you very much, Alfonso," said Judy coldly. "Now go ahead and put Bilblox back on the phone."

Alfonso handed the phone over to Bilblox and, as he did, he felt about as low as he had ever felt in his life.

Bilblox pressed the receiver to his ear and listened intently. He nodded his head repeatedly and said "yes, ma'am" no less than a dozen times. Finally, he clicked off the phone and dropped his head, as if he were in pain.

"What happened?" asked Alfonso.

"She made me swear on my honor that I wouldn't let any-thin' bad happen to ya," said Bilblox.

"So why are you so upset?" asked Alfonso.

"Because," said Bilblox wearily, "I got no business makin' a promise like that."

CHAPTER 9

INTO THE STORM

AFTER CROSSING THE GREEK ISLANDS, the Twin Otter headed up
along the western coast of the Black Sea. They skimmed along
at a low level to avoid radar and landed for fuel and supplies on
the outskirts of the Romanian harbor town of Constantja. The
Twin Otter touched down in the early evening in a farmer's
field that was encrusted with a thin layer of snow and ice. The
ever-resourceful Snej took off on a bicycle that she stored in the
Twin Otter. She carried a basket, a rifle, and a bag full of cash.
She returned two hours later followed by a heavy truck filled
with drums of high-octane airplane fuel. In her basket she had
several different types of Romanian cheeses, grapes, warm flat
bread that smelled like olive oil and oregano, and several links
of pencil-thin smoked sausage. Alfonso, Bilblox, and Snej ate

dinner in the airplane. As they ate, Alfonso stared out the window as the two truck operators filled the Twin Otter's extra tanks with fuel.

Before boarding, Bilblox said grimly, "Alfonso and Snej, take a good look around—and do some lookin' for old blind Bilblox as well—cause this is the last peaceful scene we'll be lookin' at for quite a while. The Urals'll be nasty this time-a year."

"But think about Somnos," Alfonso replied. "Imagine what it looks like, now that the Founding Tree is fully grown. It ought to be a paradise."

"Yup, should be nice," said Bilblox grimly. "Assumin' we can make it there. I sure hope that you remember the right coordinates."

"I'd never forget them—64° North latitude by 62° East longitude—they were encoded in Uncle Hill's old watch," declared Alfonso confidently. "Don't you remember? From there it's just a few hours' hike."

"Hmm," said Bilblox. He was visibly worried.

Neither of them spoke for a while and eventually Alfonso opened the rosewood box that he had taken from the crypt in Alexandria. He wanted to check on the floating seeds. The glass vial containing the bluish liquid was intact, but to his dismay, the seeds were lying on the wood, dried out and cracked. One of them had partially disintegrated into gold-colored dust. An hour or so later, Alfonso checked on the seeds again—hoping foolishly that their condition might have improved—but instead he discovered that the seeds and the gold dust were gone and all that remained was a light-colored stain on the wood. It was as if the seeds had simply evaporated or melted into the wood.

"Not good," muttered Alfonso.

"What's the matter?" asked Bilblox.

"Well," said Alfonso, "the seeds that were in the rosewood box seem to have decomposed and then kind of evaporated or something."

"Hmm," said Bilblox with a yawn. "I hope we didn't need 'em fer anything."

Alfonso was about to close the box when he noticed something. The bottom of the box was pockmarked with thousands of minute indentations. At first, the indentations appeared to be arranged randomly, but, upon closer inspection, Alfonso sensed that they formed a pattern. But he couldn't grasp its complexity. It was like a puzzle with too many pieces. It would take a computer to analyze something this complicated. The only other solution was for Alfonso to enter hypnogogia, that magical state of mind in between waking and sleeping in which he was able to tap in to his special powers as a Great Sleeper. But he wasn't ready to do that. Not yet. The last time Alfonso had entered hypnogogia, nearly two years ago, it had almost killed him.

☙

It was mid-morning on December 12 when the Twin Otter neared the Urals. December 12! It was Great Wandering Day! At this very moment, the gates of Somnos were ajar and Wanderers were parading out onto the snowy slopes of the Urals. And, in all likelihood, Hill was standing there, just waiting for Alfonso to arrive.

Alfonso's thoughts snapped backed to reality as the Twin Otter began to shake with turbulence. The view out the window of the plane was enough to make the hairs on the back of his neck stand on end. As far as the eye could see there were dark, billowing clouds, which were illuminated every few seconds by brilliant flashes of lightning.

Bilblox and Alfonso crept up to where Snej was sitting. Her normally cool demeanor was gone. She muttered Persian curses under her breath, and Alfonso could see that her knuckles had turned an angry red from the strain of keeping the Twin Otter on course and level.

"Very bad weather ahead," said Snej in a voice that strained to keep calm.

Bilblox nodded. "Should we turn around?" he asked.

"I'm afraid not," said Snej. "I've been listening to military cargo planes a couple hundred miles behind us, and they're in much worse shape than we are. They report hail and hundred-mile-an-hour winds. We really have no choice but to continue on. If we find a place to put down near the coordinates you gave me, I'll do it, because we are quite close actually. Otherwise, I'll just keep going east to Nizhnevartovsk. We've been there before."

"All right," said Bilblox. "Do you need anything?"

The plane fell abruptly and then evened out. "Just sit down," said Snej.

Bilblox smiled and clapped Snej on the shoulders. "You betcha," he replied.

They made their way back to the main cabin and strapped themselves in.

"I'm always getting you into trouble," said Alfonso quietly. "This is my fault."

"We both made the decision," replied Bilblox with a shake of his head. "We're in this together."

The plane rattled fiercely and both of them fell into a prolonged silence. Alfonso looked out the window and watched the storm clouds draw closer. He imagined the ferocity of the blizzard that was raging below. The blizzard made him think of all the times that he had used the sight of swirling snowflakes as a means of entering hypnogogia.

The last time Alfonso had tried to enter hypnogogia, he had ended up in a coma. The memory of this awful episode still gave him the heebie-jeebies. It all started with Alfonso catching a bad flu. That night, his mother sent him to bed early, put a humidifier in his room, and covered him with blankets. As hard as he tried, however, Alfonso couldn't fall asleep. Eventually, out of pure boredom, he decided to enter hypnogogia. He focused on the mist that was coming out of the humidifier until he could see each individual particle of moisture. The particles flowed and swirled around him and Alfonso studied the intricate patterns that they made. Every time he reached out to them, he was overcome with a delightful feeling of weightlessness. And then suddenly, without warning, everything went black.

Alfonso woke up several weeks later in the hospital in St. Paul. He had been in a coma the whole time and had fractured his collarbone. His mother told him that he had fallen out of bed and hit his head on the floor. The impact of this blow to the head had put him into a coma. But this made no sense because his bed was only two feet off the ground. Besides, it wasn't Judy who had found him. It was Pappy. According to Pappy, he had walked into Alfonso's room and seen his grandson "floating" near the ceiling.

Afterward, Alfonso was rushed to the hospital. Pappy repeated the story of what he had seen, but Judy and the doctors dismissed this as a figment of his imagination, saying his mind wasn't as sharp as it used to be.

One morning in the hospital, toward the end of his stay, Alfonso awoke to the sound of the chief neurologist whispering to his mother. Alfonso was tempted to open his eyes, but for some reason he didn't. The neurologist was whispering, ". . . And so your son is very lucky to be alive. It was a very severe coma. We use something called the Glasgow Coma Scale, which rates comas in severity on a scale from three to fifteen, with three being the worst. Alfonso experienced a level-five coma. Most patients experience considerable brain damage at that point. Alfonso's chances of partial recovery were less than twenty percent and his chances of full recovery—which he somehow managed— were barely two percent. What I can't figure out is how a mere fall from his bed could have caused such a severe coma."

"I don't know what to tell you," whispered his mother, exasperatedly.

At this point, Alfonso opened his eyes. His mother and doctor rushed over to his side and gushed over how well he was doing. There was no more discussion of what had caused the coma and Alfonso decided that, for now at least, this was for the best. It was all too scary to think about.

Quite suddenly, Alfonso's mind snapped back to the present, as the seaplane began to plunge. Loose items flew around the cabin. A book hit Bilblox in the head and he let out a shout. The plane tilted downward at an ever steeper angle. The sound of screaming engines filled the air. Lightning flashed in the windows. Alarms blared. Oxygen masks dropped from the ceiling. The overhead lights blinked off and were replaced by harsh red emergency lights. Alfonso felt weightless and then nauseous. Snej was yelling something, but it was impossible to hear her. Bilblox's seeing eye dog, Kõrgu, had apparently woken up and was now barking furiously from her kennel in the back of the plane. The plane tore downward through the clouds. The force of gravity had pinned Alfonso into his seat, but he was still able to turn his head to look out the window. It was pure white. Then, for a moment, the storm relented and he could see the rocky, snow-covered ground. It was close—perilously close—and Alfonso knew at that moment that they were going to crash.

CHAPTER 10

SNOWBOUND

THE TWIN OTTER slammed into the snow with tremendous force. The plane tore apart—glass exploded into thousands of shards, the windows blew out, sections of the roof peeled away, and vast amounts of powdery snow engulfed the cabin. Finally the plane shuddered to a stop, and the loud noises of the crash were replaced by the groan of rapidly cooling metal.

Some time later, Bilblox came to. Perhaps just a few minutes had passed, or perhaps it had been hours. It was impossible to know. At first, Bilblox wondered if he had died, but then the biting cold brought him back to his senses. He tried to move his toes, and after some effort he could feel them brushing against the inside of his boots. Something trickled down his neck, and he discovered a bad gouge there. He unbuckled his seat belt and stood up gingerly. He sniffed the air for the telltale signs of smoke and fire, but felt only the sting of a bitterly cold wind.

"Alfonso?! Snej?!"

No response.

Bilblox groped his way forward. It was at moments like this one, in the thick of a crisis, that he most hated being blind. He felt so helpless. Even without his eyesight, Bilblox could sense that the plane was basically level. Inside the remains of the plane's cabin, chunks of foam, sheared-off metal, shards of glass, and other detritus from the crash littered the floor. Of course, being blind, Bilblox couldn't see any of this. He simply felt his way around the cabin and, every few seconds, shouted the names of his friends. Eventually, he heard a low moan from several feet away. He stumbled toward the sound and discovered it was Alfonso. Bilblox ran his fingers across Alfonso's face. The boy's eyes were closed and his hair was sticky and wet.

"Alfonso?" Bilblox whispered, voice shaking. "Come on now, open your eyes. Y-You're fine." He grabbed a handful of snow and used it to dab Alfonso's face.

Alfonso's first thought was that he was back home in World's End, and his mom was trying to wipe dirt from his face. For some reason, though, he found it almost impossible to move. It took a great deal of focus to open his eyes and weakly utter Bilblox's name.

When he heard Alfonso, Bilblox yelled gleefully. "Hurrah!" he exclaimed. "Ya just got the wind knocked outta ya!"

Alfonso coughed weakly and managed to gasp, "I'm okay."

He saw Bilblox peering down at him, his white eyes gleaming like frosted ice. The longshoreman gently grabbed hold of Alfonso and lifted him to his feet. They both sighed with relief.

"You're all right then?" Bilblox asked.

Alfonso said nothing. He stood there for a few seconds and felt his body and head throb with pain. However, he soon realized that nothing was broken, and that the wounds on his head—and the one on Bilblox's head as well—were superficial. They were both okay.

"Where's Snej?" asked Alfonso. "Is she still in the cockpit?"

"Dunno," replied Bilblox. "You're the first one I came across."

Alfonso staggered to a large hole in the wall of the plane where a window once existed. He peered outside, but could see nothing but snow and ice. It was as if the world had turned white.

"Snej!" yelled Bilblox. Alfonso ducked back inside. There was no response.

"You better go check on 'er," said Bilblox.

Alfonso nodded and began to make his way to the front of the plane. He entered the cockpit cautiously. Most of the dials, buttons, and levers were either smashed or burnt. Snej sat slumped over in her seat. Her head looked strange, almost doll-like. It hung loosely from her torso. Alfonso touched her shoulder.

"Snej, are you okay?" he whispered. "Snej?"

Bilblox's pilot lay there motionless. Alfonso drew closer and tried to ignore what he knew had happened, but there was no denying it: Snej's neck was broken. A cold tingling sensation crawled up Alfonso's spine and he felt sick. This was the second dead body in just three days, and in both cases he'd played a role in the deaths. The taxi driver he had killed. Murdered. Even if it was in self-defense. And Snej, well, if Alfonso hadn't insisted on going to the Urals in the depths of winter . . .

"What's going on?" asked Bilblox.

"She didn't make it," replied Alfonso. He was dimly conscious of his heart pounding. Panic began to take hold of him, and his hands started to shake.

"What?"

"Snej is . . . she's dead."

"Dead?"

Alfonso just stood there.

"Oh fer the love of Magrewski," said Bilblox. His voice cracked. "Of all the stinkin' rat luck. Poor Snej. Poor Snej."

"It's my fault," said Alfonso weakly.

"*No it ain't!*" snapped Bilblox. There was a ferocity in his voice that Alfonso had rarely heard before. "I'm the one who made the call. I didn't have to listen to ya. I was the boss."

But I forced you to go, thought Alfonso. He shivered and stepped aside to let Bilblox into the cockpit. The longshoreman-turned-smuggler tenderly maneuvered Snej's body into an upright position and then placed the pilot's hands on the Twin Otter's steering wheel.

"This is the way she'd want to go," said Bilblox with a choked sob. "Pilotin' the Twin Otter, doin' her job expertly to the end. She saved us." Silently, he drew a blanket over Snej's body.

A few seconds later, this moment was interrupted by a frightful sight. A very large wolf, roughly six feet in length, had suddenly wandered behind them into the main cabin of the plane. It had gray fur, blue eyes, and terrifying fangs. "Don't move," whispered Alfonso tensely. "There's a wolf in the plane."

"Oh, that's nothing to worry about," he said. He stepped out of the cockpit and into the main cabin. "Come here, Kõrgu!"

The wolf immediately leapt into Bilblox's outstretched arms from the middle of the cabin. It was an astounding jump. The wolf must have leapt fifteen feet. Only a man the size of Bilblox—who was roughly 350 pounds of solid muscle—could have absorbed the wolf's momentum and not toppled over.

"What the . . ." began Alfonso.

"This is my seein' eye dog," explained Bilblox. "She's quite a jumper. That's why her name is Kõrgushüpe. It means 'high jump' in Estonian."

"That's no dog," protested Alfonso.

"Fair enough," said Bilblox. "Technically she's a Mongolian wolf, but I don't like to advertise that fact, because people tend to get scared by the word *wolf*."

"I see," said Alfonso.

"She's perfectly friendly when she's not sinkin' her fangs into somethin'," said Bilblox. He let the wolf jump out of his hands back into the cabin, and then turned back to the cockpit. "We've got work to do," said Bilblox suddenly. "There are a number of things that we gotta do immediately. We gotta patch up some of the holes in this plane, find some blankets, and gather up some food. Maybe we'll even try to light a fire. I don't know what time-a day it is, but it feels like the sun is going down. We musta both blacked out for a while. Anyway, night'll be here before we know it, and I ain't gonna let us freeze to death."

"What about Great Wandering Day?" asked Alfonso.

"Don't matter," replied Bilblox. "The name of the game now is survival."

68

And that was that.

They immediately set to work converting the Twin Otter cabin into a shelter against the cold. First they unpacked their baggage and put on every last article of clothing that they had with them. Alfonso then searched the plane for supplies. In a storage area at the rear of the plane he found an emergency bin that included matches, a flare gun, a set of flares, a medical kit, a dozen or so blankets, two pots, a pair of binoculars, a flashlight, a compass, a container of powdered milk, and two dozen packages of freeze-dried chili. Alfonso dragged the entire bin into the main cabin of the plane. In the meantime, Bilblox had discovered Snej's rifle and three boxes of ammunition.

"It's an ol' thirty caliber, bolt-action Enfield," explained Bilblox. "It belonged to Snej. It was an antique that I bought for her in England on account of her heroism in several adventures. It's in perfect workin' order. I can't use it, but you may have to at some point. Let's hope not. Also, you might as well fire off the flare gun, just in case. I reckon we'll have to escape this jam ourselves, but you never know, maybe someone is watchin'."

Alfonso stepped outside and fired off two flares in rapid succession. He watched the flares cast a muted glow against the swirling snow. Perhaps someone would see them. After all, today was Great Wandering Day. But there were several serious problems. Somnos could be far away—ten or even fifty miles away. What's more, visibility was very bad. What were the chances that anyone would actually see these flares? Finally, it was evening now. The day was over. Most likely the gates had already closed shut and would stay shut for the next twelve years.

Alfonso and Bilblox spent the next hour stuffing cushions and other materials into the gaping holes in the Twin Otter's walls and ceiling. Visibility was nil but there was no doubt that it was getting colder and darker. They settled down to eat some rations, and then tried to rest.

Bilblox sank heavily to the floor of the plane. He suddenly looked very tired and haggard. He began to massage his forehead with his fingers as if he had a migraine.

"Are you all right?" asked Alfonso.

"I'm fine," muttered Bilblox.

"You have a headache?"

Bilblox nodded. Alfonso knew that his friend must be in serious pain because he rarely if ever complained of discomfort or even showed any signs of weakness.

"You started getting these headaches after your eyes turned white?" asked Alfonso.

Bilblox nodded. "Just give me a few minutes," he muttered. "I'll be all right."

Alfonso said nothing more. Instead, he tried to fall asleep, but this proved impossible. Eventually, out of sheer boredom, Alfonso grabbed the rosewood box that he had found in Alexandria and opened it up. Once again, he studied the thousands of tiny indentations that covered the bottom of the box. He eyed them with great frustration. Alfonso knew that if he just entered hypnogogia he might be able to decipher what hidden patterns or codes were embedded in these markings. For roughly two years now, however, he had avoided entering hypnogogia. He had been too afraid. Afraid that he might wind up back in the hospital. Afraid that he'd break his bones or end up in a coma again. But now, suddenly, he felt disgusted with himself. He was tired of being afraid.

Alfonso composed himself. He took several deep breaths. His heart rate began to slow. He relaxed his eyes and then focused on a single indentation. His mind became totally clear. Then something clicked deep within his consciousness—clicked almost like a key turning in a lock—and milliseconds later, Alfonso was in hypnogogia.

Right away, Alfonso could hear the faintest of noises—the sound of individual snowflakes colliding, the drip of water rolling down Bilblox's boots, and the slight groan of a metal screw loosening from the wall of the plane. He could smell everything, too—the odor of jet fuel leaking into the snow, the twang of paprika in the freeze-dried chili, and even the scent of iodine in the medical kit.

But there was no time to waste on any of this. Alfonso didn't want to stay in hypnogogia for long. Immediately, he directed his attention toward the rosewood box and the pattern of indentations. Some of the indentations were octagons (eight-sided) and some were nonagons (nine-sided). When he blocked out the octagons and focused only on the nonagons he saw that the nonagons clearly formed a doorway complete with a handle. There was no mistaking it. Then, to Alfonso's utter astonishment, the doorway actually swung open, as if the bottom of the box had transformed into an animated cartoon. The shock of this realization made Alfonso sit up and snap out of hypnogogia.

"What's wrong?" mumbled Bilblox. He had heard Alfonso stirring.

"You wouldn't believe me," replied Alfonso breathlessly.

"Go to sleep," muttered Bilblox. "We're gonna need our rest."

Bilblox instantly drifted back off to sleep. Kõrgu slept next to her master, with her head in Bilblox's lap. Alfonso shut the rosewood box, pulled several blankets over himself, and closed his eyes.

⧂

The mysterious currents of Alfonso's sleep whisked him into a dream. It was an unpleasant dream and one that he had actually experienced several times in the past few days. Alfonso and his classmates were about to enter the Eiffel Tower. They were on the ground below, among the hawkers selling wind-up plastic birds and fluorescent wristbands. Everyone wanted to take the elevator except for Alfonso. Instead, he took the stairs, climbing upward floor by floor. It was thrilling to be so exposed to the wind and sun, and to go up a different way than everyone else did.

Alfonso kept walking, cheerfully ignoring the shouts from his friends. They'd be quite impressed when he met them up above. In fact, he'd probably be waiting for them, since the line for the elevators was quite long. The wind and sun blew in his hair and he could see the distinctive Haussmann-era apartment buildings shining in the light of a crisp, clear day.

Then the dream took an unexpected turn. The sky clouded over. The wind abruptly became colder and Alfonso started to shiver. He looked around and noticed that the Eiffel Tower had begun to sway. Angry dark clouds covered the sky and in the far distance, Alfonso could see a disturbance, as if the ground was being churned up by a squadron of earthmovers. He felt his heart begin to pound. He tried to shout below, to warn his classmates, but no sound came out. The churning drew nearer. It buckled the earth, destroying whole city blocks. The air filled with dust and smoke. Alfonso held on to the superstructure of the Eiffel Tower as it vibrated rapidly. One leg of the massive tower was pushed up by this churning, and the entire structure began to bend.

As the Eiffel Tower began to fall, the air cleared and Alfonso could see the extent of the sudden devastation. In place of an orderly city, fires raged and people fled everywhere. What had been a flat city had turned into ruins pockmarked with giant bumps, as if something within the earth was trying to get out. Trees along the Champs-Élysées became skeletons and the water along the Seine turned black and began draining away. All that was green and living died in the blink of an eye. A great, screeching noise besieged Alfonso's ears. He looked and saw the graceful metal latticework of the Eiffel Tower tearing apart just above him. It was at that moment that Alfonso was finally able to scream.

Alfonso opened his eyes in terror. He found himself staring at a very anxious Bilblox.

"Stop screamin' 'n' get up!" Bilblox said. "Someone's pokin' around outside the plane."

"W-What?" asked Alfonso.

"Listen," said Bilblox. "You'll hear 'em."

Alfonso held his breath and heard footsteps. Bilblox was right. Someone or *something* was definitely out there.

Kõrgu began to growl. Her body trembled with anticipation of a fight.

"You better take this," whispered Bilblox as he handed Alfonso the Enfield rifle.

Alfonso took the gun and set it across his lap. An instant later, one of the cushions that they had stuffed into the wall popped out and a tall figure stepped into the plane.

"Who's there?!" demanded Alfonso as he grabbed the Enfield rifle and pointed it toward the intruder. "Bilblox, quick, turn on the flashlight!"

The intruder laughed in a very familiar way. "You wouldn't shoot an old man like me, would you?" he asked.

Bilblox flicked on the flashlight. Standing in the wreckage of the plane was Alfonso's one and only uncle, Hill Persplexy.

CHAPTER 11

A LAND TRANSFORMED

"UNCLE HILL!" exclaimed Alfonso. He ran to him and they exchanged a fierce hug.

"My dear boy," replied Hill with a smile. He wore a white fur-covered jacket, a thick wool hat, his battered pilot's goggles, and brown leather gloves. His mustache had grown longer and whiter. Otherwise, life in Somnos seemed to agree with him—Hill appeared to be in fine health.

"Alfonso, it's splendid of you to drop in on us," he said. "And just in time. We were about to close the gates on Great Wandering Day when one of our deployed scouts described a 'steel bird dropping out of the sky.' A steel bird—don't you love it? No one in Somnos has ever seen an airplane, of course. And then another scout saw the flares and, of course, we came over as fast as we could."

Another person, a tall woman, stepped through the same opening Hill used to enter the plane. She had jet-black hair that curled away from her cheeks, a noble face, and beguiling blue eyes that glittered in the dim light. She stood ramrod straight and glanced quickly at Hill, then Alfonso and Bilblox.

"Is everyone all right?" she asked in English, which was tinged with a squeaky Dormian accent. "And what is that wolf doing here?"

"That's my pup," replied Bilblox. "Don't worry, ma'am, she's had all 'er shots, and is as well trained as a mammal with fangs can be. As fer our condition, Alfonso's got a cut on his head and I've got one on my neck but otherwise we're okay." He paused. "The pilot—Snej Duhamel—didn't make it. If it wasn't fer 'er, we'd all be dead."

"My condolences," replied the woman drowsily. Her eyes were now half-closed and she appeared to be asleep. She was clearly a Dormian knight—those elite soldiers who vacillated between sleeping and waking every few seconds. "I will ask my knights to prepare a burial site." She then turned to face Alfonso, saluted, and bowed. Her eyes sprang open. She appeared to be taking a series of five-second naps.

"Colonel Nathalia Treeknot at your service, though please just call me Nathalia," she said. "I'm in charge of the Dormian Expeditionary Corps, part of the Order of the Dormian Knights." Her eyes closed. "On behalf of the Order, I'd like to welcome you home."

The colonel's words were welcoming enough, but there was something in her demeanor that seemed rather harsh. She barked several terse orders and her knights, who were all dressed in long fur coats, immediately snapped to. They gathered up whatever could be salvaged from the airplane—including the luggage, the Enfield rifle, and the contents of the emergency kit, while the others dug a burial site for Snej. Like the colonel, the knights switched between being asleep and awake every five seconds.

The funeral for Snej happened almost immediately. The group only had time for a brief ceremony before setting out through the snow, since the sky loomed gray with another blizzard. Bilblox was the only one to speak and he recited the same pilot's prayer that he had heard Snej utter so many times.

> *Oh, I have slipped the surly bonds of earth.*
> *And danced the skies on laughter-silvered wings,*
> *Sunward I've climbed and joined the tumbling mirth*
> *Of sun-split clouds—and done a hundred things . . .*

"I can't remember the rest," said Bilblox hoarsely. Tears gleamed on his face. "The prayer was written by a nineteen-year-old Canadian airman during World War Two."

"That's all right," replied Hill. Suddenly, he began reciting the verses of the poem where Bilblox left off.

> *. . . and done a hundred things*
> *You have not dreamed of—wheeled and soared*
>   *and swung*
> *High in the sunlit silence. Hov'ring there,*
> *I've chased the shouting wind along and flung*

My eager craft through footless halls of air.
Up, up the long delirious, burning blue
I've topped the windswept heights with easy grace,
Where never lark, or even eagle, flew.

Hill placed his arm tenderly around Bilblox.

"You knew the prayer?" asked Bilblox. "How?"

"You forget, my old friend—I too was once a pilot," said Hill with a smile. "I used to say it before every flight during my air force days." He looked up at the angry gray sky. "We've laid Snej to rest, and we'll mourn her later. But now it's time to go home. This weather won't hold much longer. "

Bilblox nodded somberly. "Let's go."

Although Alfonso and Bilblox were both exhausted and more than a little shaky, they blocked out their pain and trudged through the deep snow of the mountain's flank, following Hill, Colonel Treeknot, and the soldiers. Bilblox put a harness on Kõrgu and she led him expertly through the snow and then across fields of ice-covered rocks. At one point, Alfonso asked Bilblox how he was feeling and whether his headache had gone away.

"I'm better now," said Bilblox cheerfully, but there was an undeniable trace of weariness in his voice.

Snow began to fall and as the wind grew stronger it whipped at them in fierce gusts. Alfonso's cheeks grew numb and his eyes stung. Colonel Treeknot, who led the group, appeared to be zigzagging along an invisible path. There were no markers, and the route they followed was incredibly steep. And yet it appeared as if she were out on a Sunday stroll. Her calm confidence reassured Alfonso, as did the thought of seeing Somnos again.

They pushed on for several hours until the night lightened into an early, sullen morning. The snow began to fall more heavily, obscuring the razor-sharp peaks of the high Urals that surrounded them. Colonel Treeknot made several subtle hand gestures, and her soldiers took positions around Alfonso and Bilblox. In polite but insistent fashion, they grabbed the two by their elbows and helped them walk even faster. Apparently, Colonel Treeknot was starting to get nervous about the blizzard.

"Almost there," said Hill with a kindly smile.

Alfonso peered into the murky light ahead of him. As they rounded a bend, Treeknot walked up to a tall boulder that looked exactly like all of the other boulders surrounding it. She stood next to the rock and then somehow disappeared inside of it. Alfonso gasped.

Hill clapped him on the shoulder. "You see!" he whispered. "The stone gate we entered last time is for Wanderers and, of course, Great Sleepers. But we have another secret entrance— much smaller, of course—that offers access to Somnos. Only the really high muckamucks know about it."

"And you too?" asked Alfonso with a smile.

Hill proudly stood up straight. "It's because of my new position, dear nephew," said Hill. "I've been appointed foreign minister of Somnos. Isn't that something?"

"You're a diplomat?!" exclaimed Alfonso. "I thought Somnos

didn't have any dealings with foreign countries or the outside world."

"Typically it doesn't," said Hill cryptically. "But this is a relatively recent appointment. Strange times have come to Somnos."

One by one they followed Colonel Treeknot into the mountain. As he drew nearer, Alfonso saw that Treeknot had opened a four-foot-high door that was recessed within the boulder. The doorway led down a narrow, hand-carved passageway. At first, they could see dimly as they walked forward, but then one of Treeknot's soldiers shut the door behind them and firmly locked it. They were plunged into absolute darkness, and only the sound of dripping water echoing from somewhere in front gave them any sense of perspective.

As he stumbled forward, Alfonso felt the passageway growing warmer. He wanted to take off his scarf and jacket, but it was too narrow to move around. Bilblox was just barely squeezing his way through. After another ten minutes of walking, Colonel Treeknot paused and warned everyone to shield their eyes. She opened another hidden door and the golden sunlight of morning shone through. The sounds of birds chirping and wind rustling through leaves filled the passageway.

Alfonso walked into the blinding light and blinked furiously to adjust his eyes as quickly as possible. The sky above him was radiant. There were clouds, to be sure, but the clouds seemed to pulse with a powerful iridescent light. In front of them appeared a world of emerald green. They were standing on a cliff covered with tall zebra grass. Beneath them lay an incredible jungle. The tops of millions of trees with electric-green leaves formed a canopy that covered much of the valley. The trees themselves were all enormously tall and their branches were so thick that they created their own individualized ecosystems. Just one branch appeared to contain its own layer of soil, grasses, and even smaller trees.

Vines linked these branches and trees together, and along them ran, slithered, and hopped animals of all shapes and sizes, including monkeys, snakes, toucans, and tree frogs. Several wide rivers cut through the jungle and only here, along the riverbanks, was it possible to glimpse the jungle's floor. Giant ferns and orchids, thirty feet in height, reached upward toward the murky shafts of light that made their way through the surrounding treetops. The floor of the jungle itself appeared to be one continuous carpet of moss, which exuded a thick steam, as if it were being cooked. In the foreground, just below them, Alfonso spotted an animal that appeared to be an elephant, only it had an extremely narrow head and a pointy snout instead of a trunk.

Hill saw his nephew eyeing the animal and he offered an explanation. "Looks like an elephant, but it's about three times the size," explained Hill. "It's actually an anteater."

"You're kidding me," said Alfonso. "How big are the ants?"

"Some of them, the most troublesome kind, have the size and athleticism of a mountain lion," Colonel Treeknot explained nonchalantly. She was now fully awake. She took off her hat, scarf, and winter jacket, fully revealing her face and slender, athletic figure. Alfonso saw that she was quite attractive, although her face was a bit too sharp to be considered conventionally pretty. It was the kind of face that invited you to stare at it. Her eyes in particular sparkled with defiant exuberance.

"It's become a problem," continued Treeknot. She reached

into her pocket, pulled out an apple, and began to munch on it as she talked. "Ever since your Founding Tree took hold, the ecosystem has gone wild, and animals with certain types of metabolisms have become outlandishly large. Apparently this happens whenever a new Founding Tree first takes root. It lasts a few decades before stabilizing. It's been challenging for us— we've had to fight back the ants a few times. They're tough and they're organized, but it's all in a day's work. Besides, there are worse things in this jungle than the ants."

"Worse things?" asked Bilblox. "What kinda worse things are we talkin' about, ma'am? I ain't scared, just curious. You know, I have a pet to look after."

"Have a look at your tree," said Hill with a smile, trying to change the subject. "She's a beauty."

Alfonso looked out across the jungle, deep into the valley, and saw that the trees eventually thinned out and turned into fields of corn and wheat. Just beyond this was Somnos—the shining city of pink marble, with its proud towers and thick walls. It was impossible to see the damage that had been inflicted three years ago when the Dragoonya had invaded. Apparently, the Dormians were wizards when it came to rebuilding.

In the middle of the city stood the Founding Tree. Its branches and leaves extended out to cover the entire city like a massive umbrella. Even from this distance Alfonso could identify individual leaves. This was his sapling, now a fully fledged Founding Tree. This was the tree he had grown near a nameless stream in the middle of the north woods in Minnesota. It was the one he had carried across North America, across the polar icecap, across the Urals. It was the sapling that Spack and General Loxoc had died to defend. And here it was, pumping life into the soil. It seemed unimaginable that on Alfonso's previous visit all of this landscape had been covered in snow.

Alfonso's thoughts were interrupted by shouts and the sound of swords being withdrawn from their scabbards. He saw that Colonel Treeknot's men were in a classic Dormian defensive arrangement, fast asleep with their eyes half-shut.

"What's goin' on?" asked a frustrated Bilblox, who had been unable to take in any of his surroundings.

"Not sure," said Alfonso.

A moment later, something large and red leapt out of the zebra grass and lunged for Alfonso. Two of Colonel Treeknot's soldiers immediately attacked, throwing their bodies into the creature's hard shell. Their swords plunged into the creature's body. Alfonso stumbled backwards, nearly falling off the cliff, and then regained his balance. On the ground lay a bright red ant that must have weighed two hundred pounds. Its legs were still twitching. Green ooze leaked out of its head. Another ant scurried out of the grass and headed toward Bilblox. Kõrgu sprang into action. The wolf leapt through the air with dazzling speed and slammed its weight into the ant's body. The ant flew backwards, as if struck by a cannonball, and toppled over the edge of the cliff.

"That's some Seeing Eye dog," observed Hill.

"She's a good pup," replied Bilblox with a smile.

"We better get going," said Treeknot as she continued to eat her apple. "The scouting ants always travel in packs of ten or twelve. And not far behind them there's bound to be a foraging party. It's at least an hour's hike down to the river."

They began walking single file toward the jungle. Bilblox, Hill, and Alfonso were in the middle, and Dormian soldiers guarded them front and back. The closer they drew to the forest, the stranger it appeared. The sound of flowing water also grew louder. Alfonso could see a river forming to his left. It was made up of several dozen streams that came together just above the jungle, and that undoubtedly were made up of melt from the high-altitude glaciers that he could see above them. Some of the jungle trees looked perfectly ordinary, but others, Alfonso knew, were unique to Somnos. All of them were much larger than any but the largest and oldest trees in Minnesota. The trunk of one tree was covered with thick black bark that glistened like oil. Alfonso looked inquiringly at Hill.

"Isn't it a wonder?" Hill said. He continued hurrying along, huffing and puffing as he spoke. "Once we planted the bloom, the entire valley transformed itself in six months. And all these trees appeared within a few days! That one with the black bark actually secretes a type of combustible oil, just like a maple tree would secrete maple syrup. And there are many other plants I've never seen before. For example, the *Arboris pierratus* drops leaves every fall that are as light as a feather and as strong as steel. We use it to reinforce the pink limestone. It would be the perfect material for building planes, but the Dormians are wary of inventions from the outside world."

They entered the jungle along a dirt path that contrasted strangely with the light greens and yellows of the incredible plant life. As they hurried down the path, Hill pointed out a heavy, looping vine that weaved and coiled around the branches of several trees. "That vine grows everywhere," said Hill. "I've seen some that are at least a mile long. It's actually delicious if grilled properly."

At that moment, butterflies the size of Frisbees began to flutter and take off from the floor of the jungle.

"What now?" asked Bilblox.

"Butterflies," explained one of the soldiers nervously. He appeared to be asleep. "They tend to take flight before the ant hordes come."

"I ain't afraid of ants," muttered Bilblox.

Not far behind them, Alfonso could hear a persistent scampering noise. It sounded like hundreds and perhaps thousands of feet moving quickly.

"Gentlemen, I don't mean to be an alarmist," announced Treeknot as she nodded off to sleep, "but let's run along, shall we?"

The entire group, except for Alfonso and Bilblox, drifted off to sleep and sprinted down the path with their eyes half-closed. Alfonso didn't trust himself to fall asleep. Out of habit, Alfonso worried about how Bilblox would manage without being able to see, but Kõrgu was leading him along beautifully. The two were very well matched, and Kõrgu seemed to anticipate Bilblox's every move.

A few minutes later, they came upon the river Alfonso had seen before. Along the riverbank was a narrow dirt road presently occupied by three gargantuan anteaters. Each of the beasts stood a good forty feet tall and was saddled with open-air riding cabins, equipped with seats.

"Wake up!" declared Treeknot. "Everyone up the ladders! Don't forget the Great Sleeper's baggage! Someone help Bilblox get his footing! Drivers, steady your anteaters! Hurry now!"

Everyone in the traveling party scurried up the rope ladders that ascended to the riding cabins. Bilblox, who carried Kōrgu on his back, was the last one up. He joined Alfonso, Hill, and Treeknot in the lead anteater. The colonel leaned out and barked orders to her knights. Alfonso reached into his backpack and took out his sphere, but the colonel caught his eye and gave him a stern look, which seemed to suggest that this was *her* fight and he shouldn't intervene.

"Hoist up the ladders!" she yelled. "Fall asleep at will and ready for battle!"

Moments later, a wave of ants crashed through the forest. There were at least a hundred of them. Most were big, about six feet in length.

The anteaters immediately broke into action, waving their snouts about violently and sucking the ants in whole. The anteaters grunted greedily and appeared to be having a good time of it. The ants charged in waves, but each time they were either eaten or pummeled by the anteaters. Using bows and arrows taken from the riding cabins, the Dormian soldiers fired round after round at the ants. Alfonso was amazed at their skill; not once did they need anything more than one arrow per ant.

"What's going on?" demanded Bilblox. "Somebody talk to me. I need the play-by-play."

"You wouldn't believe me," said Alfonso breathlessly.

The battle raged for another ten minutes until the ants beat a hasty retreat into the jungle. Colonel Treeknot watched them leave and then turned to those in her cabin.

"It's time to leave," she said. "The ants will be back and in greater numbers."

The three anteaters traveled down the dirt road toward Somnos. The road followed the meandering river, although at times they lost sight of it because of the incredible vegetation growth. Treeknot and her soldiers were on guard the entire time; once in a great while, they encountered ants dropping down from the trees. But these ants were alone and they scurried away without causing any trouble.

The road along the river was very indirect and so it took the traveling party the better part of the day to reach their destination. Alfonso and Bilblox both napped on and off over the course of the journey. Eventually, the jungle thinned out and they entered a series of orchards filled with apple, pear, and peach trees.

Nestled in one of these orchards, right by the river's edge, was a five-story mansion made of pink marble. The house was built like a Japanese pagoda, with each successive floor being smaller than the one below it. Wide porches wrapped around the top two stories of the house. A rope and wood-planked bridge stretched from one end of the fifth-floor porch to the nearest tree. Alfonso could see a network of ropes and ladders extending from that tree onto other trees. It was twilight. The sun had just vanished behind the High Peaks of the Urals, and the last rays of sunlight shimmered gently off the marble walls of the house. Songbirds darted from the roof to the porches and filled the area with music. Alfonso stared blankly—it was the most beautiful house he had ever seen.

"What do you think of my house?" asked Hill. The anteaters had stopped on the road, right near the house. Bilblox and Treeknot were already making their way down the ladder.

"It's incredible!" replied Alfonso.

"I'm glad you like it," said Hill proudly. "After all, it's the official residence of the foreign minister of Somnos." He looked at Alfonso and his eyes twinkled with delight. "Let's go inside, shall we?"

Alfonso looked around and saw that for a moment, they were alone.

"What's the matter?" Hill asked.

"Before we go in, I have to tell you something," said Alfonso. Then, as quickly as he could, Alfonso retold the events of the last few days, starting in Marseille and ending with the astonishing discovery in Alexandria that Leif might actually be alive. Hill listened quietly.

When Alfonso finished, he stared at Hill and waited for him to respond. Hill sighed heavily, as if the weight of the information he had just received was too much for him.

"I'm speechless," he eventually replied. His eyes gleamed, and Alfonso knew he was thinking about his brother, Leif. "At the same time, I'm not completely surprised."

Alfonso nodded, a bit confused.

"You said you found something in Alexandria," said Hill. "Do you have it with you?"

Alfonso reached into his backpack and withdrew the rosewood box. Hill took the box and ran a finger over the intricate carvings. "Josephus will want to hear your entire story, every detail," said Hill at last. "You did the right thing in coming here immediately." In a soft voice he said, "To think that my brother might still be alive!"

"We have to find him," said Alfonso.

"We will," he replied quietly but with great feeling. "I'd give anything to see Leif again."

Alfonso smiled and nodded appreciatively. He knew returning to Somnos was the right thing to do.

"Now, let's go to the house," said Hill. "It's time to rest—you and Bilblox have had a tough few days. We'll have a nice dinner, you'll see Resuza again, and I'll introduce you to my wife, Nance!"

It was Alfonso's turn to be surprised. "You're married?" he asked. Alfonso had assumed Uncle Hill was not the marrying type.

"A lot has happened in Somnos since you left," he said with a hesitant smile. "Lo and behold," added Hill exuberantly, "here is my wife now."

Hill's wife, Nance, emerged through the front door and skipped happily down to where her husband was standing. She was a beautiful woman, with hazel eyes, long brown hair that framed her sculptured face, and skin the color of copper. She looked far younger than Hill. If Alfonso had to guess, he would say that Nance was in her early thirties. Hill and Nance embraced passionately and Alfonso took a step back, rather awkwardly, trying to give them as much space as possible.

As he backed away and averted his eyes, Alfonso noticed a second figure emerge from the house. She was a young woman wearing an elegant saffron-colored dress. The fabric around the neck and arms was embroidered with purple and green vines.

The young woman had luxuriant blond hair. She was tall—a good three or four inches taller than Alfonso—and was smiling mischievously. This smile triggered Alfonso's memory.

He was staring at Resuza.

Alfonso suddenly felt even more awkward. It had been three years since he saw her last. In that time, they had both grown up, but Resuza had transformed the most. She had become, well . . . very pretty.

Resuza ran down to where Alfonso was standing and threw her arms around him. "You came back!" she exclaimed. "I knew you'd come back."

CHAPTER 12

DINNER AT THE FOREIGN MINISTER'S RESIDENCE

DINNER THAT EVENING was an elegant and sumptuous affair, as was the case with all of Hill's meals now that he was foreign minister. Alfonso, Bilblox, Resuza, Hill, and Nance all sat around a large circular table that dominated the second floor of the mansion. The wooden table groaned under the weight of the dishes and platters of food. In the middle lay ten different meat and fish dishes, festooned with skewers of fruit and surrounded by elegant arrangements of flowers. Arrayed in a semicircle around each plate were crystal glasses containing several types of sparkling juices. Torches made of a sweet-smelling amber wood flickered from limestone perches above them. In the corner of the dining hall sat a trio of harpsichordists playing music that sounded remarkably similar to a fast-flowing stream. Standing next to them were a dozen heavyset men, all fast asleep and snoring in perfect harmony. According to Hill, these men comprised the Royal Chorus of Snorers.

The snoring chorus was led by a pudgy, red-faced man with at least six chins. His name was Chrapać Głośno and his snoring was the loudest and most distinct. He would snore, then wheeze, then cough, then snuffle, then whistle through his nose, and finally both grunt and clatter his teeth simultaneously. This strange sequence set a rhythm for the other snorers, who provided a chorus of purrs and hisses to accompany him. Oddly enough, the overall effect was rather pleasing.

"Mr. Głośno comes from a long line of distinguished snorers," explained Hill. "His great-great-grandfather was also in the Royal Chorus of Snorers. He was a famous baritone. He snored so loudly that the army actually used him to help trigger avalanches. There is actually a long history of snorers . . ."

"Sweetie pie, let's not ruin dinner with a history lesson," said Nance softly. She yawned, as if just waking up from a long nap. "They've just arrived after a *terrible* journey. Let them eat and relax!"

Hill then changed the topic of conversation to a subject that Nance seemed to prefer—namely, herself. Nance, explained Hill, was a legendary singer in Somnos and she had married Hill shortly after the great Battle of Somnos, three years ago. Her marriage to Hill was considered somewhat scandalous, given that she was half Hill's age. Some said Nance had only married Hill because he had become a hero and the toast of the town. Hill knew of the rumors, of course, but he paid them no mind. He was fond of saying, "People are fools for the most part—and no one is more foolish than the fools who listen to the gossip of their fellow fools."

Out of the corner of his eye, Alfonso saw Resuza staring at him. Their first encounter a few hours ago had been strange. Upon seeing Alfonso walk up from the river, Resuza had run out of the house and thrown her arms around him. For those initial seconds, Alfonso felt elated. But once the hug came to an end, Alfonso felt unsure of what to say to her. Her beauty made him feel clumsy and uncertain. In the swirl of introductions and tours, they had said nothing more to each other.

"It's really quite a treat that Mr. Głośno is with us tonight," explained Nance. She lowered her voice to a whisper. "He's been quite ill."

"Nance!" Hill exclaimed.

Nance smiled. "Mr. Głośno had a period where he relapsed as a 'tired Dormian.'"

Alfonso nodded. This was the same problem Spack had had. For Dormians, it meant that they slept without doing *anything at all,* just like non-Dormians. It was considered to be a severe handicap.

"I had been warning him for years that this might happen," continued Nance. "All that stress, poor nutrition, and lack of exercise. Fortunately, it was temporary, and now he's back to his old form."

They all stared at Mr. Głośno as he snored in his pleasant manner. As if they knew that they were the object of attention, he and the Royal Chorus of Snorers delivered a rousing crescendo of snores that rattled the crystal glasses.

After dinner, they all climbed to the top-floor porch to drink Dormian herb tea as a digestive. They listened to the sounds of birds and other animals in the jungle while Hill talked about reconstruction efforts in Somnos and the remarkable changes brought on by the new Founding Tree.

"Excuse me, dear," said Nance at one point. "Are the guards at their stations? The jungle seems unusually noisy tonight."

"Yes, yes, yes, of course," replied Hill. He then turned toward Alfonso and Bilblox and explained: "You see, living so close to the jungle as we do, we have to be especially careful about the animals—the ants mainly—but other things as well. Of course there's nothing to worry about . . ."

"That's not exactly true, dear," said Nance. "You see, Hill insists on living in the country, but it really isn't entirely safe out here. A sugarcane plantation half a mile from here was overrun by ants just last month. Several people were terribly wounded, and one of them later died . . ."

"Yes," said Hill, "but they only had two anteaters, my dear."

"I'd prefer living in the city," Nance insisted. "It's so much safer there."

Hill sighed. Clearly, this was a recurring argument between him and Nance. Alfonso changed the subject and asked about Colonel Treeknot. Hill looked relieved to talk about something else. He explained that three years ago, she had distinguished herself in the Expeditionary Corps' mission to explore the Founding Tree's collapsing root system and to search for any

94

lingering Dragoonya soldiers. In addition, she came from a distinguished Somnos family. Josephus was her uncle, and they were quite close.

"Why did they bother going down there?" asked Alfonso. "Didn't the entire root system eventually collapse? No one could have survived that."

"Sometimes the roots collapsed but left tunnels and caves in their place," Hill explained. "In other cases, the roots had taken the path of least resistance, and had filled naturally occurring caves. These places remained after the collapse of the roots and the Expeditionary Corps had to search every one, to make sure no Dragoonya remained. We couldn't take the chance of any Dragoonya skulking around the city. And as it turns out, we made the right decision."

"What do ya mean?" asked Bilblox.

"They captured Kiril alive," interjected Resuza.

"Kiril?" exclaimed Alfonso. Kiril was the Dragoonya's second in command, behind Nartam. He was an expert tracker and master swordsman who had stalked Alfonso during his trip to Somnos three years ago. Alfonso had once seen Kiril fight off four men at once, ultimately killing all of them. Kiril had also slain General Loxoc, the head of the Dormian army. And like Nartam, Kiril was born Dormian and had turned against his own people.

"Don't worry," said Hill. "Kiril is in a specially constructed, maximum-security wing of the old prison."

Bilblox snorted. "You kiddin' me? You remember Kiril in Barsh-yin-Binder, or in the battle at the walls of Somnos? He's the best killer there is. You can't keep him in this city! Eventually, that fella'll find a way to wreak havoc."

"He has to stand trial," said Hill somewhat defensively. "We're an honorable society. We can't just execute him! Plus, what can one man do against an entire city of Dormians? He's guarded by two sets of soldiers, both awake and asleep."

Hill went on to explain that several weeks after the Battle of Somnos, Kiril had been captured in one of the semicollapsed root tunnels. "It was Colonel Treeknot who found him," explained Hill. "She and two of her knights discovered him sitting on a block of ice, with blood streaming from his head. He had a severe concussion and he was incoherent. No one knows how Kiril became injured, and he refused to say what happened. The fact is, he remained silent and uncooperative for the better part of three years until two months ago, when he suddenly started to talk. "

"Kiril's trial started a few weeks ago!" Nance exclaimed. "We can go to the court! Just think, the Great Sleeper confronts his enemy! Somnos will be all abuzz!"

Alfonso looked uneasily at Hill. He had no interest in seeing Kiril again.

"We'll see," Hill replied diplomatically. "Kiril is past history. There are other, more pressing issues at hand."

"*Marcus Firment,*" whispered Nance with a mischievous smile. Apparently, this was a woman who thrived on gossip.

Hill nodded. "Three days ago, a Wanderer—one of an illustrious group that left thirty-six years ago—arrived at the main gate just before Great Wandering Day. When the Dormian knights found him, he was suffering from severe frostbite and hypothermia, and even though he was over six feet tall, he weighed less than a hundred pounds. He refused all help until he spoke with the Grand Vizier."

"What did Marcus Firment tell her?" asked Alfonso.

"That's the truly mysterious part," declared Nance. "No one knows except for the Grand Vizier and Hill, who was also there. But neither of them will breathe a word of what was said. You see what a killjoy I have for a husband!?"

"It's a sad business," said Hill quietly. "Soon after his arrival, Firment died from exposure."

Their conversation was interrupted by a loud snort from one of the anteaters. The gigantic animal was standing nearby and it was just barely possible to see its silhouette in the moonlight. Steam rose off its back. Everyone strained their eyes and peered into the darkness. Everyone except for Hill.

Instead, Hill glanced at Alfonso and gave silent thanks that his nephew was alive and well. Hill had been eagerly hoping that Alfonso would return to Somnos and he had been disappointed when his nephew failed to appear at the city's gates on the morning of Great Wandering Day. Later, when he rescued Alfonso from the downed airplane, Hill was overcome with a rare feeling: joy.

During the last three years in Somnos, Hill had achieved more than he ever dreamed possible when he had been a locksmith in Chicago. Hill had been made foreign minister of his homeland, married a famous singer, and lived in a beautiful mansion. He remained a national hero.

Still, something was amiss.

In recent months, Hill would sometimes wake in the middle of the night and find that he had sleepwalked all the way to the ancient cemetery in the Trunk District of Somnos, at the foot of the Founding Tree. He'd be standing at the moss-covered gravestones of his grandparents and parents. Next to them was also a gravestone for his younger brother, Leif, even though there was no body buried beneath the stone. Hill had insisted on this, as a way to honor the memory of his brother.

On other nights, Hill would wake and find himself in the Delirium Quarter of the city—a spooky and rat-infested area dominated by old warehouses. The Delirium Quarter was also home to Somnos's few pickpockets and criminals. On his excursions here, Hill typically awoke in front of a small, plain doorway. Engraved on the door was the curious symbol of a plant growing out of the spine of an open-faced book.

Once, Hill found that the door was open, and he climbed a narrow set of stairs leading to a warehouse filled with thousands of bronze canisters stacked in neat, orderly piles. The canisters looked like oversize tablets of aspirin. Two elderly men were picking up the canisters, inspecting them, and then restacking them one by one.

"What is this place?" asked Hill. The old men explained that this was the Arboreal Research Vault, a place containing rare tree and plant specimens. They came from all over the world, but especially from the Dormian cities and from Straszydlo Forest. The specimens, which were all stored in the bronze canisters, included strips of bark, sap, dried leaves, and seeds.

"Are you doing some kind of inventory?" asked Hill.

"Yes sir, Foreign Minister," replied one of the men. "You see, during the recent Battle of Somnos, it looks as if the Dragoonya raided the vault. Apparently some canisters are missing, but the records are bad and we're trying to figure out what or if anything was taken."

This made no sense. Why would the Dragoonya bother with this old warehouse? And why did Hill keep coming here in his sleep? There had to be a reason—there always was—but Hill couldn't decipher it.

In the last months, Hill felt as if his mind was becoming increasingly muddled. His attention span seemed to be diminishing. Even during his waking hours, Hill became restless and fidgety. He stopped eating properly and his moods became increasingly somber. He began muttering to himself and complained frequently of feeling overly drowsy. Nance had insisted that he visit the doctor, but the doctor declared that the foreign minister suffered from no diagnosable ailments. "Perhaps I am just getting old," Hill told his wife. "Old and a little crazy."

Lately, Hill's sleeping-self was becoming even more erratic. The Marcus Firment situation was weighing very heavily on Hill. And now came the news that Leif might still be alive. Hill felt sure that these were all pieces to the same puzzle. Perhaps Josephus could help decipher what all of this meant.

Hill rubbed his eyes tiredly. These were serious times in Somnos—most Dormians acknowledged that—but only Hill and Grand Vizier knew just how precarious the fate of Dormia truly was.

CHAPTER 13

IMAD'S ANTECHAMBER

After finishing his tea, Alfonso made his way to the cozy little guest bedroom on the third floor of the mansion. Most of the bedrooms in Hill's mansion weren't actually bedrooms at all because they contained no beds. In fact, the Dormians called these rooms "waking chambers." Dormians, of course, almost never slept in beds. They spent their sleeping hours out of the house and busy at work, doing tasks that required high levels of concentration and precision. When they returned home and spent time in their waking chambers, Dormians tended to engage in quiet, contemplative behavior—like playing music, painting pictures, writing poetry, meditating, or simply reading a good book.

Perhaps because he was only half-Dormian, Alfonso enjoyed

a good night's sleep. Alfonso was relieved to see that his guest bedroom was furnished with a bed. It also had a small desk and a balcony overlooking the river. Alfonso unpacked his backpack and carefully hid both his sphere and his rosewood box underneath the bed. He was just getting ready to get under the covers when he heard a faint noise at the window. It sounded like someone whispering.

Alfonso walked over to the window, opened it fully, and listened to the sounds of the night. At first, he heard nothing but the distant snorts of the anteaters, but then he heard the strange noise again. It sounded like a cross between whispering and the wind blowing in the trees. This time the words were quite audible: *Did you see it? Did you see it? Did you see it?*

Alfonso wondered if his mind was playing tricks on him. "Did I see what?" he asked out loud.

The response was immediate: *The place where the Wanderers have gathered—the deep hole in the ground.*

"Y-Yes," he stammered. "I saw it." A prickle of fear ran up Alfonso's neck.

It will happen again. You've come late, perhaps too late.

"Where are you?" demanded Alfonso. "Who are you?"

Do you not know me?

Alfonso stuck his head out the window to get a better look around. He saw no one, only the orchards and fields and then beyond this, the towering silhouette of the Founding Tree. He decided to go wake his uncle. Maybe he had been hearing the same noise.

Deep inside his head, he distinctly heard the response to his thoughts: *It will do no good. There is only one who can help you. And he is far away.*

101

"Who?" asked Alfonso nervously. "Who are you talking about?"

There was no response.

Alfonso was overcome with a creepy feeling. A question bubbled up from his subconscious: had he just been conversing with the Founding Tree? His Founding Tree. It was an absurd thought, but then again, Alfonso's life was filled with many absurdities. Other questions soon flooded his mind as well. Was it the Founding Tree that had drawn him into the catacombs beneath Paris, to the place where strange holes burrowed down into the earth? And, if so, why?

Moments later, the door to his room resounded with a crisp knock. Alfonso opened the door and found Resuza.

"You look like you've just seen a ghost," said Resuza.

"Sorry," muttered Alfonso. "I'm a little tired."

"Can I come in?" asked Resuza.

"Yeah, of course," said Alfonso.

As she entered the room, Alfonso marveled at how much Resuza had changed over the last three years. She was now sixteen years old, and a far cry from the orphan who had helped them navigate the streets of Barsh-yin-Binder.

"I hope I didn't wake you," she said. "It's just that our house has this lovely pool . . ."

"You want to swim now?" asked Alfonso. "It's dark."

"You're not made of sugar—you won't melt in the water," teased Resuza. "Come on, we have a first-rate diving board." She held up two long towels and smiled. She looked beautiful in the murky candlelight of the bedroom. It would have been impossible for Alfonso to say no.

"Okay," he said with an awkward shrug of his shoulders.

They walked upstairs to the fifth floor of the mansion and out onto a deck that overlooked the property. The far end of the deck connected to a swinging bridge made of thick ropes and wood planks, which rose steeply up into the canopy of a nearby palm tree.

"Come on," said Resuza, as she swished her towel impatiently.

"Where are we going?" asked Alfonso.

"Don't worry, it'll be fun!" yelled Resuza. She began skipping across the swinging bridge.

"What about the ants?" asked Alfonso. Resuza was already out of earshot, however, and Alfonso hurried to catch up. He stepped across the wooden planks of the bridge. It was incredibly dark; the only lights came from the occasional flickering of fireflies. Alfonso inhaled deeply. The night air smelled like honey. The bridge continued to climb steeply, until it reached the trunk of a large tree, and it ended at a wooden platform that was built into the tree itself. From here, a second swinging bridge led the way over to another nearby tree. It appeared as if there was an entire network of walkways connecting dozens of treetops.

Suddenly, Resuza spun around and leapt into the darkness below. Several seconds later Alfonso heard a loud flapping noise and then, several seconds after that, he heard a splash. Alfonso peered down, straining his eyes as hard as he could, but it was impossible to see anything in the blackness of the night.

"Come on!" yelled Resuza from what sounded like far below. "The pool is big—you can't miss!"

Alfonso hesitated, but then took a deep breath and leapt into the darkness. He fell for several seconds and then—quite miraculously—he felt himself traveling back up. This was short-lived. He was soon heading back down and then, *splash,* he was immersed in warm water.

"How'd you like that?" asked Resuza.

"What happened?" sputtered Alfonso as he tread water and struggled to get his bearings.

"On the way down you hit a giant leaf—Hill and I put it there deliberately to break the fall—and it bounces you upward, like a springboard, and then you come back down into the water."

Alfonso looked behind him and, now that his eyes were adjusted to the darkness, saw a giant leaf suspended over a corner of the pool.

"Awesome," said Alfonso. "I could do that all day!"

"I have a secret for you," Resuza suddenly whispered.

"Okay," said Alfonso.

"Two days ago the Grand Vizier dropped by unannounced for dinner," Resuza continued. "Afterward, she asked to talk with Hill in private. They went up to his study on the fourth floor and I kind of tagged along, you know, eavesdropped. Well, I couldn't hear everything, just bits and pieces. Apparently Firment encountered a large army of Dragoonya during his travels. 'Enormous' was the word he used. He was convinced that they were searching for something they considered extremely valuable. 'A mad, frantic search' is how he described it," explained Resuza.

"What do you think is going on?" asked Alfonso.

"I'm not sure," replied Resuza. "We'll have to keep our eyes peeled and ears open. Meanwhile, I'm so happy you're here!" She splashed him playfully. "We've got to go on some adventures while you're here. I'm desperate for some excitement."

"Come on," said Alfonso. "It can't be that bad here. I mean, you live in a mansion!"

"That's what you'd think," said Resuza. She quickly explained that life in Somnos was comfortable, but frightfully boring. Occasionally, she managed to sneak out and go hunting with some of the old Dormian hill dwellers who roamed the jungle on their anteaters, looking for ant colonies. There was one hill dweller in particular, an old woman named Misty, whom she especially liked. Misty was her only real friend. Resuza didn't regret her decision to stay with Hill in Somnos, but she felt increasingly certain that at some point she would have to leave.

"I was going to sneak out on Great Wandering Day," said Resuza, "but I wanted to see if you showed up. So you really do owe me. Now promise that you'll come with me on some adventures." Her voice dropped to a whisper. "And then I'll tell you the strangest part of what I overheard."

"I promise," replied Alfonso. "Now what else did you hear?"

Resuza took a deep breath.

"Firment said the Dragoonya were being led by a young teenager," said Resuza. "He was a boy just about your age."

"A boy my age?" asked Alfonso.

"Yeah, weird, isn't it?"

Later that night, when he had returned to his bedroom, Alfonso found himself sitting on the edge of his bed, holding the rosewood box in his hands. He couldn't sleep and his thoughts returned to this curious box that he had found in Alexandria. Alfonso sensed that, somehow, this box was the key to finding his father.

Once again, he studied the thousands of indentations that were imprinted on the floor of the box. Before he even fully realized what he was doing, Alfonso felt himself slipping into hypnogogia, and soon all of his senses came fully alive. He concentrated on the box and trained his mind to focus only on the indentations that were nonagons, or nine-sided. Almost instantly, the image of a door came into focus and, moments later, the door swung open.

This time, instead of pulling out of hypnogogia, Alfonso urged his mind to move through the door. Ten or perhaps fifteen seconds passed until suddenly Alfonso found himself in a small, windowless room, with marble floors and wood-paneled walls. The room had several candelabras, which cast a soft yellowish light. The only piece of furniture in the room was a narrow, wooden desk. On top of this desk was a piece of parchment. Alfonso walked over to the desk and took a closer look at the parchment. It contained a note, which read:

My dear Alfonso,

Welcome to my antechamber. My name is Imad, and while I have been dead for untold centuries, I am still very pleased to meet you. Though, I shouldn't welcome you too heartily because, in truth, you really aren't here. This room doesn't exist, except in your mind. In a sense, you are dreaming, but it is a very special kind of dream. You have found your way into this antechamber because you are a Great Sleeper. You have saved the city of Somnos—a great feat—but now you have a far greater task at hand. A cataclysm is coming. You sensed it. The Wanderers in Paris sensed it. Even the Founding Tree here in Somnos has sensed it. And so, now, there is much for you to learn.

When you stop reading this note, turn around and you will notice three doors.

Don't look yet—I have more to tell you. You may only enter this antechamber three times. On each of these three occasions, you must exit through a different doorway. Each doorway offers you a unique lesson.

Finally, and this is of the utmost importance, do not discuss the secrets of this antechamber with anyone—except, perhaps, another Great Sleeper. This is for your own good.

Your loyal and eternal servant,
Imad

When he was done reading the parchment, Alfonso turned around and, sure enough, he noticed three wooden doors that hadn't been there just moments before. The doors were all identical, except for their brass doorknobs, each of which was emblazoned with a unique image. One doorknob was marked with a cloud, another was marked with an ocean wave, and a third was marked with the image of a brick wall.

"This is crazy," muttered Alfonso to himself.

He walked over to the doorway on the far left, the one with the doorknob that bore the image of the cloud. He grabbed the doorknob and opened the door. On the other side of the threshold, he saw nothing but utter darkness. He stepped into the darkness and, almost instantly, began to plummet down, through air that turned moist and humid.

Alfonso began staring at a curious droplet of water that was falling with him. Moments later, Alfonso could see billions of water particles swirling around him. The particles all seemed to be connected by undulating currents of energy. Alfonso could not see this energy, but he could hear it crackling like a radio transmitter that is only picking up on static. Without even thinking about it, Alfonso reached out his arms and spread his fingers. He could feel tendrils of energy pulsing through his fingertips as they brushed upon and then touched the water particles. Alfonso did the same with his feet, and noticed how placing them on the particles began to slow him down. Then he felt weightless—as if a parachute had opened up above him.

An instant later, Alfonso found himself back in the guest room at Hill's mansion. He was sitting on the edge of his bed, with the rosewood box in his hands, and it appeared as if absolutely nothing at all had happened. The only sign of the incredible journey his mind had taken was Alfonso's hands, which were quite pale and trembling violently.

CHAPTER 14

SOMNOS

THE FOLLOWING MORNING, Hill saddled up his favorite anteater—a massive animal with gleaming black eyes, narrow slits for ears, and a tail as long as a tree. Her name was Bataar and Hill insisted that she had saved his life on no less than three occasions. "She's quick on her feet and she can suck down three dozen ants without batting an eye," he proclaimed. "She'll get us to Somnos swiftly."

Alfonso, Bilblox, and Resuza followed Hill's lead and climbed up the rope ladder that ascended to the open-air riding cabin on Bataar's back. This was a different cabin from the one they had ridden in the previous day. Instead of wooden seats, it was furnished with ornate carpets and large, cushy pillows. A breakfast of fruit and freshly baked banana bread was spread out on a small coffee table.

For roughly an hour, Bataar trotted down a narrow country road winding toward Somnos. Alfonso couldn't help staring at the city. The walls shined a lustrous pink and the Founding Tree's bright green leaves shaded the rest of the city. The fields directly in front of the city's walls were occupied by hundreds of giant anteaters, who were stationed there as a precaution, in case the ants became too bold. These anteaters moped about lazily and didn't even take notice of Bataar.

They left Bataar at the southernmost gate to the city and proceeded directly to the library, where Josephus was expecting them. Alfonso was able to pick out the guest tower where he had stayed on his previous visit, and he recognized a few other landmarks, including the Tree Palace, the Iron Pillow, and City Hall with its two identical buildings: one for the "waking mayor" and the other for the "sleeping mayor." Alfonso also noticed a large marble statue dedicated to Spack of Barshyin-Binder—the "lazy Dormian" who had helped Alfonso find Somnos and then died defending the city against the Dragoonya.

The biggest change in the city was the presence of water. The largest streets had all been flooded and turned into canals. In fact, the most common way to travel around the city was by gondolas, which were pulled by large turtles. Hill had hired a gondola with a team of six turtles to take them down the main canal to the old library. The driver of the boat was a short, squat man who snored loudly as he called directives out to his turtles.

The water in the canals was perfectly clear and sweet-smelling. If you looked closely enough, you could see lost coins that sat thirty feet beneath the water on the pebbly bottom of the canal. In fact, water was everywhere—flowing in the canals, spurting from faucets on the sides of buildings, and falling in graceful arcs from fountains perched on rooftops. The sun's rays glimmered through the water droplets and, as a result, hundreds of rainbows adorned the sky. Many residents were sleep-swimming in the canals for exercise. Compared to the bitter, famished city of three years ago, the new Somnos was nothing short of miraculous.

"Quite a change," remarked Hill as their gondola cut through the water of the main canal. "Amazing, isn't it?"

Alfonso nodded.

"As soon as the roots of the new Founding Tree took hold, the snow started melting and we got more water than we knew what to do with," said Hill. "It's like everything else since the new tree was planted—we just had to adjust. The old tree had been dying for such a long time that no one knew the full effect of a young, healthy one."

Alfonso was soon distracted by the sight of several men sleepwalking on a promenade alongside the canal. Their movements were extremely jerky, as if they were all simultaneously having muscle spasms or fits of epilepsy. "What's with those guys?" asked Alfonso.

"Oh nothing," said Hill. "They're having some hypnic jerks—you know, a case of the twitches—that's pretty common in the Drowsy Quarter."

"The Drowsy Quarter?" inquired Bilblox.

"Oh yes," said Hill. "You see, the city is divided into four quarters, and each quarter is known for a certain type of sleep."

Bilblox and Alfonso looked confused.

"There are four stages of sleep," explained Hill in a professorial tone. "In the outside world, scientists call those stages N1, N2, N3, and REM sleep. Here we prefer Drowsy Sleep, Deep Sleep, Dreamer's Sleep, and Delirium Sleep. In the course of a single night's worth of sleep, all human beings cycle through each of these four stages."

"And all of these stages are different?" asked Bilblox.

"Absolutely," replied Hill. "Drowsy Sleep is the lightest level of sleep. Your body is usually jerking and twitching quite a bit—much like those fellows you just saw back there. This is the kind of sleep that the Dormian knights typically enter when they hop back and forth between waking and sleeping. Deep Sleep is, of course, the deepest and most subconscious kind of sleep. This is when people tend to sleepwalk and do all manner of highly focused activities—from shooting arrows to tightrope walking. Dreamer's Sleep occurs when we have rapid eye movement and visions. It is the most creative, artistic, and inspired stage of sleep. Dormians tend to be most creative while awake, but a few of us—the really gifted ones—are capable of great artistry and imagination while asleep. And, finally, Delirium Sleep is, well, it's the worst kind. It's the sort where we toss, turn, and have night terrors or nightmares. But, thankfully, most of us only spend a few minutes in Delirium Sleep each night.

"Anyway, each of the city's four quarters is devoted to a different type of sleep," continued Hill. "Of course, you don't have to be in Drowsy Sleep when you're in the Drowsy Quarter. But, for the most part, people tend to gravitate toward the quarter of the city that corresponds to the type of sleep they're in."

"What if you're awake?" asked Bilblox.

"Then you go wherever you like," replied Hill. "But when we Dormians go to sleep we are typically drawn to one of these four quarters. Don't ask me why. It has something to do with the roots of the Founding Tree being different beneath the soil of each quarter. And the quarters themselves are as different as can be. For example, the Drowsy Quarter is popular with the sleeping knights and it's where their hangout, the Iron Pillow, is located. The Deep Sleep Quarter is kind of like the downtown—you know, full of intense, bustling activity. The Dreamer's Quarter is where the artists, musicians, and writers go to compose their work." He smiled. "That's where I first met Nance. It's a lovely place. And then there's the Delirium Quarter. Since people don't spend much time in Delirium Sleep, that quarter is pretty empty—mainly it's warehouses, graveyards, and deserted streets."

"It's an awful place," added Resuza, who had been listening quietly up until now. "The few people who go there are usually in a panic or even crying. I hate that place. I don't know why anyone would live there. I think Josephus lives there, doesn't he?" Hill nodded, but said nothing. Resuza shuddered. "Why he'd want to live there is beyond me."

Moments later, the turtles pulled up to a dock just below the library. A parking attendant was waiting for them and jittering nervously—obviously in the throes of Drowsy Sleep.

Josephus's office looked out upon a large courtyard filled with many types of tropical vegetation, including birds of paradise, bullhorn acacia, rough maidenhair, and many curious fernlike plants that had long, spindly stems and moved around slowly in order to get the best sunshine. The walls of the courtyard were covered with a vine featuring bright purple flowers that snapped shut whenever anyone passed by. In the center of the courtyard stood a towering pear tree that grew pears the size of bowling balls. A great big parrot, about the size of a flamingo, perched in the tree and mimicked a voice that sounded decidedly like Josephus's. *"I have so much to do and such little time,"* said the parrot. *"Quickly, bring me my quill!"*

The view from Josephus's office also offered a glimpse of the distant jungle surrounding the city of Somnos. Just like every other part of Somnos, Josephus's office showed a completely different city from the one Alfonso had visited three years ago.

The old historian greeted Alfonso and the others warmly and invited them to sit down in the half-dozen or so wooden seats that were scattered about his office. Josephus's bald head, long nose, and luxuriant green robes gave him the look of an old forest king.

"Well, here you are, reunited with your old chums," Josephus said to Alfonso. "Everyone looks quite well."

"You haven't aged a day," said Alfonso. And it was true. Josephus looked exactly the same as he had three years ago.

The group exchanged pleasantries for a few more minutes. Josephus began to fidget in his seat and suddenly he fixed his gaze on Alfonso and declared, "Friends, let us dispense with the chit-chat for now and get down to business. I am most eager to hear about the events that led the Great Sleeper back to Somnos. These are unsettling times in Somnos, especially with the arrival of Marcus Firment. I cannot help but suspect that the timing is related."

"My thoughts exactly," said Hill.

"Indeed," said Josephus. "So tell me everything, Alfonso. Spare no detail—even the most minor occurrence might reveal the key to these events."

For the next hour Alfonso related everything that had happened to him since falling asleep in the catacombs beneath Paris. Everything except the whispering he had heard the night before. In the light of day, it sounded ridiculous. He also remained tight-lipped about his visit to Imad's antechamber.

Josephus was particularly interested by Alfonso's discoveries in Alexandria. On more than one occasion Josephus slammed an open palm onto his desk and exclaimed excitedly, "Fascinating—just as I suspected!" Moments later, they could all hear the parrot in the courtyard below repeating this phrase, with the exact same enthusiasm.

"This is interesting and revelatory news," said Josephus, when Alfonso had finished. "My head is spinning with so many notions that I hardly know where to begin."

"Good," said Hill. "I was hoping you could make sense of this."

"Well," said Josephus, "for starters, it appears clear that Leif—like Alfonso—is a *Great Sleeper*." He proudly beamed at Alfonso.

"Over the course of Dormian history there are several examples of families producing multiple Great Sleepers," explained Josephus. "The most famous of these is the Yablochkov clan from Minsk. Occasionally, in the past, the Founding Trees from several cities died in rapid succession, and during such times entire families of Great Sleepers tend to emerge."

"But it doesn't add up," said Bilblox. "I thought Somnos was the last of the Dormian cities. So how could Leif be a Great Sleeper, huh? There ain't any other cities left. I mean, where would he be goin'?"

Josephus smiled and leaned back in his chair. "That's a most excellent point, Master Bilblox. The answer, I believe, lies in Alexandria. I believe that Alfonso and Leif entered the legendary Depot of Alexandria. If my research is correct, it is one of four places where the people of Jasber have always stored the seeds to their Founding Tree."

"Jasber?" whispered Hill.

"I'll explain," replied Josephus. His words were deliberate, but his jumpy tone betrayed his true feelings. "If you recall, Jasber is the oldest city of Dormia. Its tree is unlike any of the other Founding Trees and its seeds, which are reputed to be both gold-colored and weightless, are very sensitive to heat and moisture. These seeds would never survive in maracas, or simple carrying cases, like the seeds from the other Dormian cities. That's why they disintegrated not long after you removed them from the depot. The people of Jasber supposedly built four depots around the world so that whenever one of their Great Sleepers emerged, they were never too far from a stash of seeds. No one has heard from Jasber for such a long time that even the idea of depots has disappeared from common knowledge. However, I have studied Jasber for decades—it's been my life's obsession, if truth be told. And early on in my research, I studied the depot system. Four depots were built—in Alexandria, Machu Picchu, Peking, and Kraków."

Josephus turned to Alfonso. "Your rosewood box came with a container of bluish liquid, is that right?"

Alfonso nodded.

"That makes sense," remarked Josephus. "The accounts of the Jasberian depots always mention a vial of dagárgala, which is an ancient Sanskrit word meaning 'water-secret.' According to legend, you cannot enter Jasber without it."

"I have a question," said Resuza. "If Jasber still exists, why haven't its citizens reached out and made contact with Somnos?"

Josephus nodded. "Because they are a secretive and deeply paranoid people," he replied. "They always believed that the rest of the world—even their fellow Dormians—wanted to rob them. And they were right to be suspicious."

"Rob them of what?" asked Alfonso.

"Now we're getting to the heart of things," said Josephus. "They feared being robbed of the most powerful substance in the world. Even more powerful than the purple ash that Bilblox put into his eyes. Imagine something a hundred times more potent, and you'll get the idea." He sighed. "Let me tell you a story."

The old scholar walked over to his bookshelf, took down a slender dusty volume, thumbed through its pages, and then began to read the following passage:

> *Once, many millennia ago, a severe winter storm passed through the Urals. During the height of the storm, a bolt of lightning struck the roots of the Founding Tree of Jasber. The lightning passed through the root system and discharged in the branches of the*

117

Jasber Tree. Several branches burned and turned in-
stantly into ash. It was green and not purple because
the Founding Tree of Jasber was different in several
ways from those that grew in the other ten Dormian
cities. It grew at an extremely high altitude, and it was
believed that the lack of oxygen in the atmosphere
stunted the tree, making it smaller, but also hardier.

After the lightning struck, the elders of Jasber faced
a dilemma: what should they do with this green ash?
Ultimately, the leaders of Jasber decided to allow one
chosen citizen—whom they called "the seer"—to sam-
ple the powder. The seer rubbed a lone granule into
his eye and then instantly entered a coma that lasted
for roughly a year. When the seer finally awoke he
could see the future in great detail.

"I'm guessin' that this seer fella saw more of the future than
I did when I used the purple powder?" asked Bilblox tentatively.

"Much more," said Josephus, as he put down the book. "Using just a single dose of the green ash, the seer saw not just one,
but perhaps as many as fifty or even one hundred events in the
future—disasters, locations of treasures, secret agreements,
deaths, births, betrayals, all different twists of fate. Rightly so,
the elders of Jasber realized the value of such a prophecy, and
they agreed that once every two hundred years a seer would be
allowed to sample a lone granule of the ash and offer a new
prophecy in order to help protect the city."

"So that's why the folks in Jasber were so untrustin'?" asked
Bilblox. "They thought people would steal their green powder
and use it for their own good?"

"Exactly," nodded Josephus. "And, at one point, centuries after the lightning struck, a Jasberian monk named Imad built a contraption—a kind of magical device called the Foreseeing Pen—that helped the seers record every detail of the future. He was never fully trusted, on account of his having only one eye"—Josephus looked around before continuing—"in the middle of his forehead."

Alfonso's eyes widened at the mention of Imad's name.

"A one-eyed monk?" interjected Hill.

"Yes, you are familiar with this Imad fellow," said Josephus. "It was his statue that Alfonso found in Straszydlo Forest."

"You mean the statue where Alfonso got his blue sphere?" asked Bilblox.

"Yes," replied Josephus. "It's too bad you didn't find the Foreseeing Pen as well! With the power of the pen, the seers could take the green ash and document not just fifty or a hundred, but tens of thousands of events that were to come.

"Before long, word spread that the city of Jasber possessed a powerful ability to foresee every twist and turn of the future. The Wanderers of Jasber are probably to blame for this. As they ventured out into the world, a few of them broke the cardinal rule of Wanderers. They spoke of Dormia and, worse yet, they spoke of Jasber's special powers. Before long, armies of thieves and fortune seekers began combing the Urals for Jasber. And, not surprisingly, some of the other cities of Dormia even sent spies to Jasber to find out more about the green ash. The backlash was swift. The elders of Jasber decided to destroy the pen prophecies and, rather mysteriously, the Foreseeing Pen was lost or stolen—no one knows which. Then came the final act: The elders decided to cut Jasber off from the rest of the world.

"The people of Jasber surrounded their city with a vast maze, or labyrinth, of razor hedges, with walls fifty feet tall, and thorns so numerous and so sharp that they would cut you to pieces if you tried to climb them. Some say the maze covered an area as big as fifty square miles. Next, they stopped sending Wanderers out into the world and decided to rely exclusively on the depots. And, finally, they built something called the Jasber Gate . . ."

"Ah yes," said Hill. He had been following this eagerly and was happy to come to something he knew. "The locked door, built deep underground, in the old Fault Roads, right?"

"That's the one," replied Josephus. "The cities of Dormia were all once connected by a series of underground passageways known as the Fault Roads. Beneath the Ural Mountains sits a web of underground faults that reach all the way to the planet's fiery core. At some point, the ancient Dormians decided to use them as an underground highway system. Basically, each Dormian city dug its own tunnel leading into the Fault Roads and then they were all linked together at a place called the Hub. The Jasber Gate is located at the Hub."

Hill looked curiously at Josephus.

"You aren't really surprised by any of this, are you?" asked Hill. "I remember now—you've always believed that Jasber still exists."

"My dear Foreign Minister," replied Josephus. "You know that I am a unifier."

"What do ya mean, 'unifier'?" asked Bilblox.

"It's a name used by Dormians," explained Hill. "You see, Josephus is among a handful of Dormians who believe, quite fervently, that there are other hidden Dormian cities somewhere in the Urals. More and more people have begun think-ing like this, especially after the Dragoonya attack. They refuse to believe that Somnos is the only place left for Dormians. Their most strongly held belief is that Jasber still exists. So, you can see why Josephus is so excited."

Josephus nodded enthusiastically. "Alfonso, you have given this old man a shot in the arm!" he exclaimed. "Your discovery in Alexandria is the proof I need. This is an opportunity! After all, Somnos must be reunited with Jasber for the exact same reason that you must be reunited with your father: We are all kin who have been cruelly separated."

Alfonso said nothing at first. Everyone looked at him. "I don't know about unifiers or Jasber," Alfonso slowly began. "All I know is that I want to find my dad. Do you know where he is?"

"Yeah," said Bilblox. "And you got any idea why Alfonso was called here? I mean, ain't he already done his job?"

"I don't know where your father is, but I have a hunch as to why you were called here," said Josephus. "There are only two instances when a Great Sleeper is summoned. The first occurs when he or she must deliver a Dormian bloom and, obviously, Alfonso has already done that. The second occurs in cases where there are multiple Great Sleepers in a family—and one of them is in mortal danger."

"Mortal danger?" inquired Alfonso uneasily.

"Yes," said Josephus. "Remember the Yablochkov clan, the family of Great Sleepers from Minsk? Well, at one point dur-ing her journey, one of the daughters, Zofia Yablochkov, fell into serious peril. She was captured by Tartar slave traders. On the very day of Zofia's capture, her father, Boris, fell into a deep sleep-trance. For the next three months, he walked across the steppes of central Asia until one day he awoke and found himself in the middle of a Tartar camp. He heard shrieks coming from a nearby tent. It was his daughter being beaten for stealing a morsel of food. Boris took out a short-sword, which he used with great skill, and freed his daughter. He was summoned, in effect, to save his daughter."

"And you think that's why Alfonso was summoned?" asked Resuza. "Because his father is in danger?"

Alfonso felt short of breath. "Where is he?" he whispered.

"Hard to say," Josephus replied solemnly. "My best bet is that he is stranded somewhere near Jasber, most likely in the maze of razor hedges that surrounds the city. This is where the Great Sleepers bound for Jasber have run into trouble."

As Josephus explained this, Alfonso instantly recalled the dream that he'd had in Alexandria. In the dream, his father lay dead in the snow, amid a vast maze of hedges.

"So we need to go to Jasber," said Bilblox. "Fine. When do we leave? Are we goin' by the Fault Roads or over land?"

"I know someone who may be able to help you," said Josephus cautiously, as if he was uncertain of what he would say next. "Why don't we meet tomorrow morning at the Tree Palace?"

"The Tree Palace?" asked Alfonso. "Isn't that where Kiril is being tried?"

"Indeed," said Josephus. "I've been interviewing Kiril for several weeks now. The Grand Vizier has given me special access to him." He paused and stared at Alfonso. "*Kiril* is precisely the man I want you to see."

CHAPTER 15

THE DEAL

LATER THAT EVENING, Resuza and Alfonso found themselves on a gondola, riding through the canals of Somnos. This trip was Resuza's idea. "I just get so stir-crazy sitting around in Hill's mansion every night," she had told Alfonso. "Let's go for a gondola ride in the city." Alfonso had quickly agreed, both because he was curious to see more of Somnos and because he was eager to spend more time talking and joking with Resuza.

Currently, their gondola was passing through the Dreamer's Quarter. The canals here were lined with art galleries, music halls, and sculpture gardens where artists both created and displayed their work. Despite that it was almost nine in the evening, many of these artists were busy working, scurrying about in the euphoric grip of their own dreams. The most striking feature of the Dreamer's Quarter was all the so-called hanging artist studios, which dangled on thick ropes from the branches of the Founding Tree, like giant ornaments on a Christmas tree. The studios were all perfectly round, made of glass, and illuminated with soft blue light. Inside the studios, artists worked feverishly on their canvases.

Cold gusts of wind were blowing in off the mountains and, when combined with the warm air of the valley, they created a heavy fog. A team of ten turtles pulled the gondola through the crystal clear waters of the Dreamer's Quarter as a lanky driver snoozed contentedly in the bow of the boat.

They sat quietly and listened to the gurgling of the water. Alfonso was somewhat distracted by everything that Josephus had said earlier that day, especially the news that his father— assuming he was alive—was likely in grave danger. Alfonso kept picturing the vials of medicine that his sleeping-self had stolen in France.

Abruptly, Resuza let out a big sigh. "Nance wanted me to take you to one of the sleeping dancehalls tonight," said Resuza. "She must be out of her mind! We'd be the only two people awake! No way—no more of that for me."

"Come on," said Alfonso, rolling his eyes. "It can't be that bad here in Somnos. It's better than Barsh-yin-Binder. I mean, you're not living on the streets."

"Look," said Resuza, "don't misunderstand me. Life here is good, but . . ." She sighed heavily. "I have other considerations."

"Like what?" asked Alfonso.

"Like my sister, Naomi."

Alfonso recalled Resuza telling him about her younger sister, Naomi, who had been captured by the Dragoonya, forced into slavery, and sent to their capital, Dargora. That had been many years ago, and Alfonso doubted Naomi was still alive. But, of course, he kept this thought to himself.

"Did you look for her?" asked Alfonso.

"Of course," replied Resuza. "After she was captured I set out to find her."

"What happened?"

"You really want to know?" asked Rsuza.

Alfonso nodded.

And so Resuza recounted the story. She began by explaining that she came from a family of reindeer herders who lived in a mountain town named Tulov in the northernmost reaches of the Urals, near the icy waters of the Kara Sea. This was a lawless area governed by feuding warlords and Dragoonya slave traders. When the slave traders attacked the village where Resuza lived, she managed to escape by hiding along the banks of a nearby river. The slavers killed her parents, captured Naomi, burned Tulov to the ground, and then headed farther north, deep into Siberia.

After the raid, Resuza followed the slave traders for a few days, but she quickly realized that, without proper supplies, her pursuit was futile. So she returned to the smoldering ruins of Tulov and picked through the debris, scrounging for copper coins and undamaged workmen's tools. She found these things and, in addition, discovered a gold cup that belonged to the village's chief herdsman. Resuza took what she found and traded it for a sled, dogs, and a supply of dried fish at an old Russian trading post.

"What's a twelve-year-old girl going to do with these

supplies?" asked the old man who ran the trading post. He wore a fur cap and an old Soviet army jacket. His breath reeked of vodka and pickles. "Where's your family?"

"Slavers got my sister," replied Resuza in broken Russian.

"You're a stupid girl if you think you can get your sister back," said the man angrily. "They'll kill you the moment they see you."

Resuza knew that the man was probably right, but she didn't care. The thought of rescuing her sister was the only thing that held back the grief of losing her entire family. It was what kept her going.

"Take this, you blasted fool," said the old Russian man. He reached under the counter and pulled out an old Cossack Cavalry rifle. "Do you know how to use it?"

"Yes."

For the next several weeks, Resuza camped out in the hills above the old coastal sled route and waited until she caught sight of another band of slave traders heading north. It was a large party of at least a hundred people. Resuza trailed them surreptitiously, staying a safe distance behind them, and following the scent of the whale blubber that they burned for heat. The landscape here was filled with thick pine forests and all manner of ice—frozen streams, lakes turned solid and glistening with snowy crystals, and glaciers that glowed a luminous blue.

Ten days into her journey, Resuza encountered an old Yukaghir woman who was living as a hermit near hot springs nestled in the woods. Resuza shared some of her dried fish and the woman invited her into a cramped cave that smelled of smoke, musk, and rank animal hides. The woman spoke some

Yakut, a dialect that Resuza knew, and she warned Resuza not to venture any farther north or she would encounter a vast petrified forest, where tree trunks—made of stone and without any branches—rose from the ground like the pillars of ancient temples. In the middle of this forest was a city so well hidden that it was visible for only several minutes each day in the waning glow of twilight.

"Is this where the slavers take their captives?" asked Resuza.

"Yes," said the woman. "But the captives never live for long."

The next day, before sunrise, Resuza was back on her sled, heading due north. To her great regret, the slavers had disappeared. Twice in the coming days she encountered starving packs of wolves and, in her skirmishes with them, she exhausted her supply of bullets.

Late one afternoon, she came upon hundreds of stone tree trunks rising out of the snow. This was the petrified forest. A tremor of fear tingled its way up Resuza's spine, but she cracked her whip, urging her dogs into the forest. They refused to go and instead whimpered feebly. "Stupid dogs!" Resuza cursed. She then trudged forward into the forest on foot. She marched for several hours, until the sun sank low on the horizon and the sky turned a sapphire blue. Then she saw it. For a minute or two it flickered into sight—a vast city made of rocks the color of dry, bleached bones. Dargora. Resuza ran forward, but the façade of the city's walls vanished and in its place she saw only swirling eddies of snow. She never saw the city again.

Starving and at the very edge of life, she turned around. Back at her sled, Resuza was startled to see the old woman hermit. "How did you find me?" asked Resuza.

"Your tracks were easy to follow," said the woman quietly.

"And if I can follow them, so can the slavers, which is why we must leave quickly."

⊛

"So what happened?" asked Alfonso, who had been hanging on Resuza's every word.

"I had no weapon, I was almost out of food, and I was scared," said Resuza. "So I turned around. The old woman led me southward all the way to Barsh-yin-Binder, where I arrived penniless and, of course, without my sister. There, ironically, I was immediately captured by the Dragoonya and forced into slavery. That's where I first met Kiril. I worked for him personally—that is, until I met you and your uncle."

The gondola slipped under a bridge and then turned down a narrow canal, leaving Resuza and Alfonso in near darkness.

"Resuza," said Alfonso quietly, "let's make a deal."

"Go on," said Resuza.

"You'll come with me to find my dad, and then we'll go looking for Naomi together," said Alfonso.

"Maybe there's no point," said Resuza darkly. "Maybe they're both dead."

Alfonso said nothing.

Resuza stared at the opulence around them. They heard laughter and the clink of wine glasses from a nearby mansion. She nodded. "It's a deal."

After touring all of Somnos's canals, the gondola arrived at the southernmost gate to the city. Alfonso and Resuza got out, paid the driver, and then walked through the darkness toward

Hill's anteater, Bataar, who was waiting for them. Resuza and Alfonso were just about to climb the rope ladder onto Bataar's back when someone called out from the darkness.

"Resuza, is that you?" asked the voice. "Resuza?"

A short elderly woman with large ears, a prominent nose, and bushy eyebrows stepped out of the shadows and into a shaft of moonlight. Perhaps because she was fast asleep, she moved in an awkward bowlegged way, as if she had been hunched over working on something for many years. At the sight of Resuza, her eyes popped open and her weathered face cracked into a wide smile.

"Well, if it ain't the daughter I always wanted t'have," she said. "How are ya, sweet'eart?"

"Misty!" Resuza exclaimed, and enveloped her in a hug. "Misty, this is Alfonso, the Great Sleeper. I told you all about him."

Misty stuck out a muscular hand that felt like coarse sandpaper. "Mistepha Blazenska at yer service," she said. "'Course you can just call me Misty, everyone 'round here does."

"Misty used to work in the mines below the city, before they closed," Resuza explained. "Now she works as an ant hunter and a healer. She's one of the old hill dwellers I was telling you about."

"An yer not bad yerself," said Misty admiringly. "Why, we found the anthill o'er near the north woods—musta been fifty feet high, that anthill—and Resuza plucked off six arrows and took down six ants, just like that." Misty chortled. "I ain't seen ya around lately. You all look just purfect, like two doves in the hand." She winked at Alfonso.

Alfonso blushed.

"What are you doing in Somnos?" asked Resuza. "I thought you hated city life."

"Aye," said Misty. "I got no love fer this place, but I got a sick aunt that I 'ad to visit in the Drowsy Quarter, and I'm just now headed back out to the hills. What about you two? Whatchya doin' in the city at this hour?"

"We spent the day with Josephus," explained Resuza. "And, later on, we went for a long gondola ride through the Dreamer's Quarter."

Misty took a step closer.

"What business did you have wit' Josephus?" asked Misty quietly.

"Just chatting," replied Alfonso. He saw no point in going into any detail.

"Come now," said Misty. "You can trust me. I ain't one to gossip or even talk much at all."

Alfonso nodded reluctantly and Resuza explained, very briefly, that they had discussed the lost city of Jasber and the old Fault Roads. She said nothing about Leif or Marcus Firment, but Misty stiffened visibly at the mention of the Fault Roads.

"He tol' ya 'bout the Fault Roads, did'e?" asked Misty.

Resuza nodded.

"Well, he's got no business talkin' about them roads," growled Misty. "Hima all people. No business at all."

"What are you talking about?" asked Resuza.

"That old bugger oughta know better 'an that—the fool!" spat Misty. "All that book learnin' and not an ounce-a integrity. Don't a promise mean anythin'?"

Without another word, Misty stalked off into the darkness.

CHAPTER 16

THE TRIAL

THE FOLLOWING MORNING, Alfonso sat in the amphitheater of the Tree Palace. The stage backed up directly against the enormous trunk of the Founding Tree. The cover of leaves and branches was so thick here that very little direct sunlight made its way into the space. The air was damp and cool, and the only substantial light came from hundreds of lanterns filled with fireflies. The seats were divided into two sections: awake and asleep. The sleeping side was occupied mainly by policemen, reporters, stenographers, courtroom artists, and other professionals who needed to maintain perfect concentration. The awake side was occupied by spectators—including Alfonso, Hill, Nance, Resuza, Bilblox, and Josephus, who all sat in the front row.

The stage had just three people on it. There was Sofia Perzepol, the Grand Vizier, who stood behind a large wooden lectern. Because of the importance of this case, she was the presiding judge. To her left stood a tall, barrel-chested man dressed in a dark green robe. His name was Lukos Treeben and he was Somnos's preeminent legal scholar, who had been appointed as prosecutor. To her right was a large steel cage. Inside the cage stood a tall, muscular man, with entirely white eyes and a hideous scar on his face that twisted and coiled like a snake.

The man was Kiril.

Alfonso knew that Kiril was over six hundred years old—a feat he had achieved by rubbing the purple ash of the Founding Trees into his eyes. The purple ash did strange things to people. It gave non-Dormians a burst of good health, several minutes of telescopic vision, and a momentary glimpse into the future, but ultimately it left them white-eyed and blind. This is what had happened to Bilblox. It was different for Dormians. They too enjoyed telescopic vision and a glimpse into the future, although they enjoyed it for longer. However, the real benefit for Dormians was that the ash could prolong life. By rubbing a pinch of the ash into his or her eyes every few years, a Dormian could live indefinitely. This is what Kiril had done. If you were Dormian, the purple ash turned your eyes white, but it did not make you blind. Kiril could see perfectly well, and currently he was surveying the crowd.

Alfonso wanted to stare at Kiril, but instead he looked away, feeling oddly guilty. Despite all of the many terrible things that Kiril had done—including killing General Loxoc—Alfonso couldn't help feeling somewhat sorry for Kiril as he stood onstage under the malevolent gaze of several hundred Dormians. Alfonso eventually forced himself to look up and confront Kiril. Alfonso was surprised to see that Kiril's eyes betrayed no sign of malice or rage; to the contrary, Kiril seemed almost eerily calm. The two of them locked eyes. And then, ever so slightly, the corners of Kiril's mouth bent upward to form the faintest of smiles.

"I hereby call today's proceedings to order," the Grand Vizier called out as she banged her gavel on the wooden lectern. "Today we will continue with the trial, and the prosecution will question the defendant directly," she explained. "The defendant has refused the aid of a barrister, which is his legal right, and so he shall answer all questions directly. The questions will be posed by myself and by the prosecutor, Mr. Treeben. My first question is a formal matter for the record and quite a simple one: Who are you, sir?"

Kiril turned and nodded at the Grand Vizier, acknowledging her for the first time, and then looked at the crowd.

"I am a Dormian by birth," he began. "I was born Kiril Spratic roughly six hundred years ago in the city of Jasber. I come from a distinguished family. My father, Kemal Spratic, was a nobleman. Our family genealogy traces all the way back to the founding of Jasber and the very birth of Dormia. All of this is a matter of public record, and your historians can verify it easily enough in the Somnos library. Everything that I tell you today is true."

"Can you tell us what happened to your eyes?" asked the Grand Vizier. Alfonso couldn't help glancing at Bilblox, who shifted his weight uncomfortably but showed no emotion.

"It would be my pleasure." Kiril explained that, when he was twelve years old, he went on a journey with his mother, brother, and sister to the city of Noctos. They traveled via the old Fault Roads to visit "Outer Dormia" as the Jasberians called it. They passed through the gate and then entered the Hub, the giant intersection where the Fault Roads from each of the various Dormian cities converged. "From there," concluded Kiril, "it was a short journey to Noctos."

"How did you get permission to pass through the gate?" inquired the Grand Vizier.

"It was easy to get," explained Kiril. "My father was the gatekeeper, as was his father, and his father before them."

"Your family maintained the Jasber Gate?" asked the Grand Vizier. "You mean you belong to one of the ancient families of gatekeepers?"

"That's correct," said Kiril. The audience rustled with excited whispers. Alfonso now knew exactly why Josephus had wanted him to be here today. If it was true that Kiril's family operated the Jasber Gate, then Kiril might know the secret code that opened the gate. And if he did . . . well, it might be possible to reach Jasber.

"Tell me," said the Grand Vizier, "what happened after you passed through the Jasber Gate?"

"We continued on to Noctos and visited a distant cousin of my mother's," explained Kiril. "She ran a large apothecary. We were meant to stay for three weeks, but on the fourth day of our visit, the city came under attack by the Dragoonya. During the battle that ensued, part of the Founding Tree burned and a cloud of purple ash rained down upon the city, blinding several hundred people, including my entire family. After the battle, those of us who were exposed to the ash were rounded up like criminals. They called us Gahnos, which, as you know, means 'untrustworthy' in the ancient tongue. They said we would burn the rest of the Founding Tree. They said we had been corrupted. They herded us through the streets and then cast us out into the maw of an angry winter. I recall, in particular, a huge man with a pug nose and a shaved head shoving people out of the gate. My mother begged him to spare her children. He hit her savagely. I remember it as if it were yesterday. He hit her and she fell backwards through the gate and into the snow. My mother, brother, and sister died there, as did a number of Dormian knights who had also been exposed to the ash. I alone was saved."

"And who saved you?" asked the Grand Vizier.

Kiril did not answer immediately. He appeared to be lost in thought. The Grand Vizier's questions had triggered a strong memory of that fateful day, although it was a memory he kept to himself:

It was Nartam, king of the Dragoonya, who had saved him.

Of course, at the time, Kiril did not recognize Nartam. He was dressed as a shepherd. He had long blond hair, a bushy beard, and two entirely vacant white eyes. He introduced himself simply as Däros. In the Dragoonya tongue, the word for "father" and "master" were one and the same: däros. He had come across Kiril in a narrow ravine, nestled in the High Peaks of the Urals. Snow glistened in the air, while the temperature kept falling. Kiril was frostbit, starving, and on the brink of death. He had not eaten in weeks. A normal person would have been dead by that point, but Kiril was no longer a normal person. He had been exposed to the purple ash of the Founding Tree and therefore he was not as weak and vulnerable as other Dormians.

When they first met, Kiril's white eyes gave him away immediately, and Nartam asked him tenderly, "My poor child, are you one of the Gahnos from Noctos?" Kiril nodded, but said nothing. He could not muster the energy to speak. "Come then," said Nartam. "I have taken in other orphans as well and I offer you shelter for as long as you like."

Kiril followed Nartam to a narrow cave. "Come, don't be frightened," said Nartam. "There is food and warmth inside." The cave burrowed deep into the earth and then opened up dramatically into a spacious cavern with dozens of hot springs. This was a small village of sorts. Several dozen people were milling about, bathing in hot springs, tending to fires, cooking meat, sewing clothes, and even playing a game with a ball. They were all children, and their eyes were entirely white. "These children are all Gahnos like you," explained Nartam. "I have taken them under my wing."

"Are you a Dragoonya?" asked Kiril timidly.

"I am," replied Nartam with a reassuring smile. "But you shouldn't be frightened! Virtually everything that you've been told about the Dragoonya is a lie. Dormians are quite adept at lying. I know. Like you, I was once one of them. Dormians profess to be noble and good, but I don't need to tell you that is a lie. You have seen the truth for yourself."

In the coming days, Kiril ate, rested, bathed, and even began to talk and play with the other children. They were all from Noctos. As it turns out, one of the places in Noctos that was hardest hit by the falling purple ash was a school, and all of the children from the school had been cast out of the city and into the snow. This partially explained why there were no adults present. But there were several children, like Kiril, who had been expelled from Noctos with their parents. They all told a similar story. Just as their families were on the brink of death, Nartam appeared and offered to take the children, but only the children. Nartam explained that he had found a warm cave stocked with food, but that there wasn't room for adults. He was saving the children first. In desperation, many of the parents agreed. Those families who refused almost certainly perished.

In the evenings, when the children gathered for dinner, Nartam talked to them and told them stories. He said that they were all family now. "Our white eyes have marked us," explained Nartam. "We have been expelled from Dormia and we will never belong there. You will be reviled as villains and freaks. My dear children, know this: we only have one another."

One day, Nartam learned that Kiril was originally from Jasber, and that his parents had been in the upper echelons of Jasberian society. From that moment forward, Nartam took an especially keen interest in the boy. As it turned out, Nartam had a special connection to Jasber.

He was born Milos Brutinov Nartam in the Dormian city of Dragoo. As a boy, he had devoted himself to scorial sciences, which explored the properties and chemistry of the purple ash. As a teenager, he traveled via the Fault Roads to Jasber, the only Dormian city that was allowed to store and experiment with the ash. Jasber's riches and advanced work on the ash made an enormous impression on Nartam. After several years of study in Jasber, Nartam returned to Dragoo and wrote a famous book called *Scorial Science and the Future of Dormia*. It argued that

Dormians should occasionally burn portions of their Founding Trees and use the powers of the ash to their advantage.

"The book that I wrote was banned," explained Nartam one evening, as the Gahno children gathered around him. "You see, the Dormians are a very fearful people. They fear change, they fear the outside world, and—as you most painfully know, my dear children—they fear one another. I tried to explain to them that the Founding Tree's greatest gift was its purple ash, which bestowed both immortality and the power to see into the future. But they wouldn't listen. There is no talking sense into Dormians. They won't listen. You know this. Did any of them listen to your cry for help as you were cast into the snow to die? No. They understand just two things: power and fear."

"But wasn't the city of Dragoo burned almost two thousand years ago?" asked one of the children. "How is it that you are still alive?"

"My dear child," replied Nartam in a kindly manner, "we here, we family of orphans, we have something very special. We have the purple ash from a secret supply that I have found. And, do you know what? I am going to share it with you. Together we shall live forever. How does that sound?"

Bang! Bang! Bang!

Kiril jumped and looked around. His mind returned to the courtroom, where the Grand Vizier was banging her gavel.

"You cannot ignore the question," said the Grand Vizier. "I will ask you again. Who saved you outside Noctos?"

"You know perfectly well who saved me," replied Kiril curtly.

"Was it Nartam?" asked the prosecutor, Mr. Treeben.

"Yes," replied Kiril. "It was he who showed me kindness after my own people left me to die."

"Kindness?" said the prosecutor pointedly. "Isn't that a bit misleading, not to mention naive, to categorize his actions as 'kindness'? It is a known fact that Nartam used the Gahnos to further his own evil purposes."

"'Evil,'" said Kiril slowly, as if he were savoring the word like a sip of good wine. "Now *that* is a most interesting choice of words, Mr. Treeben. Forgive me, but the only true act of evil that I see here is casting out your own kind—Dormians who risked their own lives for you—and tossing them into the snow to die."

"That is a most shameful and regrettable chapter in our history . . ." began the prosecutor.

"Regrettable?" snarled Kiril. "That is how you describe the murder of innocent men, women, and children? You may be an officer of the court but it's quite clear to me, sir, that you haven't the foggiest sense of what justice is or isn't."

"And what about you?" asked the prosecutor. "You who have murdered so many men, including Gilliad Loxoc and his brother, Johno Loxoc. Does your pain give you free license to punish and murder as you please?"

"I have suffered," replied Kiril calmly. "But I ask for no special treatment or exemption from punishment because of this. I have slain many Dormians, including your precious General Loxoc and his brother, Johno the Wanderer, and I would gladly do it again. I have been at war with Dormia for almost six centuries. And long after you are dead, sir, I will still be at war with your people—if they should be so lucky to still exist."

CHAPTER 17

THE GREATER GOOD OF DORMIA

AT LUNCHTIME, the proceedings were gaveled to a close, and the orderly crowd of Dormians headed for the exits. Josephus approached Alfonso and whispered into his ear, "I believe that Kiril wants a word with you." Alfonso glanced around to look for Hill. He couldn't imagine that his uncle would want him to get very close to Kiril. Hill, however, was making his way out of the amphitheater and was well out of earshot. Even most of the courthouse guards seemed to have temporarily disappeared. The only one who remained was Bilblox, who was blind and unable to see what was going on. Alfonso wondered whether Josephus had planned it this way. It was all very odd.

"Well?" asked Josephus.

Alfonso stood up and walked toward the stage. But before he

could reach it, several Dormian knights approached him and stood in his way.

"I'm sorry, Master Great Sleeper," said one of the knights. "But we are under strict orders not to let anyone near the prisoner."

Alfonso paused, gathered himself, and then asked with all the confidence he could muster, "Who is the head of your order?"

"You are, sir," replied one of the knights.

"Then step aside," said Alfonso calmly.

The knights did as they were told and Alfonso continued on his way to the stage. Kiril watched Alfonso approach but said nothing. His face betrayed no expression. Alfonso drew within five feet of the cage and stopped.

"You wanted to speak with me?"

"How's your father?" asked Kiril calmly. "Still presumed dead?"

Alfonso's gut tightened, but he said nothing.

"He seemed like an able sort of fellow," said Kiril. "Tremendous stamina he had." Kiril smiled to himself. "We have some unfinished business, he and I."

"You met him?" asked Alfonso.

"In a manner of speaking," replied Kiril.

"Is he alive?" blurted out Alfonso. As soon as he spoke, he regretted sounding so young and eager.

"Possibly," replied Kiril. "One thing is for certain, though— he made it all the way to Jasber."

"How would you know?" asked Alfonso.

"Because I am meticulous when it comes to gathering information about Dormia, and Jasber in particular," Kiril replied evenly. "You see, for the last several centuries, I have dispatched spies to monitor the four ancient Seed Depots. These spies waited for a Great Sleeper to arrive, in the hopes that when one did, we would simply follow him or her back to Jasber. But none ever showed up. I began to suspect that Jasber had perished. I stopped looking for my old hometown. Then, about a decade ago, the first Great Sleeper arrived at a depot. Several came, and we followed each of them, but none succeeded in making it all the way to Jasber. Then, finally, your father arrived. We picked him up in Alexandria and then, well . . . we lost him. But no other Great Sleepers came after him. Typically a Founding Tree of Jasber summons Great Sleepers one after another until one of them succeeds in delivering a new tree. No more passed through the Seed Depot in Alexandria after your father. Therefore, he must have succeeded."

"But his life is in danger?" asked Alfonso.

"You wouldn't be here otherwise," replied Kiril calmly. "I assume that Josephus told you about the Yablochkov clan from Minsk?"

Alfonso nodded.

"Then you understand your purpose," said Kiril. "I don't know what kind of dire situation your father has fallen into, but it's quite apparent to both me and Josephus that you've been summoned to save him."

"Where is he?" demanded Alfonso. "Still in Jasber?"

"Yes," replied Kiril. "I believe he's in a very, how shall I put it, *remote* part of the city."

"What do you mean?" demanded Alfonso.

"Patience, my young friend, you must have patience," said Kiril. "Right now there is another matter—it involves the Jasber Gate. Once we pass through it, I know the way through the Fault Roads to Jasber. I can lead you to your father."

"Why would you do that?" asked Alfonso. "What do you want in return?"

"You'll have my offer soon enough," replied Kiril. "Naturally, no one will trust me when it comes time to make a deal—no one ever trusts a Gahno—but I thought you might have a slightly more *enlightened* perspective."

Alfonso said nothing. His mind was reeling, and, above all, he felt a terrible anxiousness about his father.

"Perhaps you see through all of this lofty rhetoric about what's right or wrong," said Kiril calmly, almost with the air of a schoolteacher. "In any conflict, both sides always believe that they are the righteous ones, and they come up with elaborate moral justifications to kill other human beings. That's why my family was driven into the snow to die. At the time, that was the 'right' thing to do. This is how leaders manipulate men into fighting wars and doing all manner of horrible things. All of these distinctions we make, these words and titles—Dormian, Dragoonya, Gahno, good, evil—these are just the tools of manipulation. In the end, there is only power. That's all that matters at the end of the day. And the powerful always protect their interests and justify their tactics. You may bristle at this, but deep down, you know I tell the truth."

"What does any of this have to do with rescuing my father?" asked Alfonso with a sigh of frustration.

"It has everything to do with it," snapped Kiril. He stepped closer so that he was almost touching the bars on the cage. "Don't you see? They're going to tell you that searching for your father is too great a risk. They'll tell you it puts Dormia in danger, that your father is just one man, that it's not worth it, even if he is a Great Sleeper. But take it from someone who has suffered greatly for the greater good of Dormia. Take it from someone whose family perished unjustly so that Dormia could be safe. In the end, they don't care about you or your father. They only care about their pathetic city of Somnos."

Outside of the Tree Palace, Hill, Resuza, and Bilblox stood on the steps amid a vast crowd of Dormians. None of them had yet realized that Alfonso was missing. The crowd was so thick that it was easy to lose sight of someone, even if that person was standing nearby. Nervous energy pulsed through the crowd. Everyone was talking about what Kiril had just said at the trial.

Despite the steady din of noise, Bilblox was still able to hear the flapping sound that the leaves of the Founding Tree made as they undulated in the breeze. He couldn't see the leaves, of course, but he could picture them in his mind's eye. He could also picture how these leaves might look if they were being consumed in flames. He could picture the purple ash that would waft down from the sky as the leaves burned. And he could imagine what it might feel like if some of this purple ash fluttered down onto his face and dissolved in the moist film of his eyes. These were awful thoughts, and Bilblox hated himself for even conjuring this scenario, but he suspected that the purple ash was the key to making his headaches go away.

Bilblox had been having his headaches for roughly three years now, ever since he first rubbed the purple ash into his eyes, while crossing the North Pacific on Vice Admiral Purcheezie's boat. Sometimes the discomfort was worse than other times. At its best, the pain was very dull, almost like a low-grade fever. At its worst, the pain was excruciating, and it felt to Bilblox as if someone were sticking needles directly into his brain. The pain had only really gone away entirely on one occasion. This happened when Bilblox had used the purple ash a second time, while crossing the Straszydlo Forest. How good that had felt! His head had felt warm and tingly and his entire body had felt light, sprightly, and almost weightless.

In recent months, Bilblox's headaches came with greater frequency, and he often fantasized about using the ash again. Bilblox was ashamed to think such thoughts, but the headaches drove him to think and act strangely. Of course, he shared these thoughts with no one, and he swore that he would never allow himself to relapse and use the purple ash again. He had given his word to Alfonso about this. And Bilblox was a man of his word.

Eventually, the crowd in front of the Tree Palace thinned out and Alfonso reappeared and joined his friends. They all walked down to one of the nearby canals in search of a gondola. Bilblox, the enormous longshoreman, with his entirely white eyes and his pet wolf, was quite a sight to behold. A small crowd of Dormians stopped to stare. Some of the onlookers obviously recognized Bilblox and knew about his heroics during the Battle of Somnos, but others stared at his white eyes with great suspicion.

Alfonso and Bilblox made their way to a gondola that was moored on a canal in front of the Tree Palace. Hill, Resuza, and Nance were already waiting for them in the boat. The crowd of onlookers parted for Bilblox and Alfonso, except for a tall, burly man with sunken eyes and thin lips that stretched tight against his teeth.

"Look at his eyes—they're white!" hissed the man. "It's a Dragoonya!"

A stir rustled through the crowd.

Kõrgu growled, bearing her fangs.

"You're mistaken," said Alfonso in a loud voice. "This is Paks Bilblox, a hero of Dormia."

"He's got white eyes and he ain't to be trusted!" shouted the man.

Two of the man's friends, both of whom were fast asleep, stepped out of the crowd and stood behind him with their arms folded. They were unkempt, with dirty clothing, stubble on their faces, and the stink of liquor on their breath. They looked like trouble. Instinctively, Alfonso reached into his pocket for his blue sphere, but realized that he had left it back at Hill's house, under his bed, alongside the rosewood box. Hill had warned him that weapons were not allowed at a trial and so he had come unarmed.

"Who are you?" demanded Bilblox.

"The question is who *you* are," insisted the thin-lipped man. "Why do you have white eyes? Don't you know what patriotic Dormians do to traitors?"

"I suggest you let us pass," said Alfonso as steadily and coldly as he could. He looked around for Hill, but the crowd had closed in around them, and Hill had disappeared. Meanwhile, the thin-lipped man reached into a satchel tied around his waist and withdrew a slingshot and several jagged rocks. In a lightning-fast movement, he loaded the slingshot, aimed it at Bilblox, and fired. It glanced sharply off Bilblox's head, and he fell heavily to the ground.

"Drop that slingshot, you blasted fool!"

Alfonso looked up.

It was Colonel Treeknot. She was standing directly to Alfonso's right with a loaded crossbow. She wore a long green cloak, the dress of a Dormian military officer, and she had a sword strapped to her waist. Her light blue eyes looked focused but unworried.

"Of all the stupid and shameful things you could have done, this was surely the worst," said Treeknot calmly to the three men. "You just attacked the Great Sleeper and his companion, a decorated hero of Somnos. How does jail sound to you? I'll escort you there myself or, if you would prefer, I can put arrows through your throats right now."

The thin-lipped man gave a fearful look and began to speak. "I'm sorry, Colonel, I didn't . . ."

"Save it!" snapped Treeknot. She then turned to Alfonso and Bilblox and said, "I'm so terribly sorry. These are emotional times in Somnos, with Kiril being on trial, and it brings out the worst in some."

Bilblox nodded grimly and got to his feet, but said nothing.

Upon returning to his uncle's house, Alfonso felt exceedingly tired. He retreated to his guest room to rest. For a while, Alfonso simply lay in bed and stared at the ceiling. His mind was buzzing and, before long, he found himself rehashing his encounter with Kiril at the Tree Palace.

Unpleasant as it was to admit, Alfonso knew that there was truth in *some* of the things that Kiril had said. The age-old conflict between the Dragoonya and the Dormians was not as neat and orderly as it first seemed to be. Alfonso was a Dormian, and this is where his loyalties lay, but it was undeniable that both sides had committed wrongs. It was true that the Dragoonya were the aggressors and that their desire to burn the Founding Trees was both short-sighted and greedy, but did that make them evil? Perhaps it did. But, clearly, the Dormians were also capable of evil, and Kiril's life story was proof of that. It wasn't black and white. Alfonso increasingly felt that this contest between good and evil was not a struggle waged between two opposing armies or two nations, but between two opposing forces within each person.

Eventually, Alfonso did something that was very rare in Somnos: he closed his eyes and fell into a motionless, thoroughly nonactive sleep. When he awoke, greatly refreshed, he got out of bed and searched around his room for something clean to wear. As he glanced under his bed, he noticed something odd. His blue sphere was where he had left it, but his rosewood box was missing. Alfonso searched every corner of the room, and triple-checked to see if it had been put into a dresser or shoved into his backpack.

The box was gone.

Alfonso ran downstairs, found Hill, Resuza, and Bilblox, and explained the situation.

"Strange," said Hill. "I'm sure it must be around here somewhere."

"Don't worry," said Resuza. "We'll find it."

"That's right." Hill nodded. "Look here, I was just about to wake you. We're meeting Josephus on the steps of the Tree Palace at sundown. Some kind of secret meeting is being held."

Alfonso didn't like the sound of that. "But we have to find that box," he insisted.

"I'll keep looking while you're gone," said Resuza.

"Why are ya in such a panic?" asked Bilblox. "This is a big house. It just got misplaced."

"I hope so," said Alfonso grimly. "My sleeping-self went to Alexandria for that box. I have a hunch it's the key to everything."

CHAPTER 18

A MEETING AT TWILIGHT

HILL AND ALFONSO ARRIVED at the front steps of the Tree Palace at sunset. The plaza in front of the palace was deserted except for an old man who was juggling six knives in his sleep.

"Who's that juggler?" asked Alfonso uneasily.

"Oh, just a street performer who has fallen asleep and forgotten to wake up," said Hill casually. "I've seen him out before."

For a long moment, both Hill and Alfonso watched with great curiosity as the old man tossed his knives high into the air and caught them gracefully, making no sound except for an occasional snore.

"Hello there, my friends," whispered a familiar voice. They spun around and saw Josephus standing in the shadows of a half-open door. "Come, come, come. The Grand Vizier is waiting for you."

They followed the historian into the Tree Palace and down several hallways until they came to a set of wooden doors with the image of a tree intricately carved into it. "This is the Grand Vizier's office," explained Josephus with a little laugh. "It makes my office look like a broom closet."

Josephus knocked twice on the door. It swung open and they entered an enormous room outfitted with three fireplaces, several sets of bamboo furniture, a library of leather-bound books, a magnificent crystal chandelier, and a running stream that wound its way through the room. The stream originated from a small waterfall that poured through a hole in the ceiling and then emptied into a series of small fountains, the last of which drained into a large ceremonial basin with gold cups surrounding it. Standing next to the basin were four attendants, all dressed in dark blue robes.

"Welcome," said the Grand Vizier, who was sitting on a nearby bamboo chair. She pointed to the basin. "The water here is quite fresh, directly from the glaciers that surround Somnos. Please, help yourselves."

Sitting to the right of the Grand Vizier were two elderly men. The first introduced himself as Dr. Nord Nostrite. He was "chief scientist and keeper of the Great Tree." Dr. Nostrite distrusted Alfonso and, even more so, Bilblox. It was Nostrite who had insisted that Bilblox face life imprisonment for putting ash from the Founding Tree into his eyes. Fortunately this sentence was never enforced. In any case, there was no love lost between Alfonso and Dr. Nostrite. The other man introduced himself as

General Tadeusz, General Loxoc's replacement as commander of the army of Somnos.

After introductions, the Grand Vizier motioned for everyone to sit down.

"I'm sorry for the last-minute nature of this meeting," she said in a quiet voice, "but I wanted to maximize privacy." The Grand Vizier glanced at her attendants and they immediately left the room.

"As you undoubtedly know, several days ago, a Wanderer named Marcus Firment made his way back to our city's gates," the Grand Vizier began. "During his recent wanderings, Firment claimed to have seen a Dragoonya army of seventy battalions—over a hundred thousand soldiers—right here in the Ural Mountains, near the northern edges of the Sea of Clouds. If this is true, the Dragoonya have amassed a force three times as large as the one that attacked Somnos."

"Do you think that they will attack Somnos again?" interrupted Dr. Nostrite.

"No," said the Grand Vizier. "If they knew our location and wanted to attack us, they would have already done so. Either the Dragoonya can't find their way back here or, quite simply, they don't want to."

"They don't want to?" scoffed Nostrite. "That doesn't make sense."

"Perhaps they have other plans," replied the Grand Vizier. "Firment said that the Dragoonya appeared to be looking for something. And, as you may well know, the city of Jasber is rumored to exist somewhere in or near the Sea of Clouds."

The Grand Vizier shot a quick glance at Josephus.

"I've consulted with Josephus, and he and I agree that it appears as if the Dragoonya are making a massive effort to find Jasber," declared the Grand Vizier.

"Do you really think that Jasber still exists?" asked General Tadeusz incredulously. "That's nothing but a myth put forth by the unifiers, and we all know the honorable Josephus is a leader. Can he realistically provide neutral counsel?"

"Until recently I would have been very skeptical," said the Grand Vizier. "But the news that Alfonso brings from the Seed Depot in Alexandria leads me to believe that the city does exist and that both Jasber and Alfonso's father—also a Great Sleeper—may be in considerable danger. Assuming Leif succeeded in delivering his Dormian bloom, where is he now? That's the question, isn't it? Josephus suspects that Leif is stranded in the maze of razor hedges that surrounds Jasber. It is also possible that the Dragoonya followed Leif on his journey to Jasber and now are very close to finding the city. This would put both Leif and Jasber in great danger. And this would explain why Alfonso was summoned."

"Are you proposing that we send an expedition to find Jasber and Leif?" asked Hill.

The Grand Vizier nodded. "This is precisely the issue we are here to discuss," she replied. "If there is a way to find Leif—and warn Jasber—I should very much like to do it. What's more, there's also the possibility of learning more about the Dragoonya plans. Josephus believes that he knows a route down into the old Fault Roads that leads to the Jasber Gate. And, as for the Jasber Gate, there may be a way to pass through it—but it would involve a considerable risk."

"Considerable risk?" inquired General Tadeusz.

"Yes," said the Grand Vizier. "Guards, bring him in!" she commanded.

At that moment, a door at the far end of the office swung open and a tight formation of roughly a dozen Dormian knights marched in. They all appeared to be huddled around something or someone. Eventually, the knights fanned out and revealed a prisoner, who wore heavy, iron shackles around his wrists and ankles.

It was Kiril.

General Tadeusz rose to his feet and placed a hand on his sword. "Do you think this is wise, Madame?" asked the General. "Kiril is extremely dangerous even with shackles on."

"There is no need for alarm," said Kiril calmly. "I haven't come to cause trouble—not tonight anyhow."

"It's all right," said the Grand Vizier. "On this occasion, I happen to believe Kiril."

"What's the meaning of this?" demanded Dr. Nostrite.

"I have a deal to offer you," replied Kiril. As he said this, he stared directly at Alfonso, as if he planned to offer the deal to Alfonso and Alfonso alone. This deal, if it were to be accepted, would need the support of the Great Sleeper. Kiril knew this. Alfonso felt as if he were being manipulated, but what could he do? After all, his father's life quite possibly hung in the balance.

"What kind of deal?" asked General Tadeusz angrily. "I can't imagine that you are in much of a position to negotiate."

"How wrong you are," replied Kiril coolly. "A man like myself, who has lived for more than six hundred years, has learned a thing or two along the way. What I have is knowledge—

knowledge that you desire. Knowledge that may help you get to Jasber. I know that Alfonso visited the ancient Seed Depot in Alexandria and retrieved one of the rare rosewood boxes it provides to Great Sleepers. It appears as if Jasber, my beloved birthplace, still exists. How touching."

Alfonso and Hill exchanged quick glances, but said nothing.

"Alfonso," continued Kiril. "I know you are keen on finding your father. I alone can help you. My family operated the Jasber Gate for many generations. The code for opening the Jasber Gate has long been hailed as the single most cryptic and impossible puzzle ever devised. I can assure you that, if you were left to your own devices, you would never open that gate. Fortunately, however, I can help."

"You know the code?" asked Hill pointedly.

"Yes," said Kiril.

"Can you prove it?" asked the Grand Vizier.

"Here is what I am ready to offer," said Kiril. "Take me down into the Fault Roads. Take me in shackles and under guard if you like. I will be your guide. I will open the Jasber Gate. In return, when I have made good on my promise, you will release me into the mountains."

"And what if you can't open the gate?" asked Hill.

"Then return me to prison here in Somnos, where I shall live out the rest of my days," he declared.

"Tell us," said the Grand Vizier. "From the Jasber Gate, how far a journey is it to Jasber?"

"As far as I can recall, you can make the trip in about four or five days," Kiril replied. "You follow the Jasber fault until you reach a place known as the Terminus, which is where the fault ends. There once was a tunnel connecting the Terminus to Jasber itself and, as far as I know, that should still be open."

"Josephus," said the Grand Vizier, "is this in keeping with what you have read about the Fault Roads?"

Josephus nodded.

"Well, that's the offer," said the Grand Vizier. "Now we must discuss it in private."

Kiril nodded respectfully. Knights closed in and led him out of the room.

"This is foolhardy, to say the least," declared General Tadeusz. "We know virtually nothing of the Fault Roads. It is a wretched place and no one has been down there for hundreds of years. There were reasons we sealed all access tunnels shut. I don't need to remind any of you about the evil that lurks down there. If we open up the way into the Fault Roads we invite trouble into Somnos."

"This is a historic opportunity," countered Josephus. "I must say, General Tadeusz, I am surprised that you are being so shortsighted about this. Aren't you the least bit curious to reconnect with Jasber, to begin the glorious task of unifying our people? I would have thought that you wouldn't be scared off so easily by a few darkened passageways."

General Tadeusz's face flushed momentarily, but he quickly regained his composure. "I would be most eager to see Jasber," said the general stiffly. "But the risk is too great. I am against reopening the Fault Roads and I am against trusting our greatest enemy. This is the man who killed General Loxoc. Have you forgotten who we are talking about? That's the problem with unifiers and scholars like you, Josephus; you fall madly in love with your theories and you have no regard whatsoever for the risks that they involve. I am sure you would like to write a great big book about rediscovering Jasber. No doubt it would make you very famous and they would build a statue in your honor in the library's Great Hall. But I am responsible for men and women's lives. This is why decisions of great importance are best left to those accustomed to the burden of weighing life and death."

"If we were to authorize this expedition," said Hill, ignoring General Tadeusz, "who would lead it?"

"I am inclined to have Colonel Treeknot lead the expedition," replied the Grand Vizier. She looked around the room. "We will put it to a vote. Josephus is not a member of the cabinet, and therefore does not have a right to vote. We already know how General Tadeusz stands. What do you say, Dr. Nostrite?"

"With all due respect," said Dr. Nostrite, "I think it is fool-hardy to risk so much on the faint hope of saving one man and finding a city that in all likelihood does not exist. Perhaps in a few decades, after our tree is well established and our strength has returned . . ."

"That's two votes against," said the Grand Vizier. "How about you, Hill?"

"I think we ought to give it a try," said Hill. "It's a risk. It will be very dangerous, of course. But, in the end, sitting here and doing nothing may be even more dangerous."

"What about you, Alfonso?" asked the Grand Vizier. "You're a Great Sleeper and our tradition entitles you to a vote. What do you think?"

All eyes turned to Alfonso and he felt the intensity of the entire discussion swivel toward him. In truth, Alfonso didn't know what he thought. He certainly did not trust Kiril. It seemed quite obvious to Alfonso that Kiril had a plan of his own. And what did General Tadeusz mean when he described the "evil that lurks down there"? None of this was inviting. Under other circumstances, Alfonso would have voted against going, but his concern for his father tipped the scales. It was quite possible that his father was on the brink of death, and when this possibility was factored into the equation, the choice was really not much of a choice at all.

"I agree," said Alfonso softly. "I think we should give it a try."

"Two in favor, two against," said the Grand Vizier. "I greatly appreciate everyone's counsel." She closed her eyes and instantly entered a sleeping trance. Seconds later, her eyes opened. The strain of making this decision was evident on her face.

"All of our considerations must focus on one question: will it jeopardize the security of Somnos?" remarked the Grand Vizier. "Clearly, Kiril has his reasons for making this offer, and they are not simply his own freedom. This smells like a trap in which all of Somnos might be caught." She looked around with an air of finality. "I have made my decision. No one will enter the Fault Roads."

"So we're just going to let my father die," said Alfonso angrily. He felt hot and flushed in the face. It was probably unwise to speak to the Grand Vizier in this manner, but he didn't care. This was his father's life they were talking about. "Both my dad and I risked our lives to save Dormia and this is the thanks that you show us?"

Alfonso rose to his feet, strode across the Grand Vizier's study, and stormed out the door.

CHAPTER 19

PAPER TRAIL

EARLY THE NEXT MORNING, Resuza woke up after a restless night of sleep and crept down into the kitchen to have a glass of placka nectar. Freshly prepared every morning by Hill's servants, it came from a tropical fruit with a nutlike exterior. Resuza loved to have a glass of it each morning as soon as she woke. Usually she was alone. However, that morning she found Hill sitting at the breakfast table with a worried look on his face. He was hunched over the table, studying an assortment of scraps of paper.

"You're off to an early start," said Resuza. "How did the meeting go last night?"

Hill looked at Resuza, and she knew at once that something was wrong.

"A half-hour ago, I received some rather grim news," Hill replied wearily. "Here, have a look at this," he said, pointing to the table. The scraps of paper were laid out like the pieces of a puzzle. Some of the pieces appeared rough, as if torn, and others appeared blackened, as if burned.

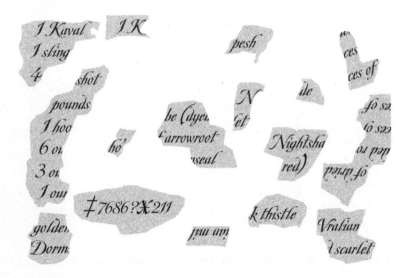

"What is it?" asked Resuza.

"These are the last traces of Kiril," replied Hill.

"What?"

"Sometime last night, Kiril escaped from his jail cell," explained Hill. "It appears to have been an inside job."

"But how?"

Hill explained that the lock on Kiril's cell required two keys. One of these keys was held by the captain of the guard unit and the other key was kept in the Tree Palace. The captain despised Kiril because Kiril had gravely wounded two of his best men, one of whom was his cousin. It was highly unlikely that the captain had helped Kiril. This meant someone had made a copy of the captain's key without his knowledge. As for the second key, Hill speculated that someone of high rank—with access to the Tree Palace—had stolen it and given it to Kiril.

"Is anyone looking for him?" asked Resuza.

"Of course," replied Hill. "Apparently, Colonel Treeknot has set out with a group of her knights to hunt Kiril down."

Hill went on to explain that the only clues they had as to Kiril's whereabouts were the scraps of paper on the kitchen table. Kiril had written in English, probably because he knew the guards would not be able to read it. He had written quite a bit in his cell; one of the guards even recalled him drawing maps and diagrams. Kiril had insisted that he was merely helping Josephus write his history of Jasber. In the end, however, Kiril managed to burn everything he had written—everything except this one, torn-up, and partially burnt page, which appeared to be a list of sorts.

"Have you put the pieces together?" asked Resuza.

"I'm still working on it," said Hill. "But I'm off to the library. I believe one of these scraps—the one with the numbers—is the reference code for a book. I know a librarian down there who is going to help me. After that, we can swing by Josephus's place and see what he makes of all this. Why don't you wake Alfonso and Bilblox? I'm sure they'll want to help."

Resuza ran upstairs and returned several minutes later with Bilblox at her side.

"Where's Alfonso?" asked Hill.

"I don't know," said Resuza, with a tinge of worry in her voice. "He's gone."

Hill looked worried as well, and remembered Alfonso's

161

stormy outburst the night before. "I'm sure it's nothing," he said grimly.

಄

Alfonso was lying on his stomach, in the snow, watching a long procession of sleds make their way across the frozen tundra. The sleds were lashed together in the form of a long, single train. Each sled carried a large metal cage, and inside were human beings—captives—who were wrapped in blankets and huddled together for warmth. Alfonso found it impossible to move. He was paralyzed with fear. After a few seconds of struggle, he gave up and simply watched with silent dread.

The ground soon began to shake with the sound of approaching hoofbeats. Six figures on horseback were galloping toward the train of sleds. The rider in front, who appeared to be the leader, was smaller than the others. In one hand he held the reins to his horse and in the other, he held a canister whose bronze surface gleamed brightly in the sun. The rider's face was smooth, tender, and almost fragile looking. He was a teenager, about the same age as Alfonso, with ash-gray hair and entirely white eyes. Alfonso knew at once that this had to be the boy Resuza had told him about—the one who was now leading the Dragoonya.

Moments later, the boy had galloped beyond view to the front of the procession. Alfonso returned to looking at the sleds. The occupants of one particular sled caught his eye. They were an older man and a young woman, and they looked very familiar. Suddenly, he knew who they were. There was no mistaking Hill and Resuza. Alfonso screamed for them. The snow and procession of sleds disappeared, and Alfonso blinked his eyes.

It was early morning, and as Alfonso woke up from his dream he realized he was on an empty cobblestone street in Somnos. Alfonso rubbed his face and looked around. Rats scurried over the cobblestones and errant scraps of paper tumbled in the wind. On one side of the street there was a rundown warehouse and a sprawling graveyard. On the other side of the street was an old stone mansion surrounded by an imposing wrought-iron fence.

Alfonso was quickly distracted by the sound of screaming. Two women, one young and the other middle-aged, were milling about at the far end of the street. The younger woman was sobbing hysterically and the older one was screaming, "Leave me alone, leave me alone, leave me alone!" Alfonso glanced about to see who else was lurking nearby. Was someone chasing these women? It didn't appear so. There was only one other person in sight—a man wandering in the cemetery, whimpering and then muttering to himself, "I'm sorry, my son. Forgive me for what I have done. I beseech you, my dear boy, forgive me!" They all appeared to be fast asleep and in the firm grip of nightmares.

Slowly it dawned on Alfonso: he was in the Delirium Quarter. Why was he here? As if in response to this question, Alfonso heard a faint flapping sound above. The noise came from the leaves of the Founding Tree. Of course, thought Alfonso, the tree has drawn me here. But why?

Moments later, the younger woman—the one who had been sobbing—woke up and began to look about in a disoriented

163

fashion. "Excuse me!" she yelled in a quavering voice. She was talking to Alfonso. "Which way is it to the Dreamer's Quarter?"

"I don't know," called Alfonso. "I just woke up myself." He smiled in a friendly manner, but the woman responded with a frown. She pointed to a sign posted along the wall of the cemetery. It read:

WARNING:

YOU HAVE ENTERED THE
DELIRIUM QUARTER.
NO ONE IS ALLOWED HERE DURING WAKING HOURS
WITHOUT SPECIAL AUTHORIZATION.
IF YOU HAVE JUST WOKEN UP,
LEAVE NOW!
DO NOT WAKE ANYONE UP AROUND YOU.
INDIVIDUALS WOKEN FROM SUCH STATES
ARE PRONE TO SUDDEN ACTS OF
VIOLENCE AND DEPRAVITY
IN THE SECONDS BEFORE THEY REACH
CONSCIOUSNESS.

"Don't stick around here," warned the young woman. "Bad things happen in this quarter." With that, she spun around and took off at a brisk pace.

Alfonso was about to follow her when something caught his eye. It was a placard on the front gate of the mansion across the street. The placard read: RESIDENCE OF THE ROYAL SCRIBE OF SOMNOS. It was Josephus's house.

Alfonso walked across the street and passed through the wrought-iron front gate. The mansion, made of gray stone, was four stories high and quite imposing. Its windows were long and narrow, almost like the arrow slits on a castle, and the roof was adorned with an enormous brass weathervane that creaked as it swiveled in the wind. The overall effect was quite somber, the complete opposite of Josephus's office in the library.

The mansion was surrounded by an elaborate rock garden of large geodes, cracked open so that the blue-gray crystals inside of them sparkled in the early morning light. The geodes were surrounded by an expanse of fine black sand that had been neatly raked. Perched on the geodes were a number of emperor butterflies. These butterflies, like so many of the other living things in Somnos, were abnormally large. Some had a wing-span as long as a man's arm.

As he approached the front door, Alfonso was surprised to discover that it was slightly ajar. He stood at the entrance and called Josephus's name several times. His cries echoed throughout the four-story house. After a minute or so of calling, Alfonso began looking around.

Not surprisingly, the house was filled with books—novels, encyclopedias, atlases, almanacs, historical accounts, scientific studies, and quite a few picture books as well—all of which were bound in leather and smelled of mildew and stale pipe tobacco. The floors were covered with thick, ornately woven carpets. The air was speckled with dust and virtually every corner of the house boasted a vast array of cobwebs.

For the most part, though, the house appeared to be in perfectly good order. The only room that appeared to be in disarray was Josephus's study. A giant pile of clothing was amassed in the center of the room; books lay scattered across several desks; wall maps hung precariously from a coat rack. It looked like Josephus was packing for a long journey.

Alfonso looked carefully at the enormous maps that covered the walls of the study. There were maps of Mongolia, the Gobi Desert, the Laptev Sea, the Great Rift Valley in Africa, and the island of Papua New Guinea. Most of the maps dated back to the 1700s and were marked with the names of countries that no longer existed.

In one corner of the room, Alfonso noticed a peculiar wooden map hanging on the wall. It was smaller than the others, no more than six inches in length, and Alfonso only noticed it because it was illuminated by a shaft of light that was pouring in from a nearby window. This particular map showed the original eleven cities of Dormia. Alfonso looked closer. He found Somnos and Jasber and the others, as expected, but something puzzled him about Jasber. The dot showing Jasber was smudgy and faint, as if the ink here had simply evaporated. This reminded him of the time he was in the Motte-Picquet subway station in Paris with his classmates. He remembered walking over to a map of the system and noticing that the dot showing the Motte-Picquet station was worn away from the thousands of people who had put their fingers there. The city of Jasber was worn in the same manner, as if it had been repeatedly touched.

Alfonso pressed his index finger to the city of Jasber. He heard a small click. Across the room, the bottom drawer of a massive bookcase swung open on a recessed hinge. Alfonso found a candle on Josephus's desk, quickly lit it, and then crawled in through the secret doorway. It led into a small, square room no bigger than a walk-in closet. The walls of the room were lined with books and maps, all of which concerned Jasber. Lying on a desk were several fountain pens, a tall candelabra, and a small book with French writing on it. Alfonso picked up the book and began flipping through its pages. Its title was written in both Dormian hieroglyphs and in French. It read:

~ Un Destin Solitaire: Les Dormeurs Géant de Jasber ~

Alfonso had always been good at French and he grasped its meaning immediately. Roughly translated, the title read, "A Lonely Fate: The Great Sleepers of Jasber." Alfonso placed the book in his coat pocket and continued looking around. Moments later, he let out a soft, barely audible cry. Lying on the floor, in the corner of the room, was the rosewood box from Alexandria. The top was gone, and had obviously been ripped from its delicate hinges. There was no sign of the vial of dagárgala. "My box," said Alfonso aloud. "He took it!" Alfonso grabbed the remains of the rosewood box and stuffed it into a small backpack that he was carrying.

Alfonso's investigation was soon interrupted by the sounds of voices coming from Josephus's study. For a moment, Alfonso panicked, but then he relaxed when he recognized them. He crawled out of the secret room and saw Hill, Bilblox, and Resuza standing in the middle of Josephus's study.

"Alfonso!" exclaimed Resuza.

"What on earth are you doing here?" Hill inquired.

Alfonso explained what had happened after he had woken up in the Delirium Quarter. Bilblox shook his head in disgust.

"It looks like ol' Josephus is in cahoots with Kiril," said Bilblox.

"What do you mean?" asked Alfonso. Hill told him about Kiril's escape, and his belief that Kiril had received help.

"If they have joined together, I think I know where they're headed," Hill concluded with a weary shake of his head. "You see, Kiril left a torn-up list of items in his cell. On the list was a numeric code. We've just come from the library. It turns out that the code corresponds to a book from the library that's now missing. It was checked out to Josephus; we came here to ask him about it. It's called *The Ancient Fault Roads of Dormia*, written by Kemal Spratic, Kiril's father."

They stood there for a moment, stunned by their discoveries.

Hill sighed and stood up straight. They looked at him expectantly.

"The Grand Vizier must be informed at once," he said. "Josephus and Kiril are headed for the Fault Roads—and Jasber. There's not a moment to lose."

CHAPTER 20

MISTY

LATE THAT AFTERNOON, Alfonso found himself riding on Bataar, along with Hill, Bilblox, and Resuza. Directly behind them were two of Hill's diplomats on a smaller anteater. They were all headed down an old jungle road that led to the northern corner of the valley, where the old platinum mines were located. Birds called out from the shadowy depths of the jungle and, occasionally, oversized monkeys scampered across the road in front of them. A thin mist hovered just above the treetops. Bataar seemed unusually skittish, looking this way and that, as if expecting trouble at any moment. Resuza sat perched at the front of the riding cabin, aiming an Enfield rifle at the treetops. This was the rifle that once belonged to Bilblox's pilot,

Snej. Bilblox had decided to give it to Resuza and she was now putting it to good use—making sure that nothing dropped down from the branches overhead.

The one thing that was conspicuously absent from the surrounding landscape was people. No one was in sight, no travelers on the road, no farmers in the field, no fishermen on any of the valley's rivers or streams. This was because the Grand Vizier had put all of Somnos on lockdown. No one was allowed to leave their homes until further notice. No one, that is, except Hill and his traveling party. They had been given explicit orders, from the Grand Vizier herself, to find an old passageway that led down into the Fault Roads, and look for a trace of Kiril and Josephus.

Under other circumstances, such a task would normally fall to Colonel Treeknot and her Expeditionary Corps, but they were nowhere to be found. Apparently, Treeknot had taken matters into her own hands and set off before dawn to find Kiril. This wasn't surprising. Colonel Treeknot liked to operate on her own. And perhaps she'd already found Kiril. But just to be doubly safe, the Grand Vizier turned to Hill and Alfonso to search for the entrance to the old Fault Roads.

Finding a way into the Fault Roads was much easier said than done. When the roads were shut down, hundreds of years ago, the leaders of Somnos went to great lengths to seal off all entrances. The official reason for this was that they posed a security risk. The year before the Fault Roads were closed, the city of Noctos was sacked by the Dragoonya. People feared that the Dragoonya would somehow find a way down into the Fault Roads and take Somnos by surprise. This was a valid concern.

But there was another reason for keeping the Fault Roads sealed off. There were rumors that creatures known as zwodszay had come to inhabit the darkest nooks and crannies of these ancient tunnels. The miners spoke of these mysterious creatures with a mixture of awe and repulsion. There had been strange incidents where miners disappeared beneath the earth, and the zwodszay were blamed.

Of course, given the length of time since the Fault Roads had closed, no one knew a way back down. Josephus had claimed to know a way in, but that was of no help now. It was Resuza who provided the most promising lead. She recalled the strange encounter she and Alfonso had with Misty on the night of their gondola ride. At the mention of the Fault Roads and Josephus, the normally genial miner became enraged. Why did Misty care so much about the Fault Roads or about Josephus for that matter? Something apparently had happened between the two.

Hill knew Mistepha "Misty" Blazenska only vaguely, but he agreed she might be of some assistance.

Hill was sitting next to Alfonso, who was rearranging the scraps of paper taken from Kiril's cell to try to find something recognizable.

"Do you think Misty will help us?" Hill asked Resuza.

"Hard to say," she replied. "She's the most stubborn person I've ever met, but there was something about Josephus she really didn't like."

"Hey, I'm pretty stubborn," said Bilblox.

Kõrgu, who was sitting on Bilblox's lap, growled in agreement.

"Yeah," said Resuza, "But wait till you meet Misty—"

"Hey!" cried out Alfonso. "I think I put these pieces of paper together—have a look." Hill and Resuza drew closer.

1 Kho'pesh
1 Kaval
1 sling shot
4 pounds of dried Vralian Nightshade
1 hooded robe (dyed scarlet red)
6 ounces of arrowroot
3 ounces of goldenseal
1 ounce of Dormian milk thistle

‡7686?✗211

"What are these things?" asked Alfonso. "I know what a slingshot and hooded robe are, but what's the rest of this stuff?"

"A kaval is a shepherd's flute," said Hill. "The nightshade, arrowroot, goldenseal, and Dormian milk thistle are all herbs."

"What's a khopesh?" asked Alfonso.

"I don't know," said Hill as he scribbled some notes on a piece of paper. "But I intend to find out." Hill tugged on Bataar's reigns and brought the giant anteater to a halt. He then called for his two aides. One of them, a young woman not much older than Resuza, dismounted the anteater and hastily climbed up Bataar.

"What do you need, Mr. Foreign Minister?" asked the aide.

"I want you to get me everything that's on this list, from the nightshade to the slingshot," said Hill. "And I want an update on what Colonel Treeknot is up to. Find out if she has returned or if there is any more information on where, exactly, she has gone."

"Right away, sir," said the aide. She scurried down and immediately ran toward her anteater.

"Why do you want those items?" Alfonso asked.

"Kiril obviously has everything planned out," replied Hill. "And if we are going to follow him, then we need everything that he has."

"How far do ya intend to follow him?" asked Bilblox.

Hill made no reply.

ᛗ

Just shy of sundown, Bataar entered a large clearing in the jungle and Misty's house came into full view. The old miner lived in a ramshackle cottage built on stilts about thirty feet high. One solitary skinny ladder provided access to the cottage. As Bataar walked closer, they all saw Misty open the door to the cottage and walk onto the wide front deck that was covered with all manner of potted plants.

"State your names and business!" yelled Misty.

Hill stood up and leaned out of the riding cabin. "It's me, Hill Persplexy! The foreign minister!"

Misty watched impassively as they climbed down from Bataar. They paused at the bottom rung of the ladder that ascended to Misty's house and looked up.

"I've got nothin' t'say t'the high 'n' mighty," Misty yelled. "But I'll let ya inside 'cause-a Resuza, who's got the only sense in this city. But I ain't toleratin' that wolf inside my house."

"She's not a wolf!" yelled Bilblox. "She's my seein' eye dog."

"No matter, she ain't a-comin' in my house!"

"Leave her here," said Hill. "She'll be fine. Bataar is here, in case anything happens."

Bilblox nodded.

They all climbed up the rickety, wooden ladder. When they arrived on the porch, they saw that not only was it covered with plants, it also had all types of mining equipment scattered about—ropes, winches, cranks, pulleys, torches, pickaxes, grappling hooks, and sledgehammers. There were also quite a few vats of a pungent-smelling liquid that could have been either kerosene or moonshine, it was impossible to say which.

"Come 'ere and git inside," said Misty. "I feel a chill a-comin' and I got a fire started in the furnace."

They all followed Misty into the cramped confines of her cottage. The walls were lined with potions and poultice wraps, all of them identified with scrawled Dormian hieroglyphs. Misty gestured for them to sit down.

"So tell me," said Misty in a sullen tone. "To what do I owe this honor?"

Hill leaned forward in his chair. "Let me be blunt. I understand you and Josephus may have some history, especially with regard to the Fault Roads," he said. "All that is in the past. My question is this: how can we enter the Fault Roads?"

Misty's face clouded over at the mention of Josephus. "I got nothin' t'say. I ain't been in the Fault Roads."

"You've never been in the Fault Roads?" Hill pressed.

Misty shook her head and glared at Hill.

Resuza tried a different tack. She relayed the news about Kiril's escape and what they had found in Josephus's house. This evoked an immediate reaction from Misty. She slammed her meaty fist on a nearby table.

"I tol' him," she exclaimed. "I tol' him to forget that foolishness. He never listened. Thought he was the smartest sleeper around. Look where it got 'im. Treason!"

"What happened, Misty?" Resuza asked in a soft voice. "What's this all about?"

"Musta been near fifty years now," said Misty with a shake of her head. "Me 'n' a coupla miners found a veina pure platinum. 'Twas a gorgeous whitish silver color and it just stretched real thin and deep like—way down into the bowels of the earth. Well they got regulations says ya can't mine beneath a certain depth fer fear a-hittin' one of the roots of the Foundin' Tree. And we was pretty close to that depth when we hit this vein. But we're miners, and we found a veina platinum, so we just keep diggin'. One day, we bust through this wall and find ourselves in a cave—only the ground is perfectly flat like we was on the floor of a man-made tunnel. We agreed: nobody says a word 'bout this."

"It was the Fault Roads?" asked Resuza.

Misty nodded and continued with the story. Before digging any deeper, she paid a visit to her great-uncle Dlugosz, who was 106 years old and, according to family legend, had been born in the mines. Dlugosz had experience mining deep, well beyond the legal limit, and it was said that he had a few encounters with the creatures known as zwodszay.

"Yes sir, indeedy," said Dlugosz to Misty. "Sounds like the

cave ya hit is a Fault Road. Mighty dangerous down 'dare—mighty dangerous. If ya gonna go, ya best take percautions. I'd take lotsa light wit' me and I'd cover meself up good with the sap-a the skelter tree—it's a greasy-lookin' tree in the jungle. Makes ya hard to track. Careful though—skelter sap wears off in 'bout quarter-day's time. Also, take just a few fellas wit'cha. No more 'an a dozen. The zwodszay don't like big groups none. Tell ya the truth, it's safest goin' alone. Don't talk either. Best to keep quiet or whisper. And keep yer eyes out for them mile markers, that's whatchya want. Ferget the platinum vein. Them mile markers is the real treasure!"

The following day, Misty returned to the mine with a crew of eleven. They took all of the precautions that Dlugosz had recommended. Just as Misty had initially suspected, the cave turned into a tunnel. Every few hundred yards or so, it had markers on its walls, which were made of solid gold. The markers had numbers on them—512.5, 512.4, 512.3, etcetera—which indicated how far it was to some destination, presumably farther down the tunnel. They couldn't believe their good fortune, and began prying the gold markers off the wall and stuffing them into their bags. Once or twice, Misty could have sworn that she sensed someone watching her.

"My goodness!" gushed Karny, the youngest of the miners. "We do this fer a week or so and we'll be richer 'n thieves."

"No!" said Misty. "We're 'ere today and then we ain't never comin' back. We'll melt down these mile markers so that no one knows where they came from, sell 'em at the exchange, pay what we owe to the Miners Guild, divvy up the profits, and that'll be the end of it!"

Misty's plan was a sound one, but it was foiled by Karny,

who pocketed one of the mile markers and attempted to sell it on his own to make a bit of extra cash for himself. A week or so later, Karny showed up for work with a thin, bespectacled, scholarly looking young man at his side. The man introduced himself as Josephus, royal historian of Somnos, and asked to speak with Misty alone.

"I know what you're up to and what you've found," said Josephus in a measured voice. He then held out the solid gold mile marker as his proof. "You could be arrested on a number of counts, including for digging so deep and for entering the old Fault Roads."

"But ya ain't turned us in," said Misty. "So ya must be wantin' somethin'. You lookin' fer a cut?"

"No," said Josephus. "My interests are more scholarly. I want you to take me back down to the Fault Roads for an hour or two so I can look around."

"That's it?"

Josephus nodded.

Misty gave a sigh of relief. She didn't like the idea of going back into the Fault Roads, but what choice did she have? Her crew escorted Josephus down the old mining shaft that led into the Fault Roads. As soon as they entered the road itself, Josephus let out a hoot of joy and broke off at a near run down the ancient passageway. Misty and her men hurried after him. They continued downward for several hours until Misty finally lost her patience.

"We've gone far enough!" declared Misty. "It's more 'an time we turn 'round. We've bin gone almost six hours and our coverin'a skelter sap is worn away. We're headed fer trouble from the zwodszay."

"That's an old wives' tale," said Josephus. "There's nothing like—"

He was interrupted by what sounded like the approach of heavy raindrops, but clearly this was impossible. Steadily the noise grew louder until it finally became evident that this was the sound of hundreds of feet and hands.

It was the zwodszay.

"They was upon us 'fore we ever saw 'em," recalled Misty with a shudder. "They went fer our torches first and 'fore we knew it, we was standin' in total blackness. Couldn't see a blasted thing. I smelled 'em though. They smelled like rottin' flesh. Then there was the screamin' of my miners. Sometimes I swear I can still hear 'em whimperin' like pups bein' eaten alive. They slaughtered us. Killed all twelve of us except fer me'n' Josephus, who were in the back and managed t'run away. We emerged from the tunnel drippin' in blood. Miners' blood. Aft'ward, we sealed up the way in wit' a boulder."

She stared at them angrily, and it was clear that the horror of that day had weighed upon her ever since.

"Why didn't you tell anyone?" asked Resuza.

"What for?" asked Misty. "No sir. I put a knife t'Josephus's throat and said if he ever tried to go back down them roads, I'd kill 'im meself. He said he'd never go back. He learned his lesson, 'n' tol' me it'd stay a secret. We agreed we'd tell folks that there was a cave-in and that's how them other miners died. There was a lot of lyin' that we done, but we didn't 'ave a choice. If we tol' the truth, some numbskull woulda tried t'get back into the Fault Roads."

"So you've never been down to the Fault Roads since then?" Alfonso asked.

"No one's got any business down there," replied Misty matter-of-factly.

"But have *you* been down there since?" asked Hill.

"I ain't gonna lie to ya," said Misty with a sigh. "'Twas a time when my nephew fell sick 'n' no one 'ad any money. Was right 'fore the Great Sleeper came and the crops was all dyin' and people was starvin'. I went in by meself, real quiet, carried lotsa light, reapplied my skelter sap three times, and came out with a bunch a mile markers. It was just t' help my nephew, you understand?"

"Can you show us how to get down there?" Alfonso asked.

"No," said the old miner. "I won't letcha go down there. And it ain't just cause of the zwodszay either. Ever since the roots of the old Foundin' Tree withered away, none of the ground beneath Somnos has been stable. Mines've been collapsin' left and right. That's why I've taken to huntin' ants fer a livin'. I haven't been down 'dere for over a year now. It ain't safe."

"Please," said Resuza.

Misty sighed heavily.

"Fine," said the old miner finally. "I'll jus' show ya parta the way. But'cha better grab a few of those rank-smellin' vats that are sittin' on my porch—we may need 'em."

"What are they?" asked Bilblox.

"Skleter sap," replied Misty with a grunt.

Later that evening, as the moon began to rise, Bataar made her way into the foothills that loomed above the jungle. The temperature here was pleasantly crisp, a perfect mix of the warm jungle air below and the icy mountain air above. Looking backwards, it was still possible to see the majestic lights of Somnos in the distance. The area they were traveling through was a barren scrubland, composed of rocks, grass, and occasional clumps of snow. No one spoke. Alfonso, Hill, Resuza, Bilblox, and Misty were each lost in their own thoughts.

For his part, Hill was busy looking through a leather bag stuffed with a slingshot, a shepherd's flute, a hooded robe, and an assortment of herbs. These, of course, were the items from Kiril's list. Hill's aide had been incredibly resourceful at finding everything on the list. She had worked at lightning speed and delivered the items to Misty's house at dusk, just before they had departed for the Fault Roads. The only item missing from the list was the khopesh—no one could figure out what this was.

"Aha!" said Misty. "Bring this 'ere anteater to a halt!"

Resuza, who had the reigns, tugged forcefully.

"What's the matter?" asked Hill.

Misty jumped to the ground and pointed to a round boulder that, at first glance, looked no different from the hundreds of boulders surrounding it. Upon closer inspection, however, they saw a small curlicue carved into the bottom of the rock.

"That's the mark I use," Misty proclaimed. She looked at Bilblox. "Come on then—help me with this thing. It's good t'have some strong folk helpin' out."

Misty and Bilblox pushed the boulder to one side, revealing a dark hole in the ground just over a foot and a half in diameter. Alfonso looked at it. The hole didn't seem particularly exceptional, certainly not like an entrance to the ancient Fault Roads.

"Any signs of Josephus or Kiril?" asked Hill.

"Impossible to say," said Misty. "Ground 'ere is all rock—no place to leave a footprint. If they came through 'ere, they musta moved dis 'ere boulder back into place and covered their tracks."

Hill looked unsatisfied.

"Whatchya' got that look on yer face fer?" asked Misty.

"We need to know if Josephus and Kiril are down there," said Hill. "I want to go down and see if we can find any traces of them."

"And what if ya do find some traces?" asked Misty angrily. "Then what? You gonna just keep goin' till the zwodszay ambush ya and eat ya for lunch?"

"No," said Hill. "I have no interest in exploring the Fault Roads. We'll just poke around a little bit. And, if we find any traces of them, we'll report back to the Grand Vizier and she can decide what to do."

"Blasted fool!" cursed Misty. "Stubborn, thick-headed, arrogant fool of a man. And they call ya a blasted dignitary? All them years ya spent in the outside world softened yer brain up like milk on porridge."

"Will you take us down there?" asked Hill.

"It'll cost ya," replied Misty.

"What's your price?"

"Let's put it this way," said Misty. "If I see any of them mile markers, ya just turn yer head, and I'll come home with a few souvenirs."

"Fine," said Hill.

Misty still looked worried, as if she knew she was making a terrible mistake, but she eventually nodded. "Well," said Misty finally. "It oughta take a few hours to git down to where ya want to go. I can show ya where them Fault Roads start. We can poke around a bit. Then we can resurface and ya can go have yer chat with the Grand Vizier."

Hill nodded.

"I got some extra packs wit' me," said Misty. "Just in case, I figre we oughta take enough supplies fer a few days."

"Why's that?" asked Alfonso. "You said it should only take a few hours."

"First rule a-minin'," said Misty. "Always plan for the worst—cave-ins—especially these days. It's real easy t'get trapped. That's why I'm insistin' on the extra food, and torches, and skelter sap, too."

Misty tied one end of a thick rope around a nearby boulder and then dropped the other end down the hole. It was impossible to see how far down the hole went. Bilblox placed a hand just above the hole.

"Do you feel that air?" he remarked. "It's cold." He shook his head and looked at Alfonso, who had his hand on Bilblox's shoulder. "Do you remember the catacombs below Barsh-yin-Binder? Afterward, I swore I'd never go underground again."

"We got no time fer storytellin'," muttered Misty. She had turned quite grumpy and her coal-black eyes glared at the group. She put on a battered miner's helmet, double-checked an overstuffed canvas bag slung around her shoulders, grabbed hold of the rope, and lowered herself down into the hole, burly hand over burly hand. When only her head peeked out of the hole, she looked around once more and let out another cackle. "Each of ya remember yer packs 'n' supplies and hurry up!" she said. "Follow me quick—you folks is liable to stand around

that hole fer hours, makin' excuses why ya won't go down!"
And with that last word, she disappeared.

They stood around the hole, listening to Misty's grunts and
half-curses as she lowered herself down. Finally, Resuza grabbed
hold of the rope, smiled at everyone, and disappeared through
the hole. Hill quickly followed. Then Bilblox, with Kōrgu
perched on his shoulders. Alfonso was the last. Suddenly,
Alfonso had a very dark feeling, as if he'd rather do just about
anything else than descend into this hole. But it was too late for
second guesses. Alfonso grabbed hold of the rope and felt its
coarseness against his palm. More noises fluttered up from below. Alfonso shut his eyes, ground his teeth together, and descended into the darkness below.

CHAPTER 21

THE DESCENT

THEY DESCENDED roughly fifty feet until they landed in what appeared to be a large, hollow cavern jagged with stalagmites and stalactites. It was completely dark, except for a solitary beam of moonlight coming from the hole above them. The stone floor was covered with dust and the air smelled musty and stale. It was cold as well—not cold enough for ice to form, but cold enough for them to see their breath and to feel the tingle of a cough forming in their chests.

Hill removed his pack and took out a lantern. Misty immediately put a restraining hand on Hill's arm. "Not now, laddy," she warned. "Ya got plentya time later when ya might need that light. No use wastin' it while we still got some above us. Now where's them barrelsa skelter sap that Bilblox was carryin'?"

Bilblox took a barrel out of his oversize backpack and set it on the ground. The barrel was roughly the size of a large watermelon. Misty uncorked the barrel and poured an ounce or so of liquid into her hands. It glowed faintly and smelled like rubbing alcohol.

"Great-uncle Dlugosz swore by this stuff," she said. "Those zwodszay 'ave an especially keen sense-a smell, but the sap covers yer scent near perfect. I'd smear this all o'er yer faces and any other expos' skin—the zwodszay don't like it. Plus it glows a little, so ya can see one another. Don' worry—the zwodszay got terrible eyesight. They'll smell ya miles away but can only see ya if yer within' kissin' distance." She looked at Kōrgu. "The wolf won' like it, but ya better cover 'er as well."

"Wait a minute," said Bilblox. "I though ya said the zwodszay were in the Fault Roads—not in ordinary mines like this one."

"That's right," said Misty. "But with all the collapsin' that's been goin' on down 'ere, it's impossible to say where the zwodszay might be. We're all lucky they ain't found a way up to the surface—otherwise Somnos would 'ave a far worse problem than those ants."

Everyone smeared the sap over their exposed skin. It went on smoothly, so that only a small amount was necessary for each person. Bilblox grabbed Kōrgu and applied the sap to her fur and snout, even though she wriggled and tried to brush it off. This task completed, Misty gestured toward a far corner of the empty cavern, where an iron cage sat almost directly over a dark mine shaft. The door to the cage hung open on one broken hinge. "There's the transportation to the mine below. Took us months to dig the shaft." They walked to the rickety cage, which was large enough to fit the entire group.

"All righty then, git inside, ladies and gents," muttered Misty. "We're not here fer a school trip, and these bonesa mine ain't gettin' any warmer with us standin' 'round and waitin'."

"Are you sure this still works?" asked Hill.

Misty let out a gruff cackle. "Well, ya got no other options, that's fer sure. S'long as the chain still holds, we'll be fine." They reluctantly crowded into the cage and felt the floorboards creak ominously. One or two appeared to be missing altogether. Misty entered last and dragged the lopsided door closed. "Hold on tight," she said. "This 'ere cage is apt to give ya a jolt."

Misty reached up and pulled down a metal rod. It screeched down, and suddenly the cage began to descend into the complete darkness of the mine shaft. At first the descent was quite slow, but after thirty seconds or so, it sped up so quickly that it wasn't clear whether the cage was still attached to its metal chain.

"MISTY?!" yelled Hill.

"Jus hol' on there," shouted Misty. "The ballast balancin' the other side is a bit light. We're goin' faster than we should." They continued their near free fall in the iron cage. Alfonso huddled in a corner of the cage. Both his hands gripped the rusty bars, and his mind whirled round and round, trying to calm his panic.

Brrraaaaacckkk!!!

The cage shuddered and began to slow. Thousands of sparks bloomed above them and rained down like falling fireflies. A loud scraping sound, like fingernails on a chalkboard, reverberated throughout the cage. Misty slapped Hill on the shoulder and shouted in his ear, "Those are the brakes kickin' in! I knew this ol' gal was still workin'! Why, she could prob'ly go fer another hunnert years!"

At that moment, the cage stopped abruptly, and they all fell to the floor. It was completely dark, except for the last sparks dying out on their packs and jackets. Bilblox moaned. "I thought Fort Krasnik was behind on the times," muttered the blind longshoreman. "That elevator's a death trap. Any broken bones out there?"

No one said anything. Slowly, the group stood back up and brushed themselves off. Bilblox reached out toward the cage door to push it open, but found nothing. "Where's the door?" he asked.

Misty lit a candle and let out a surprised whistle. "Good thing we didn't move around in the cage!" she exclaimed. "That cage door musta snapped off. Well, nothin' we can do now. Let's get movin'."

She lit a lantern and walked out of the cage into a small room with a low, hand-dug ceiling. A narrow tunnel led out of the room and a great many rocks lay strewn across the floor.

"Hmm," said Misty. "These rocks've all been moved 'round. This tunnel used to be almost totally blocked."

"Maybe Josephus and Kiril moved them," suggested Alfonso.

"Not by 'emselves," said Misty. "It'd take more'n two men to move these rocks." Misty scrambled into the tunnel, moved aside several smaller boulders with practiced ease, and then motioned for them to follow.

"So you don't think Josephus was here?" asked Hill.

"Impossible to say," said Misty. "Mebbe he was, mebbe he wasn't, who could . . ."

Just then, their voices were drowned out by an enormous rumble, which sounded unmistakably like an earthquake. The ground shook and small rocks fell from the ceiling.

"What was that?" asked Resuza nervously.

"Oh that's just the ground shiftin'," said Misty. "It's like I told ya's—ground ain't stable anymore after the old Foundin' Tree died." Her voice trailed off in the midst of another rumble.

They walked down a long tunnel lit only by Misty's lantern. After about two hours, they were stopped by what appeared to be a cave-in. The tunnel was completely filled in with smashed wood timbers, cracked chunks of marble, and hundreds of boulders.

"The mines keep goin' past this spot, but that's many years ago," Misty said. She rubbed her chin and looked around, as if she were lost.

"Should be 'round here somewhere," she muttered. Misty set down her lantern and began groping around on the floor. "Yup, 'ere it is. And no rocks or pebbles on it either. Someone mighta been through 'ere recently—quite possible."

Everyone clamored around Misty to see what she had unearthed. On the ground before them was a rusting metal door with a hefty sliding bolt. "I put this 'ere door in after the disaster with Josephus," explained Misty. "Didn't want any trouble clawin' its way up, if ya know what I mean."

"This is the door to the Fault Roads?" asked Bilblox.

"Yup," said Misty. She smiled. "Now, my dear Foreign Minister, ya may want to reconsider whether ya really wanna open this 'ere door. Maybe we all can 'ave a drinka water and ya can mull it over."

Hill nodded somberly.

Misty patted her pockets. "Ah crimminy!"

"What is it?" asked Alfonso nervously.

"I misplaced me satchel with me cigars in em," said Misty. "Oh, I musta put 'em down about five minutes back, when I stopped to 'ave a drink. I'm gonna go grab 'em real quick. You all wait 'ere. Have a good look around, mebbe have a little snack, and then we can formulate a plan. Keep mullin' it over, Mr. Foreign Minister. I'll be back in a jiffy!"

Misty traipsed off into the darkness.

"Lunch, anyone?" asked Bilblox as he groped around in his backpack. "Feels like Misty packed us some beef jerky and . . . some more beef jerky."

"I'll have a piece," said Resuza.

"The jerky is excellent," said Bilblox as he chewed loudly. "Must be venison, maybe with a bit of paprika or garlic."

"Okay," said Alfonso. "Give me a piece, I'd like . . ."

Brrrrrrrrrrrrrrunnnn!

There was a deafening rumble. Everyone was knocked off their feet. Dust fell thickly from the ceiling and pebbles flew through the air. Kōrgu started barking ferociously.

About a minute later, Hill managed to light a torch and together they surveyed the damage. There had been a large cave-in and much of the ceiling had crashed down around them. The most obvious and immediate problem was that the way back to the elevator—the passageway that Misty had just walked down moments before—was now completely sealed off with enormous boulders. Alfonso, Hill, Bilblox, and Resuza immediately set to work trying to move the boulders. They worked feverishly for several hours, but it was no use. Even the mighty Bilblox, who was famous for lifting six-hundred-pound containers with ease, couldn't budge the massive rock pile.

"What are we gonna do?" asked Bilblox finally.

"We don't have much of a choice," Resuza said grimly.

"What are you suggestin'?" asked Bilblox. "You wanna open that door and go down into the Fault Roads? Where's that gonna take us?"

No one spoke for a moment.

"It could take us to Jasber," said Alfonso quietly.

"And it could take us straight to hell," retorted Bilblox. "I got a strong feelin'—a very strong feelin'—that we don't want to open that door."

"We're going to have to open it," said Hill wearily. "And it has nothing to do with Jasber, or the zwodszay, or Josephus, or Kiril. The thing is, if we don't open that door, we're going to run out of oxygen."

"He's right," said Resuza. "The air is beginning to feel a little thin in here."

"And what do we do once we're down there?" Bilblox demanded.

No one replied.

❧

Hill slid the bolt on the old door and heaved it open. A blast of warm air blew into the cavern, as if they had just opened the door to an oven. "Heaven have mercy on us," muttered Bilblox. "Who's goin' first?"

"I will," said Hill. "Everyone remember their packs with the supplies. And reapply some of that skelter sap, just in case." That done, Hill fastened a rope to the door and lowered himself into the darkened hole below. Alfonso went next, followed by Resuza, and then Bilblox with Kõrgu around his shoulders. They touched down on a cobblestone floor. It appeared to be an ancient storeroom, filled with shards of pottery, several intact plates, and a number of items that glittered in the dim light of Hill's torch. The storeroom opened into a tunnel that glowed with a faint light.

Hill set down his pack, pulled out his Colt .45 revolver, and stuck it into his belt so he could grab it quickly if need be. He then pulled out a sturdy wooden club. "This was in one of Misty's packs," explained Hill as he handed the weapon to Bilblox. "It should work very well in short-range combat, even when wielded by a blind man."

Bilblox nodded appreciatively.

Resuza took out her Enfield rifle and expertly moved her hands around the stock, muzzle, and firing mechanism. She glanced through the sight, and slid a bullet into position. "I'm all set," she said. "Hopefully I won't need it." She slung the rifle across her shoulders, and it hung loosely across her body, at the ready.

Hill turned to Alfonso. "Do you have your blue sphere?"

Alfonso nodded.

"Good," said Hill. "Make sure you can access it quickly."

"What's the plan?" asked Bilblox.

"Well, let's have a look around before making any decisions. All right?" Hill asked.

Everyone nodded.

They followed Hill into the tunnel. It soon ended and they entered a vast expanse. They were aware of space stretching out in all directions, and at first it was unclear where the floor ended and the open space began. Alfonso looked up and at first saw nothing. He waited, and after a few seconds, the whole picture snapped into focus. They were standing on a cobblestone road, about fifteen feet wide, carved into the side of a sheer cliff. Along the outside edge of the road ran a knee-high wall, also made up of cobblestones. It protected the group from a breathtaking chasm that dropped downward into the depths of the earth. The far wall of the chasm was the mirror image of their side minus the road. Above them, the walls of the chasm stretched away from each other, much like the sides of a *V*, which gave the entire area an astonishingly open perspective. There was no ceiling or roof visible—just gaping blackness above. Alfonso had never been to the Grand Canyon, but he imagined that the scale was probably similar, and he had to remind himself that he was still underground.

All of them spent the next few minutes staring at the Fault Road and the chasm in dumbstruck amazement.

"I don't understand," said Resuza at last. "Why are we able to see?" Alfonso looked around and realized she was right. The light appeared to be coming from the chasm itself. Alfonso peered over the edge and noticed a faint red glow at the bottom. Alfonso felt a pebble under his shoe, picked it up, and threw it over the edge. They all listened in silence, waiting for the sound of the pebble landing. Nothing. The pebble just fell, and fell, and fell—deep into the fiery bowels of the earth.

"No one knows how deep it is," whispered Hill. "Some say whatever's thrown into the chasm keeps going until it reaches the middle of the earth and burns up."

"Which way do we go on this road?" asked Resuza very quietly.

"I don't think we have a choice," whispered Alfonso.

To the left, the road slanted downward, deeper into the earth. To the right, the road climbed upward, back toward Somnos and the surface. The only problem was that the road to the right only stretched for a hundred yards before it tapered off into empty space. Clearly, perhaps long ago, someone had destroyed this road, making it impossible to reach the surface and Somnos.

"Looks like we ain't gonna be surfacin' anytime soon," whispered Bilblox.

The road to the left was passable. Hill said it probably led to the Hub, where the Fault Roads from all eleven cities once converged. This was where the Jasber Gate was located as well.

"What now?" asked Resuza.

"I say we head for the Hub," said Hill. "Either we'll find a way to the surface there or we'll stumble across Josephus and Kiril."

He looked at Resuza's quizzical expression and continued defensively. "I don't see any other options. We can't just wait around in that old mining tunnel up above because sooner or later there's bound to be another cave-in, and we'll all be crushed. And if that didn't kill us, the lack of food, water, and oxygen would. We have to press on to the Hub."

Bilblox nodded with a sudden determination. "All right," he said. "'N' what happens if we meet a zwodszay?"

"We run and then, if necessary, fight," said Hill. "Unfortunately, I don't know anything about them."

"I do," said Resuza. "Misty told me about them once before. Supposedly they were humans once, but you wouldn't know it, because they've been down here for centuries—eating only bats and moldy algae. Somehow, by mistake, they entered the Fault Roads, and they've never been able to leave. Although they've adapted to life underground, they haven't lost the taste for freshly butchered meat, like lamb sizzling over a fire. So they turn to the only meat they have left: themselves, and any other unlucky souls who stumble down here."

"It just gets better 'n' better," said Bilblox with a grimace.

Moments later, Bilblox put his arm around Alfonso. "Come on," he said. "Let's go find your dad."

CHAPTER 22

THE FAULT ROAD

DURING THE FIRST HOURS along the Fault Road, the travelers spoke very little to one another and spent much of their time looking around, spellbound by the incredible distances above and below them. The road had obviously fallen into disrepair, but it was still apparent that it had once been the transportation route for a very wealthy kingdom. Every several hundred feet, solid gold markers were embedded in the wall. In addition to this, Alfonso occasionally noticed diamond-encrusted murals depicting feats from the annals of Dormian history—generals with their swords in hand, Great Sleepers arriving, and new Founding Trees being planted. At the foot of one of these murals, Hill discovered an elegant fountain pen lying on the floor. It was in perfect condition and the ink on the stylus was still wet.

"What do ya make of it?" whispered Bilblox.

"It must belong to Josephus," replied Hill. "They can't be more than a day ahead of us, if that."

The traveling party pressed ahead into the darkness. As the hours wore on, Alfonso found himself straining to hear any out-of-the-ordinary sounds. At times, he thought he heard scampering noises, like those from rats, but he never saw anything. Being deep underground, they had no sense of day and night. Out of habit, Hill occasionally glanced at his old watch issued by the U.S. Air Force, but without any trace of night and day, the numbers and movement of the hands meant nothing.

At one point, Alfonso definitely heard something scurrying just behind them. It was the scampering noise again, but somehow it sounded . . . heavier. Kõrgu growled and turned to face whatever was behind them. Her fur bristled. Alfonso looked at Resuza, who was staring intently for any sign of movement. Her Enfield rifle lay at the ready in her arms.

"They haven't made up their minds yet," she remarked in a matter-of-fact tone.

"Who?"

"The zwodszay," she replied. "I think they picked us up a few hours ago. They're somewhere above us, on the rocks. It's that noise you hear once in a while. There are only two or three of them right now."

"Why can't we see them?" Alfonso asked.

"I think they're biding their time," said Resuza very quietly.

"I don't understand," whispered Bilblox. "If they found us, why ain't they attackin'?"

"Because they're pack hunters," replied Resuza. "They won't attack until they're sure that they can overwhelm us."

On the first night, they set up camp at a wide bend in the road, which allowed them to see in both directions for quite some distance. It was a relatively easy place to defend and Hill liked the spot for this reason. Hill and Bilblox moved some old stones into the middle of the road, creating a small defensive wall that they could crouch behind during an attack. At this part of the Fault Road, the light was also fairly strong. It appeared as if the fiery red glow at the bottom of the fault was getting brighter.

While Hill and Bilblox finished building their fortifications, Alfonso and Resuza worked together to pitch two canvas tents. It seemed odd to Alfonso to be camping out in the middle of what was once a busy thoroughfare. But, of course, no one had used this road for centuries. Once the tents were up, Hill insisted that everyone apply a fresh dose of the skelter sap.

After covering himself in sap, Bilblox sank to the ground and sighed heavily. He looked uncharacteristically weary and he massaged his forehead with his fingers as if he was in a great deal of pain. Apparently, his headaches had returned.

"Are you all right?" asked Alfonso.

"Don't worry about me," said Bilblox with a forced smile. "I just need a good night's rest."

"We've all got to sleep," said Hill. "We'll take turns standing watch so we don't get ambushed. We'll do hour-long watches. I'll go first."

"I'll sit with you for a while," said Alfonso.

Hill nodded appreciatively.

The two of them gathered up some old planks of wood that they had found by the side of the road. They built a small fire and once it had burned down a bit, they put a kettle on the coals and brewed some mint tea they had found in one of Misty's packs. They sat there cradling their warm tin cups and talked in low, hushed tones.

"The fire ought to help keep those beasts away," said Hill. "I wouldn't mind some more of that beef jerky, but I think we ought to conserve our supplies."

Alfonso stared pensively at the fire. After a long pause, Hill spoke up.

"What are you thinking about?" asked Hill.

"Lots of things," Alfonso replied. "I'm wondering about Misty, and what happened to her." He looked at Hill. "I was also thinking how funny you used to be. You used to make me laugh a lot. Do you still do those crazy things when you're asleep—like make big meals in the middle of the night? I guess it's not that crazy, now that you live in Somnos. Everybody must do those kinds of things."

Hill chuckled. He stretched out his legs and looked at the fire a bit wistfully. "Sleeping is when I do my best work on the house," he replied. "I don't cook as much, but my sleeping-self has a knack for mechanical things. Do you know that I'm sleep-building an elevator in the house? It'll be the first one ever in Somnos! I guess that's what happens when you've got a bit of money and your sleeping-self has a fix-it personality."

He sighed. "Sometimes, I have to admit, I miss my old life—

living as a bachelor in Chicago, fixing watches, and sleep-riding around the city on my motorcycle. Being a foreign minister can certainly be wearisome. But lately, since your arrival, I've been feeling better. I've been more energized."

"Why's that?" asked Alfonso.

"Because I thought my brother was dead," replied Hill. "And now, for the first time in decades, I have a hope that he's alive. My goodness, I haven't seen Leif since he was younger than you are. Funny, isn't it, that both of you are Great Sleepers and I'm not?"

"That reminds me," said Alfonso as he stood up and grabbed his pack. "I found a book in Josephus's secret room. I think it's about the Great Sleepers of Jasber."

He rummaged through his pack and came across the rosewood box. For a moment, he was sorely tempted to take it out and tell Hill about the secret antechamber that the box allowed him to enter. But then Alfonso recalled the warning that he'd found inside the antechamber; and so he put it aside and took out the book.

Together, Alfonso and Hill flipped through the pages. The only picture in the book was a full page, hand-drawn rendering of a snow-covered cottage at the beginning of chapter 12, titled "La maisonette au centre du labyrinth."

They studied the text below it carefully. Each page of the book was divided in half. The upper half was written in Dormian hieroglyphs and the lower half was written in French. Hill could read Dormian hieroglyphs, but not very well, so Alfonso read the French text and translated it into English for his uncle:

CHAPTER XII:
THE COTTAGE AT THE CENTER
OF THE LABYRINTH

During the time known in the outside world as "The Iron Age," which began around the Dormian year 2100 (or 800 B.C.), the city of Jasber went through a period of great turmoil. Rumors spread throughout Central Asia that the legendary seers of Jasber possessed strange tools to predict all manner of things to come. For example, they predicted that in the Dormian year 2247 (or 653 B.C.) Yezdegird III, the last king of the Sasanian dynasty of Persia, would be murdered. This information was leaked to the outside world by a wanderer from Jasber and the prophecy turned out to be true. Incidents like this encouraged many attempts to find the magical city of Jasber.

Not surprisingly, the leaders of Jasber became afraid. They worried that outsiders would discover one of the two secret gates that led into their city. One gate was known as the Great Sleeper's Gate and it was used exclusively by Great Sleepers bearing Dormian blooms. The other was known as the City Gate and it was used by wanderers, soldiers, and dignitaries who, from time to time, had reason to venture into the outside world.

In order to better protect themselves, the Jasberians surrounded the two entrances to their city with a vast labyrinth, or maze. To create this maze, they employed a rare plant indigenous to the swampy valleys of the Urals known as razor hedge. When planted in the vicinity of the Jasber Founding Tree, this fast-growing plant began to change in incredible ways: it grew to more than one hundred feet in height, and its branches sprouted long thorns that could easily pierce armor. The razor hedges became impenetrable and unclimbable.

For the Jasberians, the only problem with this maze was that it made matters quite difficult for Great Sleepers who were trying to deliver a Dormian bloom to Jasber. A good number of these Great Sleepers entered the maze, got lost, and failed to deliver their plants. A solution was needed. Eventually, the leaders of Jasber handpicked a group of the city's most able-bodied young men and women and declared that they would be "labyrinth sweepers" with two basic responsibilities. First, they were charged with maintaining the labyrinth, which meant trimming the razor hedges with a special tool known as a khopesh, which is a combination of a sword and a sickle. Second, and more important, the labyrinth sweepers were responsible for searching the labyrinth and finding anyone who had wandered into the maze and become lost. Intruders who weren't Great Sleepers were expelled. Great Sleepers, on the other hand, were escorted immediately to Jasber via the only gate that remained, the City Gate.

You may ask: what happened to the Great Sleeper's Gate? It was closed forever in the name of tightening security—after all, one gate is easier to defend than two.

Despite these precautions, the Jasberians grew ever more fearful. This came to a head when the Dragoonya sacked the Dormian city of Loptos. It was destroyed when a Great Sleeper arrived and turned out to be a Dragoonya in disguise. This episode frightened the leaders of Jasber to the core. In response, the Jasberians took a rather extreme measure: they decided that no Great Sleeper would ever be allowed to enter the city of Jasber again. Instead, the labyrinth sweepers would find the Great Sleeper in the maze, take possession of his or her Dormian bloom, and deliver it to Jasber themselves.

And what would then become of the Great Sleeper?

The leaders of Jasber refused to allow these Great Sleepers to return to the outside world. "Simply put, these people—

although they are the true heroes of Jasber—know too much," wrote Karlovo Wachterovsk, who was the Grand Vizier of Jasber at the time. "For that reason, we ask them for a final sacrifice: they must spend the rest of their lives in the maze." And so the Jasberians built a tiny cottage at the center of the maze, and it was here that each and every Great Sleeper was meant to stay until he or she died.

Escaping this cottage was impossible. The maze was simply too vast. Dormians in the remaining cities of the kingdom—which included Quartin, Ribilinos, Noctos, and Somnos—objected vehemently to this practice and decried it as inhumane, cold-hearted, and contrary to the noble spirit of Dormia. But the Jasberians would not be dissuaded. And so, in the ensuing centuries, many Dormian poets have composed odes to the lonely fate of the Great Sleepers of Jasber. Perhaps the most famous of these writings is the following passage by an unknown poet from Quartin.

> *Robbed of family, hearth, and home*
> *Nothing but the Labyrinth to roam*
> *A more tragic fate is not known,*
> *Than of these heroes who die alone.*

"Did you know about all this?" asked Alfonso when he finished reading.

Hill sipped his mint tea. "No," he said. "I remember hearing about how the Jasberians were paranoid, but I didn't realize that they were quite this paranoid."

"Well," said Alfonso, "at least now we know a bit more about Kiril's list and what a khopesh is. Why do you think he needs it?"

"I'm not sure," said Hill. "Clearly Kiril plans on going all the way to Jasber."

"Yeah," said Alfonso, "but why?"

"Don't know," said Hill. "I'd always presumed that his only goal was to escape. He can't take on Jasber by himself, even if he is the world's best swordsman."

"What about Dad?" asked Alfonso. "Do you think he's in that cottage?"

"It's funny," said Hill with a sad smile. "As you were reading, a memory of your father came into my head. I haven't thought of it in years! I once locked him in the closet when we were both boys—we couldn't have been more than five and seven—and as small as he was, he split one of the wood panels on the door just trying to get out. He never gave up."

"You think Dad's going to try and escape?" asked Alfonso. Hill nodded.

"You seem pretty certain," remarked Alfonso.

His uncle shook his head. "Leif won't accept staying in that cottage for the rest of his life, especially when he has a wife and son waiting for him."

Alfonso looked worried. He had just remembered something.

"I forgot to show this to you," said Alfonso. "My sleeping-self stole it back in Marseilles." Alfonso reached into his backpack and pulled out the tin containing the Polyvalent Crotalid Antivenin and two syringes.

"Hmm," said Hill with a worried look. "Antivenin—it's what you take to counteract the venom from a spider or a snake."

"Do you suppose . . ."

"Hush!" said Hill.

"What is it?" whispered Alfonso.

"Turn around and have a look," said Hill.

Very slowly, Alfonso turned around. At first, he saw nothing. Then he noticed that the road behind them was now blocked by several dozen giant, gnarled boulders that seemed to have materialized out of nowhere.

"Where did those boulders come from?" asked Alfonso.

"I have no idea," whispered Hill hoarsely. "Quickly now, let's build up the fire."

Alfonso felt a shiver run up his spine. He shoved the tin back into his backpack, double-checked that his sphere was readily available, and turned to work on the fire. He and Hill worked together for several minutes, throwing scraps of wood onto the fire, until the flames roared to life and crackled greedily. Alfonso rubbed his eyes wearily. He felt tired.

"It's the strangest thing," said Alfonso, as he stared into the now roaring fire. "Every time I start to feel sleepy, I almost feel like some force is pulling me deeper into the Fault Roads."

"Hmm, that is very curious," said Hill. "I've had the exact same feeling—like something is tugging on me—almost as if I were a puppet."

This conversation was interrupted by a slight rustling noise.

"What is it?" asked Alfonso.

"Those boulders," said Hill nervously. "Am I going crazy, or did one of them just move?"

CHAPTER 23

LEIF

MANY MILES AWAY—at this exact moment in time—fifty-one-year-old Leif Perplexon struggled forward into the maw of a howling snowstorm. Visibility was so bad that he could barely see ten feet off into the distance. Miniature cyclones of snow crystals roared across the icy surface of the ground. The shrieking of the wind was punctuated only by the sound of Leif's feet chafing against and cracking the ice. Instead of boots, blankets were bound around his feet with ropes. This jury-rigged footwear made him prone to slipping. He proceeded slowly down a narrow corridor hemmed in on both sides by hundred-foot-high hedges. Razor-sharp thorns, some as long as two feet, stuck out from every branch. Some were covered with long icicles, and on occasion the gusting wind caused the icicles to fall and shatter into glasslike shards.

Leif was a tall, lanky man with heavily freckled cheeks, a flat nose, and a broad, sweeping forehead beneath an unkempt shock of black hair. He was quite slender, but what he lacked in muscle mass he made up in endurance. When he lived in World's End, Minnesota, he regularly made day trips of fifty and even sixty miles on his cross-country skis. Once he made the two-hundred-mile trip to Minneapolis-St.Paul on skis. During the summer, he could swim for hours at a time. It was this stamina that allowed him to make the journey from Alexandria, Egypt, to the High Peaks of the Urals mostly on foot. However, the journey had taken its toll. He was now terribly fatigued, and the reserves of strength he had enjoyed his entire life were ebbing away. Only one desire kept him moving: to see his wife and son again.

As he plodded onward, Leif's woozy mind returned again to the events that had uprooted him from World's End and landed him here in this godforsaken maze. On the day that he supposedly drowned in the lake near his home in Minnesota, Leif Perplexon did in fact go for a swim. As usual, he slept while swimming, although when he woke up he found himself in the oddest of places. He was sitting in front of a television monitor at the international departures wing of the Minneapolis/St. Paul Airport, dressed in a suit and hiding behind a pair of dark sunglasses. In his hands were two carry-on bags, a passport, and an envelope stuffed with $3,000 in cash.

Leif looked around and saw a copy of the *Minneapolis Star Tribune* sitting next to him. After glancing at the date, his jaw dropped. He had been asleep for three days straight. Leif had done many crazy and bizarre things in his sleep, but never anything remotely like this. As he flipped through the paper, he came upon an article in the regional news section that caught his attention . . .

Lake of the Woods Man, Known for Swimming Skills, Dies in Lightning Storm

By Benjamin Soskis

World's End, MN – Leif Perplexon was known for his ability to swim longer and farther than most men could canoe, but three days ago, he met an untimely end when a freak lightning storm passed over the sleepy hamlet of World's End. After 72 hours of nonstop searching, authorities have stopped looking for a body and Mr. Perplexon has been presumed dead. He leaves behind a wife and son who . . .

Leif dropped the newspaper and headed directly for the nearest pay phone, but he had barely taken six steps when sleep overtook him. He didn't wake up again until his plane landed in Cairo, Egypt. Upon landing, he again made a dash for the nearest phone, and again sleep overtook him before he could call home. This is how it went for several days. Every time Leif Perplexon tried to alert anyone to his whereabouts, he was instantly overcome by sleep.

His memories from Egypt were fuzzy because he slept most

of the time. Leif recalled flashes of being awake—diving into a turbulent sea, finding a box of seeds in a basement of some kind, and walking through a desert in the light of the moon.

Eventually, Leif realized that the key to staying awake was not fighting the plan that his sleeping-self had devised. First and foremost this plan involved safeguarding a curious plant that Leif had hatched in his sleep from the seeds he'd found in Alexandria. The plan also involved walking hundreds or even thousands of miles northward and not talking to *anyone* along the way. Leif had a strong suspicion about where he was headed. He knew that he and his brother hailed from a kingdom in the Ural Mountains known as Dormia. Now he was being drawn there by an almost gravitational pull. There was no resisting it. And so, gradually, Leif resigned himself to making the journey. He began staying awake for longer stretches and pushing himself to move as quickly as possible; after all, the sooner he made his delivery, the sooner he could return to his old life.

Or so he thought.

Leif gradually became aware that his sleeping-self was obsessed with traveling stealthily. In his sleep, Leif tended to travel at night, or through crowds, or over rocky terrain on which he left no footprints. Leif even wondered if his sleeping-self had deliberately faked his death back in World's End in order to ensure that nobody would follow him.

Leif soon realized that there was good reason for his stealth. Every so often, he noticed that he was being followed by a tall man who wore a wide-brimmed hat and a heavy fur cloak. The man followed him like an apparition through the deserts of Syria and Iran, over the Köpetdag Mountains and into Turkmenistan, down along the plains of Uzbekistan, and across the

Aral Sea to the foothills of the Urals. Often the man was no more than a flickering speck on the horizon. This mysterious pursuer tended to keep his distance; but on one occasion, as Leif entered the Urals, he had a face-to-face encounter with the man. Leif had lost his way and was forced to turn around and backtrack along a series of steep cliffs. At one point, Leif rounded a corner and ran directly into the man. The man's hat fell off, revealing his eyes, which were entirely white.

"Who are you?" demanded Leif. "Why are you following me?"

"My name is Kiril," replied the man calmly. "I am your friend. If you let me help you, you'll return faster to World's End, where your wife and son grieve your loss."

"What makes you think I have a wife and son?" asked Leif.

"Dishonesty doesn't suit you," replied the man. "I know a great deal about Judy and Alfonso and you."

At the mention of his family, Leif stiffened. He knew on some deep, instinctual level that this man posed a danger—not just to himself, but to Judy and Alfonso. This realization stoked a fury that was smoldering deep within him. His life had been hijacked. What's more, he was powerless to alter the course of his own fate. And now, on top of everything else, Leif sensed that his wife and child could be in danger. Something inside of Leif snapped. He set down his plant very carefully, and then he charged Kiril.

Kiril quickly reached for his sword but then, rather mysteriously, he stopped himself as if he had forbidden himself from using it. A second later, Leif's body slammed into Kiril's and the two men toppled to the ground. It was icy—very icy—and Kiril slid and fell backwards off the edge of a cliff. Leif was stunned.

Had he just killed this man? It had all happened so fast. Before he could think another thought, however, Leif fell into a deep and prolonged sleep.

On the morning that he finally awoke, Leif found himself alone in a cottage, which was surrounded on all sides by towering walls of razor hedges. The plant that he had cared for was missing. His cottage was equipped with plenty of food, firewood, and warm clothing. It took a while before Leif realized that there were no socks or shoes anywhere in the house and this, he presumed, was to ensure that he didn't step outside.

There was also a note.

The note was written in Latin, French, English, and one or two other languages that Leif did not recognize. The note informed him that this cottage would serve as his new home. It explained that a "labyrinth sweeper" would visit him once every new moon to replenish his food, though it cautioned him not to converse with the sweeper. Above all, the note stressed that he was *not* to venture outside. The corridors of the surrounding maze were vast and dangerous, the note explained, and he would not last long if he tried to explore them.

Like clockwork, the labyrinth sweepers arrived once every month or so. They were mysterious figures who wore scarlet-red robes and carried strange-looking swords. They never spoke, except once, when Leif attempted to follow one of them out into the snow. The sweeper drew a line in the snow with his sword and mumbled a phrase in Latin: "Mors ultima linea rerum est." Leif had taken Latin in college and he understood what the sweeper had said: "Death is everything's final limit." It was unclear whether the sweeper was threatening him directly, or simply warning him about the dangers that awaited him if he stepped outside, but the message was clear: don't cross this line.

A great deal of time passed. Many years, perhaps as many as five or even six, came and went. Occasionally, Leif ventured outside, but he never made it very far without shoes or any sense of where he was going. And so he waited. Gradually, Leif came to realize that there were fates worse than death, and staying forever in that lonely cottage was one of them. It was time to escape. He began hoarding his food, preparing for a long journey. He even made a pair of makeshift shoes. Then, one clear crisp day, he made a break for it. That was several weeks ago. He had been wandering the maze ever since.

As he plodded onward through the snowstorm, Leif tried to picture his son's face. He couldn't do it. Somehow the image had become lost, like a coin that falls through a hole in the pocket. His mind was softening and he knew it was the result of the cold and his fatigue. Leif had to stay focused. Truth be told, he wasn't exactly certain of which way he was headed. He knew only that he was in the middle of a vast labyrinth, and while he had no idea where the exit was, he was determined to find a way out—or die trying. He was almost out of food. He wouldn't last more than three or four days. He had to stay alert and look for . . .

Leif stopped in his tracks. Something had snagged his leg. He looked down at the ground and to his astonishment he saw a pale white hand grabbing his ankle. It was connected to a skinny arm that stuck out from underneath the razor hedges. Leif kicked his foot frantically, but in his weakened state the grip of the pale white hand was too firm to shake loose.

CHAPTER 24

ALEXANDER'S BRIDGE

MORNING IN THE FAULT ROADS came without any indication that somewhere, miles above, the sun had begun to rise over the horizon. Alfonso, Hill, Resuza, and Bilblox all sat around a campfire, gnawing on beef jerky, sipping tea, and staring in gloomy silence at the flames. No one had slept well. Hill and Alfonso seemed especially edgy, and they had good reason to be. The boulders that they had seen—the ones that had mysteriously appeared the night before—had since vanished.

"Are ya sure you really saw them boulders?" Bilblox had asked.

"Yes," replied both Hill and Alfonso at once. That was the extent of their morning conversation.

The group broke camp quickly and pressed forward. As they walked on, the road dipped downward and the chasm within the fault itself widened until it appeared to be at least half a mile across. The air also grew noticeably warmer and they all began to sweat. The sweat washed off the skelter sap and they had to reapply the green oil hourly.

An hour or so later, they came upon a bridge that spanned the chasm. It was, without a doubt, the most impressive architectural structure that Alfonso had ever seen. The bridge, which was made principally of chiseled black stone, spanned the fault and appeared to be nearly a mile long. Giant spiraling support beams carved into the forms of snakes rose from the depths of the fault and held up the bridge. The bridge was also lined with a dozen spindly stone towers topped with weathervanes that creaked and swiveled ominously. The path on the bridge itself was quite narrow—just wide enough for a single lane road. Halfway across the bridge sat an abandoned stagecoach. The road they had been following crossed the bridge and continued onto the other side of the fault.

"That must be Alexander's Bridge," said Hill. "It's named after a precocious teenage engineer from Somnos who solved the mathematical equations necessary to construct a bridge of this size. I remember reading about it when I was in school in Somnos. All the teachers used it as an example of the incredible feats we can do when asleep. Apparently the idea for the bridge came to Alexander when he was lost in the jungle and he came upon a slithering mass of snakes. Dormian historians say it's the oldest bridge of its length in the world. When Europe and Asia could barely make two-story buildings, Dormians built this bridge, complete with the first example of flying buttresses. Without it, Somnos would have been cut off from the rest of the Dormian cities and would never have become the capital."

"We gotta cross it?" asked Bilblox uneasily. "Ya sure it's still workin' after all these years?"

"I'm sure it is," Hill replied. "I mean, I think it is."

"You *think*?" asked Alfonso.

"Come on, you babies," said Resuza. "Must I always lead the way?"

Resuza walked forward, heading down the road toward the bridge. The others followed closely behind. Upon closer inspection, the bridge did not inspire confidence. In many places, the stonework had crumbled away, leaving gaping holes. The entire structure also groaned and creaked loudly as if it were straining simply to hold its own weight. At one point, Hill reached out and grabbed the stone guardrail to steady himself and it crumbled in his hands. Occasionally, Alfonso peered over the edge and looked down. It was an eerie thing to look into a seemingly bottomless depth and see a faint red glow miles below. Long tendrils of fire rose up, as if trying to lick the underside of the stone bridge.

Midway across, they came upon the abandoned stagecoach. One door was ajar. Resuza readied her rifle and crept up to the vehicle slowly, half expecting someone to jump out. The coach was made of fine cedar and its interior was upholstered with red velvet and blue silk. She brushed her hand across the plush silk and it disintegrated into a gritty powder. Startled, she fell backwards against the door. It splintered loudly and fell off its hinges. Although the stagecoach looked beautiful, it was in an advanced state of decay.

Just beyond the stagecoach, they came upon a section of the bridge—perhaps fifteen feet in length—that looked as if it had been repaired somewhat recently. The stonework here was lighter in color and the texture of the stones was coarser and less polished.

"Who do you think did this repair work?" asked Resuza.

"No idea," said Hill.

"Do you think it's sturdy?" asked Alfonso.

Hill extended a leg and tested one of the stones with his foot.

"It feels solid enough," replied Hill.

He walked forward and crossed this section of the bridge in several jaunty steps. Resuza followed him. Alfonso stared at the stonework suspiciously for a moment. Something about this section of the bridge looked wrong, but he couldn't put his finger on what was giving him pause. He hustled across and joined Resuza and Hill on the far side. The only one left to cross was Bilblox. He was having a hard time because Kõrgu—who had been quiet for most of the journey—whimpered and refused to go forward.

"Oh, fer cryin' out loud!" griped Bilblox. He reached down, scooped Kõrgu up in his arms, and began to walk forward. Suddenly the stones beneath his feet began to shift and give way. It looked as if they were going to collapse, but they didn't, they simply undulated and jiggled like giant cubes of jelly.

"What's happenin'?" yelled Bilblox.

The stones were all moving now, as if somehow they had lost their stonelike properties and had become gelatinous. They began changing form into something altogether different. Alfonso thought back to the boulders that had materialized mysteriously on the road the night before. He gasped as he realized what was going on. They weren't stones at all—they were alive! At that moment, a hand emerged from the shifting stones and grabbed Bilblox's leg. Stones were now transforming rapidly all around him. These creatures had been lying face-down on the ground, masquerading as part of the bridge. They seemed to be chameleons—able to take on the color and texture of their surrounding environment. But as they sprang into motion and blood coursed through their veins, their gray rocklike appearance dissolved and their true form became visible.

They looked vaguely human, although horribly deformed. Their arms and legs were covered with a great many bulges, stumps, and nodules where the creatures' bones had apparently grown in bizarre and unnatural ways. More abhorrent than this, however, was the creatures' skin, which was transparent and slimy-looking—like the yolk on an uncooked egg. It was possible to look directly through their skin and see their muscles and tendons and even some of their inner organs. The creatures wore tattered pants but no shirts. Their bluish-red hearts throbbed rapidly in their chests.

"ZWODSZAY!" yelled Hill as he whipped out his Colt .45 and began to blast away. A bullet struck the zwodszay that was clinging to Bilblox's leg. For a brief moment, Alfonso watched in sickened fascination as the blood rushed through the creature's veins and pulsed toward the wound. Then Alfonso snatched his blue sphere and began hurling it. Resuza loaded her Enfield rifle and began firing.

"OFF THE BRIDGE!" yelled Hill. "RUN!"

Bilblox roared with fear and rage and pushed his way forward through the mob of a dozen or so zwodszay that were clawing at him. Kõrgu snarled and snapped her jaws ferociously every time a zwodszay reached for her master. One of the zwodszay clawed at Bilblox's backpack and, in one powerful stroke, tore it open. Instantly, the barrel of skelter sap fell out and crashed against the bridge. The impact caused the barrel to splinter and viscous sap exploded everywhere. The zwodszay shrieked. Bilblox took advantage of this momentary confusion and ran toward the others.

Once Bilblox reached them, they all set off in a panicked run. Hill led the way, followed by Alfonso, Resuza, and Bilblox. Kõrgu led his master dutifully. They crossed the remainder of the bridge quickly and sprinted down the Fault Road for as long as they could until exhaustion overcame them.

The road was silent—both ahead of them and behind them.

"They're gone," panted Alfonso.

"For now," gasped Bilblox. "But we've lost the skelter sap."

Hill looked at everyone. They were all sweating profusely. It would be child's play for the zwodszay to track them now.

CHAPTER 25

ONE HUNDRED KNIGHTS

SEVERAL MILES DOWN the Fault Road, ahead of Alfonso and his companions, a convoy of one hundred armed soldiers was marching toward the Hub. They were Dormian knights from Somnos and they looked as if they were setting out on a long journey. They all shouldered packs crammed with weapons, rope, grappling hooks, a range of other spelunking equipment, and food provisions. All of their faces and arms were covered with the same gleaming green sap. Oddly, though, the entire formation had only two torches. The first was held by a soldier walking about ten feet ahead of the procession. His eyes were wide open and he constantly scanned the road, the walls, and the fault that began only feet away. The second torchbearer was also wide awake, and he trailed the entire convoy by about ten feet. Walking backwards, he too scanned every inch of his environment, watching for anything amiss. These soldiers weren't awake so that they could see better. Without question, their senses would be sharper when they were asleep. However, these scouts had to think, anticipate, and predict when an attack might occur, and these types of cerebral activities were always best done while awake.

The rest of the soldiers marched in perfect formation. They all held their swords in the same manner, gripped in their right hand and resting loosely on their outstretched left arm. A soft, strangely delicate sound came from the soldiers. It was a mix of hypnotically rhythmic breathing and light snoring.

All of them were fast asleep.

In the middle of the procession a number of soldiers were grouped closely around a prisoner in shackles. That prisoner, of course, was Kiril. Meanwhile, at the front of the procession, just behind the wide-awake scout, walked two people who appeared to be in charge. The first was Josephus, who carried a bulky leather rucksack and an old wooden walking stick. The other was his niece, Colonel Nathalia Treeknot. They appeared to be awake.

"You know, Great-uncle," Nathalia Treeknot was saying, "one of my men can carry that rucksack for you. It looks rather heavy."

"That's quite kind of you, Nathalia," replied Josephus. "But I'm up to the task."

"What's in that rucksack anyway?" asked Nathalia.

"An assortment of things," replied Josephus cryptically.

"Things from Kiril's list?" asked Nathalia.

Josephus nodded, but offered no further explanation.

"Do you know what purpose Kiril has in mind for those items?" asked Nathalia.

"I know enough," said Josephus testily.

"I see," replied Nathalia. After a few seconds' pause, she continued. "I still can't believe that the Grand Vizier changed her mind about this mission. How did you convince her?"

"It wasn't anything I said," Josephus quickly replied. "We agreed that Kiril could not be trusted, but the Grand Vizier also understood the historic opportunity that we had. And opportunities always involve risk. However, we've managed the risk. There is no way Kiril can escape."

"Yes, of course," replied Nathalia. She didn't seem entirely satisfied by her great-uncle's logic or his explanation, and it showed on her face. Of course, Nathalia loved her great-uncle, even though he wasn't exactly a warm man. He had always buried himself too deeply in his books to pay much attention to her when she was a child. She could remember visiting his mansion in the Delirium Quarter, when she was no more than five or six, and feeling as if she were in a museum. "Don't touch anything in your great-uncle's house," her mother had told her. "He is a very strange man and is likely to fly into a rage if you disturb so much as a cobweb." Later on, when she was in school and doing extremely well in her classes, Josephus began to take a more active interest in her. He bought her books, and maps, and even play-swords. He delighted in her obvious military talent. He wasn't affectionate, but he was very fond of her, far more so than of any of the other nieces and nephews in the family. "You have an incandescence," he told her occasionally. "You remind me of myself when I was young."

At one point, when she was nineteen, Nathalia briefly fell in love with a carpenter who was doing work on her parents' house. He was much older than she was, and far less educated, but he had a quiet strength about him that Nathalia greatly admired. He also wrote poetry, and Nathalia, like Josephus, was a lover of sonnets. Nathalia's parents naturally disapproved of her affections, but this made little difference to her. She proclaimed that she intended to wed the carpenter. It was Josephus who convinced her otherwise.

"Don't do it," he told her bluntly one afternoon.

"I am *thoroughly* tired of trying to make my parents happy," she replied. "I have to do what's best for me."

"I couldn't agree more," said Josephus. "You are one of the brightest stars in our family's illustrious history. But to achieve, you must take risks—bold risks—and getting married at the age of nineteen is far too conventional and it doesn't suit you. Becoming a general does."

Nathalia had bristled at her great-uncle's advice but, eventually, she was won over by it. Ultimately, what the two of them shared more than anything else was ambition—a burning desire to do something great, something worthy of being remembered. Of course, this was precisely why Nathalia felt a growing unease about her great-uncle as they proceeded along the Fault Roads. She sensed his hunger to reach Jasber and it unsettled her.

"Is there something that you aren't telling me?" she asked Josephus.

Her great-uncle slowly shook his head. "Nathalia," he said in a low voice, so as not to be overheard, "I have told you everything and I don't know why you insist—" Josephus was interrupted by a shout from behind them. Nathalia immediately ordered the convoy into defensive positions and dashed back to see what had transpired. Josephus followed as quickly as he could. The soldier at the back of the formation had dropped the torch and pointed his trembling sword into the darkness.

"What did you see?" demanded Nathalia.

Sweat ran freely down the soldier's face. Clearly, he was terrified. "C-Colonel Treeknot, for the last few minutes I thought I've heard something scurrying in the darkness, just beyond the reach of my torch. And then I just saw something. It was a face or an arm or something like that. Whatever it was, it gave me a start. It looked like clay but it was alive. And it's not alone. I think there may be, well, hundreds of these things." He shook his head furiously, as if trying to rid himself of the memory. "It's th-the most awful thing I've ever seen." Tears dripped down his dirty face. "I-I'm sorry, Madame Colonel. Begging your pardon."

"Don't worry, soldier," Colonel Treeknot softly replied. "You can rejoin the others. You've been awake for a few hours now and I know it's stressful. We'll wake up your replacement."

"That'll be most appreciated," the soldier gratefully replied. "I could do with a few hours of sleep-marching." He paused. "Do you think it was a zwodszay?"

"I'm not sure," Nathalia replied. "But don't worry, they won't bother us. We have the sap that Josephus provided and what's more, we're a hundred knights strong. If they wanted to attack us they would have done so already. They're probably just curious. Ignore them and you'll be fine."

Several of the knights who had also woken up were nodding their heads. They seemed to be reassured. But the calm that

Nathalia had restored did not last long because it was interrupted by a hoarse but deep laugh. The soldiers looked around for a moment—incredulous that someone would laugh at the words of their commanding officer—and then realized that it was Kiril. His mouth was contorted in a bitter, twisted smile and his white eyes gleamed brightly.

"I always find it funny when commanding officers lie to their soldiers with an air of such unflappable confidence," said Kiril. "Always have to keep the soldiers calm, right, Colonel? Fear is an insidious thing—a kind of sickness—and it can't be allowed to fester among the troops."

"You will bite your tongue," said Nathalia sternly. "My soldiers aren't scared and what's more, they're far too smart to be rattled by your antics."

"Come now," replied Kiril. "You know as well as I do that the zwodszay are showing all the signs of being classic pack hunters. They are just biding their time until they outnumber us by a ratio of three-to-one or perhaps even ten-to-one and then they will attack."

"And what makes you an expert on the zwodszay?" inquired Josephus. "They weren't around when you last entered the Fault Roads."

"I am an expert on survival," replied Kiril coolly. "And I know a thing or two about the minds of soldiers. I know, for instance, that the Colonel is worried—and not just about the zwodszay either. Tell me, Colonel, do you truly believe that the Grand Vizier approved of this little adventure? How much do you trust your beloved great-uncle?"

The colonel stepped forward and slapped Kiril across the face with the back of her hand. It was a hard blow and blood trickled from Kiril's mouth. A shiver of rage rippled across Kiril's face. His long, coiled scar pulsed red, but he remained perfectly still.

"That's enough!" Nathalia roared. "You will keep quiet if you want to make it out of here alive."

"Now that's funny," said Kiril with a rueful shake of his head. "Colonel, you must have realized by now that *I* am the only one who will make it out alive."

"What do you know?" asked Josephus. His voice rose with a barely perceptible tone of panic. "What aren't you telling us?"

"Now, now, now," replied Kiril soothingly. "My dear Josephus—surely a man of your intelligence understands that weighty secrets, matters of life and death, are never to be given freely."

As the convoy continued on its way down the Fault Road, Kiril licked his lips to clear his mouth of the metallic taste of his blood. The wound bled for a long time—far too long for Kiril's liking. It made him sick to his stomach, and it took all of his self-control not to gag.

Ever since he was a child, Kiril had suffered from a blood ailment known since ancient times as "the royal disease." Those who suffered from it could not stop bleeding when they were cut. Many of the royal families of Spain, Germany, and Russia had it. In modern times, the disease was known as hemophilia. It could be quite dangerous, especially for someone like Kiril who often fought with a sword. Fortunately, for Kiril, when he took the purple ash on a regular basis, the disease went into remission. And so, for almost all of his life, he had suffered from no sickness, not even a common cold.

But this was changing.

Within the last year or so, his body had begun to break down, even though outwardly he appeared strong. Arthritis had set into his joints. He was constantly sick with colds. He suffered from migraines. And, most troubling of all, his hemophilia had returned. The reason for all this was quite simple: the supplies of purple ash were gone.

"The ash is our lifeblood," Nartam had told Kiril and all the other orphans from Noctos, more than six hundred years ago. "That is why my secret supply is so precious."

Many years passed before Kiril discovered exactly how Nartam had come upon his secret supply of purple ash. Slowly the truth came out—that Nartam had sacked a number of Dormian cities and had, in fact, even burned the Founding Tree in his own home city of Dragoo. By the time that Kiril had learned all of this, however, he was already addicted to the ash. Twice a year, Nartam gave his closest followers, all of them former Dormians, a pinch of the ash to rub into their eyes. Kiril was soon hooked, both to the ash and to the immortality that it bestowed. Kiril didn't resent this. To the contrary, he revered Nartam, because he was the giver of life and because it was Nartam who first allowed him to have the sweet, heady taste of revenge.

Roughly one month after Nartam had first found him, Kiril was still living in the cave with the other orphans from Noctos. The place already felt like home. Then, one morning, Nartam explained that his other, "grown children" would be arriving.

The following day, several dozen soldiers—both men and women—arrived in the cave. The soldiers were quite friendly and they began to teach the orphans the arts of war, swordplay, archery, and hand-to-hand fighting. In the evenings, the orphans were asked to recall everything they knew about Noctos. They were asked to draw maps of streets and diagrams of buildings. It became increasingly obvious that Nartam, and his soldiers, were preparing to launch a fresh attack on Noctos. On the previous attempt, they had infiltrated the city and burned part of the tree, but then they had been driven back.

"The city of Noctos has two gates," explained Nartam. "The main one is heavily guarded and we can't take it. But there is a second gate—I believe this is the gate through which you children were cast—and if we can push through that gate we can enter the city." Nartam paused and looked about. "Now," he said finally, "is anyone's memory good enough to help us find the way back to that gate?"

A lone voice spoke up.

"Yes, Däros," said the young Kiril meekly. "I am certain I can find the way back."

"Very good, my boy," said Nartam with a smile. "My dearest son of Jasber. You shall lead the way with me."

"Excuse me, Däros," said a boy of six or seven. He was one of the children from the school that had been drenched in purple ash. "My parents still live in Noctos. Will I be able to see them once we take the city?"

"Did your parents save you or do anything for you when you were cast out of the city to die?" asked Nartam pointedly. "Did they run to your rescue? Did they look for you? Do you

226

honestly think they would love you with your hideous white eyes? Have you learned nothing from me?" Nartam walked over to the boy, placed his arm around him, and talked to him tenderly. "I know it is hard to accept," said Nartam softly, almost in a purr, "but we are your only family now."

Two weeks later, the rest of Nartam's army arrived. The vast majority of them were not Dormians. Most of them were slaves whom Nartam had bought as children, taken in, trained, and groomed to be soldiers. They were all fiercely loyal to him. On the day of the invasion, Kiril rode at the front of the procession with Nartam. They shared a horse, riding on a single saddle. Kiril swelled with pride that was magnified when he found the small mountain gate through which he and the other Gahnos had been expelled. In the snow around the gate, there were the bodies of a great many Gahnos who had died, and, amid the frozen carnage, Kiril saw the body of his sister.

She was frozen in a block of ice. The inhuman sight kindled a fire in Kiril that many centuries of fighting still had not extinguished.

Kiril stayed by Nartam's side as Nartam led his force into Noctos and burned the city to the ground. Nartam galloped through the burning streets at great speeds shouting orders, and Kiril clung to him fiercely. At one point, quite by chance, they came upon a tall man with a pug nose and a bald head. He was fleeing down a side street. It was the man who had hit Kiril's mother and shoved her out into the snow. Kiril tugged on Nartam's sleeve. "That man pushed us out into the snow," said Kiril as he pointed to the bald man. Nartam said nothing in reply. He simply goaded his horse into a gallop and caught up with the bald man. The man looked up and showed an expression of terror. Then, in one clean sweep of his sword, Nartam took off his head.

"You have nothing to fear, my son," said Nartam as they galloped away. He tenderly placed his arm around Kiril. "No one will ever hurt you again."

These words rang in Kiril's ears as he marched along the Fault Roads, surrounded by a hundred Dormian knights. Very soon, he would repay Nartam for all his many gifts, and the world would at last recognize Däros as leader and father, just as Kiril had. Very soon.

CHAPTER 26

THE HUB

AFTER THEIR ENCOUNTER with the zwodszay, Alfonso, Hill, Re-suza, and Kõrgu and Bilblox half-walked, half-ran, for hours. In the darkness, their minds played tricks on them. At times, one of them would cry out that they heard something, but in the end, there was never any absolute proof that the zwodszay were following. The heat underground seemed to increase, and as sweat gathered around their necks and under their packs, they felt the loss of the skelter sap.

They pressed on. Their brains shut down and their entire existence focused on putting one foot in front of the other. For this reason, it took several minutes before they realized that the actual pavement underfoot had changed. The cobblestones were replaced with a rough marble, and the road began to climb and widen. The air grew cooler and began to smell faintly of smoke. It also became darker until suddenly they realized they could no longer see one another, even though they were only several feet apart. Hill lit a torch and they stopped to look around. The Fault Road had turned into a tunnel with smooth marble walls and a low ceiling that glittered from the torchlight. It ended in a room with seven passageways from which to choose.

"Which way?" asked Resuza.

Without saying a word, Alfonso yawned, shut his eyes, and began to sleepwalk down the passageway on the far right.

"I guess that settles that," said Resuza.

Alfonso awoke several minutes later and found himself standing in a vast, darkened space. Hill, Resuza, and Bilblox stood just behind him.

Kõrgu began to growl.

"Everybody light your torches," commanded Hill. "We need more light in here."

Resuza lit two torches and held one in each hand. Alfonso lit another two torches and handed one of them to Bilblox. The combined light of their torches partially illuminated the cavernous space. They were in a giant eleven-sided hall. A towering stone pillar stood flush against every intersection of the eleven walls and rose up to the ceiling. The ceiling itself was so high that it escaped the light of their torches and lay hidden in blackness. It took a moment for Alfonso to realize that the stone pillars were actually built to resemble the trunks of Founding Trees and—when he strained his eyes to see more carefully—he realized that these stone trees had a great many stone branches that radiated upward and served as support beams for the ceiling. The effect was powerful and more than a little spooky. It felt as if they were standing underneath the intertwined stone canopy of eleven Founding Trees. And if this wasn't strange enough, the walls had countless ledges and perches. Most were occupied by stone gargoyles.

In the center of the hall stood a gigantic wooden stump, at least thirty feet in diameter. The stump was bleached pale white, almost like driftwood, and gave off a soft but distinct smell of juniper.

"What's everybody starin' at?" asked Bilblox. "Don't get all silent on me, you know that gives me the willies."

"We're in a massive hall with a tree stump in the middle," explained Alfonso.

"It's much more than just a tree stump," said Hill in a whisper. "I think it's the remains of the original Founding Tree of Dormia. They brought it here from Jasber. It must be tens of thousands of years old."

Resuza walked toward the stump to get a better look.

"Be careful!" cautioned Hill. "Even though it has been dead for ages, its core still possesses great power. They say that the stump draws you to it in your sleep. I think it has been pulling at Alfonso and me ever since we entered the Fault Roads."

"Like a big magnet," observed Bilblox.

"That's the idea," said Hill. "Back when the Fault Roads were still used, it enabled Dormians to sleepwalk all the way to the Hub without having to wake up or consult a map. I have no idea what effect it would have on non-Dormians."

Resuza continued to walk around the base of the stump and she stopped short and gasped in shock.

"What's the matter?" asked Hill.

"C-come see," whispered Resuza.

They rushed over to where she was standing.

"Oh no," whispered Hill.

On the far side of the stump lay a pile of weapons, helmets, and body armor. Much of the equipment was battered, scratched, and badly dented. After a few seconds, Resuza realized what was strange about the scene. While there had obviously been a great battle here, there were no victims and no blood. The air was pungent with the smell of human sweat, and strands of torn human hair lay scattered across the floor.

"A battle was fought here very recently," explained Hill somberly.

"Something doesn't make sense," said Resuza. "Why is there no blood? Where are the bodies?"

"I don't know," said Hill. "Perhaps—"

Hill was interrupted by the unmistakable sound of footsteps. They all spun around with their weapons drawn.

"Who goes there?" demanded Bilblox.

The footsteps, which had been coming from their left, abruptly stopped. The light of their torches extended for perhaps as far as thirty feet. Just beyond this, on the periphery of the shadows, it was apparent that something or someone was lurking. Alfonso peered into the darkness but saw nothing. Soon the figure in the shadows took one tentative step into the light. It was a ghastly sight. At first glance, the figure resembled a boy about four feet tall. Yet his bones were horribly deformed and his skin was so translucent that they could see his throbbing heart. It was a lone zwodszay.

The creature's face was the color of ash and lined with purple veins that bulged just underneath his skin. He had no hair any-where, and his eyes were tiny, approximately the size and shape of raisins. His nose, however, was perhaps twice as big as a hu-man's, and both nostrils flared in and out, as if the cartilage had disappeared and only the translucent skin remained. The crea-ture took a step forward but lifted its arms to shield itself from the light, which obviously was making it uncomfortable. Al-fonso felt sick just looking at the creature but for some reason he focused most on its fingers. The tips were long and delicate and tapered off like the partially melted ends of candles.

The creature opened its mouth and began to speak in a soft, kindly voice that sounded like a kitten purring. His liver-red tongue darted out of his mouth and constantly coated his lips with viscous saliva.

"T' šuži b idmi śęd ver šere," said the creature.

"What?" demanded Hill.

"T' šuži b idmi śęd ver šere," repeated the creature.

"What's that noise?" asked Bilblox nervously. "Is someone speakin'?"

"Yes," said Hill grimly. "It's a zwodszay and I'm about to kill it."

"Wait!" said Resuza. "He's saying, 'I was born in this black forest.'"

Hill looked at her incredulously. "You can understand him?"

"More or less," replied Resuza. "He is speaking some strange dialect of Komi. It's a Uralic language spoken by herdsmen in some parts of the Urals. There was a Komi village not too far from the town where I was born."

"So what's he trying to tell us?" asked Alfonso.

"I think he's trying to say that he was born in this room,"

said Resuza, "Look around. This room is probably what he calls the 'black forest.'"

The creature was talking rapidly now in his strange tongue.

"Well, with all these stone trees, it is a forest of sorts," said Alfonso. "What else is he saying?"

"I'm not exactly sure," said Resuza. "But he keeps repeating two words, one is *nebeg* and the other is *mort*."

"What do they mean?" asked Bilblox.

"Well," said Resuza, "I think *nebeg* means 'book' and *mort* means "human.'"

"That doesn't make a licka sense . . ." began Bilblox.

"What was that?" asked Alfonso.

They all heard at the same time a terrifying sound. Alfonso felt his skin crawl. It was the sound of many footsteps, so many that as it grew nearer, it was like the roar of water over rocks. As this sound grew, the creature began jumping up and down nervously. "Sjurs!" exclaimed the creature nervously. "Sjurs!"

"What does *sjurs* mean?" asked Hill.

"It means 'thousands,'" explained Resuza.

"Thousands of what?" asked Bilblox.

"Zwodszay," said Hill. "I think they're coming for us."

The creature was now waving his hands wildly and begging them to follow him. He obviously hated the light from their torches, since he kept shielding his eyes, but still he moved a little closer.

"I think he wants to take us somewhere," said Resuza.

"Bad idea," declared Bilblox. "Isn't this guy a zwodszay like the others? This could be a huntin' trick. Send one first as a scout and then lead 'em into a trap."

The sound of the footsteps grew louder. Kõrgu let out a mournful howl.

"You may be right!" shouted Resuza. "But what choice do we have? We know nothing about the Hub, and if we stay here, we'll be slaughtered! Without the skelter sap they'll find us in no time."

Hill nodded. "She's right. Let's go!"

An instant later, Hill, Resuza, Alfonso, and Kõrgu and Bilblox were following the creature across the floor of the massive hall and up a narrow, recessed staircase.

They continued up the staircase for some time and then turned off down a nondescript passageway for several minutes. At the end stood a wooden door reinforced with a spider web of iron latticework. The creature pushed the door open and gestured for the rest of them to enter. Hill, who was in the lead, hesitated for a moment and then walked through the doorway with his weapon at the ready. The rest of the group followed. The creature entered last, then closed the door behind him and locked it by sliding a large bolt into place.

Alfonso glanced around the room. In the glow of their torches, he was able to see fairly well. They were in a perfectly circular room, with an opening opposite them that led into a larger area filled with floor-to-ceiling shelves of rotting books. The circular room they stood in was empty, but the walls were painted with elaborate, intricately drawn murals depicting what appeared to be the Hub during its heyday, when throngs of men, women, and children traveled here en route to the other cities of Dormia.

The most elaborate of the murals depicted a river of lava at the bottom of a narrow fault. Just above the lava flew strange birds with wide, swept-back wings and vaguely rectangular faces. Another wing that looked like the dorsal fin on a shark jutted out of the birds' backs. Although the mural was probably not to scale, the birds appeared massive. Their skin was made not of feathers but of interlocking scales.

Hill immediately crossed the circular room and stopped just inside the entrance to the larger room. "Must be some sort of ancient library," Hill declared. "I guess these are the books that the zwodszay was talking about."

The zwodszay slid his pointed fingertips lovingly over the mural. He purred deeply, as if the images gave him great pleasure. He then looked at Hill and walked into the other room. "Mort," it purred. "Mort."

They followed the creature to the far corner of the larger room, where a pungent, faintly glowing moss covered the floor. Here they came upon a most unexpected sight. Lying on the moss was a soldier wearing a tunic emblazoned with the symbol of Somnos. The soldier looked up weakly and regarded Hill. His face was streaked with dirt and tears. His eyes were red and wide open, although he blinked slowly.

"F-Foreign Minister Persplexy," gasped the man. "It's you, isn't it?"

The man breathed slowly and with great effort.

"Indeed it is," replied Hill. His face had gone white. "How did you get down here? *What happened?*"

"W-We were attacked by the zwodszay," said the soldier, lifting his head off the mat. "Th-They slaughtered us . . . We were a hundred knights strong, but there were thousands of them.

They attacked from all directions and destroyed—" His head fell back and a deep, painful sigh rattled through his body.

"What unit are you from?" asked Hill.

"Somnos Expeditionary Force, Sergeant Ryszard Yelexovf," said the soldier. "I j-just need to sleep. I've always been much happier while asleep, truth be told. I-I've been trying, sir, but . . ."

"Give him some water," commanded Hill.

Resuza walked over to the sergeant and unscrewed her flask of water. Tenderly she supported his head and poured the water directly into his mouth.

"I was wounded and this zwodszay carried me to safety," continued the sergeant. "This creature . . . If it weren't for him, I'd be dead . . . like the others."

"Who exactly are the others?" asked Hill. "And what were you up to?"

"Colonel Treeknot said we were supposed to open the Jasber Gate and take the prisoner back," whispered the soldier. "But we were attacked . . ."

"Colonel Treeknot!" exclaimed Hill.

"What about the prisoner?" asked Alfonso. "Do you mean Kiril?"

The soldier nodded.

"Was Josephus there as well? Is he alive? How about Kiril?" asked Hill.

Sergeant Yelexovf's eyes fluttered and he groaned in pain. "I don't know . . ." he said. "I think they all must be dead."

CHAPTER 27

KYN

"WHAT ARE WE GOING TO DO NOW?" asked Resuza. "Eventually, we'll have to leave this room and find the Jasber Gate."

Hill was busy tending to the soldier's wounds with bandages and ointment. He looked up at Resuza and regarded her wearily. "I know, but first let's regroup here for a while," said Hill. "It'll give us a chance to think. I'm trying to make sense of this. I can't imagine Colonel Treeknot doing this . . ."

At that moment, the zwodszay began chattering away again and, on cue, everyone looked to Resuza for an explanation. The creature stood just beyond the range of their torch's light. Alfonso was glad for this; the creature was terrifying to look at.

"I can't understand what he's saying," said Resuza. "He's talking too quickly."

The creature, perhaps sensing that he was not being understood, squatted down on his haunches and used a knobby index finger to draw several letters on the dust of the floor, just inside the light. This is what he wrote:

кась

"What does that mean?" asked Alfonso.

"The writing is Cyrillic. I think it's the Komi word for 'home,'" explained Resuza. "Maybe he's telling us this is his home."

Resuza then asked the creature a question in what sounded like his own strange tongue. The creature replied and this time he spoke more slowly, drawing out all of the syllables, making every effort to ensure that he was understood.

"He says that we will be safe here," explained Resuza.

The creature drew another word in the dust.

кынь

"I think it's his name," said Resuza. "It's pronounced Kyn. It means 'polar fox' in Komi."

"Polar fox," said Bilblox. "I kind of like that."

"Trust me, old boy," said Hill with a shake of his head. "You wouldn't like it quite as much if you could see this fellow. He's about as far from a polar fox as you can imagine."

"Don't be unkind," scolded Resuza. "Kyn has just saved our skins, unless you have forgotten."

"True enough," Hill replied. "See what else you can learn from Kyn, especially the location of the Jasber Gate."

"All right," said Resuza. "But what are we going to do about the soldier?"

"I've treated his wounds," replied Hill. "Now he needs to rest."

"He sounds like he's in rough shape," said Bilblox.

"Wait a minute," interrupted Hill. "Where's Alfonso?"

They looked around.

"ALFONSO?" yelled Hill. There was no answer. Hill looked concerned. "That's not like him. I'll go look."

"Let me go," said Resuza. "I'll be quieter on my feet and, besides, I'm a better shot with my rifle."

Hill hesitated. "Very well," he said. "But be quick about it."

⊛

At that very moment, Alfonso was tiptoeing down the staircase and out into the vast emptiness of the eleven-sided hall. He walked slowly but with great purpose, heading directly for the massive stump at the center. The area was entirely dark, but this made little difference, because Alfonso was fast asleep and he was being guided by a force that did not require him to think or watch where he was stepping.

Upon reaching the stump, Alfonso paused for a moment, then climbed onto it, still in the grip of his sleeping trance. Alfonso's eyes blinked softly. He saw a flash of light, and then a series of images flickered across the ceiling of the eleven-sided room like a movie, only the images were three-dimensional.

The first images were those of a hunchbacked woman dressed in rags, stumbling across a field of snow with a Dormian bloom in her hands. She eventually knelt down, dug a small hole, and planted the bloom into the frozen soil. Immediately, the snow began to melt. Somehow, Alfonso knew that he was staring at the very first Great Sleeper. The woman disappeared and, seconds later, a young man appeared walking along a frozen river. He too had a Dormian bloom. The man eventually planted his bloom along the riverbank and instantly the ice on the river began melting.

Similar scenes involving Great Sleepers danced and glimmered overhead at an increasingly rapid pace. And then came a scene that was unlike the others. It featured a teenage boy with a delicate face, ash-gray hair, and entirely white eyes. It was the same boy, the leader of the Dragoonya, from Alfonso's nightmare in the Delirium Quarter. The boy stood in a small clearing surrounded by a vast Boreal pine forest. The boy had a Dormian bloom in his hands, only it didn't look right. Its leaves were thin, shriveled, and an ugly charcoal gray. The boy bent down and gently placed the strange bloom into a shallow depression in the earth.

As soon as the boy finished planting the bloom, hideous slimy roots emerged and began to churn their way through the soil like snakes. Soon all the surrounding trees in the pine forest began to wither and die. They died by the millions. A fierce wind blew, loosening countless dead pine needles, which fluttered down from the treetops and swirled in the sky, creating a cloud that eclipsed the sun. When the pine needles finally settled, all that was left were the skeletal remains of a dead forest, which stretched as far as the eye could see.

"Alfonso! ALFONSO!"

Alfonso was brought back to reality by a voice calling for him. It was Resuza yelling at him to get down from the stump. She held a torch in one hand and a rifle in the other.

241

"What are you doing up there?" she called.

"I-I-I've had some kind of terrible vision," replied Alfonso.

"Come quickly," beckoned Resuza. "It's not safe for us to linger here."

Alfonso climbed down from the stump as quickly as he could. His entire body was quivering. He was so happy and relieved to see Resuza that he hugged her tightly. She hugged him back. Alfonso smelled her warm skin and hair and his cheeks flushed in the darkness. They stared at each other, both suddenly aware of a tension between them. Alfonso looked at the curve of her lips. Resuza's eyes sparkled and Alfonso was suddenly aware of just how beautiful she was.

"I'm glad you're okay," she finally whispered. "You should be more careful."

&

They ran back to the library where the others were waiting. Kōrgu yelped, ran to Alfonso, and licked his hand affectionately.

"What happened to you?" asked Hill.

"Nothing," said Alfonso. "Just a bit of sleepwalking." He glanced at Resuza but said nothing more.

"We're going to have to keep a closer eye on you," said Hill wearily. "Your sleeping-self is getting restless."

The only one who didn't react to Alfonso's return was Kyn. The creature stood in the half-darkness, chewing greedily on a biscuit. Alfonso looked on with repulsed amazement while Kyn's throat contracted and expanded as he swallowed.

Resuza began talking with him, and after a few minutes she summarized her conversation. "It's pretty hard to understand him, but I've learned a few things. The zwodszay primarily live on režofi, which are bats. Apparently, when they get tired of eating bats, they hunt their own. It's a sport for them. Kyn was one of those who was thrown out to be hunted, but he's managed to avoid being caught."

"Can he take us to the Jasber Gate?" asked Bilblox impatiently.

"I think so," said Resuza. "He said he could take us down a passageway to a big locked door. I'm assuming that's the Jasber Gate. He said a few of the Dormians escaped down that passage, but he's not sure if they made it through the big locked door."

"Ask him if he knows of any vents to the surface," said Hill.

Resuza translated Hill's question and Kyn shook his head.

"He says there is no way to the world above," said Resuza. "If there were a way, he would have taken it long ago."

"How's the sergeant doing?" asked Alfonso.

"He's resting," said Hill. "Which is exactly what we should be doing. Let's get a few hours of shuteye. It'll help immensely."

While everyone settled down to rest, Alfonso rummaged through his backpack until he found the rosewood box. He'd been waiting eagerly until he had a spare moment to tinker with the box again. The top had been ripped off, and the vial of bluish liquid was gone, but the rest of the box was intact. Alfonso stared at the floor of the box and eased his way into hypnogogia. With great concentration, he studied the thousands of indentations along the floor of the box. Almost instantly, he saw the optical illusion of the door swinging open and then—presto—he once again entered the secret antechamber.

The antechamber was slightly different from how Alfonso remembered it. The room was the same size and the desk was still there, but now a small fireplace burned brightly against one wall. Also, instead of three doors in the room, there were now just two—the one marked with the drawing of an ocean wave and the one marked with the drawing of a brick wall. The third door with the cloud, which Alfonso had entered on his previous visit, was gone.

Alfonso walked over to the desk and discovered a new note written on a piece of parchment:

Alfonso;

The window to change the course of events is closing. You must get to Jasber quickly, although you must also master the art of hypnogogia before you arrive. Hypnogogia offers portholes into other realms. Some scholars mistakenly believed that hypnogogia is merely an extremely heightened state of perception, in which it is possible to see, hear, and smell with supernatural abilities. Although this is true, a truly skilled Great Sleeper can also use hypnogogia not just to see the smallest particles of matter, but to alter and manipulate them as well.

The world is made of minute particles known as oms, each of which contain two layers. In the outside world, this concept, known as omism, was first described by an Arabic alchemist named Jabir ibn Hayyan in the 8th century A.D. Dormian scientists, of course, knew about omism long before that.

The most important concept of omism is this: if a person manages to see oms with the naked eye, the outer layer immediately disintegrates, and small pockets of nothingness are created. These voids don't exist for very long, but while they do, they allow for the laws of physics to be altered. Gravity, for example, can occasionally be disobeyed. Of course, the only way to see oms with the naked eye is to enter hypnogogia, which only Great Sleepers can do.

Good luck, my friend. Your humble servant,
Imad

P.S. Look for the ageling. She will take you to your father and together you can save him—if you arrive in time.

Alfonso read Imad's note several times, and wished he knew more about omism. Eventually, he turned his attention to the two remaining doorways. He focused on the one marked with the drawing of the brick wall. Alfonso opened the door and discovered that, sure enough, a sturdy red brick wall blocked the doorway.

How am I supposed to pass through this? wondered Alfonso.

Alfonso then recalled the line from Imad's note about altering "the laws of physics" and knew what he had to do. He concentrated on the smallest speck that he could see on the grainy exterior of the brick wall. Then he forced himself to peer even deeper, until all he could see were billions of minute reddish particles. The air crackled with electricity and the particles of brick began to waver, as if their solidity had been compromised. Alfonso cautiously inserted a fingertip, his hand, and then his entire arm into the wall.

Seconds later, his eyes opened and he found himself back in the room with Hill, Resuza, Bilblox, Kyn, and the wounded Dormian soldier. Alfonso was exhausted and wanted only one thing: sleep.

Soon everyone in the room was slumbering—everyone but Kyn.

CHAPTER 28

A VISION FROM THE CHAIR

SEVERAL HUNDRED MILES AWAY, the city of Jasber began waking up. The city's inhabitants, known as Jasberians, were finishing their work, returning to their homes, and sleepwalking into their kitchens to prepare food. It was dinnertime, the first waking meal of the day, and Jasberians always spent this meal with their families. When they woke up, Jasberians all heard the exact same sound, that of rushing water. Jasber was situated at the foot of a massive waterfall and shrouded in a perpetual cloud of mist. This waterfall emptied into a roiling river of whitecaps, which then forked its way around the three islands that made up the city.

Each of the three islands of Jasber had a distinct purpose. One contained virtually all the city's residents. This was Jasber Isle. The second contained only the city's Founding Tree. This was Tree Isle. And the third contained a palace with five tall, spindly towers, the tallest of which sparkled as if it were inlaid with thousands of diamonds. This palace was the city's monastery, and the island on which it sat was known as Monastery Isle.

On this particular morning, as on all mornings, the monks on Monastery Isle were performing their ancient chanting ritual. They assembled in the monastery's main hall and chanted in Dormian to the slow beat of a giant bronze gong. All the monks were gathered there except for the chief monk, or abbot, who was busy conducting a ritual of his own. He was escorting a redheaded girl, who appeared to be no more than eight or nine, down a stone promenade to a rocky point at the tip of Monastery Isle. At the far end of the promenade stood a thin stone tower with a commanding view of Tree Isle. This is where they were headed.

"You need to stay focused, Marta," the abbot was saying. He was a kindly, gray-haired man with a slight limp. He was smoking a pipe and talking quietly as he led the way forward. "Your powers of clairvoyance will be of no use to us if you do not stay focused," he said. "You must look at the tree and only at the tree. That is what matters. And, of course, when you have your visions, you must look at the astrological clock just beneath the tree so that—"

"I know, I know," said Marta. "To get the exact date."

"Yes, my dear," said the abbot with a smile. "After all, what good is it to have a vision of the future if we do not know when the events in that vision will take place?"

"Master Abbot, you've told me all this before," said Marta with a sigh.

The abbot paused for a moment, turned, and looked at Marta. She was tall for her age, with bright green eyes, a face full of freckles, and a pointy little chin. The abbot didn't speak at first and the only sound was that of the waterfall and the rushing river. He looked kindly at the young girl and patted her head. "Marta, I have seen you, from time to time, glancing elsewhere," he said. "That won't do. When you are sitting in the chair you must stare only at the tree."

"But I get so bored!" protested Marta. "A kid isn't supposed to sit in a chair for hours just staring ahead."

"I know, my child," replied the abbot. "But your task is to protect the most valuable living thing in the world, our Founding Tree. And I think you know full well that you are no ordinary girl."

And, of course, Marta knew this was true. She wasn't a normal girl. A little over two years ago, the abbot had selected Marta to be the thirty-third seer of Jasber. Seers were chosen once every two hundred years and the selection process was rigorous. Every child in Jasber was tested. Marta still recalled the test well. She and a group of other children boarded a rowboat for Monastery Isle. Once there, they were led into a small cellar in the monastery illuminated by a dozen paper lanterns. Inside stood a long banquet table with a large clay urn filled with silvery-colored water in the middle. One by one, they were invited to look into the urn.

Marta did as she was told. At first she saw nothing, but then she noticed an eyeball floating just beneath the surface of the water. It was large, easily twice the size of a normal human eyeball.

"Whose eye is that?" asked Marta. "It belonged to Imad the Great," replied a monk who was standing next to the urn.

"You mean the Cyclops?" asked Marta.

"Yes," replied the monk. "Now look into it and tell me what you see."

Marta did as she was told and stared into the eyeball. To her astonishment, in the black pupil of the eyeball she saw the tiny image of Imad himself. He was hunched over a desk and writing feverishly.

"I see Imad," said Marta matter-of-factly. "He is scribbling something."

"Really?" replied the monk. He seemed very pleased. "Can you tell what Imad is writing?"

"Yes," replied Marta. "Shall I read it to you?"

"Please," said the monk.

She peered closer and said, "'What exactly does the future hold? Its many secrets remain untold. Hidden in the burning hot and biting cold is the key to a future foretold.'"

"As I live and breathe!" exclaimed the monk.

"What's the matter?" asked Marta. "Did I not read it correctly?"

"No, to the contrary," replied the monk. "You're the only child in Jasber who has seen anything in that dead eyeball, let alone read the verse that Imad was writing."

"What does that mean?" asked Marta.

"It means that you must speak with the abbot," replied the monk excitedly.

Several days later, Marta traveled to Monastery Isle by herself to meet with the abbot. They met in his office, a dusty room full of books, cobwebs, and a dozen half-finished cups of tea.

"My dear girl, you are second-sighted," announced the abbot. "You have the ability to see what we all see, but you also have the ability to look at things and see what is hidden to everyone else." He smiled with great excitement. "You can perceive the detail in things that others cannot. You are destined for great things as our new seer. Do you know what this entails?"

Marta nodded somberly. Every man, woman, and child in Jasber knew exactly what it meant to become a seer. Once chosen, seers were asked to drop a lone granule of the green ash from the Founding Tree into each of their eyes. The result was a deep coma. Upon emerging from their comas, seers had the power of clairvoyance. When they stared with great concentration at a given object they could, from time to time, see glimpses of that very same object at some point in the indefinite future.

Once, long ago, the seers of Jasber had far greater powers. With the use of the Foreseeing Pen they could write highly detailed prophecies that spanned thousands of years into the future and included the entire world. The one-eyed monk, Imad, had designed the pen himself. But the pen and ash combination ultimately brought trouble—foreign spies and mercenaries came looking for it—and so the leaders of Jasber did away with the pen. Nowadays, the seers of Jasber had limited visions of the future that never spanned more than two centuries. What's more, in modern times each seer of Jasber was charged with just one responsibility—staring at the city's Founding Tree for several hours every day. The purpose of the ritual was to ensure the safety of Jasber. The logic went as follows: As long as the Founding Tree was alive and well, then, presumably, the city was okay. On the other hand, if a seer foresaw a problem with the tree—saw it being burned, for example—then the people of Jasber would have time to alter this fate before it came to pass.

"Do you know what being a seer entails?" the abbot asked again, summoning Marta from her thoughts.

"I won't be able to see my family again if I become a seer," said Marta, "will I?"

"It's too dangerous. Once you can see into the future, you are a resource . . . and a danger," replied the abbot. He paused awkwardly and then smiled rather sadly. "We here on Monastery Isle will become your family."

⸎

Marta and the abbot continued their stroll to the end of Monastery Isle until they reached the stone tower. The abbot fumbled for a key to the locked wooden door at the tower's base, and when it opened they walked carefully up a spiral staircase that led to the roof. It was perfectly flat, and in the middle sat a giant wooden chair. Without saying a word, Marta scurried over to the chair and climbed up into it. The chair was so tall that it had a ladder with six rungs built in to make it easier to climb up and take a seat. Once she was in the chair, Marta had a perfect view of Tree Isle and the Founding Tree. She stared across the river to this massive tree and sighed rather wearily. She would be here like this—just staring and staring—for the next six hours.

There was no rhyme or reason to when Marta had her visions. Sometimes she had five or six in a single day. Sometimes she had none. On this particular day, she had been staring at the tree for almost four hours and she still hadn't had a single vision. Finally, out of boredom, she glanced down at the abbott to see what he was up to. He was sitting cross-legged at the base of the tower. He appeared to be deeply engrossed in a book.

Marta's heart began to throb in her chest as she realized what she was about to do. She took a deep breath, exhaled, and then turned her entire body around so that she could get a glimpse of Jasber Isle. She drank in the sight of the delicate wooden buildings with steep, sloping rooftops that formed the city's skyline. She saw the city's armory with its four distinctive domes. She strained her eyes and barely, just barely, she could see the five-story townhouse where her parents and siblings lived. Home. Just the sight of it filled her with a deep longing. Marta was about to return her attention to the Founding Tree when, suddenly, she began to feel cold and slightly nauseous. There was no mistaking it—a vision was coming.

Flames.

There were flames racing up the sides of the armory. A tall man with white eyes and a gruesome, coiling scar across his face was holding a torch and starting new fires wherever he went. The flames spread quickly, devouring much of the neighborhood surrounding the armory. Her family's townhouse was burning, and she saw her mother and father trapped on the roof. Marta was terrified, but somehow she kept her calm and remembered the most important rule that one could follow when having a vision. The date. She needed to know when this would happen. A tower with an astrological clock stood at the north end of the armory. Marta turned to it. Although it was difficult to see through the flames, in the waning seconds of her vision she glimpsed the date when the fire would take place. It was just seven days from now—one week into the future.

CHAPTER 29

THE ELEVEN-SIDED HALL

Deep underground in the Hub, Alfonso suddenly awoke with his heart beating loudly in his ears. It took a second to realize that a struggle was taking place in the dimly lit room. Muffled curses and loud, gasping noises filled the air. Alfonso jumped to his feet and peered around, trying to determine what was happening. A few seconds later, the gasping noises stopped. By that time, Alfonso had taken a candle from his backpack and lit it.

Kyn lay pinned to the floor. Hill's elbow was at Kyn's throat, and his full weight pressed down upon him. Dark blood pooled at the zwodszay's neck and coated his lips. Kõrgu had one of the zwodszay's thin, knobby arms between his fangs.

"Spit it out," Hill commanded.

Resuza stood next to them, her face pale and sweaty. She

stammered a translation of Hill's words to Kyn. He tried to respond, but could not because of Hill's elbow.

"Let him speak," said Resuza.

"What could he possibly have to say?" snarled Hill. "This—this beast was licking the sergeant's blood. Look at that blood covering his mouth. Even now he's smacking his lips, trying to taste it." He shook his head but then relaxed his grip on Kyn.

Kyn lay motionless. They could all see blood flowing from the veins of his upper body to his throat. He tried to say something, but only faint rasps came out. Finally, he managed to sputter a few words.

"He says the soldier was already dead," said Resuza. "It's not their custom to waste food."

Kyn looked up at Hill with wide, round eyes and said a few more words that sounded like a kitten purring. Hill's shoulders relaxed. He stood up and shook his head in deep disgust. "Tell him that we do not eat our dead," he told Resuza. "Tell him to promise that he will leave the sergeant's body alone."

Kyn nodded eagerly. Hill ignored him and walked to a corner of the room, where the sergeant lay. Hill and Alfonso wrapped his body in a blanket. Once this task was finished, Hill banished Kyn to the circular room and told him not to return. When he was gone, they sat together silently. The only person who suffered an injury during the melee was Bilblox, whose leg had been cut slightly. Resuza washed the cut carefully and then wrapped a piece of raw cotton around it. As they sat there, the presence of the dead soldier weighed heavily upon them.

"When did the sergeant die?" Alfonso asked.

Hill shrugged his shoulders. After several minutes of silence, he finally spoke. "We have to leave now. The Hub is filled with danger—I feel it. I don't trust Kyn, but I think he's telling the truth about there being no way to the surface. That leaves only one option."

"The Jasber Gate," said Resuza.

Hill nodded.

"We should probably go then," said Resuza. "I don't know why we haven't been attacked yet—and I don't see any reason to stick around here."

From the other room, Kyn began making noise.

"What's the matter now?" asked Bilblox.

Kõrgu bared her fangs and began a low growl.

"She senses danger," replied Bilblox. "Time to move."

Commotion broke out in the room, as everyone gathered their belongings and made sure their weapons were at the ready. They joined Kyn in the circular room.

"*Sjurs!*" exclaimed Kyn. "*SJURS!*"

"He just keeps saying 'thousands,'" explained Resuza. She seemed exasperated. Kyn unbolted the door and ran into the hallway. He gestured for them to follow him downstairs.

"Why should we go downstairs into the big room?" Alfonso asked. "It's too open. We just left there to come up here to hide."

"The noise is coming from above us," Bilblox quickly replied.

"What about the sergeant?" asked Alfonso.

"I wish we could give him a proper burial, but we can't," said Hill quietly. "We need to go."

The group ran down the staircase and entered the eerily silent hall. Alfonso felt very exposed standing in this vast, wide-open space. He glanced up at one of the sturdy, treelike pillars and followed its trunk up into the darkness of the ceiling. Along the walls of the room, the countless stone gargoyles stood on their perches.

"Now where?" asked Resuza.

Kyn shrank against one of the stone pillars. "KYK MORT!!" he screeched.

"What's he goin' on about?" demanded Bilblox.

"I don't know," snapped Resuza. "He's saying something different from before. Something about two humans, but I don't know—"

"Well, I reckon the feller is talkin' 'bout us," said a creaky old voice that came out of the darkness. "Was a foolhardy idea comin' all this far. Most others woulda given ya up fer dead. But I know ya got strong stock in those youngsters, and I said if I was still breathin', I'd help ya."

A moment later, two figures emerged from the shadows. One was Misty. The other was an extremely thin man, so thin that his bones seemed to stick out of his skin like tent poles. He had a wildly unkempt head of bushy hair. Both were covered with thick layers of skelter sap.

"MISTY!" shouted Resuza. "You made it! I knew you'd survive that cave-in!"

Misty gave a gap-toothed smile. "That's right, little lady." Her smile quickly disappeared and she became all business. "I knew ya'd go t'the Hub and try to fin' Josephus. Luckily, ol' Misty knows the mines better'n anyone, 'n I followed ya in as soon as I could. Took me the better part of a day to round up some miners and clear out that landslide that separated us. But here I am."

"And you told the Grand Vizier what happened?" Hill interjected. "What did she say?"

Misty shook her head dismissively. "Pshaw. I never asked anyone's permission fer anything, and I ain't startin' now. I don't trust those high 'n' mighty fools, but I figured ya might be intent on goin' to Jasber—and passin' through that locked gate—'n' so I brung this 'ere feller. He's Clink, m'second cousin on me mum's side and the best picklock in the city. He's also the only other person I trust in Somnos, after Resuza. I don't much care fer 'im, but he's family all the same."

"Did you say *Clink*?" asked Bilblox.

"That's right, Leafy," bowed the thin man with the prodigious head of bushy hair. Bilblox recognized his old friend right away. On his first visit to Somnos, Bilblox had been branded as a "leaf burner" and he was briefly imprisoned. During his time behind bars, Bilblox's cellmate had been a picklock named Clink. The two of them had become friends and, eventually, they escaped the prison together.

"It's your old cellmate, the one and only Clink," explained Clink. "Once again, I've come to save the day. My only interest is aiding you, of course, and perhaps liberating a bit of treasure along the way. Just think, Leafy old boy, I'm on my way out of Somnos—finally!"

"Any signs a Josephus 'n' Kiril?" Misty asked.

Hill frowned. "We came across a badly wounded soldier from the Somnos Expeditionary Force. Before he died, he said Josephus, Kiril, Colonel Treeknot, and a hundred soldiers came through his area but were attacked by zwodszay. They may have all been killed."

Clink's jovial face turned somber. "Colonel Treeknot and her soldiers were with Josephus and Kiril? So they're all a bunch of traitors?"

"We have no idea," Hill quickly replied.

"Sjurs!" Kyn interrupted. "SJURS!!" He entered the light and they could see the grayish-purple muscles of his heart pounding in his chest. His tapered fingers wavered nervously.

"Hmm," said Misty as she eyed Kyn suspiciously. "Ya think it's a good idea t'be pallin' around with a stray zwodszay?"

"Let's find the gate and then we'll talk about it," said Hill. Sweat poured down his face.

"I'd have to say the gate is this way," said Clink confidently as he pointed to a large, darkened stone archway. Directly above the archway there were three images carved into the stone: a silver pen with an enlarged barrel, a vine containing many clusters of berries, and a bolt of lightning striking a tree. "I believe those are the symbols of Jasber, aren't they?"

"They were on the cover of the rosewood box," said Alfonso.

"Then follow me," said Clink. "We'll be through the gate in a flash."

"Before we go . . ." said Hill. "Misty, did you bring any more skelter sap with you? We're all out."

"A-course I did," said Misty, as she set down her pack and pulled out a small wooden barrel filled with sap. "Why doncha lather yerselves up?"

Misty was about to uncork her barrel when something darted through the darkness and snatched it away from her. It was Kyn. He had moved so quickly that his steps had barely been visible. Kyn was now clutching the barrel with both arms and holding it protectively as if it were a great treasure.

"Hey, ya varmint!" hollered Misty. "Give that back."

"Quiet!" yelled Resuza. "Look up."

Everyone in the party glanced up to the shadowy ceiling of

the eleven-sided room. The upper walls of the room were crawling with movement. Alfonso was the first to realize what was going on. The hundreds of ledges and the perches where the stone gargoyles had once been were all now empty.

"The stone gargoyles are gone," gasped Alfonso.

"That's because they ain't gargoyles," said Misty. "They were all zwodszay!"

"It's a trap," exclaimed Alfonso. "Kyn has led us into a trap."

"RUN!" yelled Hill. "Run for the Jasber Gate!"

CHAPTER 30

THE LOTUS BERRIES

AN EXHAUSTED LEIF PERPLEXON violently kicked his leg, but he couldn't loosen the grip of the hand that clutched his ankle. "Let go!" hissed Leif. But it was no use, and as Leif continued to flail about, he lost his footing and hit the ground with a heavy thud. The hand tightened around Leif's ankle and pulled his entire body under the razor hedge. Leif felt himself sliding down into darkness. He suddenly felt very warm and moist, as if vapors from a hot bath were dampening his face. Slowly, his eyes adjusted to the darkness and Leif was able to get a decent look at his surroundings. He was lying in a spacious foxhole that had been dug out beneath the razor hedge. The air was filled with steam, which appeared to be coming up from the ground. Lying in the foxhole, just several feet away, was the person who had clutched Leif's leg. He was a gaunt man with a nose that had obviously been broken several times, droopy eyes, and filthy long black hair. He wore a heavy piece of cloth that he had wrapped around himself like a toga, and a grimy brown turban was parked securely on his head. The only splash of color on the man came from his eyes, which were a sparkling red-brown.

"You speak English?" asked the man, in a heavy accent that soundly vaguely Arabic.

Leif nodded dumbly, uncertain of what to say.

"You're no sweeper," said the man. "Who are you?"

"Leif Perplexon, from World's End, Minnesota."

"Minnie-sota? Strange name. Did you come to this labyrinth bearing a plant?" asked the man.

Leif nodded.

"And they took it from you?"

Again Leif nodded.

"So you succeeded," said the man with a smile, which revealed a partial set of yellowing teeth. "That is more than I can say." The man reached behind himself and took out the brown withered remains of a plant. It looked as if it had been dead for months, perhaps years. "This was my bloom," said the man with a sheepish shrug. "I came very close to delivering it, but I was starving, and I had to take refuge under the hedges. I was stuck here for some time—days, weeks, months—how is one to know? Ayyy! Anyway, when I came to my senses, the plant was dead. Luckily, the roots of these hedges warm the earth and my den, so I did not freeze to death. As you can see, my friend, I am still very much alive." He said this as if he didn't quite believe it himself.

Leif nodded, despite the fact that the man's story sounded far-fetched.

"My name is Zinedine Hanifa," said the man as he reached out his hand. Leif shook it. "I walked here from Algeria," he continued. "I am a Berber. I come from the Atlas Mountains, perhaps you have heard of them? I am a schoolteacher, and I am pleased to speak English and French. I have a wife and three children there. The children are . . ." Zinedine paused abruptly and scratched his head as if he were profoundly confused. "What year is it now? Do you know, my friend?"

Leif told him what year it was.

"My God!" gasped Zinedine. "Could it be? I left home ten years ago. It's impossible! But maybe not. How could I really know how many moons have passed? The berries have taken away all sense of time. Ten years. That means my daughters may be married. Oh my goodness, I must get out of here . . ." With great effort he raised himself to rest on his elbow, but after a few seconds he groaned and returned to lying flat on the ground.

"I know the feeling," interjected Leif. He stretched out his legs to enjoy the warmth of the foxhole, and for the first time in days he began to relax. "That's exactly what I am trying to do. I have a wife and son back home that I would like to see as well. I was trying to escape, but I am just about out of food. Which reminds me—how have you survived all these years? Didn't you say something about berries?"

"Ah yes, the lotus berries," replied Zinedine with a smile. He reached into his toga and pulled out a leather satchel filled with bright red berries. "That is what I call them. They grow in the hedges. If you know where to look for them they are easy to

263

find. I can show you how to pick them. They have kept me alive, although most unfortunately, they have also kept me *here*."

"What do you mean?" asked Leif.

"The berries are delicious," explained Zinedine. "So delicious in fact that I am incapable of stopping myself from eating them. The problem is . . . how to put it . . . well, whenever you eat the berries you are sent somewhere else. Somewhere very pleasant, oh yes, my friend, very pleasant indeed. Often I am sent back to a beautiful little lake in the Atlas Mountains, a place I knew from my youth. It is where I met my wife, when we were both sixteen. We spend hours talking and laughing and . . . holding hands. And every time I kiss her it is like the first time. Oh, it is wonderful! But then when I wake up, I am in this miserable hole in the earth, covered in snow and dirt. The berries are so delicious. You will see . . ."

Zinedine reached into his satchel, scooped out a handful of berries, and handed them to Leif.

"Go on and try them," urged Zinedine. "I am curious where you will be sent."

"Are you addicted to these berries?" asked Leif skeptically.

"Perhaps," replied Zinedine. "But what choice do we have here, my friend? If we do not eat them, we die."

Leif picked up a berry, studied it closely, and contemplated whether to eat it. His stomach was aching for food. Perhaps he could have just one of these little red fruits. After all, what harm could there be in eating one berry?

CHAPTER 31

THE JASBER GATE

ALFONSO AND HIS COMPANIONS all took off at the same time, like a startled flock of birds. Hill arrived at the archway first. There, he encountered an extremely tall zwodszay who appeared out of the shadowy gloom, almost as if he had been waiting for them there all along. Like Kyn, he had no hair and his skin was pale and translucent. It stretched tightly over the many ridges and bumps of his malformed bones. Hill could see his heart beat slowly beneath his chest.

Apparently, this zwodszay was not scared in the least.

Hill also noticed that half of the creature's mouth was fixed in an intelligent smile. Hill felt slightly reassured by this, until he realized that the smile was frozen due to the fact that the zwodszay's lips had been badly mangled. His frozen lips alternated between pale white and blue, as his blood flowed through them. He carried what appeared to be a three-foot-long stone club sharpened to a razor point. Although thin, the zwodszay was incredibly strong. He carried the club as lightly as if it were made of paper.

Hill unholstered his Colt .45 and took aim. Before he could shoot, however, the tall zwodszay jumped up, soared through the air, landed on top of Hill, and forced him to the ground. The creature salivated at the sight of Hill's bare neck. It opened its mouth, revealing a row of jagged teeth. Hill squeezed off a shot and missed, but the sound startled the zwodszay and it jumped away.

"HILL!" Alfonso screamed. He had just arrived along with the others. "Hill, are you okay?"

They gathered around Hill underneath the archway. Alfonso helped his uncle struggle to his feet.

"Oh no," whispered Hill.

Alfonso followed Hill's gaze, and the blood drained from his face. They were now surrounded by thousands of zwodszay. The great hall flickered with the ghostly pulsing of their blood as it coursed through their translucent skin and glittered evilly within their tiny red eyes. Moments later, the zwodszay began to move in for the kill.

"Listen to me," yelled Bilblox authoritatively. "This ain't the first time I've been outnumbered in a gang fight. We gotta stick close together and keep our backs to one another. Understand?"

"He's right!" affirmed Misty.

"Come on now, ya blasted, infernal zwodszay!" yelled Bilblox ferociously. "Old Papa Bilblox has got some strong medicine for ya!"

At that very moment, two zwodszay—as if answering Bilblox's taunt—rushed the blind longshoreman. Bilblox heard them coming and shuffled to his left and then swung his club in a wide arc. At full extension, the club slammed into the chest of both advancing zwodszay and sent them flying backwards.

Seconds later, Alfonso heard a soft, swishing noise. A zwodszay landed nearby and then swept Alfonso's legs out from underneath him. Kõrgu leapt through the air, knocked the zwodszay off Alfonso's back, and then sank her fangs into the creature's neck. Alfonso staggered to his feet and looked around. The zwodszay were moving in.

At that moment, Alfonso thought of his dad. A great, sorrowful choke of regret welled up in his throat. He roared in anger at the injustice of it all. His right hand gripped the sphere and he began to hurl it into the zwodszay masses. The sphere, which glowed blue in the darkness, flew through the air in a blur of light and returned each time to Alfonso's outstretched hand. Hill and Resuza fired off a flurry of rounds with their rifles. In the midst of this onslaught of strange weapons, the zwodszay hordes wavered. A few of the creatures retreated and, as they did, they created an opening toward the archway that—hopefully—led to the Jasber Gate.

"Quickly now!" yelled Misty. "Follow me."

The old miner sprinted into the darkness of the tunnel and the others followed. It was a vaulted passageway with a slick stone floor and a low ceiling. The walls were coated with bat droppings, which resembled a mudlike paste. Eventually, the passageway began to narrow and, as it did, the bat droppings disappeared. At this point, Misty paused and hurled her lantern back into the tunnel behind them.

"Get ready fer some fireworks!" yelled Misty. "Them bat droppins burn like gunpowder."

Seconds later, there was a massive explosion and a wave of fire raced back down the tunnel, toward the hordes of zwodszay.

"That oughta buy us a few minutes!" yelled Misty exuberantly. After a minute of running, they came upon a small cast-iron door that was locked from the inside. The door was ancient-looking, but very solid. It would be impossible to break it down without a giant battering ram or great deal of force. Misty grunted a sigh of disgust. They had reached a dead end.

"Now what?" asked Bilblox.

Without saying a word, Alfonso approached the cast-iron door and studied it very carefully. He remembered the brick wall in Imad's antechamber and the note about omism. Then something happened that everyone present would remember for the rest of their lives. Alfonso took a deep breath, entered hypnogogia, and slowly thrust his arm *into* the iron door just above the doorknob. Seconds later, they all heard the sound of a rusty deadbolt sliding along its runner. Alfonso withdrew his hand and shook it for a second as if even he didn't believe what just happened. He turned the doorknob and the door immediately swung open.

"I reckon I spent one too many dark and dreary days in them mines," remarked Misty. "Fer a moment there, I'd a-sworn on m' own grave that Alfonso just passed his hand through that door like a ghost."

"That's exactly what he did," said Hill in disbelief. "But how?"

"It's just an old Great Sleeper's trick," said Alfonso nonchalantly. He was breathing heavily. "Come on, I think we've found the Jasber Gate."

Everyone walked through the small doorway and Clink, the last person through, closed and locked the cast-iron door behind him. They had now entered a perfectly square chamber with twenty-foot-high stone walls. In the center of the room stood a hefty, waist-high, bronze candelabra with three prongs, each of which contained a large, half-used candle. Hill lit each candle with his torch. These were no ordinary candles: when lit, they threw off an intense light that bathed the room in something close to daylight. For the group, who had been traveling in near darkness for almost a week, the light was both welcome and uncomfortable. They hoped it would also deter the zwodszay from entering, at least for a while.

For the most part, the room was quite plain. The floor was dirt and three of the four walls were bare. Yet the fourth wall, the one they were all facing, was adorned with a complex mosaic comprising thousands of square tiles. Most of the tiles were colored a drab gray, although a number of black tiles were scattered throughout the mosaic, usually grouped in curlicues of five or six tiles.

"I reckon this 'ere wall with the tiles is yer gate," said Misty with a cough. Like everyone else, she was winded from running. "D'ya think Kiril 'n' Josephus an' maybe Treeknot got this far?"

"I don't see any sign of them," said Alfonso. "Those tiles look like they form some kind of pattern." He looked at Resuza. "Is it some kind of language?"

Resuza stared at the black lines of tile that soared and danced across the gray. "Nothing I've ever seen," she replied.

Hill walked over to the wall and pushed one of the black lines. It wouldn't move. He spent a few minutes feeling and

269

pressing every part of the tiled wall that they could reach. The wall was intact, with no trace of hidden doors.

Meanwhile, Clink was examining the wall as if it were a piece of fine art. He tried to loosen individual tiles, but nothing budged. Eventually, he walked back to the entrance, spun around, and stared at the tile wall from a distance. After a minute, his mouth began to move, but no sound came out.

"Da-ta-da-*dah*-daaaa-ta." Then Clink began to hum.

The others looked puzzled.

"Thank goodness you have me around!" exclaimed Clink. "Did you know that I am not only an accomplished safe-cracker, but I'm also one of Somnos's finest musicians?"

"This is no time for boastin', ya foolhardy braggart," muttered Misty.

"Clink! You're a genius!" Alfonso exclaimed. "Those black lines are musical notes, aren't they?"

Clink nodded proudly.

"Never made it past the second grade," said Clink proudly. "But I do what I can."

"Quick," said Alfonso. "Take out the kaval—the shepherd's flute—and play it. "

"Fer the love of Magrewski, ya better hurry up," said Bilblox nervously. "I think I hear them zwodszay comin'."

Seconds later, they could all hear the sound of stone clubs smashing against the cast-iron door.

The zwodszay had arrived.

Resuza took out her Enfield rifle and walked over to the doorway where Bilblox was also standing. She pointed her rifle at the doorway, poised to shoot.

Wham! Wham! Wham!

The stone archway around the door began to crumble and give way.

Clink wet his lips and began to play the kaval.

The notes echoed in the room and seemed to get louder and crisper instead of diminishing. The room was built for music, and each crystal clear note hung in the air, perfectly balanced with the other notes. Clink repeated the same simple arrangement several times until they all heard a grinding sound.

"The wall is opening!" yelled Alfonso.

They all watched as the tile wall descended slowly into the floor. It took a minute before the wall had dropped enough for them to see what was behind it. Hill groaned. It revealed *another* wall. It was the same size as the tile wall and set back several feet. Alfonso ran over and examined this new wall. It was made up of a row of extremely narrow doors. Each door, made of smooth yellow marble, was approximately six inches wide. All together, there were about a hundred doors, each of them identical. Alfonso tried opening a few, but they all appeared to be locked.

Wham! Wham! Wham!

The cast-iron door toppled over. Screeches and yowls came from the passageway. They looked back and saw thousands of tiny red eyes staring at them.

"They won't come in because of the light," yelled Hill.

A grinding sound came from the tile wall. The top emerged from the floor and began to rise quickly toward the ceiling.

"This is our chance!" shouted Hill. "Quick, everyone, we'll get on the other side of the tile wall before it closes."

"But we'll be trapped between the two walls!" protested Clink. "If we can't open those doors, we'll be stuck."

"We'll worry abou' that later," yelled Misty. "Come on, ya numbskull!"

They all ran to the tile wall and jumped over—first Misty, then Clink, Alfonso, Resuza, Bilblox, and Kõrgu. Hill came last. By the time he reached the wall, it had risen to almost six feet. Just as Hill was about to climb over, the room was plunged into darkness. The zwodszay had reached the candelabra. A hideous burning smell filled the room, followed by a heart-rending moan. Apparently, one of the zwodszay had sacrificed himself to ensure that the candles were extinguished.

Hill grabbed the top of the wall and began to pull himself over. It was now over eight feet tall and rising quickly. Hill let out a cry of pain. His hands slipped and he began to fall backwards.

"Th-They've got me," Hill shouted. "I-I can't make it . . ."

Bilblox sprang into action, leapt toward Hill's voice, and grabbed hold of Hill's hands, which gripped the top of the rising wall. The burly longshoreman pushed off the wall with his feet and yanked Hill toward them. It was hard at first, but then the zwodszay holding Hill on the other side lost its grip, and Bilblox and Hill fell heavily onto the ground.

The zwodszay all began to screech and snarl as if, perhaps, they had turned on one another. It was such a terrifying sound that tears dripped down Alfonso's face and he hugged the ground. Then the first wall closed completely. The sounds of the zwodszay abruptly disappeared, leaving Alfonso and the others in the silent, completely darkened space between the two walls.

CHAPTER 32

SEEING THE STARS

ALFONSO REACHED into his backpack and pulled out his blue sphere. He spun the object in his hand and it soon began to glow with the flickering image of the one-eyed monk placing a scroll of parchment into a locked box. This was strange. Alfonso hadn't seen this particular image before, but he was concerned with more pressing matters. He held the blue sphere out so that it might cast some light into the surrounding darkness, but its meager light could only trace the basic outline of the enclosure. Resuza lit a candle, which generated a bit more light.

Hill sighed. "Now what?" he asked. "Josephus's list doesn't have any keys." He looked at Clink. "What do you make of all these doors?"

Clink stood up, took the candle from Resuza, examined one of the locked doors, and nodded thoughtfully. He extracted a wire spool from his pocket and inserted it into one of the keyholes. Over the next few minutes, he moved the wire back and forth in the keyhole. Finally, he looked up. His face was streaked with sweat.

"There's no obvious triggering mechanism, which means even Alfonso couldn't do that nifty trick of his." Clink looked annoyed. "This is ridiculous! Who knew that Jasberians were such good locksmiths? Somnos is filled with weak, flabby locks!"

"Even if we could unlock one of these doors, we still got problems," said Bilblox as he felt the dimensions of one of the doors. "The doors are too narrow. Probl'y only Alfonso and Resuza can fit through."

"You're right about that," chuckled Misty, who had been listening to the conversation. "Me 'n' you got meat on our ol' bones, and we can't be fittin' through doors like them!"

Clink examined the entire length of the wall and confirmed that all the doors were identical; each was made of smooth marble and contained a keyhole with no obvious triggering mechanism. Clink unsuccessfully tried every tool in his satchel, but he did notice one curious thing. Small amounts of fog or mist appeared to be seeping through several of the keyholes. "It's as if there are a bunch of clouds on the other side of this wall," concluded Clink. "Though I don't know how that helps us."

They sat on the stone floor and watched Resuza's candle drip away. Clink and Hill chewed on some beef jerky. Bilblox was rubbing his head with his fingers and breathing rather heavily. Apparently, the old longshoreman was fighting off another one of his awful headaches. Alfonso squeezed Bilblox's shoulder in a gesture of sympathy and Bilblox grunted appreciatively. The others in the traveling party simply rested. The only person doing anything remotely productive was Misty. She had a small pad and pencil out and she was composing a sketch in the flickering light.

"What are you drawing?" asked Alfonso.

"Oh nothin' special—just a drawin' of that bridge we passed o'er," said Misty. "I like to sketch a bit just to keep mah hands from bein' idle."

"Mind if I draw something?" asked Alfonso.

"Sure," said Misty, as she handed the pad and pencil to Alfonso.

Alfonso was not especially fond of drawing, but he wanted to get a vision onto paper before he forgot the details of it. It was the vision that he'd seen in the Hub while standing on the giant stump—the vision of the white-eyed boy and the spooky-looking plant that the boy had placed in the soil. Alfonso worked quickly. He drew the boy, the plant, its hideous roots, and the dead trees that surrounded it all. His sketch was rough, but evocative.

"That ain't a bad renderin' of the Coe-Nyetz Tree," said Misty appreciatively. Alfonso hadn't noticed, but the old miner was looking over his shoulder. "Ya did a nice job drawin' them roots."

"What are you talking about?" asked Alfonso.

"That's what ya drew, ain't it?" asked Misty. "Oh, I used to be mighty interested in that bit of 'istory when I was a wee girl."

"The Coe-Nyetz Tree isn't history," interjected Clink condescendingly. "It's a fairy tale. There's a difference, you know."

"Call it what you like," said Misty. "It's a true tale."

Suddenly, everyone in the room was paying avid attention to what was being said.

"What's the story?" asked Resuza.

"Oh, it's just a bunch of nonsense about an evil Founding Tree that spreads death and destruction," said Clink dismissively. "It's peasant lore. Miners and bricklayers love that kind of stuff. Only simpletons like my cousin here put any stock in such tales."

"Why, ya ain't even got the story right," sniped Misty. "It's a tale about Dormia—that's what it is. It's about the elders, in their *infinite* wisdom, makin' a helluva stupid mistake. It's about the high 'n' mighty always thinkin' they're too smart t'have any problems. Ya see, ever since the beginnin' of our times, the elders been tryin' to grow a Foundin' Tree from nothin' but scratch. Ya know, without the aid of a Great Sleeper. Just in case a feller in yer shoes don't show up." She looked at Alfonso. "I don't mean to insult yer groupa Great Sleepers, but it's happened. Anyhow, I don't need to tell ya, they ain't never succeeded in growin' a tree in this manner. They came close once, though, and that's what the Coe-Nyetz Tree was all about."

"Go on," said Alfonso eagerly.

"Well, a few thousand years ago, there was a fella—a Dormian—who went by the name of Resže," continued Misty. "He got ahold of some ether from a Foundin' Tree—that's the magical sap that grows inside the tree's trunk. Anyhow, he gets special permission t'sprinkle some of that ether on the seeds of a Colossal Carpathian fir."

"What's that?" asked Alfonso.

"They came from Straszydlo Forest," explained Misty.

"They're extinct now, but when they lived, they was dark, mysterious trees. Grew only razor-sharp needles that made ya tremble jus' t'look at 'em. Resže traveled into the forest to get some-a these seeds. Then he went into Siberia t'conduct his experiment."

"A-course, nothin' much is known about what Resže accomplished, other than that he failed. All they ever figured out came from a follow-up expedition. They found ol' Resže's bones all right, but here was the spooky part: every tree, shrub, 'n' blade a grass hundreds a miles from the site was dead, and farther out, vegetation was only just beginnin' to return. Along the way, they encountered some peasants who spoke of a 'circle of death' that destroyed all life."

"A bunch of hogwash," said Clink. "The fairy tale also says that the Coe-Nyetz Tree is regenerative. Oh, they say all kinds of things . . ."

"Regenerative?" inquired Bilblox.

"That's just a fancy waya sayin' that the tree can grow back," explained Misty. "You can grow it, cut it, burn it, and it'll grow right back. Not like our Founding Trees where, if you cut 'em, they'll never sprout new limbs."

"So, what you're saying is, this tree could give you an endless supply of purple ash?" asked Alfonso.

"I suppose it could," said Misty.

"Look here, Alfonso," said Clink. "This is what miners do when they're bored—they spin ridiculous yarns."

"Oh, it's a true tale," countered Misty. "Mister Foreign Minister, ya heard of the Coe-Nyetz Tree, aintcha?"

"I know the first lines from an old nursery rhyme," said Hill. He closed his eyes and recited it from memory:

Old man Resže much toil did he spend,
A seed and some ether he did blend,
An ominous fate this did portend
A dark shadow tree and the world's end.

"Yup, that's the rhyme," said Misty.

"World's End," muttered Alfonso to himself. "Strange—that's the name of my hometown."

"I haven't recalled that rhyme in years," said Hill. "Alfonso, how did you hear about this tale anyway?"

"It's rather odd," muttered Alfonso almost to himself. "I saw it in a dream very recently."

Misty stared at Alfonso. "A Great Sleeper saw that tree in his dream? 'N' ya never read nor heard about it before?"

"Never," replied Alfonso.

"Well that ain't good," declared Misty. "Ya jus' gave me the shivers."

Clink snorted, but said nothing.

Resuza's candle began to flicker. It was almost out. Resuza reached into her backpack for another. Hill shook his head. "Don't bother," he said. "I think we're all tired. Let's just have some darkness for a bit. We'll sleep and maybe figure a way out in our sleep."

Alfonso nodded, although it was a strange thing to watch the candle go out. He couldn't help feeling helpless and panicked as the candle sputtered, the flame disappeared, and only the faint reddish tint of the dying ember remained visible. Seconds later, even that light disappeared.

Then something most unexpected occurred: two incandescent, glowing images appeared in the darkness. The first image, which was a painting of the night sky, was emblazoned on the ceiling. It glowed a lustrous blue and looked amazingly like the real night sky, despite the fact that they were trapped deep underground.

The second image, which was a drawing of a lion, was emblazoned on the tile wall that had just risen into place. The lion looked proud and regal. Several white dots, the same shape as the stars above them, illuminated different parts of his body. Beneath the image of the lion, the same phrase was written in three different languages:

قلب الأسد * 轩辕十四 * *Cor Leonis*

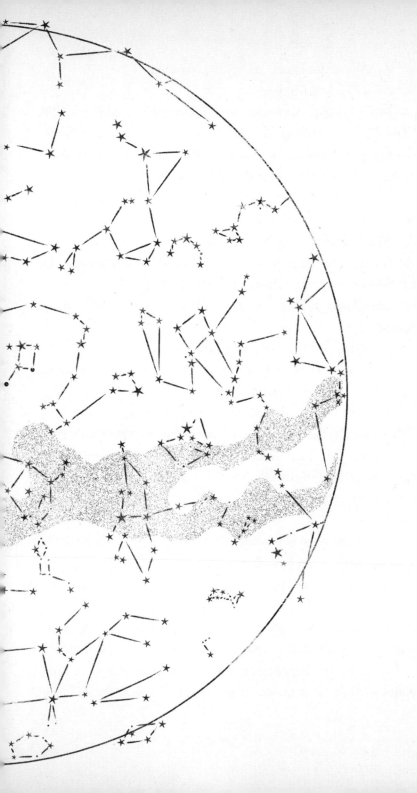

"Would you look at that!" Hill exclaimed.

"What?" asked Bilblox.

"Two glowing drawings just appeared," explained Hill. "There's one on the ceiling of the constellations of the northern sky and the other is of a lion with stars at different places on his body on the back of the tile wall."

"The lion is Leo," explained Clink. "That's one of the constellations in the northern sky."

"What's that writing beneath the lion?" asked Resuza.

"The first language is Arabic," explained Hill. "The second is Chinese or Korean I believe. And the third is . . ."

"Latin," said Alfonso excitedly. "I've taken a bit of Latin in school."

"What does it say?" asked Resuza.

"Well," said Alfonso, "*Cor* means 'heart' and *Leonis* means 'lion.' So I guess it's 'heart of the lion.'"

"What on earth is that about?" asked Bilblox.

"Obviously, that's referring to Regulus, the star that's right at the lion's heart in the Leo constellation," Clink proclaimed. "It's the bottom-right star on the drawing of Leo. You've all seen it before, I'm sure. It's one of the brightest stars in the sky."

"That's some second-grade education you got," said Bilblox.

"I probably could have been a top-notch professor or a certified genius," said Clink matter-of-factly. "But I'm simply too fond of stealing, cheating, and rule-breaking."

"It seems like they want us to find Regulus on the map of the northern sky above us," remarked Resuza. "Can you find it?"

"Sure, it's in the bottom left-hand corner above us," explained Clink. "Just match up the shapes. Do you see it?"

"I see it!" said Resuza.

"What do you suppose is so special about that star?" asked Hill.

"Not sure," said Clink.

"Maybe we're meant to touch it or press it," suggested Clink. "But I suppose the ceiling is too high for that . . ."

"Come on—use your brain. That's what the slingshot is for!" said Bilblox wryly. "The slingshot was on the list of things Josephus brought along. This is probably what it's for."

"By Jove, that's right!" said Hill. "Resuza, have a go at it. You're the best shot among us."

Hill took the slingshot out of his backpack and handed it to Resuza.

"Resuza, do you see Regulus?" he asked. "Can you hit it?"

"Sure," she replied. She loaded the slingshot with a single rock, aimed carefully in the pitch-black darkness, and let the rock fly. *Ping!* The rock hit the lion's heart dead-on. Half a second later, they all heard something fluttering in the air and then landing softly on the ground. Hill immediately lit a candle and they gathered around the object that had fallen from the ceiling. It appeared to be a key, although it was by no means an ordinary one. It was extremely long, curved like a *J*, and appeared to be made of a crinkled, brown paper.

"Careful," Hill warned. "This thing looks incredibly fragile." Clink edged closer, picked up the key, and held it lightly in his palm. "I've heard stories about these, but I never imagined they actually existed," he said in a voice tinged with wonder. "These are leaf keys. When you put them into the keyhole and turn them, it unlocks the door but it also destroys the key. You get one chance and that's it."

"Why don't we just use the slingshot a bunch of times?" Bilblox asked. "That way, we'll get enough keys, just in case."

"Good point," said Hill. "Resuza, why don't we try to get another one? Just in case." She nodded in agreement. After Hill blew out the candle and their eyes adjusted, she aimed carefully and fired again at the lion's heart. *Ping!* They all waited for another key to drop, but nothing happened. Hill lit the candle and shook his head.

"As I suspected," said Clink. "You get one key and that's it. Each party that enters this chamber only gets one key—one chance to open the second gate."

No one spoke for a minute or so.

"I have an idea," said Alfonso finally. "Clink, you're saying that the leaf key disintegrates. Well, if anyone used a leaf key recently, there's got to be a trace—you know, a bit of leaf left in the keyhole."

"I didn't see anything like that," replied Clink. "The keyholes were clean."

"Maybe I can look a little closer. Hand me that candle," said Alfonso.

Hill gave the candle to his nephew and everyone backed away from Alfonso as he focused carefully on the flame. The flame danced and flickered and Alfonso became lost in the complexity of its movements. He slipped into hypnogogia and walked toward the wall of doors and began examining each door's keyhole. He approached each keyhole with his eyes wide open. Then he squinted his eyes, effectively zooming in, as if his eyes were two telephoto lenses, until the faintest of dust particles appeared as big as beach balls. Finally, at the twelfth door from the left, he found something. In the flickering light of the candle, he saw a microscopic wafer with an intricate pattern of veins on it.

He didn't recognize what it was at first but then it hit him—he was staring at a particle from a leaf. Alfonso straightened up, relaxed his focus, and sensed the familiar spinning that always meant he was returning to normal.

"Well?" Hill asked anxiously. "Did you find anything?"

"Twelfth door from the left," said Alfonso confidently. "Someone used a leaf key in that lock."

"I hope you're right," said Clink. "Otherwise, this place'll become our tomb." He laughed nervously. His breezy confidence was gone. Clink took a deep breath, carefully inserted the key into the keyhole, and turned it. It crinkled and disintegrated immediately. Seconds later, they heard the most beautiful sound in the world. It was a grinding noise. The entire wall of doors descended into the floor.

The group stumbled out of the darkness and onto a wide, broad ledge made of the same marble as the doors. One by one they fanned out across the ledge and gazed out at the view in front of them.

"Oh my heavens," said Hill in amazement. "Have you ever seen anything like this?"

CHAPTER 33

RIDING THE CURRENTS

"THE OL' MINERS in Somnos'll never believe me when I tell 'em about this," Misty said in a hushed voice. "They'll say I made it up."

"*Incredible,*" whispered Clink.

Just beyond the marble ledge gaped a vast chasm. Across this chasm hung a thin layer of clouds, and far beneath, lava from the earth's core had formed into a vast river. The light from the river of lava was uncomfortable to look at—just like the sun—and after a few seconds they turned their attention to the ceiling. In complete contrast to the furnace below, the ceiling, which looked to be almost a mile above them, was covered with a thick, dark blue ice, the kind that forms only after many years of below-freezing conditions.

"What kinda magic is this?" asked Misty. She looked worried. "Why are there clouds underground?"

Clink took a few steps forward, nodded, and turned to Misty. "What you are witnessing here, my superstitious, backwoods cousin, is nature at its strangest and most incredible," explained Clink with a professorial air. He obviously had recovered from his tongue-tied state. "The cloud layer is the equilibrium between the two extremes, where the rising heat from the lava interacts with the cold air coming off the ceiling. Cold air falls, and hot air rises. That cloud is where the two meet. Pay attention, dearest Misty, and you'll emerge from these subterranean depths an educated woman. Better late than never, I say."

"Don't get too uppity," grumbled Misty. "I remember when ya tried to rob the mayor's house and ya locked yerself inside a closet by accident. Did yer book learnin' help ya then?"

"Hey," said Resuza. "What's that shiny stuff farther along the walls? Is that . . ."

They all followed her gaze. Misty cackled and rubbed her hands together. "I know the good stuff when ah see it! That's gold! Hah! I thought it was just the stuffa fairy tales. 'The way t' Jasber is covered wit' gold.' Well, I guess they was right."

Alfonso looked at the walls carefully. Thick lines of something bright and yellow zigzagged in between the rock like cracks in a broken window. It was an enormous vein of gold, equal to the richest mines of Siberia and South Africa. Combined with the cloud layer, the glistening of the gold-veined walls gave the area an otherworldly feel, as if Alfonso and the others had stepped into another dimension or planet.

"I'm sure it's mighty impressive," said Bilblox matter-of-factly. "But I get the sense we don't have any roads to walk on,

287

like on the other side. Gold and clouds won't help us get any-where. What's the plan, ladies and gents?"

"We don't need roads," said a voice from above. "We've got something much better." They looked up. It was Hill. He was standing on what appeared to be the upper level of the marble ledge, which was accessed by a tiny set of stairs just below where he stood.

"What's up there?" Alfonso shouted.

"You're not going to believe this," Hill replied with a grin.

&

When they arrived on the upper level, Hill was standing next to a row of twenty large chests, four feet long by three feet wide. Several of the chests were empty. Scattered across the floor were strips of cloth, tied together to form a strange-looking rope that gleamed blue, and rough-hewn beams of wood. Presum-ably the items on the floor came from these chests. Hill exam-ined an elaborate pictograph chiseled on the inside of one chest.

"What are these things?" asked Alfonso. He was the first to reach Hill.

Hill wore an excited, schoolboyish smile.

"Alfonso, this is *quite* interesting." Hill gleamed. "These pic-tographs clearly explain how to build a glider. Or at least, the Jasberian equivalent of a glider."

"What?"

"At long last, I've found Dormians interested in modern technology!" exclaimed Hill. "Maybe it'll be easier now to con-vince the Grand Vizier that Somnos needs an air force."

"And what exactly are we supposed to do with these gliders?" Resuza asked. "We're not outside, and we don't have a motor to take us in the right direction."

"True enough," said Hill. "Still, they're here for a reason."

Clink walked to the edge of the upper level. He stared at the ice on the ceiling, then at the cloud layer, and then at the lava below. After thinking about this for a while, he turned back around, but as he did so, he noticed something unusual in the wall behind them. Very near the ceiling of the fault a perfectly round vent jutted out from the wall. The entire structure was constructed of a smooth material, perhaps marble, and it looked to be about a hundred feet in diameter. Clink watched the vent until a small icicle hanging from the ceiling—not far from the vent—broke away and began to fall. Yet instead of falling straight down, it flew toward the vent and then disappeared inside.

"Aha!" exclaimed Clink. He jabbed a finger toward the vent. "That's how they do it."

"That's how they do what?" asked Misty.

"That vent above us is drawing in air," explained Clink. "Thus it creates a current that can pull the gliders toward it. It must be a very strong pull. Look—the vent is actually pulling in large icicles."

They watched another icicle fall from the ceiling, veer toward the vent, and disappear inside.

"Why does that help us?" Resuza asked. "Even if there is a current going into that vent, it doesn't matter. It's going in the wrong direction. We want to go the other way, away from here."

"True enough," replied Clink. "But I bet there's a separate current going in the direction we want to go. And I'll wager all the gold in this fault that there's one of those vents on the other end by Jasber." He walked to the edge of the platform. "Does anyone have something they don't need, like a piece of cloth?"

Alfonso searched through his pack and handed over a cloth sack from Somnos that contained their used tea grounds and other bits of trash.

"That will do splendidly," said Clink. "Now pay close attention. There should be two currents—an upper one and a lower one." Clink took the sack from Alfonso and tore it into two pieces. He then took one piece and threw it high into the air. Almost immediately, it was sucked upward into the vent. "That's the upper jet stream and it appears to be bringing air toward the Hub." Clink then took the second piece of cloth and hurled it into the chasm below. They watched as it fell toward the cloud layer. Just as it was about to pass through the clouds, an unseen force gripped it, and it sped away from them, just above the cloud layer.

"That's the lower current!" declared Clink exuberantly. "And it's blowing toward Jasber. All we need to do is assemble these gliders, drop them toward the clouds, and let the wind do the rest!"

"Ridic'lous," proclaimed Misty. "You'll never get me steppin' one foot in that pile-a wood on the floor, no matter how well ya hammer it together."

Hill shook his head in amazement. "I'm trying to think of some other explanation, but I can't," he said.

"Why don't we put the gliders together and then we'll make a decision," said Bilblox.

As it turned out, the gliders proved remarkably easy to assemble. The frames were made of sturdy wooden beams that lashed together with the aid of the gleaming blue rope joints. The wings of the aircraft were made of a soft cloth that looked and felt like silk but was so resilient that it could not be punctured, even with the sharpened tip of a sword. Each glider contained three seats. The forwardmost seat was for the pilot, who apparently was meant to steer the glider with just two levers. Each lever was connected to rope that pulled on flaps attached to the wings and fin of the plane. A crude parachute at the rear of the glider could be used to slow down its momentum, and a set of wooden wheels screwed onto the underside of the vehicle. Amazingly enough, that was it. It took them four hours to assemble the first glider and only two more to assemble the second one.

"Well done," proclaimed Hill as he looked at the completed gliders, which sat wing to wing on the main marble ledge. "And now . . ." His voice trailed away.

They walked to the edge of the platform and looked down into the fault. Below them hung the layer of clouds. They were conscious of a slight wind pushing the clouds forward, but it didn't seem nearly strong enough to support the gliders.

"Don't worry," said Clink. "All we have to do is board the glider, push off, and fall toward the clouds. The wind will do the rest."

"That's what ya think, do ya?" said Misty glumly. "I don't mind danger, but fallin' into a field-a lava with only the hope of havin' some wind is plumb crazy." She turned in desperation to Resuza. "This cousin-a mine, he ain't right in the head, ya see? He's fulla crazy idears, and people in Somnos don't pay him no mind. 'N' we're trustin' our lives to 'im!"

Hill broke the silence that followed Misty's outburst. "I

don't see any other option," he replied. He said he would pilot the first glider, with Bilblox and Resuza riding in back as passengers. Kõrgu would sit next to Bilblox. Alfonso, the only other person besides Bilblox with experience in planes, would pilot the second glider. Clink and Misty would ride with him.

"As far as I can tell, flying these gliders ought to be easy," said Hill confidently. "One lever will turn you left or right and the other will bring you up or down. It all seems pretty straightforward. I believe these gliders are meant to be flown by inexperienced pilots."

Alfonso nodded, but felt none of Hill's confidence.

They rolled the two gliders to the far end of the platform, which extended out into the fault. This part of the platform was made of well-polished wood that still shone even after centuries of disuse, and it slanted down toward the fault below. Hill boarded the glider first, followed by Bilblox, Kõrgu, and Resuza. As Hill nodded off to sleep, Alfonso gave their glider a soft push and it slipped easily off the platform and into the air. The aircraft dropped like a lead weight. Kõrgu barked mournfully. Seconds later, the current just above the cloud layer grabbed the glider and pushed it forward just as easily as it had whisked away the sack that Clink had thrown. The glider flew steadily and safely just above the cloud layer until it became only a blip in the distance.

Alfonso looked at Clink and Misty.

"It works!" Clink exulted. "Let's go—we have to keep them in sight." They ran to their glider and maneuvered it into position. Misty gave it a good push, and the aircraft began its slide down the smooth wooden launching pad.

"I love you, Misty," whispered Clink with a choked sob.

"You're a fine cousin. You've always been the most supportive of all my family."

"I still say ya ain't as clever as ya think y're, but I reckon I am fond of ya," said Misty. "Now we best nod on off t'sleep, so we can focus better and not get all riled up." Her eyes promptly shut, as did Clink's. Their bodies relaxed ever so slightly as the glider fell into the fault.

Just as it neared the cloud layer, the current grabbed the glider and sent it skimming along the surface of the clouds. The wind roared in their ears, but otherwise, the journey seemed remarkably peaceful. Alfonso tentatively pulled on the pilot's gears. Hill was right; one gear moved the plane left and right and the other moved it up and down. Luckily, Alfonso had room to experiment, since the fault was about a mile wide. Alfonso only hoped it didn't get much narrower.

Up ahead, Hill's sleeping-self was showing off. His glider banked upward. The glider's momentum carried it up for several hundred feet before it began to falter. Then, just as the glider was about to plummet down, the upper current blowing in the opposite direction grabbed the glider and began whisking it back toward the Hub. Hill's glider rapidly approached Alfonso's until Hill threw his glider into a steep descent and smoothly returned them to their original course. Although spectacular, these aerial acrobatics did not sit well with Bilblox. From his vantage point, Alfonso could see a red-faced Bilblox shouting at Hill. It woke up the former air force pilot, and from then on, Hill steered the glider without incident.

Several hours later, both gliders approached a stone ledge on the left side of the gold-veined wall. The ledge was equipped with a long landing strip that was clearly intended to function as a runway on which gliders could land and then take off again. Hill's glider landed gracefully with hardly a bump, while Alfonso's landed with a great deal of jostling. Both gliders were stopped by an old rope that stretched across the runway. Hill observed that this rope functioned exactly like an arresting wire on an aircraft carrier. It caught the gliders, slowed them down, and brought them to a quick stop. Incredibly, the rope itself was made of several hundred intertwined strands of gold string, and it still functioned well after several hundred years of neglect.

Alfonso and the others exited their gliders, stretched their legs, and took a good look around. Earlier in the day, while they were still in flight, they had passed over a number of ledges. Most were small and contained only a scattering of rocks. This particular ledge, however, was remarkably different. It was at least four times as large as the previous ledges and it contained something they hadn't seen in several days: water. Most of the ledge was taken up by a small lake bordered by a scattering of moss, shrubs, and waist-high grass. All of this plant life was the same color, a bright reddish brown. The lake itself contained water that was perfectly clear and the floor of the lake was covered with starfish. The water looked very clean and eminently drinkable. In the middle of the lake sat a man-made gold dome.

"At last we've run into some good luck," exclaimed Clink as they all took in their surroundings. "This is a perfect place for a rest."

"Careful," warned Hill. "We have no idea what we've landed on. For all we know, this water is a trap built by the zwodszay."

By the time Hill had finished his sentence, Clink had already walked to the edge of the pool. He leaned over, stuck an inquiring finger into the water, and then brought it to his lips.

"Absolutely, lip-smacking delicious!" he declared jubilantly. "You could make a fortune bottling this stuff. I suspect it's ice melt. Look at the edge of the lake, next to the wall." Although difficult to make out, it appeared as if melt from the ice-covered ceiling above them was steadily running down the wall and merging with the lake.

"This don't make sense," muttered Misty. "In the middle-a this god-fersaken place, we got an oasis?"

"And what about that gold dome in the middle of the lake?" asked Resuza. "What do you suppose that's all about?"

She was interrupted by a splash. Kõrgu had jumped in the water and begun swimming around. It soon became apparent that she was headed directly for the dome.

"What's yer wolf doin'?" Misty asked.

"I don't know," replied Bilblox.

They all watched as Kõrgu approached the curious gold dome. She swam around it several times, pawing at its gold walls. She barked loudly at the group and then dove underwater. After a few seconds, they heard her barking again, although this time they couldn't see her. Her barks sounded muffled.

"She's inside!" shouted Resuza. "There must be an underwater entrance!" Resuza took off her backpack and proceeded to take off her socks and shoes. She glanced at the others. "Come on—let's see what's inside."

"Wait a minute . . ." began Hill.

But Resuza was not to be deterred. She walked briskly into the small lake and within a few feet, the cool water rose above her waist. Resuza began swimming toward the gold dome. Once she was only a few feet away from the man-made island, she disappeared under the water. A few seconds later, they faintly heard her voice. "It's perfect! *Come on!*"

Alfonso quickly followed and in no time he neared the hut. When he dove under the water, he saw a murky light. He swam up toward the light and then bobbed up into the dome itself. He hoisted himself out and sat down, dripping wet, to take in his surroundings.

"Incredible," said Alfonso. "It's just like a beaver lodge, only it's for people."

The lodge was only one room but it was large, perhaps twenty feet in diameter. There was a thick glass window overhead, and through this skylight a dim light shone through. The entire circumference of the round hut was lined with bunk beds. They were plain-looking, but each bed was covered in soft piles of the same fluorescent blue fabric that tied their gliders together. The floor of the lodge was covered with a soft yellowish moss that seemed to function like a carpet. In the center of the hut, next to the hole that led back down into the water, was a fireplace with a grill for cooking. Alfonso peered through the half-light and saw Resuza resting in one of the bunk beds.

"How's the bed?" he asked.

She raised her head and smiled at him. "It's very comfortable," she said. "Try it out."

Alfonso stood up and walked toward her. He avoided Kõrgu, who was sitting contentedly on the floor by the fireplace chewing on what appeared to be a *very* old piece of meat. Alfonso took the bed to Resuza's left and lay down so that their heads were less than a foot apart.

"Not bad," he admitted. "I could stay here for a while." He paused. "I wonder why they have beds. Wouldn't the Jasberians be active sleepers, just like Dormians from Somnos?"

Resuza stretched out her arm and playfully tousled Alfonso's head. "Even if they didn't sleep, they'd still need to rest. Anyway, look above you. This is Dormian for sure."

Alfonso stared at the bottom of the bunk above him. It was covered with intricate pictographs. The pictographs showed people with their eyes half-closed flying gliders down a fault. The illustrations were done in beautiful gold leaf and a light blue ink that glowed like pale moonlight.

A gurgling noise came from the water entrance. Hill appeared and then, within the next few minutes, Bilblox, Misty, and Clink all came through the porthole in a hubbub of excitement.

"As nice as this lodge is," said Hill, "I'm afraid it's bad news."

"How do ya figure?" asked Bilblox.

"There's only one reason the Jasberians would've constructed such an elaborate lodge with an underwater entrance," said Hill. "They must have used it to protect themselves from the zwodszay, which means there could be more zwodszay lurking about."

"He's right," said Misty. "The zwodszay hate water. That must be the purpose of this here strange domed abode. We're safe fer now. But them beasts is probably lurking about somewhere not too far away."

No one said anything else. They quickly unpacked and tried to get some rest. Hill stretched out his legs. Alfonso heated up some slabs of salted pork, an activity that drew Kõrgu's rapt attention. Resuza boiled water for tea. While in the relative safety of the lodge, Misty and Clink were busy calculating the amount of gold contained in the Jasber fault walls. "At least a hunnert tons!" Misty exclaimed. "We could buy every buildin' in Somnos fer that."

"Pshaw, that's nothing," said Clink with an excited giggle. "We couldn't spend all that gold in Somnos. We'd have to strike out into the world. Maybe we could go to Barsh-yin-Binder and buy that whole city. Hah! We could put gold dust in handkerchiefs and blow our nose with it! I'll found a university in my name and we'll both get honorary degrees!"

The two cousins continued to plan all the possible ways to spend their riches. The others just listened to their chatter as they ate their dinners. Toward the end of their meal, Kõrgu's ears pricked up. She growled and looked up through the skylight.

"What is it?" Resuza asked.

"She hears somethin'," Bilblox said. "And I heard somethin' too, like a very quiet flappin' noise."

"What kinda flappin' noise?" Misty asked. She looked excited. "Like wings?"

"Sorta," replied Bilblox. "It sounded like—like dried leather flappin' in the wind."

"Hoo boy," replied Misty. "I was wonderin' if we'd see any of them creatures. Bilblox, ya may have heard the magmon flyin' nearby. They usually stick close to the lava, but they're curious types, I reckon."

"What are you talkin' about?" asked Bilblox. "Magmons? Is this more miner lore?"

"Ah, don't ya worry," replied Misty. "They're like kittens compared to the zwodszay. These are flyin' reptiles that love the heat. They're purty big but gentle. Or so I've been tol'."

"Are you serious?" inquired Hill.

"'Course I'm serious," replied Misty. "Here—I'll draw ya a picture." She pulled out a sketchbook, nodded off to sleep, and began to draw. Ten minutes later, she woke up and revealed her drawing.

"As ya can see fer yerselves," said Misty, "they're purty big. Them little birds is seagulls, so that should give ya some sense-a scale."

Now Alfonso's curiosity was truly piqued. The flying creatures that Misty drew were identical to those depicted in the murals back at the Hub. The rectangular faces, the back-swept wings, the dorsal fins jutting out from the middle of their backs—it all matched.

"How do you know about them?" Alfonso asked.

"Ever' Dormian miner knows about 'em," Misty replied. She looked at Clink with a sly grin. "I guess they're another *myth* comin' t'life. Josephus knew about 'em. Don't rightly know how they live down there or how they feed. 'N' I only seen one once. They're the silent type. Only noise they ever make is that sound Bilblox jus' heard—kinda like dried leather flappin' in the wind."

Hill stared up at the hole in the ceiling and shivered. "Even if they're only curious, let's hope we can avoid them," he said. "Come on now, let's enjoy these beds."

Within an hour, they were all in the comfortable bunk beds that lined the solid gold hut. Hill had brought a pair of torn trousers with him, and he was snoring gently as his sleeping-self expertly repaired the tears. Misty's sleeping-self was muttering to herself while Clink's was apparently in the throes of an epic fantasy in which he was conducting an entire orchestra.

Meanwhile, Resuza, Bilblox, and Kõrgu lay motionless in their beds.

Only Alfonso was still awake. He stared at the underside of the bunk bed above him and at the luminescent pictograph of the gliders etched into it, and as he did, the pictograph came alive. The pilots of these gliders swooped and plunged in complete mastery of the countervailing wind currents. Alfonso soon realized that what he was seeing was an optical illusion. The pictograph functioned like a holograph that simply created the illusion of depth and motion.

Alfonso eventually closed his eyes, but just as he was drifting off to sleep, he happened to glance up through the skylight and saw an enormous head covered in reddish scales staring down at him. Alfonso let out an involuntary gasp.

"Just lie still, lad," said a voice through the darkness. Then came a cackle. It was Misty. "Yer starin' at a magmon. Now ain't that an incredible sight?"

CHAPTER 34

THE TABLES HAVE TURNED

FARTHER DOWN THE JASBER FAULT, perhaps a day's journey by glider, another stone ledge jutted out from one of the fault's gold-streaked walls. This ledge lay directly below a series of stalactites that hung down from a giant bulging rock. Similar to the station where Alfonso and the others currently were staying, this place also had a runway for gliders. Near the wall, water trickled out of a dark cave, and a few cattail-like plants grew there in the mud. In the middle of the ledge sat a dilapidated, rectangular building that was surrounded by several dozen gnarling, shrieking zwodszay.

The building was only a single, dingy room, illuminated by a sputtering candle. It was occupied by two men and a woman.

These three people sat on the floor, breathing heavily and stealing glances at the room's lone door, which was rapidly giving way.

Qt-Thud! Qt-Thud! Qt-Thud!

This was the sound of bodies—the bodies of hungry zwodszay—pounding on the other side of the door with maddened vigor. The door was not going to last much longer. Its rusty hinges were starting to buckle under the pressure. The three people in the room—Josephus, Nathalia Treeknot, and Kiril—exchanged glances but said nothing.

Josephus and Nathalia were utterly exhausted. The historian's face was pale and coated with sweat. His fingers trembled and it appeared as if he had aged at least a decade in the past week. It took Nathalia great effort to rise to her feet and draw her sword in preparation for combat. Kiril, who wore shackles around his wrists and ankles, appeared to be in moderately good condition. And, oddly enough, he didn't seem concerned with the dire situation.

"The zwodszay are going to break down that door any minute," said Josephus weakly. "It's hopeless—this is the end. We have no more soldiers left to defend us. The zwodszay have slowly cut us down. Th-they just never give up."

Nathalia looked at her uncle wearily, but said nothing to contradict him.

"There's an alternative," replied Kiril calmly. "You could unchain me. I can't fight in shackles, not very well anyhow, but if you unchain me I can help defend us. I'm rather good with a long sword . . ."

Qt-Thud! Qt-Thud! Qt-Thud!

Two rusted, decaying screws popped out of the door's top hinge.

Nathalia reached into her pocket and felt the set of keys that unlocked Kiril's shackles. Josephus eyed his niece sharply.

"You can't do it, Nathalia," said Josephus. "This man is our worst enemy. No matter the cost, we cannot let him go. I forbid you! Somnos forbids you!"

"I'm afraid it's too late for that now, Uncle," said Nathalia. "This is our only chance to survive."

"Nathalia, we can fight these zwodszay off," added Kiril calmly. "The doorway is narrow. They can only come in two at a time. If you and I each wield our swords, we will cut them down as they enter."

Qt-Thud! Qt-Thud! Qt-Thud!

A slat of wood broke off the door and the gray tapered fingertips of a zwodszay entered wormlike through the hole in the door.

Nathalia took the keys out of her pocket.

"Don't you dare!" screeched Josephus. "A-All of Somnos will hold you responsible if Kiril escapes."

"I am at my wits' end with you, *Uncle*," snapped Nathalia. She stared furiously at the old historian. "I have lost every single one of my soldiers—the best and bravest Somnos had to offer. And for what? So we could find a city that may not even exist? What's more, I have serious doubts whether the Grand Vizier ever approved of this mission in the first place. I think you lied to me and my men so that—"

Wham!

The door exploded off its hinges and slammed to the ground.

Without a moment of hesitation, Nathalia tossed the keys to Kiril and then slid a long sword across the floor for Kiril to use. Quickly, but with great precision, Kiril unlocked the shackles around his wrists and then around his ankles. Meanwhile, Nathalia ran to the door to attack the zwodszay.

The first two zwodszay to enter the room were relatively scrawny creatures with faces that were grotesquely deformed by strange, knobby growths that lined their foreheads. They lunged at Nathalia, but she parried them expertly and counterattacked. Seconds later, a massive zwodszay burst in through the door and charged Josephus. Josephus cowered helplessly and readied himself to die. Yet, just in the nick of time, Kiril leapt in front of the zwodszay and sank his sword deep into its chest. Kiril then dashed over to the door and took a position next to Nathalia. Together they cut down the zwodszay as they entered the room.

Nathalia was a very skilled fighter, perhaps better with a sword than anyone in the entire army of Somnos, yet when standing next to Kiril she seemed positively sluggish. Kiril's movements were so dazzlingly fast that, by comparison, Nathalia seemed old and sickly. Nonetheless, the two of them worked quite well together. They fought valiantly, using every last bit of their strength, and after several minutes of heated battle the few remaining zwodszay retreated, scurrying away from the glider station and into the darkness of the fault.

"My goodness, you've done it!" said Josephus exuberantly. He was still in the corner, but he had managed to struggle to his feet.

"Don't celebrate just yet," said Nathalia as she clutched her stomach. "I'm sure they'll regroup and come back eventually."

"What's the matter?" asked Josephus. "Have you been hurt? My dear, dear niece . . . what has happened to you?"

"I'm fine," said Nathalia softly.

"Let me have a look . . ." began Kiril.

"Stay away!" ordered Nathalia. "I'll not have you near me. Just because we fought together doesn't mean I trust you."

"You may not trust me, my dear colonel," said Kiril, "but I'm afraid you need me."

"I suppose we won't be putting Kiril back in his shackles," said Josephus softly, almost to himself.

"That's correct," replied Kiril coldly. "That would clearly be against your best interest—and mine. Besides, you are no longer in a position to say what I must or mustn't do. Of course, if the good colonel wishes to challenge me, then so be it, but something tells me that she is smart enough to know the limits of her powers."

Nathalia glowered, but made no reply.

"As I thought," said Kiril. "Well, let's have a bit of rest and a bit of food perhaps, and then be on our way."

"Where are we going?" asked Josephus.

"That no longer concerns you," replied Kiril, with the briefest of smiles.

Within a short while, Kiril had built a crackling fire in the room's stone hearth. For firewood, Kiril used the remains of an old table and chairs that had fallen apart and lay in many broken pieces in the corner. The wood was extremely dry and it lit easily. Once the fire had burned down a bit, Kiril used the coals to warm up a few slabs of salted beef. Josephus took out their remaining provisions—which included a flask of wine, a loaf of dried bread, a bit of cheese, and some potatoes—and spread them out on his sleeping mat. Nathalia, who appeared both exhausted and haggard, lay nearby and stared blankly at the ceiling.

"Would you care for some food?" asked Kiril in a friendly, almost lighthearted manner.

"A bit of meat would be nice," said Josephus as he took some of the salted beef.

"I hope you enjoy your meal," said Nathalia weakly. She clutched her stomach and winced before continuing. "It's bound to be your last," she gasped. "I can't imagine that Kiril intends to drag an old man and a wounded Dormian officer out of these tunnels with him."

"That would be a bit cumbersome, wouldn't it?" replied Kiril.

"Indeed," said Josephus grimly, as he began to chew on his salted beef. "Tell me, if I am not to live to see it, what is to be done with the remaining items on the list? The khopesh, the hooded robe, the four pounds of Uralian nightshade, and the herbs—arrowroot, goldenseal, and Dormian milk thistle. What plans do you have for them? They will be used to enter Jasber?"

"You are a most curious fellow," replied Kiril with a cluck of his tongue. "And the fact that your insatiable curiosity has led you to your demise seems to have no effect on you whatsoever."

"Everything on that list has a very specific purpose. I realize that," said Josephus. As he said this, Josephus eyed a large leather rucksack containing all the items on the list. The rucksack sat on the floor in a far corner of the room. Through much of the journey Josephus had carried the sack but, alas, the tables had turned and now it was in Kiril's control. "What frightens me," continued Josephus, "is that there are so many remaining items on the list which we have not used. You don't seriously plan to destroy Jasber, do you? After all, it is your birthplace!"

"My plans have been thought out much further than yours," said Kiril with a smile. "That's all that matters."

Perhaps the single most important lesson that Kiril had learned in his six hundred years of life was that survival depended entirely on carefully planning for the future. Nartam had said this innumerable times. "If we are to live forever, then we must think centuries and even millennia into the future," Nartam had told him, soon after his army had sacked the city of Noctos. At the time, Nartam was leading a march back to the city of Dargora with his plunder. Kiril, still a boy, rode on Nartam's horse with him. They were at the head of a massive procession that included hundreds of carts filled with gold, slaves, and, most important, purple ash from the Founding Tree of Noctos, which had been burned to the ground. This plunder would lead to centuries of Dragoonya ascendancy.

"The ash that we have recovered from Noctos will last us four hundred years," explained Nartam matter-of-factly. "Perhaps it will last five hundred years if we are careful. But we mustn't be complacent. We need another source of ash. The time will go by more quickly than you think. It always does."

"What will we do, Däros?" asked the young Kiril.

"We need a source of ash that will not run out," replied Nartam. "There was such a source once, many centuries ago. It

307

came from a magnificent tree. A shadow tree. If we had it again, Europe and Asia would be ours. Think of the destiny we could forge for ourselves!" His white eyes shone and his entire body tensed.

"The source is gone?" asked Kiril.

"For now," replied Nartam cryptically. "But someday we will grow it again."

In the centuries since then, Kiril, son of Jasberian nobility and orphan of Noctos, became Nartam's most trusted son. For the Dragoonya, one's rank depended entirely on Nartam's favor. In general, Nartam preferred former Dormians above all others. They made up a small portion of Dragoonya society— the top 1 percent. Nartam called these people his family and they alone were given the purple ash. His "family" comprised his old comrades from Dragoo, the orphans from Noctos, and child refugees who were captured and converted after the sacking of other Dormian cities. Within this group, everyone vied for Nartam's trust and affection. This was especially true, in more recent centuries, as the supply of purple ash began to dwindle and attempts to procure more ash failed. By the late 1800s, Nartam's supply was dangerously low and he began to panic. "We don't have enough for everyone," Nartam told Kiril. "It's time to start reducing the size of the family."

It was Kiril's job to tell those members of the family that they were officially cut off—that they would no longer be receiving any ash—and that their immortality was over. The time had finally come for them to die. A few took this news passively. They skulked off into the darkness, grew sick, and died. Others became enraged, even violent. Kiril killed them. This was his job. And no one was his equal with a sword.

That was well over a hundred years ago. Now the ash was completely gone, and there were few of the elite Dragoonya left. There was no margin for error. Kiril could make no more missteps. He had failed to follow Leif to Jasber. He had tracked Alfonso all the way to Somnos, but failed to destroy the city. There was only one hope to fulfill, at last, Nartam's fondest dream. It all came down to the shadow tree. Everything now depended on what Kiril did in the next few days. His plan was difficult, but it was working so far. Most importantly, he had to make sure he did not receive a serious cut, the kind that would really make him bleed.

"Kiril, I want to know something," said Nathalia through gritted teeth. She was sitting near him and appeared to be in considerable pain. "I am good with a sword, but you are the best I have ever seen. Then who . . ."

"You want to know who cut my face," said Kiril.

Nathalia nodded.

"Before they die, many of those who fall under my sword ask the same question," replied Kiril with a slight smile and a shake of his head. "I will tell you only this: I am going to visit the man responsible."

"To kill him?" asked Nathalia.

"Nathalia is such a beautiful name," said Kiril quietly, almost to himself. He ignored the question. "The name is very worthy of you."

Kiril looked at Nathalia tenderly for a moment, reached out, and ran his finger across her cheek. Nathalia shivered. Kiril stood up. "In a time of war," continued Kiril, "there is, unfortunately, no room for empathy or affection. The only pleasure I give myself is vengeance. It is—"

Kiril stopped midsentence. "Where is Josephus?"

Josephus had been lying on the dirt floor of the room, but at that moment, he was nowhere to be seen.

Kiril's eyes flashed with anger. "You drew my attention away so Josephus could skulk away! And where is my leather rucksack? Josephus!"

Kiril rushed out the door and cursed his mistake in not keeping an eye on the historian. On the ledge, the glider that they had been using was parked at the edge of the runway. It was in perfect shape—the zwodszay had left it alone. But where was Josephus? He couldn't have gone far; after all, he was nearly dead from the stress of the journey. Kiril strained his eyes into the darkness. The only light was the ever present red glow radiating up from the depth of the fault.

Kiril heard Josephus before he saw him. The old historian was on the runway and staggering toward the edge. He dragged the large leather rucksack behind him. Kiril broke into a run and sprinted toward him.

"What do you think you're doing?" gasped Kiril, when he finally caught up with Josephus at the edge of the runway.

Josephus stood four or five feet from the edge of the fault with the leather rucksack dangling from his arm. Inside the bag were all the remaining items from the list. Kiril eyed the bag greedily.

"Keep your distance," Josephus warned in a trembling voice. Clearly, he was at the end of his strength, and it took all his effort to stay conscious and inch forward. "You know I can't let you have this rucksack."

"I am disappointed in you," said Kiril calmly. "I thought you and I had an understanding."

Josephus didn't reply immediately; instead he inched closer to the edge of the fault. He was now just two or three feet from the precipice.

"Give me that bag!" Kiril demanded.

"Never!" hissed Josephus.

As he said this, Josephus turned toward the edge of the fault. Yet, before he could take a single step, a sudden blow knocked his legs out from under him. Josephus found himself on his back, staring up at Kiril. Kiril reached down, grabbed the leather rucksack from Josephus's hands with commanding force, and then opened the sack to inspect its contents.

"Where is the vial of dagárgala and the lid to the rosewood box?" demanded Kiril.

"I-I threw them over the cliff," stammered Josephus.

"LIAR!" bellowed Kiril as he grabbed Josephus by the throat. "Hand them over or I snap your neck!"

Josephus's face turned red, then blue, then purple. He slumped to the ground. Kiril reached into Josephus's coat and found the rosewood lid, with the glass vial securely tied to it.

"No," gasped Josephus.

"Goodbye old man," said Kiril.

The last thing that Josephus saw was Kiril's fist coming down and smashing him in the face.

Much later, Josephus awoke with a thundering headache. He rolled onto his back and managed after much effort to lift his head. There were no signs of Kiril, but he saw something else just above the cloud layer. It was a glider, *their* glider! And though Josephus could not see who was in it, he knew perfectly well that Kiril was the pilot.

He had left them.

Josephus was now alone with his wounded niece and a mob of hungry zwodszay who were lurking in the darkness. He turned back to the lonely hut.

"N-Nathalia!" he yelled, his voice cracking with sorrow. "NATHALIA!"

CHAPTER 35

HOME AGAIN

Leif Perplexon's tan and lanky body cut through the cool waters of Lake Witekkon, trailing millions of bubbles. After gliding for several feet, he expertly dolphin-kicked up to the surface, which shimmered with the sun's reflection. His head exploded through the surface into the dazzling light of day. The sky was a spotless blue. Towering evergreens lined the rocky shore. A slight breeze rippled across the water, carrying along inquisitive dragonflies. A family of loons called to one another in the distance. By all appearances, it was an absolutely perfect summer day in northern Minnesota.

Leif blinked. It was all still there. It was perfect. Even the taste of the lake water was vivid with its tang of minerals from the glacier-scoured bedrock. He was swimming in the elixir of life. Leif glanced about. About a hundred meters away lay the rocky beach and, just beyond it, he saw the small cottage and modest greenhouse.

Home!

Leif did a furious front crawl until he reached the beach. As he swam, he felt fit and strong. The ache in his bones, the weariness of his muscles, the numb feeling in his brain—all of it was gone. He pulled himself up onto the beach and there, standing just feet away, was his wife, dressed in shorts and a tank top. She looked slim and girlish, the way she was when they first met.

"Thank goodness you're okay," said Judy as she rushed over and hugged her husband. "I got so worried when that lightning storm passed through. It happened so fast! Did you get out of the water in time? You must have. I'm just so glad you're back."

"Yes . . ." stammered Leif. "I'm fine—I just . . ."

"Dad!"

Leif looked up and saw his son, Alfonso, sprinting toward him. Alfonso looked exactly the same age as when Leif had seen him last.

"Dad!" yelped Alfonso as he leapt into his father's arms. "I knew you'd be okay."

"Come on," said Judy. "I have some egg salad and roast beef on the table. Let's have lunch."

"I'll get Pappy!" shouted Alfonso, as he dashed toward the greenhouse.

Leif and Judy walked over to a picnic table at the far end of the beach that was loaded with a large pitcher of iced lemonade and platters of egg salad and roast beef sandwiches, as well as watermelon, and warm chocolate brownies.

"This is the day I drowned," Leif said, almost to himself.

"What?" asked Judy.

"Nothing," said Leif. But he was certain of it now. He was reliving the day, over six years ago, when he had disappeared from World's End. It was as if someone had turned back the clock; only now, in this version of history, Leif emerged from his swim and returned to his family.

"This isn't real, is it?" asked Leif.

"What?" inquired Judy. "What are you talking about?"

"This isn't really happening," said Leif. "This is some kind of dream."

"Don't be silly," said Judy, as she pinched her husband affectionately on the cheek.

"Don't do that," said Leif with a laugh. "You know I hate it when you pinch me."

"But it felt real, didn't it?" asked Judy.

"Yeah," confessed Leif, "It did." He sat down at the picnic table in front of an egg salad sandwich and sank his teeth into the soft, doughy rye bread. It was delicious. In his right hand he gripped a brownie that gleamed with rich chocolate. "My goodness," said Leif, "it's good to be home."

Leif heard a dog barking in the distance and he looked up. A playful golden retriever bounded toward them. The dog looked familiar, but Leif couldn't figure out why, because he never owned a dog in World's End.

"Is that . . . but it couldn't be . . . is that Sockeye?" asked Leif. Judy nodded.

"But Sockeye never lived in World's End," protested Leif. "He was the dog that lived in the orphanage where I grew up. Sockeye would have to be more than . . . well, more than thirty years old. And look at him—he looks like a puppy."

"Alfonso loves him," said Judy resolutely, ignoring what her husband had just said.

"None of this is really happening," said Leif rather forlornly. "It's not real."

"What does it matter?" asked Judy as she kissed her husband on the head. Leif felt the warmth of her lips against his lake-cooled brow. She stared at him.

"And what does 'real' mean anyway? You're here, I'm here, Alfonso is here, Pappy's coming from the greenhouse. What else do you want?"

"No," protested Leif. "In the real world you and Alfonso are suffering."

"Look at me," said Judy sternly. She grabbed her husband by the shoulders. "I am Judy. I am your wife. Do I look like I am suffering? I'm so happy to see you. Don't you dare leave me now." Her face softened and she kissed him lightly on the lips. "Besides, we have a surprise for you at dinner. Your parents are coming over from Somnos and your brother will be here too. You haven't seen them in decades. Stay for dinner, *please*."

A lone tear ran down Leif's cheek. "Okay," he murmured softly. "I'll stay."

"Make yourself at home, my love," said Judy soothingly. For a moment, she seemed almost crafty, which Leif knew was very much unlike her true nature. "Besides," she added with a knowing smile, "you've already eaten a lotus berry and you'll soon be eating another. I suspect that you'll be here for a very, very long time."

CHAPTER 36

CROSSING THE RIVER

SEVERAL HUNDRED MILES AWAY, in the ancient city of Jasber, Marta's entire body was shaking. The color was gone from her face and her breathing had turned shallow and rapid. The vision of what she had foreseen—the fire that would soon devour Jasber's armory and her parents' home—was still vivid in her mind's eye. This horrible fate would come to pass in just a matter of days. Her parents would likely die. Marta had to do something. The man with the white eyes and the hideous scar on his face had to be stopped. Marta had to do something before he set the armory ablaze. But how? She struggled to maintain her concentration as she descended the narrow spiral staircase of the tower to the stone promenade where the abbot was waiting for her. She felt tired and suddenly quite old. Her bones creaked as she stepped downward.

The abbot was smoking his pipe and humming a sleepy lullaby to himself. He noticed Marta coming down the staircase and woke up. When he saw her face, his content expression turned worried.

"You had a vision," said the abbot. "An upsetting one?"

Marta nodded.

"And the Founding Tree?" asked the abbot. "What will happen? When?"

Marta said nothing. The fatigue was so overwhelming, she could barely think.

"What's the matter, my child?" asked the abbot. "Tell me what you have foreseen."

"Something awful," whispered Marta.

The abbot nodded. He placed his arm around Marta in a kindly, grandfatherly way. "Now, now, now," said the abbot soothingly. "No matter what you have seen—no matter how bad it is—there is no cause for alarm. We can intervene and change the course of fate. That is what we do. Now tell me, *when* did this vision of yours take place?"

"One week from now," replied Marta.

"My goodness," said the abbot. Despite the fact that he was trying to remain calm, there was a trace of panic in his voice. "W-What happens to the Founding Tree just seven days from now?"

"Nothing happens to the Founding Tree," replied Marta quietly.

"What?" said the abbot. Then comprehension bloomed on his face. "Marta, you didn't! Please tell me you didn't!" He stared as she buried her face in her hands. "You had a vision unrelated to the tree. My child! You know that is strictly forbidden!"

"I had a vision about my parents!" Marta blurted out. "There will be a terrible fire in the city, and my parents' house will burn—"

"Silence!" thundered the abbot. The old man seemed more frightened than angry. "You must *never* speak of this again, not to me or anyone else. This is sacrilege."

"But—" began Marta.

"No!" said the abbot. "Seers may only use their powers to make prophecies about the Founding Tree. This is the rule that cannot—*must not*—be broken! Without this discipline, what is to stop seers from using their powers recklessly and as they see fit—telling people who will die, who will prosper, who will be betrayed, who will be exalted, and in what manner? Such wide-ranging prophecies bring anarchy. That is why the Foreseeing Pen was hidden away millennia ago. The alternative is chaos!" He was breathing heavily and his face had turned red. The abbot leaned in close to Marta.

"I don't care *what* you saw; if it doesn't involve the Founding Tree, then it is no concern of mine—or of yours. Tell no one. The survival of our people depends on it." He paused and his expression softened. "You must not speak of this to *anyone*."

Marta nodded despondently.

"Oh my dear, dear girl," muttered the abbot. "Whatever am I going to do with you?"

Several hours later, Marta lay in her bed staring at the ceiling. She was in the Seers' Room, the traditional octagon-shaped bedroom that all seers had lived in for thousands of years. In keeping with the goal of protecting the seer's powers, the room was windowless, so that the seer's visions would be focused only on the Founding Tree. However, given the exalted status of the seer, the bedroom was exceedingly comfortable. Marta's bed was spacious, immaculately clean, and piled high with pillows and soft blankets. A silk fabric draped high over the four extended posts of the bed gave the bed a cozy, tentlike feel. The floor was carpeted with soft rugs. The walls were adorned with intricate tapestries depicting seers from ages past. In the corner stood a tall water chime, which gurgled peacefully. Although meant to inspire soothing contemplation, at the moment the water chime had the opposite effect on Marta. She wanted to knock it to the ground. Her pounding heart reverberated in her head, and she clenched her hands into angry red fists.

She had to do *something*.

Marta stood up and began pacing around her large room. Three of the room's walls were lined with floor-to-ceiling bookcases, containing ancient books from all around the world. The abbot was obsessed with foreign languages and, when he learned that Marta was a very quick study, he insisted that she learn as many foreign tongues as possible in order to keep her mind sharp.

The other walls in the room were hung with tapestries, except for one final wall, which was bare but for an ornate gold curtain that covered the opening to a ledge set within the wall. The ledge was empty, but centuries ago, it was the resting place of the Foreseeing Pen, which the seer would use to write down all manner of prophecies, from the smallest flick of a butterfly's wing to the eruptions of volcanoes. Now the pen was gone, and the seer could predict only what was in her line of sight. And that had been bad enough, thought Marta.

Suddenly, she stopped her pacing and rushed to the bookcase nearest her bed. There was just one thing that would calm her down. She knelt down and shoved heavy books out of their resting places. They tumbled to the carpeted floor before her. She coughed a little from the swirling dust and then found what she was looking for: a folded piece of parchment.

The door reverberated with a sharp knock. "Marta?" It was one of the monks stationed near her door. Obviously, he had heard the thud of the books falling to the floor.

Marta breathed deeply and composed herself. "Everything is fine. I found the book I was looking for. Be at peace, kind monk."

"Be at peace, kind seer," came the melodious reply.

Marta brought the parchment to her bed and quickly unfolded it. If the monks knew she had this, they would be furious. It was a serious breach of rules to possess any reminder of the world she had left behind. And after the vision Marta had today, if the abbott saw she had a drawing of her family . . .

She sat on her bed, skinny legs dangling, and traced the outline of her family. Her mother, father, and two brothers. Her older brother, Stoven, was almost a man and had nearly reached her father's height and weight, while Danyel, the younger one, was still a boy. She smiled at Danyel's hair, which always stuck straight out in wild formations.

A polite tapping interrupted her thoughts. It was the abbot. Marta knew she had only seconds. She tumbled off the bed, ran to the bare wall, and hid the parchment in the alcove behind the gold curtain. The door opened and the abbot appeared, looking concerned.

"I heard reports of noise in this room," he said. "Obviously, you are welcome to do whatever you would like, as long as—"

"As long as the rules are respected." Marta finished his sentence.

The abbot nodded. He looked at the pile of books scattered across the floor near her bed.

"Dearest Marta," he said in his most gentle voice. "I know you are suffering because of your vision. Believe me when I tell you that the only option is to put it out of your head. You are our seer. Your mind must be strong enough to forget."

Marta nodded. She *would* forget the vision, she said to herself. After she warned her family.

CHAPTER 37

RESCUE

THE FOLLOWING MORNING, in the gloomy darkness, Alfonso and the rest of the group were preparing to move on. They gathered around their parked gliders, getting ready to take off. They stowed their bags and double-checked all the bindings that lashed the glider together. A distant, dry noise interrupted their concentration. Misty barked for everyone to hit the ground.

"Nobody move," hissed Misty. "Them magmons is comin' back!"

The dry-sounding noise grew louder and more distinct. They could make out the sound of flapping wings and as they did, a windstorm began to blow all around them.

"Please no," whimpered Clink. "It's too soon for me to die. I've finally made it out of Somnos. My life has just begun—"

"Shut yer trap and lay quiet!" snapped Misty.

The wind was blowing furiously now. Dust, bits of ice, and other debris swirled angrily around them, and the sound of the flapping wings grew deafeningly loud.

At one point, in the thick of the windstorm, Alfonso dared a glance upward. He saw the belly of an enormous creature flying overhead. The creature looked a bit like a bird, but it had scales like a reptile, and a long slithering tail like a snake. It was huge, at least one hundred feet long. It looked as if several of these creatures, perhaps as many as five of them, were flying together in a tight formation. They passed quickly overhead and did not seem to notice or care about the human beings below.

"That was close," gasped Misty, once the magmons had passed. "Musta been that food we were cookin'. Didn't I tell ya they're curious creatures! Well, I 'ope that's the last we seen of them!"

They spent an anxious half-hour clearing off debris from their gliders and then set off again down the Jasber fault. As they flew along, hour after hour, Alfonso kept peering ahead for an end to the fault. According to a pictograph traced on the inside of Hill's glider, they would reach the end of the Jasber fault after twenty-four hours of flying.

Alfonso strained his eyes, and at last he saw something, although it wasn't what he expected. In the distance, perhaps half a mile away, he saw a glider station that was swarming with perhaps as many as fifty zwodszay. The zwodszay all appeared to be clamoring around a large rectangular rock that jutted out into the fault just above the station.

Alfonso wondered what these zwodszay were after. A few seconds later, he had his answer. The zwodszay were getting ready to eat. Their meal, perched at the top of the oddly shaped rock, was an old man whom Alfonso recognized immediately: Josephus.

Hill's glider, which was about a hundred feet ahead of them, dove for the spot where Josephus was perched. The zwodszay looked up, saw the incoming glider, and quickly sprang into action. They had no intention of forfeiting their meal. Within seconds, the zwodszay began snatching up loose rocks and hurling them at Hill's glider. Almost all of these rocks fell short. Hill expertly steered his glider just over Josephus's head. Meanwhile, Resuza leaned over the side of the glider, extended her arms, and reached down toward Josephus's outstretched hands. At the last moment, however, Josephus panicked and withdrew his hands. The glider whizzed past and Josephus remained on his perch.

"Blasted fool!" cursed Hill. "What'd he do that for?"

Hill navigated his plane back around in order to do a second fly-by. This time, both Bilblox and Resuza reached over the side of the glider to grab hold of Josephus. Success! They clasped his hands and yanked him off the ground. The plane began to climb upward.

"Where's Colonel Treeknot?" yelled Resuza. "And Kiril?"

"My d-darling, darling niece—" cried Josephus with a sob. His body went limp and he lost his grip on the glider. In order to keep him from falling, both Bilblox and Resuza had to lean farther out of the plane. At that instant, the glider hit an air pocket and dropped. Resuza thrust out her hands to reach for support, but found only air. She screamed and tumbled out of the glider, crashing down some fifteen feet onto the runway of the glider station below.

Two zwodszay who were standing near where Resuza had fallen moved toward her quickly. Hill spun around in his seat, whipped out his Colt .45, and fired off several shots. The two zwodszay dropped dead.

"I'm out of bullets!" Hill said.

Alfonso, who was circling far above, watched in horror as all of this transpired. Immediately, he directed his glider down, diving toward the spot where Resuza was stranded.

"Misty, Clink!" Alfonso yelled. "You're going to have to pull Resuza up and into the glider."

The glider shot toward the runway below. Alfonso set his sights on Resuza. She had gotten to her feet—apparently she wasn't injured too badly—and she was now limping down the runway toward the precipice at its end. A mob of zwodszay was closing in on her.

"Nice and easy," whispered Alfonso through gritted teeth. He felt himself becoming drowsy, his body's usual response to extreme danger. This helped. His hands were steady, steadier than they had been all day. The glider swooped down over the heads of the zwodszay and continued on toward Resuza. Misty began to climb out onto the wing of the plane, but Clink interceded, and pointed at himself, indicating that he would do this. "You're too old to be hanging out of gliders, old girl," said Clink. "Let me do it, I'm very agile."

Misty nodded.

"We're too high!" shouted Clink. "Bring her down a bit and I'll grab her."

The glider dropped down, almost landing on the runway.

Resuza ducked. Clink extended a lone, sinewy arm and grabbed her wrist. The glider continued straight ahead, causing Clink to fall backwards against the wing. Somehow, he managed to keep hold of Resuza and, in so doing, yanked her up onto the glider.

This sudden shift in weight caused the glider to lurch to one side, but Alfonso gripped the controls with white knuckles and managed to level the glider. He glanced backwards one last time and saw the zwodszay tearing into one another in frustration. There was no sign of Kiril or Colonel Treeknot.

"Egads, that was a close one," whispered Misty.

CHAPTER 38

THE FIERY DEPTHS

THE BRIEF ENCOUNTER with the zwodszay rattled everyone and, for a while, no one in either glider spoke. Alfonso simply focused on maintaining a three-hundred-yard distance between his glider and Hill's. They continued down the fault for another hour or so until Hill's aircraft began to wobble in a strange manner. Alfonso could see Hill yanking furiously at the controls.

Seconds later, Alfonso's glider became just as difficult to handle.

"What now?" yelled Misty.

"I don't know!" replied Alfonso. "I think we're losing speed."

"The wind has vanished!" shouted Clink.

He was correct. The wind current, which had pushed them

along at an even, steady tempo since the Jasber Gate, had suddenly disappeared. The noses of both gliders dipped down and they began to drop toward the thin layer of clouds below.

Hill yelled something and seconds later a parachute came flying out from the tail of his glider. Alfonso quickly followed suit. He yanked a small lever in his cockpit and a parachute deployed from the rear of his glider. This slowed the velocity of their descent, but they kept sinking. They descended closer to the cloud layer and then entered it. Everything turned white, but they soon left the clouds and saw far below them a vast, bubbling river of lava. The walls of the fault were sheer, with no ledges, and there was no safe landing place anywhere. Resuza shuddered at the awful sight. If their descent continued, they would soon fall into the burning stew below.

"It's all over," intoned Clink. He shook his head. "All hope is lost. Even a Great Sleeper cannot make the wind blow."

"D'ya always have t'be so blubberin' negative?" Misty snarled. "It t'aint over yet."

"You old fool of a miner," whimpered Clink. "Don't you get it? Must I explain everything to you? This is Kiril's doing. He must have closed the air vents at the far end of the fault. That's why the wind has died. Kiril has done us in. After all this, he's outsmarted us yet again."

"Ya always got all the answers, dontcha?" replied Misty bitterly. "Well if you was so bloody smart, how come ya ain't figured a way to avoid this? Sometimes, I can't believe we're related."

The two gliders sank deeper and deeper into the abyss of the fault. Several minutes passed in silence. Alfonso looked hopefully at Hill's glider, but he could see by the slouching of his uncle's shoulders that he was out of ideas. The air grew steadily warmer until it became obviously uncomfortable. They started to sweat and their faces took on a reddish glow. It grew so bright that it began to hurt their eyes.

"If you gents don't mind, I'll be taking my coat off," said Resuza. As always, she was keeping her cool, even in the direst of situations. "It's a bit warm for my liking."

"You might as well keep it on," muttered Clink morosely. "We'll all soon be ashes anyway."

Alfonso glanced down. It now appeared as if they were only a mile or so from the lava, which glowed and crackled as terribly as the surface of the sun. It was a swirl of red and orange, laced through with large, slow-moving black ribbons. The heat was so intense that Alfonso's eyesight faltered and he began to see little specks bloom and flicker across his field of vision. He closed his eyes, but the specks became worse. He considered going into hypnogogia, but why? There was nothing he could do. He crouched lower in his glider seat. Every pore on his body pumped out sweat in a vain attempt to cool him down.

Suddenly, Alfonso heard a loud howling. It came from Hill's glider, which was nearby. It was Kõrgu. The wolf was howling so loudly that those in Alfonso's glider could hear her as easily as if she were right next to them. Poor wolf, thought Alfonso. She's probably burning up under that heavy coat of fur.

"Well hold yer pickaxes, lads!" gasped Misty. "Take a gander down below because that surely is the wildest thing I've ever seen in all my days."

Alfonso, Resuza, Clink, and Misty all peered tentatively over the side of their glider and took in an astonishing sight. What they had initially thought were black ribbons of ash and charred matter were actually hundreds of giant birds coasting lazily above the lava. Only they weren't birds, they were magmons. They were going in both directions, like vehicles floating above a glowing highway of lava.

"Makes sense," said Misty. "Them magmons prolly love the heat, bein' that they're reptiles 'n' cold-blooded. They love goin' to the lava to warm their freezin' organs."

"Where'd you read that?" asked Clink skeptically.

"I can't read, you fool," hissed Misty. "It's jus' common sense."

"Have a look at Hill," said Resuza. "Looks like he's got a plan in mind."

They all glanced down. Hill was leaning out of his glider with a long piece of rope in hand. One end of the rope was lashed to the glider, while the other end formed the lasso loop.

"He's not really going to . . ." began Alfonso.

"Yes, he is!" yelled Resuza. "And we better get ready to do the same."

Hill began to twirl the lasso over his head. Alfonso could hear the rope cutting through the air, but the sound was soon drowned out by the massive flapping sound coming from the wings of countless magmons. The magmons seemed totally unconcerned with the gliders. Seconds later, Hill's glider descended directly into a swarm of the flying behemoths. Hill twirled his lasso a final time and then released it. The loop of rope flew through the air and fell squarely on the head of a nearby magmon. It was a perfect throw. Unfortunately, the reptile wiggled its head in such a way that the loop slipped off.

The loop fell and then, quite by chance, hit another Magmon and caught the giant reptile by its left leg. Hill yanked the rope and the loop cinched tight around the ankle, just above its massive claw. The reptile let out an unconcerned harrumph, turned its head to look at the strange thing attached to its leg, and then continued moving steadily onward.

Hill's glider was immediately drawn into motion in the right direction, toward Jasber. The magmon was so strong and powerful that the glider appeared to have no effect on its flying.

Meanwhile, back on Alfonso's glider, Resuza had crawled onto the wing with a lasso in hand. She too was trying to lasso one of the massive flying beasts. She tossed the rope several times and missed on each occasion. Magmons were all around them and they seemed as unconcerned with this glider as they had with Hill's. Then suddenly Alfonso and the others realized that they were no longer falling toward the lava. Improbable as it seemed, the glider was skimming along rapidly toward Jasber, as if the wind had suddenly reappeared only a mile above the raging fire.

"Wh-Wh-Wh . . ." It was all a weakened Alfonso could manage to say. Resuza was slightly more aware of her surroundings. She looked around and realized that the glider was lying on what appeared to be a large smoldering sheet of leather. Apparently, one of the many incredible properties of the wood from the glider was its resistance to heat. To the left and right the smoldering leather undulated in a steady rhythm. And about a hundred feet in front, a rectangular head bent backwards upon itself to look at what had just landed on its back.

"W-We're on the back of a magmon," whispered Resuza. "Look around. They're enormous, bigger than elephants."

Clink and Alfonso stared at the reptile's wings, which had a blackened, charred look to them, as if they had been singed by fire. The eyes in the massive creature's head glowed a sickly yellow.

"Do you think we can step off the glider and examine the creature?" Clink asked. "The scribes of Somnos would pay dearly for a firsthand account of a magmon's skin. Either that or I could sell my story to the newspapers."

Without waiting for an answer, Clink stepped out of the glider and onto the creature's broad back. Looking quite pleased with himself, Clink took a few exploratory steps around.

"CLINK!" shouted Misty. "You're livin' proof that book sense and common sense ain't the same thing. Get back on this 'ere glider!"

"Why?" he yelled back. "I'm just as safe as you are." It was at that moment that he noticed what everyone else had already seen: his leather moccasins were burning up from their exposure to the magmon's skin. Clink let out a shriek and ran back to the safety of the glider.

⟋⟍

An hour or so later, the two magmons carrying the gliders began to fly up toward the cloud layer and away from the blisteringly hot area above the lava field. This was a great relief to everyone. They had been worrying about how much longer they'd be able to tolerate the heat. In comparison, the air above the clouds felt downright wintry, and they all began to shiver. The walls on both sides of the fault narrowed considerably.

Soon a floor of rock appeared directly below, and their view of the lava disappeared. The magmons flew only feet above the ground while about a mile ahead loomed a solid wall of rock.

It was the end of the fault.

Hill detached his glider by cutting the rope of his lasso. He guided his aircraft to the rocky floor. In one seamless motion, the reptile carrying Alfonso's glider shrugged its back. The glider gently flew off and wafted down to the rocky ground with barely any impact. It was mysterious behavior, as if the reptile knew exactly where and how to release the glider. Alfonso wondered if the Jasberians had trained them to do just this long ago. Little else would explain the magmons' ease around the gliders, and their knowledge of where to discharge them. Released from their charge, the mysterious reptiles continued upward until they disappeared into the darkness.

The two gliders had arrived at a final landing station, which consisted of a long runway and a dozen or so old, dilapidated stone buildings. A third glider sat on the runway—evidence that Kiril may have already arrived. Everyone happily jumped onto the solid, rocky ground. Bilblox carried Josephus, who looked terribly pale.

"How is he?" Alfonso asked.

"Not good," replied Hill. "He's been drifting in and out of consciousness the whole time. Why don't you put him down, Bilblox."

Bilblox laid Josephus on the ground.

"Did he say anything about Kiril or Colonel Treeknot?" Resuza asked.

"It's hard to figure out what he's saying," Hill replied. "He keeps muttering something about Jasber, but mainly he's incoherent."

"My friends," said Clink with a sigh. "Of course I share your heartfelt concern for the old historian, esteemed scholar that he is, but in the name of self-preservation, might I ask how exactly we plan to get out of here?"

"Apparently, this is where the Jasber fault ends," said Hill. "I believe this place is called the Terminus. The Grand Vizier told me about a connecting tunnel that led from the Terminus directly to Jasber, but she suspected that the Jasberians may have destroyed it."

"That must be it over there," said Resuza, as she pointed toward the remains of the mouth of a tunnel, which was blocked by tons of rubble.

"It'd take six teams-a miners to move them rocks," declared Misty.

"There must be a way out of here," said Clink. There was more than a hint of desperation in his voice. "After all, we don't see Kiril lurking around and it looks like his glider is here."

"I suspect that Kiril, being a Jasberian, knew how to get out of here," said Hill. He paused and frowned. "Apparently he also knew how to close the air vent that cut off our jet stream." Hill gestured upward. They all looked up and saw two massive vents, one on top of the other, both of which resembled the vents they had seen at the Hub. The lower vent was closed—covered with a series of horizontal copper flaps. Much higher up, they saw the second vent. This one was open.

"Come on," said Hill. "Let's look around and see if we can find a way out of here."

They fanned out to look for any sign of recent activity in the Terminus. It was Resuza who saw something first. Just below the lower vent, the rock wall was scarred, as if someone had chiseled away at it with a pickax. The ground here was littered with pebbles and broken tiles. Resuza bent down and began sifting through these pieces.

"What is it?" Alfonso called.

"There was something on this wall," she said. "Maybe a mosaic or a painting? These pebbles on the ground are colored and shiny. Whoever destroyed it did a thorough job. And the damage looks pretty recent."

Alfonso helped Resuza look through the debris. After several minutes of searching the ground, they collected a number of painted pebbles. They were mostly different shades of blue, although there were scattered greens and reds. Hill and Clink joined them in the search, and it was Hill who found something of greater interest.

Buried underneath a layer of dust and dirt, Hill found a small metal plaque. It was dark and streaked with ribbons of green, oxidized metal. He rubbed a finger over the surface and found the faint traces of Dormian hieroglyphs. After he cleaned the plaque thoroughly, the following markings stood out:

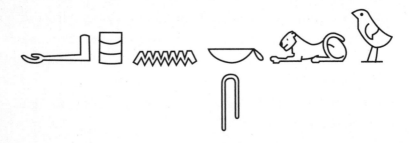

"A New Sailing Route to Jasber," Hill translated. He whistled in amazement. "The map was probably *new* a thousand years ago."

Clink sighed. "That map would've been useful," he said. "So of course Kiril destroys it, just in case we'd have any chance of getting out of here and following him. What a very clever fellow that Kiril is. A truly worthy adversary! First chap that I have encountered in a very long time with the acumen and mental gifts to rival my own."

"The two of you oughta go into business together," quipped Misty. "It'd be less than thirty seconds before one of ya double-crossed the other."

Everyone laughed, including Clink. Alfonso realized that this was the first time in days that he had smiled. It felt good.

Resuza looked up at the closed vent. "I wonder if it's a coincidence that the map was just underneath this vent." Without uttering another word, she free-climbed up the twenty feet of stone wall to the vent and pulled at the nearest copper flap. It was about two feet wide and it moved quite easily, though the on-rushing air kept pressing it back into place. Resuza shimmied herself into the vent through the open flap.

"Wait a minute!" yelled Hill. "You don't know where that leads. Come back!"

But it was too late—Resuza had already disappeared into the vent.

CHAPTER 39

ESCAPE

THE DOOR TO MARTA'S ROOM opened silently, throwing a thin ray of light over her bed. Moments later, the abbot poked his head in. He saw that Marta was in bed, resting. This was actually quite unusual. Typically, whenever Marta fell asleep, she sat at her desk and read. She rarely, if ever, used her bed. The one notable exception was when she had a vision. On those occasions, like today, she was often so exhausted that she simply collapsed and lay motionless for extended periods of time.

The abbot nodded his head and closed the door as noiselessly as he had opened it. He assumed that Marta would be knocked out for many hours; seers, and especially young ones like Marta, often needed as much as a day to recuperate after a vision. The abbot would check on Marta again in about ten hours and, in all likelihood, she'd be the same curious, intelligent child that she had been prior to having the vision of her family and the fire. The abbot was not an unfeeling man. He could well understand Marta's distress. Yet he reminded himself that the ancient codes of the seers had to be followed. There could be no exceptions. Even still, his heart ached for Marta. How much could she be expected to bear?

When the door closed, and the room fell back into a heavy darkness, Marta cautiously sat up, fully awake and dressed. She sat in her bed for a few minutes and listened for any noises. Satisfied that everything was quiet, she glanced at a wind-up clock that she was holding in her hand. It was ten minutes to midnight. She sighed and continued to wait. Other than the ticking of the clock, the only sound was the gurgle of the water chime. Beyond that, she could just barely hear the far-off rumble of Jasber's many waterfalls.

She thought about her time in the monastery. It wasn't fun—that was for certain—but Marta had tried to make the best of it. After all, being the seer was the greatest honor imaginable. Her family was very proud of her. What's more, the citizens of her hidden, treasure-filled city were counting on her to keep them safe. So she did her best and counted her blessings. Overall, life in the monastery had been comfortable. The abbot was kind to her, the food was exceptionally good, and her lifelong curiosity was satiated by the volumes upon volumes of accumulated wisdom that sat in the monastery's rich collection of archives and manuscripts. It was an honorable life. It was a life Marta fully accepted.

Until today.

Marta glanced at her clock again. It was exactly midnight.

The monks who patrolled the shores of Monastery Isle would be changing their shift.

Now was her moment!

She threw off the covers, sprang to her feet, and put on her robe and sandals. She took a deep breath, cracked open the door, and tiptoed down a long stone corridor. Torches flickered every twenty feet and water dripped steadily from an unseen leak.

A minute later, she appeared at the top of a stone embankment that sloped down to the monastery's small harbor. Tied to a wooden pier were half a dozen sturdy rowboats with high gunnels, built to keep out turbulent waters. The boats were all painted a distinctive bright red. Marta had never rowed a boat before, but how hard could it be? She had seen others do it with relative ease. Besides, she only had to go several hundred yards. That's how far it was to cross the river and reach Jasber Isle, where her parents lived. She couldn't imagine what they would say upon seeing her.

Marta crouched behind the embankment and searched for any signs of the monks. The area was deserted. She took a deep breath and then dashed for the harbor. Her dark cloak and small size made her difficult to see even if anyone had been looking in her direction. Soon she arrived at the pier and jumped into the closest rowboat. She untied it and, within seconds, the boat was free. It took only a few strokes before the rowboat exited the harbor and began drifting downriver with the current.

Marta did her best to control the rowboat, but the oars were much heavier than she expected. The current was powerful, and as the turbulent water slammed into the hull of the boat, the tiny vessel shook and trembled. Marta pulled as hard as she could. Her life and the lives of her family depended on her success. She had gone over this route in her head: it was crucial to meet the current at an angle so that the waves broke harmlessly across her bow. A wave hitting the boat broadside might tip it, sending her and therefore her family to their deaths.

Five minutes passed, then ten. Marta's back and arms began to ache. Her hands burned and, in several places across her palm and thumb, she felt the onset of painful blisters. She was panting heavily and despite the cold water that frothed around her, sweat gathered in the small of her back and under her hair. In a moment of panic, Marta looked up and noticed that she was barely halfway across the river. A dark realization began to settle upon her.

She wasn't going to make it.

She struggled mightily for another ten minutes and succeeded in going forward no more than another thirty feet. It was a lost cause. Still, she kept going. Her mind willed her body to move, but it began to ignore her commands. Her arms felt like iron and slipped off the oars.

The rowboat drifted and ran smack into a wave. The jolt threw her to the bottom of the boat. Pilotless, the rowboat and its light cargo were carried away by the swift current. The current took command and smoothly forced the boat downstream, away from both Monastery Isle and Jasber Isle. Marta licked her suddenly parched lips. She crawled into a fetal position at the bottom of the boat, as water broke furiously over the top and drenched her. Her last conscious thought was that she had failed. The tall man with white eyes and the gruesome, coiling scar across his face would succeed in burning Jasber to the ground. Her family would be among the first to die. There was no way to prevent it.

∿

A few minutes later, on the shore of Monastery Isle, a young monk who was on patrol glanced out across the river and, quite by chance, caught sight of a wooden rowboat being pulled downriver. The boat's red color indicated that it had come from the monastery. The young monk squinted into the darkness. Who was in that boat? It was hard to see clearly.

In the coming days, the abbot would question the young monk many times about what he had seen. The monk was hard-pressed to say for certain, but his overriding impression was that the boat was empty.

"But I can't be sure," concluded the young monk during one such questioning. "Although certainly there was no one at the oars."

The abbot thrust his hands into his tunic. He withdrew a piece of parchment he had found in Marta's room, in the former resting place of the Foreseeing Pen. He stared at the drawing of Marta's family and then in a fit of despair crumpled it in a white-knuckled fist.

Where is Marta?

Jasber's very existence lay in the hands of a young girl gone missing.

And there was another matter. The fire. In just a few days, the abbot knew that Marta's prophecy would come true and a fire would sweep through Jasber Isle. People would die. What's more, the fire would start near the house of Marta's family— and near the old armory, where the city's single most valuable treasure was stored and preserved. For a brief moment, the abbot was sorely tempted to share his secret, but soon his sense of propriety returned and he knew that, in accordance with his monastic vows to protect only the Founding Tree, he wouldn't say a word.

CHAPTER 40

THE SEA OF CLOUDS

ALFONSO AND THE OTHERS followed Resuza's lead and, one by one, entered the large vent. Here they found rusted metal rungs that led the way up. In the distance they could hear Resuza's footsteps and, more encouragingly, they could see the faint, murky glow of daylight. Bilblox carried Kõrgu, who appeared quite comfortable and at ease on the longshoreman's shoulders, while Hill managed with some effort to carry Josephus, who remained unconscious. The others carried Bilblox's and Hill's packs.

The walls of the vent were covered with ice and the floor was wet with a constant trickle of cold water. For most of the time, they climbed straight up. Toward the end, however, the vent turned into an incline that they could walk up. At this point,

Kõrgu began walking and Bilblox picked up Josephus. The old historian was pale and his white hair was matted to his damp head. After some time, they caught up with Resuza, and then they all paused to catch their breath.

"What's wrong with him?" Bilblox whispered. "He's so light, and he's shiverin'."

"He's got two fur coats, but he's soaked them through with sweat," replied Hill. "Outside of a few bruises, I don't see anything the matter. Maybe he's got internal injuries. I wish we had a doctor among us."

The others stood or sat nearby in silence.

"C'mon now, let's get goin'," said Bilblox finally. "Can't ya jus' taste the outside!?"

They continued onward and gradually the tunnel changed into what appeared to be the inside of a cave. The walls grew rougher and the ground flattened out almost completely. The skeletons of animals lay scattered across the floor and light green algae began to appear in small patches. A mist of water vapor hung in the air and the darkness began to recede.

When they arrived at the mouth of the cave, a strong wind, flecked with ice and rain, greeted them. At first they saw nothing because they weren't used to being aboveground. As they stood there, waves crashed around them and lapped at the floor of the cave. It appeared that the cave ended at water level. They huddled against the sides of the cave and grew progressively wetter. The way forward was unclear. There were no boats and they certainly couldn't enter the freezing water.

Eventually, Alfonso discovered a series of tiny steps carved into the rock. Shouting over the wind, he showed them what he had found and then carefully began to climb. After about thirty steps up the sheer cliff, Alfonso emerged onto a flat, rocky surface. He looked around and saw that they were on a tiny rock-strewn island no more than two hundred feet in diameter.

Alfonso peered into the gray light of day and stared at the waves advancing on the island from every direction. Farther out, slabs of ice floated heavily, barely visible above the crashing water. A heavy layer of clouds hung so low in the sky, it seemed to Alfonso that he could climb through them with a short ladder. And on the horizon, they saw what appeared to be land or other islands. It was too distant to tell.

"I'm freeeeeezin'!" yelled Bilblox, who had just emerged from the narrow stairway. Josephus was still slung over his shoulder and Kõrgu followed behind. "Where in the name of Ivan Magrewski are we?"

"I assume we're in the Sea of Clouds," said Hill, who was the next to emerge. "Now we just have to find a big island. Supposedly Jasber is on a mountainous island in the middle of this sea. It can't be that far away. Of course that map would've helped." He looked back at the stairway, from which Resuza, Clink, and Misty emerged. The stairway was nearly impossible to see unless you were standing right next to it.

"How's Josephus?" asked Alfonso.

"Still out like a busted light," replied Bilblox. "But he's breathin' steadily."

It began to snow lightly and Bilblox began to mutter. Alfonso scanned the horizon, but saw no indication of where to go, or any possible way to get off the island. It looked as if they were marooned in the middle of a vast icy sea. Alfonso's spirits were beginning to plummet until he heard Misty cry out, "Well, look-e-here!"

346

The old miner had found another set of steps on the other side of the island. It led to a small cave also at water level. Just like the other cave, the entrance to this one was well hidden. Inside they found a row of six sturdy wooden rowboats. The wood was oddly translucent so that you could almost see through it. The boats were provisioned with oars, tarps, and old navigation devices known as sextants. The ground had been recently disturbed and there was obviously room for one more boat. Alfonso and Hill exchanged glances—Kiril had likely found this cache and taken a boat.

"I bet these boats are Dormian-made," said Hill as he ran his fingers over the gunnels. "Look at how light they are! And they haven't decayed at all. I'd wager they were made with wood from the *Arboris pierratus* tree."

"Which way do you suppose we're meant to go?" asked Resuza.

"Probably toward that light," Clink said confidently.

"What light?"

"That one," said Clink, pointing off into the distance.

Clink was right. Flickering on the horizon directly in front of them was an orange light that glowed like a faint torch. It looked to be two or three miles away, but it was impossible to know for sure.

"Let's go," said Clink. "Finally, some adventure in the open sky!"

"Yer crazy!" exclaimed Misty. "Jus' think of it—bobbin' around in that ocean like a buncha frozen ice cubes."

Ten minutes later, they were all piled into a single boat, moving steadily in the direction of the orange light. Bilblox and an ashen-faced Misty were working the oars and Alfonso was navigating. The others, including Kõrgu, sat on the floor of the boat shivering and watching the freezing water pass ghostlike underneath the boat's translucent bottom. On several occasions they collided with giant slabs of ice and almost tipped, but Bilblox and Misty's strength with the oars kept them afloat. As they drew nearer to the light, it became increasingly obvious what it was they were approaching—a towering stone lighthouse. A dozen or so cannons poked out of battlements along the walls. Hundreds of gargoyles glared stonily from ledges along the tower.

They maneuvered closer and saw that two torches burned in front of a portcullis that blocked any entrance into the lighthouse. It seemed to be the only way in. The rest of the stone base was filled with thousands of steel spikes, which made the tower look like an evil porcupine.

"Who wants to knock on the front door?" Alfonso joked.

To everyone's astonishment Clink immediately volunteered. "I'll do it," he said. "Anything this well protected has a lot to hide. *Treasures,* if you catch my drift."

Misty and Bilblox paddled the boat onto the lighthouse island, to an area out of sight of the entrance. From the untouched look of the area, no one had set foot there in recent days, perhaps months. Clink was the first ashore. He splashed through the ankle-height water and onto the pebbly ground. It was covered with great masses of frozen sea kelp. He cursed to himself as he trudged through and sank several feet down.

"This is a fine mess to be stuck in!" he snapped. Suddenly, he stood up straight and stared at a pile of sea kelp in front of him. "Hullo, what's this?" He leaned closer and then began to shout. "Huzzah!" he yelled. "Happy days!"

"What's he carryin' on about?" asked Bilblox.

"I don't know," said Hill. "But we better have a look."

They clambered out of the boat and made their way toward Clink. There, nestled amid the frozen kelp, was the object of Clink's happiness. It was the unmistakable skeleton of a man clad in a leather overcoat, and frayed ropes of cloth. Thick black hair still clung to his skull. Given the man's exposure to the weather, he might have died anywhere from months to years ago.

"Clink, show some respect," said Resuza.

"Oh, I respect this fine man," replied Clink happily. "Just look at what he is about to give me!" Clink knelt down to the skeleton, took hold of an arm bone, and pried off a glittering bracelet that appeared untouched by the passage of time. It was a band of thick silver. Delicate lines of gold and sparkling inset diamonds ran along the length of the band. It had to be worth a fortune.

"Now this is worth the whole adventure," Clink proclaimed. "Can you imagine me walking the streets of Somnos with this bauble! There won't be a woman who'll be able to take her eyes off me!"

"Put it back," said Hill. "It's not yours."

"True enough," replied Clink. He looked at the skeleton lying before him. "But this poor sap can't use it. Tell you what— if he wakes up and demands it back, I'll return it. Otherwise, I'll keep it for a while." With that, Clink set off whistling through the sea kelp, toward the lighthouse.

"Where are you going?" demanded Hill.

"Why into the tower, of course," replied Clink. "I can just imagine what goodies might be inside."

"Wait a minute!" said Hill. "You can't go in alone."

"Of course I can!" replied Clink with a laugh. "You forget, this is my business. I am a thief, a pickpocket, a purse-snatcher, a kleptomaniac, a burglar, a purloiner, a pilferer. You get the idea—I break into places! And I'm always successful because I'm so clever! However, I always work alone. Let me go inside. I'll check it out, secure the premises, and then we'll all have a nice rest."

Clink walked up to the portcullis and knocked loudly on its iron latticework. After a minute of knocking, the portcullis opened with a loud clanking noise. Clink waved a friendly goodbye and disappeared into the darkness of the entranceway.

CHAPTER 41

KIRIL'S HOMECOMING

THE ROUGHNESS of the Sea of Clouds didn't bother Kiril in the least—he simply rowed right through the waves, deftly avoiding the ice as he went. One of the many advantages of being over six hundred years old was that he had centuries' worth of experience to draw upon. Kiril had spent entire lifetimes of normal humans dedicated to the pursuit of various skills. This was part of the reason that he was so good with a sword—he had been wielding one since the Renaissance. The same was true of boating. He had been navigating boats ever since the early 1500s, when he had sailed alongside the famous Portuguese sailor Fernão Mendes Pinto, who explored much of China. Kiril was an expert marksman, a skilled archer, a connoisseur of poisons, a master craftsman, and a scholar of over two dozen languages. He was, in short, a man who had made good use of his immortality.

Kiril had been rowing now for almost six hours, heading due west the entire time, in the direction that the sun had set. When night fell, and the clouds cleared very briefly, Kiril used his sextant to confirm his whereabouts. He was on course. It was all going so well.

For centuries, Kiril had contemplated trying to find his way back to Jasber, but it had always proved impossible. The High Peaks of the Urals were sprinkled with hundreds of lakes. Of course, Kiril had been aware of the legend that Jasber existed on an island in the Sea of Clouds, but how could he have known that the legend was true? After all, Jasber's location was kept hidden even from its citizens. Even if he had known the location, it would have been impossible to know which island was home to Jasber. Most of the islands lay in the Ferramentum Archipelago, where Kiril was currently rowing. It was a cluster of thousands of islands, all of them filled with impassable marshland, razor hedges, and other traps that had caused the death of so many explorers.

The surrounding landscape looked familiar to Kiril, but only vaguely so. Truth be told, his memories of leaving Jasber were vivid but incomplete. He recalled a stormy boat ride—he even recalled how the boat looked and smelled—but he had no recollection of the route that the boat had taken. Fortunately for Kiril, he had found the mosaic map in the Terminus; this had given him all the information he needed to find his way.

Kiril glanced over his shoulder. He was almost there. Just

a mile off his bow he saw a series of sheer, algae-covered cliffs that pierced the waters and rose like a giant mossy tombstone jutting out from the sea. It occurred to Kiril that after centuries of wandering the globe, he was on the cusp of returning home. He briefly allowed his thoughts to shift to his mother and father.

Although his mother had died outside of Noctos after she and her children had been branded as Gahnos and cast out into the snow, his father, Kemal, had remained in Jasber. Typically, Kemal spent part of the year in the Hub, maintaining the Jasber Gate, and the rest of the year back in Jasber with his family. Kiril often wondered what had become of his father. Did he travel to Noctos to search for his family? Did he seek vengeance against those Dormians who had mistreated the Gahnos?

Very occasionally, Kiril allowed himself to wonder what his father would say about the man Kiril had become. Certainly his father would disapprove, but then again, his father had been fortunate. He had not witnessed the slow, agonizing death of his family. Kiril had witnessed this. And this was the kind of thing that changed a person. Kiril knew this, but it could not be helped. *They* had done this to him. The people of Noctos. The Dormians. He could not forget this as much as he sometimes wanted to. And this, of course, was the curse of living for six hundred years in fine health. Kiril's memory was stunningly lifelike in its intensity. He could recall the last breaths that his mother had taken as if it had been yesterday. He could see her face, feel her breath, smell her perfume. It was fresh in his memory. Always fresh. And this freshness was what fueled his undying bitterness. Kiril's only reprieve was exacting vengeance. This was his tonic, his drug. It was one of the few things that made Kiril feel truly satisfied—that and rubbing the ash into his eyes.

As he neared the cliff-hung island that was his destination, Kiril caught sight of something that gave him pause. A heavy fog was rolling in, and visibility was very poor, but Kiril could have sworn that he had seen an empty rowboat drifting several hundred yards off his starboard bow. This was very odd. The Sea of Clouds was an extremely remote and untraveled corner of the world. No one sailed these waters except for fools, bandits, and naive adventurers hell-bent on courting death. What was this boat doing here, so close to Jasber?

Kiril stopped rowing and strained his eyes to see through the fog. The boat reappeared for an instant, and Kiril saw the distinct image of an old woman sitting in the stern. An instant later, the boat disappeared. The fog began to grow even heavier and Kiril knew that he ought to be going. His eyes ached from a combination of nervousness and prickly fear, as if he had just seen an apparition. He was tired and his mind was playing tricks on him. That was the only explanation. "I'm seeing things," muttered Kiril as he picked up his oars and began to row away. "Fatigue always brings out the ghosts."

Kiril navigated his boat into a protected inlet along the coast of the island. The water here was calm, so calm that he was actually able to see his own reflection in the glassy surface. It was startling. His slender, youthful face had turned gaunt, and his raven-black hair was now gray. All this had happened in just a few months. More than anything else, however, Kiril noticed the awful scar along his face. It looked larger and uglier than before. Inevitably, he thought of the man who was responsible for giving him this grotesque mark.

◈

Leif Perplexon was one of the most worthy adversaries Kiril had ever faced. It wasn't because he was skilled with a sword, or a gun, or a weapon of any sort. He wasn't especially fast or strong. But his stamina was *astounding*. Kiril had followed him day and night for the better part of a year as Leif made his way from Alexandria to the Urals. Leif hardly ever rested or slowed his pace in the least. Several times along the way, Kiril lost his trail, but then he always picked it up again. As they entered the Ural Mountains, Kiril's hopes began to rise. He knew that he was on the cusp of rediscovering Jasber. He was close—so close—and then disaster struck. Kiril was following Leif too closely along a series of cliffs and, for some reason, Leif turned around. The two men faced each other several feet apart.

"Who are you?" demanded Leif.

Kiril remained cool, and assured Leif, as calmly as he could, that he meant no harm. He suggested, as was his usual tactic, that he was protecting the interests of Dormia. Leif appeared convinced until out of the blue he charged Kiril. Kiril reached for his sword, but then stopped himself. The whole point was to follow Leif to Jasber, not kill him. A brutal fight ensued. Under other circumstances, Kiril would have been able to subdue Leif easily, but two things were working against him. First, he was exhausted from the walking he had done. Second, there was the fact that Kiril's rations of the purple ash had been cut severely.

He still had the ash in his blood, but not much of it, and he was feeling weak. After many centuries of life, Kiril was slowing down—the grim specter of mortality had reappeared.

At one point, Kiril appeared to be on the cusp of beating Leif. He had managed to bash Leif in the head several times with a rock in the hopes of knocking him out. At the last minute, however, Leif used his long legs to kick Kiril away. Kiril stumbled backwards, fell off the cliff, and landed twenty feet below on a small ledge.

Kiril survived, but Leif vanished.

Weeks later, Kiril was forced to bring the news to Nartam that he had failed and lost their last chance of reaching Jasber. "You have failed me," said Nartam quietly. He drew close to Kiril. He held a dagger in his hand. Kiril sensed what was coming and he braced himself. Nartam took the dagger and in a slow, deliberate motion, he sliced a hideous snakelike gash across Kiril's face. Kiril shuddered in pain. His cheek tore open and blood gushed out. And then something miraculous happened—something that only happened when the magical power of the purple ash was coursing through your veins. The bleeding stopped. The skin around the gash closed. And in a matter of seconds, a purplish scab formed and hardened.

"Däros, Däros, Däros—forgive me!" cried Kiril.

"I forgive you," said Nartam soothingly. "And when we get more ash, I will give you enough so that this revolting scar will vanish from your face altogether, but until then, this scar will mark your failure—and remind you of what we must do *now*."

"Tell me what must be done," said Kiril eagerly. "I will do it."

Nartam nodded with satisfaction and outlined his plan. He began by explaining something that Kiril already knew—

namely, that the Founding Trees of Jasber and Somnos were botanical cousins and their life cycles were roughly synchronized. In other words, when one tree died, the other usually followed suit. It only stood to reason that the Founding Tree of Somnos would soon wither, and, when it did, a new Great Sleeper would emerge in order to deliver a Dormian bloom to Somnos's gates. This new Great Sleeper, explained Nartam, would most likely be a relative of Leif Perplexon. "Don't ask me why this is so," added Nartam. "It has always been this way with Founding Trees that share a life cycle. They summon Great Sleepers from the same family. I have seen it happen several times over the course of my very long life."

"It will be Leif's child?" asked Kiril.

Nartam nodded. "The parent is often called first, and then the child. And you say that he is just a young boy? Excellent— he will be easy to follow. How marvelous, isn't it? For the first time in my very long life, the jewel of Dormia—Somnos—is almost within my grasp."

"I will observe the child in the place where he lives," said Kiril.

"Yes," said Nartam. "Then you must follow him to Somnos and lead our attack on the city. Yet before the city burns, you must obtain something very important—a cannister of Colossal Carpathian fir seeds from the Arboreal Research Vault. I want those seeds," said Nartam very slowly and deliberately. "*Everything* depends on those seeds."

Kiril said nothing for a moment. Then slowly, the realization dawned on him. "You intend to use them to grow a Coe-Nyetz Tree!"

As a boy in Jasber, Kiril had heard the legends about this

tree. It was grown by taking the seeds of a Colossal Carpathian fir and infusing them with the ether from the Founding Tree of Jasber. Only the ether from this particular Founding Tree was powerful enough to do the trick. Once grown, the tree was a monstrosity. It sucked life out of the soil and, instead of spreading life wherever it reached, its root system resulted in devastation. Or so the legend went. No true scholar in Jasber really believed it. The Coe-Nyetz Tree was just a myth—and now he said as much to Nartam.

"It's no myth," replied Nartam with a smile. "I know. I was alive. I was there when Reşze did his experiment and grew his Coe-Nyetz Tree. Much of northern Asia and Europe turned into a vast wasteland. I was living in Barsh-yin-Binder at the time. I still remember how the trees wilted and the crops all turned a sickly gray. The peasants all said that this plague came from the north, from the great Siberian tundra, and so my men and I rode toward the heart of it. Eventually, we found the place where Reşze had grown his Coe-Nyetz Tree. Reşze was a Dormian scientist and a fool! By the time that we arrived he was in the process of destroying it. My men and I tried to save it, but we were too late. Yes, that tree existed once, in an imperfect state. It can again, and this time, it will be perfect. Most important, it will not be destroyed."

Kiril was confused. "But why would you grow a tree like that?"

"Violence in the name of survival can be honorable, even beautiful," replied Nartam softly. "And make no mistake—without the ash, we will die quickly. The Coe-Nyetz Tree produces an endless flow of it. You can burn one of its limbs and, unlike the Founding Trees, the burned limb will grow back. When we came upon its remains, I saw the ash everywhere. There was so much of it that entire fields had turned purple." Nartam leaned in closer and his white eyes gleamed fiercely. "If we control this tree, then we control the entire area that it affects—Asia, even Europe. No more scrabbling like paupers. We would have everlasting life *and* dominion over the riches and miserable lives of those two continents. We will teach the world to ignore us at their own peril."

Kiril nodded. "And the seeds to this Carpathian fir are in the Somnos vault?" he asked. "And you're sure about this?"

"You forget, my son," replied Nartam calmly. "I was once a respected Dormian scholar. I studied the Founding Trees. In my youth I traveled to Somnos and saw these seeds with my very own eyes. They will be there. Rest assured, they will be there."

Kiril nodded his head deferentially, but he seemed unconvinced.

"And what of Jasber?" asked Kiril finally. "How will we get there? In order to grow a Coe-Nyetz Tree, don't you need ether from Jasber's Founding Tree? That was how the myth . . . I mean story . . . that is how it was always told to me. And we've missed our chance . . ."

"You will make amends for your failure," said Nartam curtly. "Once the city of Somnos has fallen, we will excavate the entrance to the Fault Roads. The people of Somnos were never so keen on closing these roads and it should be easy to find a way into them. Then you will guide us through the Jasber Gate. You will take us to your old home. You will help us grow the tree that gives bountiful ash. You shall save us all."

And the plan had almost worked.

Kiril had found Leif Perplexon's son, Alfonso, and had followed him all the way to Somnos. Kiril's army had attacked the city in full force. During the battle, Kiril's trusted lieutenant, another Gahno by the name of Konrad, had raided the Arboreal Research Vault and obtained the proper canister of seeds. But then, at the crucial moment, the Dormians had staged an astoundingly fierce counterattack. Kiril's army faltered and then broke into retreat. In the chaos of that retreat, Kiril stumbled upon Konrad. "Hold on to the seeds," Kiril told him. "I am going back into Somnos."

Konrad looked at him uncomprehendingly. Konrad was short and sinewy, all coiled muscle. His black hair lay wet against his head, and his chest heaved with exertion. "No," he protested. "We're in full retreat. You'll be killed if you go back."

"Perhaps," said Kiril, as he ran a finger along the scar that marred his face. "But perhaps not. I must find a way into the Fault Roads. I *cannot* fail. Not again."

"What shall I do, master?" asked Konrad.

"Find Nartam," said Kiril. "And tell him I've gone after his ether."

The hull of Kiril's rowboat scraped to a halt. Low-lying, gloomy clouds hugged the island, muffling all sound. Anyone else in this particular inlet would have been overcome with a deep melancholy. But Kiril's mood was a strange mix of euphoria and despair. The details of his plan were crystallizing in his mind. He would soon be back in Jasber, walking down the ancient streets. But first he would swing by the lonely cottage at the heart of the labyrinth. He would pay his old friend Leif Perplexon a very quick visit—and finish matters between them.

Kiril stepped out of the boat and drew it onto the pungent dried kelp that littered the shore. A tiny, rust-flecked snake curled around a submerged rock near his ankles. Kiril sighed heavily. In that instant, the image of his mother's face leapt into his mind, and it came with such suddenness that Kiril almost flinched.

"Mother, I have come home with malice in my heart," whispered Kiril to himself. "Please forgive me for what I must now do."

CHAPTER 42

A SURREAL DINNER

LEIF WAS AT HIS DINING ROOM TABLE in World's End, Minnesota. To his left sat his wife, Judy, and his father-in-law, Pappy. To his right sat his son, Alfonso, and his long-lost brother, Hill, who was now a grown man in the very prime of his life. Across from him were his parents, Stephanek and Kata, whom he had not seen since he was six years old, when he left Somnos. All of them were carrying on—talking, joking, laughing, even toasting glasses—as if there were nothing in the least bit strange or impossible about this gathering.

"I say, this is magnificent lamb kabob!" gushed Stephanek. Stephanek looked much older than Leif remembered him. His hair was thinner, his face was pudgier, his eyelids droopier, but there was no mistaking him—this was Leif's father. "I don't know what kind of spices you use, Judy, but they are simply wonderful," Stephanek was saying. "Every time we come over for dinner I think I gain another few pounds."

Leif took a bite of his lamb and realized, at once, that it was the best he'd ever had. He was also overwhelmed with happiness that his parents had met Judy and his son, Alfonso. Tears streamed down his cheeks, but no one seemed to notice.

"I wish Stephanek liked my cooking half as much as he likes yours," said Kata. Leif's mother had barely aged a day. She was a bit thinner perhaps, and a bit grayer, but otherwise unchanged. "You must share your recipes, Judy."

"Of course I will," said Judy with a fond smile. "After all, you're family. I hope you have room for dessert: blackberry tart and vanilla ice cream. Leif, Alfonso, and I picked the berries yesterday!" Judy stood up, but before heading into the kitchen, she leaned over and whispered to Leif: "Someone on the back porch is waiting to speak with you."

Leif smiled. It was probably an old friend. "Please excuse me," he said. "I'll just say hello."

He made his way to the back porch and there, in the moonlight, he found a large hulking man. The man was standing with his back to Leif.

"Can I help you?" asked Leif with a smile.

The man turned around slowly and revealed himself. He was dressed in a simple monk's robe with ordinary features—other than the one very large, bloodshot eye situated directly in the center of his forehead. Leif recoiled at the sight of this Cyclops.

"Well, hello there," said the monk in a friendly manner, as if he were just a neighbor stopping by. "As I'm sure you realize, none of this is really happening. What's more, this is your dream. I really have no business being here, and I certainly haven't come to cause any trouble. After all, I've been dead for a very long time."

"Who are you?" asked Leif. He couldn't stop staring at the monk's eye. It twitched furiously whenever the monk spoke.

"My name is Imad," replied the monk calmly. "Many centuries ago I lived in the city of Jasber. But that is neither here nor there. My interest is in you. I am simply curious regarding your intentions. Will you stay in this ditch below the razor hedges and willfully ignore the world outside?"

"What does it matter to you?" asked Leif sharply.

"It matters quite a bit," replied Imad. "I must say, I'm surprised that a Great Sleeper like you would give up so easily." Imad clucked his tongue. "Such a disappointment."

Leif took a deep breath. He sensed that Imad was manipulating him, trying to draw him out of his dream and back into the labyrinth. But why?

"Do you know what's coming?" asked Imad pointedly.

Leif made no reply.

"A cataclysm," continued Imad matter-of-factly. "All of Europe and Asia will suffer terribly—to the point of extinction. It will be the end of life as you know it. It will be the World's End."

"Why are you telling me this?" asked Leif.

"Because," replied Imad, "you are among the few who can stop this from coming to pass."

"What makes you so certain?" asked Leif.

"Once, many centuries ago, I wrote a prophecy with the aid of a magic pen," explained Imad. "The prophecy was not comprehensive, it did not foretell everything, but it foretold of this cataclysm. And it foretold that only a man by your name and his son could stop this from happening."

"His son?" inquired Leif.

Imad nodded.

"You must be mistaken," said Leif. "My son is just a young boy, a child. Besides he is far away—in Minnesota—with his mother."

"No," Imad replied simply. "Your son is actually quite near Jasber, and drawing nearer by the day. And I am afraid he is not safe. His bravery and his love for you have goaded him to take many risks."

"The World's End," whispered Leif.

"Yes," replied Imad. "Alfonso will try to stop it—with or without you—but he will not succeed on his own." The terrifying monk stared at Leif. "Enjoy your blackberry tart," he said, and then strode off into the darkness.

When he finally woke up, Leif was lying on his back in the dark. He groaned through parched, cracked lips. The air was warm and rank. He leaned up on one elbow and pushed his tired brain to think. Above him was a dirt ceiling, its outlines barely visible in the darkness. And outside . . .

Then he remembered. Outside were the snow-covered razor hedges, the glistening red berries, the cottage in the middle of the labyrinth. And beyond this was the world at large—the real world.

Someone stirred nearby. It was Zinedine, the failed Great

Sleeper. "Finally, you are awake," said the North African. "I have wanted to take another berry, but first I wanted to see where you had traveled to in your dream. Was it a pleasant place? Did you see your family?"

Leif sat up and rubbed his dry eyes. "H-How long have I been here," he asked.

"Several days, maybe a week," replied Zinedine. "I was in the Atlas Mountains! You should have seen my son. He is now a man. No matter, I will describe him to you. But first, tell me, did you enjoy the dream? Wasn't it nice?"

Leif did not reply. Instead, he turned and clawed his way out of the foxhole and back to the snowy surface of the labyrinth.

"Don't leave me!" yelled Zinedine, his muffled voice hoarsely echoing through the labyrinth. "We are friends now! Where are you going?"

There was only one answer to this question. Leif had wasted precious days and already he felt an overwhelming urge to try another berry. He shook his head violently. That was finished. If he was to press on, if he was to escape the maze, then he needed more supplies. He needed to restock. And that meant returning to the cottage at the center of the labyrinth.

CHAPTER 43

THE LIGHTHOUSE

STANDING IN FRONT OF THE LIGHTHOUSE, Hill seemed oblivious to the breathtaking scenery of ice, rock, and sea that surrounded him. He was fixated on his wristwatch. Clink had now been inside the lighthouse for almost thirty minutes and there was still no sign of him. In Hill's estimation, this long absence meant one of two things: either Clink had stumbled upon a great trove of riches that he intended to hoard for himself or he had met an untimely end.

Misty shifted her weight uneasily. "He's a plum' fool, is what 'e is," she muttered. "Clink's a goner. How'm I gonna tell the rest-a the family about this?"

"I'm sure he's fine," said Hill immediately. The clouds had

thickened and grown darker. A heavy snow had begun to fall, and a paper-thin layer of frost covered their clothes. Hill wondered if Josephus would survive a night in the open. The old historian's breath had turned erratic.

They continued staring at the portcullis until another half-hour passed and the portcullis opened at last. A tall, gangly, gaunt-faced man, dressed in a top hat and shabby black overcoat, stepped out. He cleared his throat, as if to make a formal announcement, and began to shout. "Velcome von et all to the Dlugosz Lighthouze," yelled the man in a very heavy Uralic accent. "I bid you enter. The master vants you come in. You vill be qvite safe."

Hill looked at the others, who were shivering in the cold. He nodded and they all walked toward the man, stopping a cautious ten feet away.

"Who are you?" asked Resuza.

"I am guard, doorkeeper, and butler," said the man. "My name is Sancholowerotamosucholeshtruvonska. But you call me First-Floor Man because I stay on first floor of lighthouse."

"What kinda name is that?" retorted Misty.

"Sancholowerotamosucholeshtruvonska is name of lake in south side Urals where I vas born," explained First-Floor Man. "Translation of lake's name is 'You fish your side of vater, I fish my side of vater, nobody fishes middle so fish can rest.'"

"That's sensible," nodded Hill.

"Very," replied Resuza.

"Come," said First-Floor Man. "Master avaits!" As he walked through the doorway, they all heard a clanking noise. It came from a long chain attached by an iron shackle to First-Floor Man's ankle. The other end of the chain disappeared inside the tower. Alfonso looked inquiringly at Resuza, but they said nothing.

They walked up the steps and through the door of the tower. Bilblox brought up the rear. He carried Josephus, and Kõrgu padded along quietly at his side. The first floor of the lighthouse was a barren, spacious, high-ceilinged room made entirely of stone. Several flickering torches illuminated the room's only distinguishing features—an empty coat rack, a small cot covered in a beaver fur blanket where First-Floor Man apparently slept, and a stairway leading to the floor above. It was reasonably comfortable but still drafty, and Hill hoped that other parts of the lighthouse were cozier.

"You leavfe coat here and go upstairs to meet master," ordered First-Floor Man authoritatively.

"What if I don't want to take off my coat?" asked Bilblox.

"You vill take off coat!" snapped First-Floor Man. "My job is taking coats. You vant me not havf job?"

"Where is our friend Clink?" asked Hill.

"I am butler, not detective," replied First-Floor Man indignantly. "Givf me coats or I begin havfing the anger!"

They each set down their packs and handed their coats to First-Floor Man. As this was going on, Alfonso noticed that First-Floor Man's long chain was bolted to the wall. Was he a prisoner in the tower? Alfonso was trying to decide how to broach this subject when Misty spoke up.

"Why in blazes are ya chained up?" Misty asked. "Want us t'free ya?"

"That iz a crazy idea. Vat are you trying to do? Kill me?"

They looked at one another, confused, and at that moment a familiar voice called down from the second floor.

"Hey, everybody, come on upstairs and enjoy a bit of ale!" yelled the voice. "There's roast lamb and some freshly braised salt cod as well. It's a feast!"

"Is that Clink?" asked Bilblox.

"It sure is," yelled the voice. "But you may have to call me Master from now on!"

They quickly climbed the stairs and entered a beautifully appointed parlor. The walls were made of a well-polished dark red wood and lined with dozens of stuffed and mounted fish. The fish were enormous, likely native to the Sea of Clouds, and they looked primordial. Each one grinned maliciously through either fangs, swordlike snouts, or pointy, razor-sharp quills.

Several large bay windows offered a stunning view of the surrounding seascape. The gold leaf ceiling shone lustrously in the waning light of day. The room was furnished with half a dozen banquet tables, several bearskin rugs, and a long wooden bar behind which was a walk-in pantry stacked with bottles of wine and barrels of ale. At the far end of the room, a fire crackled in a large stone hearth and warmed a steaming caldron that smelled deliciously of lamb, apricots, sage, and nutmeg.

"Make yourselves at home," said Clink, who sat at one of the banquet tables wearing a starched napkin around his neck. He was devouring a plate full of lamb and salt-crusted cod. "The lamb is excellent, and the cod is unlike anything I've ever tasted before."

Seconds later, a burly, rosy-cheeked, blond-haired man popped up from behind the bar. The man wore pants and a matching vest made of animal fur and he held a bottle of red wine in each hand.

"Good news! I think I've found that vintage cabernet for

you, Master," said the man cheerily in a crisp English accent. "It ought to go just splendidly with your lamb."

The man walked toward Clink's table with the two bottles. As he walked they heard a scraping noise. He too had a shackle around his ankle and was chained to the wall with a much shorter chain of roughly thirty feet. After placing the bottles on the table, he whispered loudly to Clink.

"Now that your colleagues and friends have arrived, shall I proceed with the champagne? I have a splendid Chateau de Compostelle that should do quite nicely. Your choice of either rosé or blanc de blanc."

"Uh, excuse me," said Hill in a baffled voice. "Can you tell me what exactly is going on here?"

The man bowed with a graceful, practiced air. "Kind visitors, my name is Second-Floor Man and I am the official cook and bartender. As esteemed friends of our new master, I bid you welcome. Luckily, I keep a few dishes ready just for these types of unexpected opportunities. Would you be interested in a light repast? I assure you that this is only to tide you over for a few hours until I can whip up something more proper, as befits your high station."

Hill looked at the others before addressing Second-Floor Man. "We'll certainly welcome some food and drink," he said.

"Why are they calling Clink 'master'?" Bilblox whispered.

"We'll figure that out later," whispered Resuza. "Right now, let's eat. I'm famished."

They all sat down next to Clink, who was grunting in appreciation as he shoveled the steaming hot food into his mouth. Bilblox laid Josephus down on a nearby couch and covered him with blankets. The old historian seemed more comfortable, and

371

appeared more asleep than unconscious. Bilblox joined the others, who were waiting with an expectant air while the delicious smell of warm food filled the room. Soon they were eating heartily as Second-Floor Man looked on with an air of professional attention.

"Ain't anyone around here got a normal name?" asked Bilblox in between chews. "Why are ya called by your floor, instead of a real name?"

"A fine question," declared Second-Floor Man, who was serving Misty extra slices of salt-crusted cod.

"Our previous master, Master Wilhelm Groh the Fourteenth, may his soul rest in peace, was an old-fashioned sort who didn't believe in getting too chummy with the servants. And I rather agree with him. He was *exceedingly* cultivated. The Lady Groh, who most sadly succumbed to the whooping cough several years ago, was an Englishwoman and therefore a stickler for protocol—matching teacups, silverware just so, beds tucked in, and everybody speaking the Queen's best English all the time. You know the type I'm sure. Anyway, the Master and Lady felt it was best—most professional that is—if we addressed them as Master and Lady, while they addressed us according to which floor each of us worked on. It all works out rather nicely, especially since First-Floor Man and Third-Floor Lady have such exceedingly long Uralic names." His voice grew softer. "You know, First-Floor Man is actually married to Third-Floor Lady and—even though they are husband and wife—they still use their professional names."

"There's a Third-Floor Lady?" asked Resuza.

Second-Floor Man nodded and, a moment later, a woman's

voice from the third floor bellowed down to them. Apparently, she had been standing at the top of the stairs and listening to their conversation.

"I am maid and houszekeeper," yelled the voice, which bore a heavy Uralic accent. "Real name is Swonighzezledkinflorij-kluzhba—means 'Being clean isz better than being pretty especially if you weren't born pretty.' I only hope they'vfe been keeping clean down there. On account ahvf my chains, I only clean turd floor. Don' worry! Is moszt important floor. You are to be sleeping moszt soundly up here!"

"All three of you are chained up?" asked Alfonso.

"Indeed," said Second-Floor Man cheerily. "First-Floor Man has an especially long chain so he can go outside, around back, do a bit of gardening, and tend to the livestock as well. The chains are really for our own good, you know? Now, would you care to try some wine with your lamb, or perhaps the preference is for ale, on account of the weather? Something tells me that the large, strapping gentlemen—Bilblox, is it?—might care for some ale."

"Ale would be nice," replied Bilblox.

"Dark or light?"

"Dark," replied Bilblox.

"A bit of ale for your wolf as well?"

"She's a seein' eye dog," replied Bilblox. "And she'd love some lamb. Probably some ale too."

Kõrgu growled in agreement.

"You're chained up for your own good?" inquired Resuza incredulously. "What on earth are you talking about?"

"Oh, my dear lady, I know what you are thinking," said

Second-Floor Man as he gave Bilblox a brimming tankard of ale and provided everyone else with wine. "But we are not prisoners. Quite the opposite actually. You see, these chains keep us free. In the past, servants here at the lighthouse have been tempted to leave, but when they do, they are invariably waylaid and killed by the sorts of villains who inhabit this lonely corner of the globe. These chains remind us of the world outside, and why we never leave the security of the tower. I count my lucky stars that we are chained up and that the chains have held over the years."

He looked out the window. They followed his gaze and saw that the weather had turned worse, and a blizzard raged across the ice-filled waters. Second-Floor Man turned back and continued. "The Sea of Clouds is absolutely lawless, scattered with bands of criminals, pirates, and slave traders. That's why it's such an event when cultured visitors, like yourselves, come to visit. Sea of Clouds is one of the largest inland seas in the Urals and, without question, the hardest to reach. Its waters are filled with bizarre and enormous fish, perfect sport for the fisherman! Of course, there are also countless islands in this particular sea. Just nearby is the Ferramentum Archipelago, a cluster of thousands of islands, all of them brimming with razor-sharp hedges and utterly devoid of anything useful. More than a few of them are inhabited by pirates and slavers who recognize other attributes, namely, that the area is a perfect place to hide."

Second-Floor Man paused a moment and looked around. "A bit more ale, Mr. Bilblox? You seem quite thirsty."

"That'd be nice," said Bilblox with a burp, "though I wouldn't mind trying the light ale."

"Certainly," said Second-Floor Man.

"I think you'll like the light ale," said Clink with a smile. "It's really my best stuff."

"Wait a minute," said Alfonso. "If everyone is locked up, how do you ever see one another?"

"Ve don't see von another," yelled Third-Floor Lady. "That is how marriage lasted. You think I vould be married turdy-four yearsz if I had to see First-Floor Man evfery day? Ha! Never!"

"It can be a bit trying at times," said Second-Floor Man. "Of late, both seem to be hard of hearing, which can make relaying messages difficult."

"I hear vell enough!" yelled both First-Floor Man and Third-Floor Lady at the same time.

"Of course," yelled Second-Floor Man with an exasperated air. He looked at the group. "Perhaps now that we have a new master life may be a bit cheerier."

Hill cleared his throat and half-smiled at Second-Floor Man. "I've been meaning to ask you . . . Why are you referring to Clink as your master?"

"Because he wears the master's golden bracelet," explained Second-Floor Man matter-of-factly. "The deed to this lighthouse clearly states that when the master dies he passes on ownership by giving the bracelet to his heir. And now we welcome the Right Honorable Lord Clink to his rightful home!"

"And you think Clink's honorable?" asked Misty with a mischievous smile.

"No matter, I am the heir," declared Clink proudly. "I have the bracelet and this is how the old master would have wanted it."

Bilblox shook his head. "I'll take another refill on the ale," he said.

"Certainly," said Second-Floor Man.

"How old is the lighthouse?" asked Alfonso. "It looks ancient."

"The lighthouse portion was built in the seventeen hundreds by a Kazakh king named Abul Khair Khan," said Second-Floor Man. "Later it was used as a way station for gold miners who were mining one of the nearby islands. And then, in the late eighteen hundreds, it was taken over by the Groh family and converted into a grand fishing lodge. I can't say exactly how old the foundation is, but quite old—several centuries for certain."

"Oh it's a great deal older than that," Josephus weakly interjected. For the first time since they had saved him in the Fault Roads, the old historian was awake and somewhat lucid. He was now sitting up on the couch and looked feverish, but alert. "I am sure this structure was built and rebuilt many times," continued Josephus shakily. "But the original foundation is probably well over four thousand years old."

"Josephus," said Resuza nervously, "are you all right?"

"Far from it, my dear," he said with a rather sad smile.

"Would you like some food?" asked Second-Floor Man.

Josephus shook his head sadly. "I'm afraid I have no appetite," he said tiredly. He looked at Second-Floor Man. "The cellar in this lighthouse—is it long and rectangular and on each end are there several deep holes in the stone, like inlaid buckets?"

Second-Floor Man looked astonished. "How did you know that? In thirty years, only myself and First-Floor Man have ever set foot down there."

"Just a hunch," replied Josephus. "That's an old Jasberian cellar, and the holes are used for storing vegetables. I'm sure you find them quite useful; they're perfect for preserving freshness during the long winter months." He looked at the rest of them and shook his head wearily. "I've been studying Jasber my entire life. The lighthouse itself isn't Jasberian, but the foundation is. I remember reading about several outposts built on islands throughout the Sea of Clouds. There were once five guard towers for Jasber."

"Jasberian?" replied Second-Floor Man. "What a strange name. Is it an old slave trading tribe?"

Josephus shook his head. He suddenly looked as if he might pass out at any minute. "There should be an island nearby," whispered Josephus hoarsely. "It has sheer gray cliffs that rise out of the water. On the top of the cliffs are thick razor hedges. Do you know the island?"

"There are thousands that fit the description in the Ferramentum Archipelago," replied Second-Floor Man. "It's within a day's sail of the lighthouse, although once you arrive in the area you could be sailing there for years before you find the right place. Do you have any other information about what the island looks like?"

Josephus shook his head sadly. "That's all I know," he replied in the softest of voices. "I-I thought that . . ." But the old historian never finished his sentence. He collapsed suddenly into the couch.

"We need to get him into bed," said Hill with great urgency.

"Is he alive?" asked Clink.

Hill raced over to where Josephus was lying and took his pulse.

"Just barely."

CHAPTER 44

SECRETS IN THE NIGHT

JOSEPHUS WAS QUICKLY TAKEN to a bedroom on the third floor and he remained there, tossing and turning in his sleep, muttering incomprehensibly. Hill stayed by his side most of the time and cooled his feverish forehead with a wet cloth. By nine o'clock that evening, the others had also made their way up to the third floor. Everyone was in dire need of rest. As much as they wanted to press on for Jasber, they simply couldn't resume their quest until the morning. They were too tired, and besides, it hardly seemed right to leave Josephus in this condition.

Most of the traveling party was euphoric at the thought of sleeping in a bed. After being underground for so long, in such desperate conditions, the idea of a bed and thick blankets was almost too wonderful to imagine. Upstairs, Alfonso and the others met Third-Floor Lady—a squat, round woman, with closely cropped white hair, a wide smile devoid of teeth, and a large white-haired mole in the middle of her forehead.

"I've nize rooms for you, but you havf to share," she said. "Come, come, I vill show you." Third-Floor Lady walked walruslike to each of the rooms as they trailed behind. Bilblox, Clink, and Kõrgu shared the master bedroom; Hill and Josephus were in the large guest room nearby. Alfonso was given a tiny room farther down, while Resuza and Misty's bedroom was Lady Groh's former dressing room on the other end of the hallway.

Alfonso's room was dominated by a large fireplace crackling with a blazing fire, and a bay window overlooking the icy seas. This far up, he could barely see the water below, and it felt as if he was in the middle of the clouds. Every so often, plumes of iced mist would crackle menacingly against the bay window. Despite being in a warm and cozy room, he wasn't able to fall asleep. He tried to shake off a sense of foreboding. Was his father alive? Where was Kiril? Would they find Jasber? The questions tormented him and kept him awake.

Eventually, Alfonso got out of bed, sat down in a small chair near the fire, and took out his dad's book about Alexandrian architecture. The familiar yellowed paper and Leif's handwritten notes calmed him down. Alfonso stared at the fire and relaxed enough to think happier thoughts and to imagine the future: he and Leif returning triumphantly to World's End. They'd work together in the greenhouse, and they'd joke about their sleeping-selves. Maybe they'd work on delving deeper into hypnogogia. As he closed his eyes, Alfonso thought of the thick forests around World's End, the mournful calls of the loons, and the delicious warmth of waking up late on a Sunday. He thought back to when he was eight or nine, and his dad's large hands gently shook him awake after a long, comfortable sleep. It was so luxurious to be in a warm house and to be protected and loved. Alfonso stared out the window as the fire warmed his legs. He sighed deeply and turned to crawl back into bed.

At that moment, a scratch and low whine came from the door. Alfonso yawned, stood up, and opened the door to let Kõrgu inside. The enormous wolf padded softly inside and raised her alert snout toward Alfonso, who began to scratch on the undersides of her furry neck. Kõrgu let out an appreciative whoof and settled down by the fire next to Alfonso's chair. Suddenly hungry again, Alfonso took out a heavy plate of food wrapped up from supper and began to eat. He fed Kõrgu as well, and the two of them sat there happily eating a second dinner.

After a few minutes, there was a light knock on the door.

"Who is it?" asked Alfonso.

The door opened and Resuza entered. She was carrying two steaming mugs. "I thought you'd still be up. I can't sleep— Misty is snoring up a racket. You want some hot chocolate?" she asked.

"Where did you get that?" asked Alfonso.

"Second-Floor Man prepared them," said Resuza. "You know, I could really get used to living in this place."

"Tell me about it," said Alfonso as he took a mug from Resuza. He took a sip and tasted the darkest, richest, and most delicious gulp of hot chocolate that he'd ever had. They both sipped their drinks and, for a few minutes, the only sound was the crackle of the fire and the distant crashing of the waves.

"It's pretty cozy in here," said Resuza.

"Yup," said Alfonso. "I know we have to leave but I'm not looking forward to it."

"Me neither," said Resuza. "I have this bad feeling, like something terrible is about to happen to us."

Alfonso stared at her for a moment and remembered his strange dream in Somnos about Resuza and Hill.

"What?" asked Resuza.

"It's weird," said Alfonso finally. "I have the same feeling."

"Well, there's nothing we can do about it so . . ." began Resuza.

"There is one thing," said Alfonso suddenly. He turned around, reached into his backpack, and pulled out his sphere. He looked at it and then handed it to Resuza. "Hold on to it," he said. "Just in case."

"What?"

"I know that you're almost out of bullets," said Alfonso.

"But I don't know how to use your sphere," protested Resuza. "It's your weapon, as a Great Sleeper."

"You'll figure it out."

"What about you?" asked Resuza.

"I can always enter hypnogogia," said Alfonso. "In fact, when I'm in hypnogogia, I seem to be able to . . ."

"Walk through walls," suggested Resuza.

Alfonso said nothing. He just shrugged his shoulders awkwardly, as if this revelation somehow embarrassed him. Resuza moved closer to him. Alfonso's heart began to thud rapidly.

"You're quite shy and secretive sometimes," she said coyly. "I find that quite endearing." They smiled and stared into each other's eyes. Alfonso suddenly felt out of breath. He became aware of his head moving toward hers. At the same time, her

381

head moved closer until quite abruptly, their faces and lips were only inches apart.

Knock! Knock! Knock!

The door vibrated with someone's heavy rapping. Alfonso and Resuza spun apart and sprang to their feet.

"Who is it?" asked Alfonso. His face was flushed.

"It's me," said Hill. "Come quick—Josephus wants to talk to you."

Alfonso and Resuza exchanged glances. That didn't sound good. Alfonso opened the door. Hill stood there with a grave and deadly serious expression on his face. He nodded sadly at both Alfonso and Resuza.

"Are you ready?" he asked Alfonso.

Alfonso nodded.

They walked to the guest room, where Josephus was lying on a bed facing the fire. At Alfonso's entrance, Josephus nodded and began to struggle to sit up.

Alfonso rushed to his side. "Josephus, don't get up. You should rest."

Josephus nodded and lay back down. His forehead glistened with sweat and he was breathing shallowly. There was a sadness to him that rose like steam off his body.

"Sit close, Alfonso," whispered Josephus. "We must talk."

Alfonso sat in a wooden chair next to the bed. Josephus extended a long bony hand and reached for Alfonso. Alfonso took the old man's hand. It was deathly cold, despite his face being streaked with sweat.

"We must talk before my mind becomes any cloudier," said Josephus. "Y-You see, my entire life, I fought against fear. We Dormians have been under threat from the outside world for

so long that we think being afraid and suspicious is normal—"
He coughed violently, and a thin line of saliva appeared between his lips. "I-I tried to change that. When I learned that
Jasber might still exist, I argued to take a risk! To reach out to
them, using any p-possible means. And if Kiril was the only
way, well then . . ."

"You should relax—" began Alfonso.

"No!" hissed Josephus. "Don't you see—we are out of time!"

Alfonso said nothing.

"I failed to see it," Josephus continued. "I failed to see it . . ."

"Failed to see what?" asked Alfonso.

"The Founding Tree tried to warn us," hissed Josephus.
"Somehow it knew . . . It led you to the hole in the ground . . .
the hexagonal hole beneath the streets . . . beneath the streets
of Paris." Josephus struggled to catch his breath. "Do you know
what those holes are?"

"I didn't at first, but now I think I do," said Alfonso. "They're
holes formed by roots, aren't they? Roots from the Coe-Nyetz
Tree."

"Yes, yes, yes," whispered Josephus. "I didn't see it at the
time, when you first mentioned it, but that's precisely what
they must be. And now the Dragoonya want to grow a new
tree. That's why Kiril is going to Jasber—to get the ether. And
I opened the door for him." Josephus wheezed and then sputtered, "Somnos and Jasber may be spared, our Founding Trees
may offer protection, but throughout Europe and Asia all will
die. It will be another cataclysm. You know what that means?"

Alfonso nodded.

"You need to stop him. *Please*—" The old historian gasped
and then his breathing stopped, like a long, drawn-out sigh.

"Josephus!" exclaimed Alfonso. "HILL!"

Hill ran to their side. Concerned voices cried out in the hall. Alfonso gripped Josephus's hands and tried to make them warm. He was frantic. He knew what was happening, but he refused to believe it.

"Josephus! NO!" Alfonso shouted. He stared at the historian's closed eyes and begged Josephus to breathe again. But he did not.

A sob erupted from Resuza, who was standing nearby. Alfonso looked up and saw Hill, Resuza, Bilblox, Misty, and Clink standing in a semicircle around his chair. Alfonso's eyes filled with tears. A warm hand touched his shoulder. It was Hill.

"May he rest in peace," said Hill.

"Did you hear what he said?" whispered Alfonso.

"Yes," said Hill. His voice was hard, like granite. "We leave at first light."

CHAPTER 45

CLINK'S CATAMARAN

THE FOLLOWING MORNING, a large catamaran cut its way across
the Sea of Clouds away from the lighthouse toward the Ferramentum Archipelago. The vessel, which was both light and
highly maneuverable, skimmed over the water and when it encountered slabs of ice it simply skated directly over them. The
catamaran's two copper-plated hulls were sturdy enough to
withstand this battering from sea and ice, while the boat's three
enormous bright red sails harnessed the howling winds and
powered the vessel forward at a tremendous speed. At times,
the catamaran shot off the tops of curling waves and literally
leapt into the air. Hill, who was fast asleep, manned the tiller
with utter certitude. The others—Alfonso, Resuza, Bilblox, and

Kõrgu—hunkered down in the small cabin suspended by thick rope between the two hulls.

The catamaran, like the lighthouse, now belonged to Clink. The boat had an interesting history. Wilhelm Groh XII had originally purchased it from a Polynesian boat maker who had settled in Copenhagen. This boat maker had been trying unsuccessfully to convince Baltic sailors that the twin-hulled structure of the catamaran (a Polynesian invention) could withstand severe winter conditions much better than the single hull design of European boat makers. Wilhelm took a chance with the boat maker and commissioned a polar catamaran, which ended up being a superb craft, very well suited to wintry conditions.

Wihelm had sailed it himself through the Mediterranean and the Black Sea; he then hired a caravan of camels to take the boat overland, across the Urals, and up to the Sea of Clouds. It had been a good investment. The catamaran handled beautifully in the fearsome winds. It was a gem of a boat and Clink was reluctant to part with it. "Take good care of her," said Clink as they prepared to set off. "She's my favorite boat."

"You just got her," interjected Bilblox. "And you've never even taken 'er out."

"I know," said Clink. "That's why I'm so nervous about loaning her to ya."

Clink and Misty had decided to stay at the lighthouse until Alfonso and the others returned from looking for Jasber. The lighthouse would serve as a home base for the expedition and the cousins would be there to help Alfonso and the others when they returned from their journey. Clink and Misty's first order of business would be to ensure that Josephus had a proper burial. Clink explained that when this was done, he would "just look around."

"Don't ya worry, we'll stay put, Mr. Foreign Minister," Misty told Hill. "That cuzin a mine s'only interested in food 'n' riches, and he's got both in ample supply if he stays here. Jus' think of it, all these people waitin' on him hand 'n' foot." From the twinkle in Misty's eye, it was clear that she was also looking forward to the hospitality of the lighthouse's servants, especially the saffron-spiced mutton stew that Second-Floor Man was already preparing.

The catamaran cut its way across the icy waters and, by midday, it reached the Ferramentum Archipelago. The skies were still overcast and the air was as frigid as before, but the wind had become less violent, and they sailed calmly among countless islands. Some were tiny and barren, similar to the spit of rock they had surfaced on after climbing through the Fault Roads' air vent. Others stretched on for miles and featured sheer cliffs the color of cement but with tufts of green nestled in every crevice. On many of these larger islands, the land away from the cliffs shone a uniform dark green. These were the razor hedges, impenetrable thickets that prevented any movement farther inland. And somewhere among these islands lay Jasber.

They anchored in the cove of a large island to have a late lunch. Hill woke up, yawned from the strain of sleep-navigating, and joined Alfonso, Resuza, Bilblox, and Kõrgu in the cabin. Second-Floor Man had prepared several thermoses of dark, fragrant tea flavored with wild honey and a few drops of goat's milk. He had also woken up early to bake several loaves of sourdough bread—the starter for the bread had been handed down through twenty generations of the Groh family, he claimed. They had dried pork sausage, as well as dill and tomato salad. It was a feast, and afterward they had to force themselves to continue sailing away from their cozy mooring.

"We'll spend the rest of the daylight looking around these islands, and then we'll hole up in another cove like this one," said Hill. "With our supplies, we have three full days to look around before we have to head back to the lighthouse."

"What exactly are we looking for?" Resuza asked. "The bigger islands all look alike."

"True enough," replied Hill. "We just have to keep our eyes peeled for anything unusual—Dormian ruins, strange rock formations, or, of course, any slight trace of Kiril."

"That's yer plan to find a lost city that doesn't want to be rediscovered?" said Bilblox with a snort. "Count me in. Of course, I can't see."

They all laughed, but Bilblox was right. It wasn't much of a plan and they all knew it.

Alfonso stared at the area around them and listened to the water lapping against the twin hulls of the catamaran. He shivered and tried to shake the sense of foreboding that hovered overhead, just like the never-changing cloud cover.

An hour or two later, they were sailing between two islands on the border of the archipelago and the open water. In the far distance, they could see the warm twinkling of the lighthouse's spotlight. As they rounded a turn back into the archipelago, Resuza let out a shout.

She climbed to the roof of the cabin, where Hill was at the wheel, and pointed due north, directly into the mass of islands.

"It's a boat!" she shouted. "I think it's quite small."

The others followed her gaze but could see nothing.

"Are you sure?" Hill said with a half-snore. "My eyesight is much better while asleep and I still don't see a boat."

"Continue straight," she ordered. "You'll see it soon enough."

"Hmm," said Hill. "What if it's pirates?"

"Too small for that," replied Resuza. "It looks tiny, like a rowboat, and I think there's only one person aboard."

Several minutes later, others saw what Resuza had first glimpsed: a tiny vessel floating aimlessly between a number of rocky islands. Hill navigated the catamaran until they pulled up alongside. Bilblox threw out the anchor and they came to a complete stop.

Alfonso and Resuza peered over the rail of the catamaran to get a better look at the rowboat. Slouched motionless across the belly of the boat lay an elderly woman wrapped in a brown cloak. She was ancient. Her face was so wrinkled that it appeared shriveled like a prune. Her stringy white hair was matted and knotted, and her pointy chin sprouted quite a few whiskers.

"It's an old woman," yelled Alfonso. "I think she's unconscious."

"Oh dear, just what we need," muttered Hill. "She's alive?"

Alfonso nodded. He lowered himself onto the hull nearest the rowboat. From there, he hopped lightly into the small craft and made his way to the old woman. Very gently, he grasped her shoulders.

"Ma'am, are you okay?" he asked. "Is everything all right? What happened?"

After a few seconds, the old woman began to stir and whispered something inaudible. Alfonso drew closer, so close that his ear was just a few inches from her mouth. She whispered again. Alfonso looked up at the others.

"She's speaking Dormian," he announced. "She's got a strange accent, but it's definitely Dormian."

"What is she saying?" Hill asked. "Does she know the way to Jasber?"

"She said she has to find her mom and dad."

Hill looked confused. "She's way too old to have living parents," he declared.

Alfonso asked her if she knew the way to Jasber.

The old woman ignored this question and instead pointed toward the clouds and asked a question of her own. "What's that?"

She was obviously delirious.

"That's the sky," said Alfonso. "The sky is covered with clouds."

"Amazing," replied the old woman. "I've only seen it in picture books."

Alfonso shivered and realized that the sun was beginning to set. It was time to make for shelter.

"I'm afraid we have to get going," said Alfonso. "Can I help you into our boat?"

The old woman stared at Alfonso, as if she were only now seeing him for the first time. Her eyes were a cloudy gray, only slightly darker than white.

"I know you," she said softly. "You're the boy who floats above the flames."

"What?" said Alfonso.

"Come on!" yelled Hill from up above. "The wind is picking up—let's get her aboard! Maybe she'll make more sense after some food and water."

"I'm sorry, ma'am, but we're in a bit of a rush," said Alfonso.

"Yes, I know," said the old woman, as she rose to her feet with surprising vigor. "So am I."

After boarding the catamaran, they quickly gave her some water and a little food, but this did not help. She refused to speak and instead just stared at her hands, as if she didn't recognize them.

"I'm sure she's just exhausted," said Hill. "Let's find somewhere secluded to lay anchor. We'll try again later."

Bilblox drew up the anchor and they set off. The instant they began to move, the old woman did something quite strange. Before they could stop her, she had climbed the main mast and huddled in the crow's nest. She began to point insistently northeast, but would not respond to any of their questions or commands. She looked increasingly frantic, as if she were suddenly in a great hurry.

"I don't know about this," said Resuza. "It could be a trap."

"Nope," said Bilblox confidently. "That ol' bird ain't gonna double-cross us. I got a good feelin' about 'er."

"She speaks Dormian," said Alfonso. "Besides, what other choice do we have?"

Hill gripped the tiller and nodded back to sleep, and the catamaran shot forward in the direction the old woman was pointing. The sun continued its quick descent into the horizon. Soon, they were in near darkness. It was time to lay anchor, but the old woman continued to point northeast. The sun set and, an hour or so later, a full moon rose. So they kept going deeper

391

into the maze of islands, losing all sense of time and place, until the woman lowered her hand and uttered a small cry.

"Now what?" asked Bilblox.

"There," said Resuza. "Look in that cove."

They were passing by another series of high cliffs. Nearby was a small cove bordered on three sides by the cliffs. It looked like the perfect place to lay anchor for the night. It was fully illuminated by the moon, which glowed brightly overhead.

Alfonso peered closer. Something in the cove didn't belong there. It was shiny and lying on the beach. Hill maneuvered the catamaran closer. Within minutes, they came quite near to what Resuza had spied. It was a rowboat with a translucent hull. In fact, it looked exactly like the boat they had used to row from the rocky island to the lighthouse.

"Kiril," whispered Resuza.

They immediately looked around and scanned the high cliffs. There was no sound or movement.

"At long last," whispered Hill. "The island of Jasber."

At that moment, the stillness of the night was broken by a loud splash.

CHAPTER 46

BATTLE AT THE GATE

"GET YOUR WEAPONS!" yelled Hill.

After a moment of furious panic, they stood on the deck of the catamaran, weapons ready.

"Where's the old woman?" asked Resuza.

They all looked around. She was nowhere to be seen. Then, all at once, they saw a figure sprinting across the rocky beach toward the cliffs. It was a redheaded young woman, perhaps twenty years old, dressed in a brown cloak. When she reached the cliff, she began climbing up a series of narrow steps and toeholds that had been carved into the rock face. They watched her dumbfounded as she nimbly scaled the cliff.

"Where did she come from?" asked Hill.

No one answered.

"That's bizarre," said Resuza. "The old woman. She's gone."

The group was frozen with confusion. The red-haired woman was quickly making her way up the cliff, while somehow, the old woman had disappeared.

"I-I—" Hill paused, utterly befuddled.

"I suppose we should follow that woman," said Resuza.

They nodded and sprang into action. It took just a few minutes to drag the catamaran onto the shore and secure it. They ran to the cliff base where the mysterious, redheaded young woman had started. Up close, the hand- and footholds were more apparent, although it still took nearly a half-hour of steady climbing to reach the top. Bilblox went first, despite his blindness. It was an incredible thing to see. Kõrgu lay placidly on his broad shoulders as the longshoreman-turned-smuggler moved up the sheer cliff face.

Standing on the cliff, he yelled for them to hurry; he had smelled the onset of a winter storm. "Trust me," he shouted. "Longshoremen have a sixth sense for weather." Sure enough, it began to snow when they were three-fourths of the way up, and their clear visibility from the moonlight was replaced with a ghostly mist.

At the top of the cliff, they had their first glimpse of the razor hedges. It was a massive barricade, around one hundred feet high, made up of thick interlocked branches. There were a few scattered green leaves, but mostly it was branches and thorns colored a dull brown. Some of the thorns were small like those on rosebushes but others were as long as three feet and curved like the swords of Cossacks. Many of the branches were cracked and broken from exposure to the elements, but the thorns were all in perfect condition, as if nothing could affect their sharpness. The ground nearby was covered with heaping drifts of snow.

"There," pointed Resuza. Her voice was strangely quiet and frightened.

Alfonso followed her gaze and saw the reason for her fear.

It was Kiril.

In the distance he was standing on a large boulder mostly hidden by the twists and turns of the hedges. He appeared to be using his khopesh to cut an entrance through the hedges.

"What should we do?" whispered Resuza, as she dropped to a crouch. The others did the same. "He hasn't seen us."

"He hasn't seen *her* either," whispered Alfonso. Alfonso pointed toward a snowbank just fifteen feet or so from Kiril. There, crawling slowly toward Kiril, was the young, redheaded woman they had followed up the cliff. "What on earth is she doing?"

Slowly, the young woman rose to her feet. She held a long, swordlike thorn in her hand. She paused for a moment, as if to calm her nerves, and then she ran directly at Kiril.

"There goes our surprise," whispered Resuza.

"Come on," said Hill as he rose to his feet and started running forward. "She's going to get herself killed!"

The young woman managed to get within arm's length of Kiril before he finally noticed her and, in one swift motion, spun around and kicked her powerfully in the chest. The woman flew backwards into the snow. Kiril turned around, saw Hill and the others running toward him, and immediately returned his attention to the narrow hole that he had carved into the side of the razor hedges. It was almost three feet deep and just wide enough for an arm. At the end of the hole gleamed a brass funnel on the surface of the wall. Kiril had spent the better part of a day cutting holes into this section of the razor hedges with the sole intent of finding this funnel. And at last, it was within reach. Now he had to act quickly.

Kiril reached into his pocket and took out the small glass vial of the bluish liquid known as dagárgala. It was the vial from the rosewood box found in the Alexandria depot. Kiril uncorked the vial and carefully thrust his hand into the hole through the razor hedges. He moved his arm with the utmost steadiness. There were thorns everywhere and, above all, he could not afford to cut himself. If he started bleeding, in his weakened condition, it might kill him. When his arm was fully inserted into the hole, he poured the dagárgala into the funnel. Not a drop spilled. He had done it. Then, ever so tenderly, he began to remove his arm from the hole. A moment later, a powerful blow knocked him sideways. He fell to the snow and saw that the young woman had recovered astonishingly quickly from his kick and had thrown her body against his. Clearly, he was not as strong as he had been even a day before. A sharp pain radiated from his hand. He looked and saw a six-inch thorn sticking through it.

The woman stood over him with a heavy branch in her hand. Kiril swept her feet out from underneath her and she landed heavily on her back. He looked up and saw the others were about fifty feet away.

A massive rumbling noise came from the razor hedges. One section of the hedges, perhaps twenty feet long, was swinging open like a giant door. The dagárgala had worked! Before him lay the maze to Jasber.

Bam! Bam! Bam!

Resuza was now shooting at Kiril, but after several shots she appeared to be out of ammunition.

Kiril crouched down for cover and hid himself beside the unconscious body of the young woman. He gripped his khopesh and waited for his attackers. Hill arrived first, charging forward at great speed. Kiril lunged into the air like a missile, catching Hill off-guard, and slashed the blade of his khopesh across Hill's chest. Blood coated the blade and spattered Kiril's face. Hill uttered a deep groan and sank to the ground.

Just as Kiril anticipated, Alfonso went directly for Hill, dropped to one knee, and checked to see if his uncle was okay.

At that moment, the rumbling stopped. The gateway leading into the labyrinth was now fully open. Kiril was tempted to flee through it, but he knew he had to hold them off for a few seconds more.

Resuza dashed toward him, followed by Bilblox and an oversize wolf. Kiril swung the khopesh in a powerful arc toward Resuza. She leapt into the air and avoided the khopesh's blade, but landed off balance. In this moment of vulnerability, Kiril floored her with a roundhouse kick. The wolf snarled and leapt at Kiril's neck, but Kiril escaped the wolf's jaws at the last second. At that moment, Bilblox arrived, swung his club at Kiril, and struck the white-eyed man squarely in the chest, sending him backwards almost ten feet. Kiril landed inside the maze itself. Bilblox roared and followed him into the maze, with Kõrgu at his side. The rumbling sound restarted, and the gate to the labyrinth began to close.

"Where's Kiril?" gasped Hill. Alfonso had turned his uncle over so that he was lying face-up on the snow. Blood covered his entire chest and turned the surrounding snow a bright red.

Hill tried to wipe his face, but his arm faltered halfway up and then dropped to the ground. "W-Where is he?"

Alfonso looked up and saw that Kiril was lying face-down in the snow, with Bilblox closing in.

"He's inside," explained Alfonso, "on the other side of the hedges. Bilblox is after him."

"Go after them," whispered Hill. "This is your chance; the door is closing."

Alfonso glanced up and saw that the gate was already a quarter of the way closed.

He shook his head.

Hill raised his head slightly off the ground. "GO," he said with as much strength as he could muster.

"It's okay," Resuza told Alfonso. She had just staggered back to her feet but was bent over, coughing violently. She had gotten the wind knocked out of her, but she seemed okay. Her eyes shone as she spoke to him. "Go on," she urged. "I'll take Hill back to the lighthouse and wait for you there."

The gate was now halfway closed. A noise nearby caught Alfonso's attention. It was the young, redheaded woman. She had regained consciousness and was crawling through the doorway into the maze.

"Hurry now," whispered Hill. "Stop Kiril. Find my brother."

Alfonso took a deep breath and darted through the doorway into the maze.

CHAPTER 47

BLIZZARD

Snow fell thickly on the scene where the battle had just taken place. Resuza sank to her knees in the snow next to Hill and examined his wound. It was not deep, but it was long, stretching from the top of Hill's rib cage all the way down to his hip. There was a great deal of blood on Hill's clothing, but it did not appear as if any major veins or arteries had been severed. The real danger, Resuza concluded, was infection and loss of blood. She needed to treat the wound and then patch it up as quickly as possible.

"Can I get up now, my dear?" asked Hill, with a faint smile. "A man my age really shouldn't be lying in the snow. I'm bound to catch a cold." His smile disappeared. "It's so quiet. I'm worried about Alfonso and Bilblox. Even wounded and old, Kiril is a terrible enemy to have."

"We need to get you back to the lighthouse," said Resuza. She glanced up at the sky. Even darker storm clouds had moved in, and the wind had begun to pick up. Visibility would only get worse. They would have to find shelter, and fast. "Do you think you can walk?" asked Resuza.

"Of course I can walk," said Hill indignantly. "Let's get going."

Very shakily, Hill rose to his feet, leaving behind a puddle of blood-soaked snow. He stumbled a bit, and began limping back in the direction of the cliff. Resuza followed closely behind Hill, giving him support whenever he needed it, and watching with dismay as a steady trail of blood dripped after him.

When they reached the cliff, Resuza took a coil of rope out of her pack and fashioned a sling for Hill to sit in. "I am going to lower you down the cliff," said Resuza. "Are you ready for this?"

Hill nodded, winced in pain, and then stepped into the sling that Resuza had made. He maneuvered himself over the edge of the cliff and then Resuza began to lower him as slowly as she could. The whole process took almost an hour.

By the time Resuza made it to the bottom of the cliff as well, a true winter storm was raging. The snow was falling so heavily that Resuza could barely see Hill, who was standing just a few feet away. Sailing would be impossible, especially given that she'd have to sail by herself.

Leaving Hill sitting under a cliff overhang, Resuza searched the area and found a small cave about a hundred feet away, just above where the waves lapped against the shore. She struggled through knee-high snow and helped Hill to the shelter.

The cave was deep, narrow, and well protected from the wind. Best of all, the floor of the cave was covered with several long pieces of dry driftwood. At one point some kind of animal had probably made a nest here, but the animal appeared to be long gone. Resuza helped get Hill comfortable and then she built a fire. The heat felt wonderful and the cave warmed up rather quickly.

As the fire crackled, Resuza rummaged through her backpack and took stock of what she had. Hill must have been pondering the same question because, as she searched, he smiled wanly and asked about their supplies.

"Well," said Resuza. "We have a pot, a knife, honey, a bit of tea, a wool blanket, a needle and thread, some cooking supplies, and a small bit of salted pork."

"What kind of cooking supplies?" Hill whispered.

"Flour, salt, pepper, vinegar, garlic, and oil."

"Wonderful!" said Hill. "And do you have any lint in your pockets?"

Resuza nodded.

"Good, we can proceed," said Hill. He instructed her to boil a pot of water. Next she cut half a dozen strips of cloth from her blanket and then placed these strips of cloth in the boiling water in order to sterilize them. Once the strips were sterilized, she used them to clean Hill's wounds.

"Okay," said Hill. "Now I want you to spread that honey thinly across the length of the wound—it's a natural antibiotic. And then I want you to take the vinegar and garlic, mash it up, and cram that into the wound as well. Finally, stuff in a bit of lint. It'll help the wound seal."

"Are you serious?" asked Resuza.

"Quite serious," replied Hill. "Variations have been used since ancient times to fight the bubonic plague. I learned it in an air force survival course. Can you do it?"

Resuza nodded. It took her the better part of an hour to do everything Hill asked. Hill passed in and out of consciousness. Resuza tried to be as gentle as she could, but still Hill winced quite often.

"Thank you, my dear," said Hill with a kindly smile, when Resuza had finished. "Now I think I shall go take a brief nap and, perhaps, when I wake, we can have a spot of tea." Hill's eyes looked watery and feverish.

"All right," said Resuza. She was worried.

As Hill closed his eyes, Resuza walked to the mouth of the cave to peek outside. The wind was howling, snow was blowing sideways, and visibility was nil. They weren't going anywhere anytime soon. She threw a few more pieces of driftwood onto the fire and then reached into her pocket and pulled out Alfonso's sphere. She doubted that she would be able to use the sphere nearly as well as Alfonso did, but it was comforting to have it, especially given that she had run out of bullets during the fight with Kiril.

Resuza aimed the sphere toward the mouth of the cave and tossed it gently in that direction. It shot out of her hand, veered off to the left, ricocheted off the walls of the cave, caused several large rocks to fall—one of which nearly hit Resuza in the head—and then came back to her outstretched hand.

"Try not to kill yourself," whispered Hill. He was feverish and drifting in and out of sleep.

"I'm afraid I won't be much good with this," replied Resuza. She then held the sphere in the palm of her hand and spun it slightly, just as she had seen Alfonso do. The ball began to glow, and moments later the image of the one-eyed monk flickered across the surface of the sphere. At first the monk was engaged in completely normal activities. He peeled what looked to be an orange, and threw the peels into a nearby fire. However, he soon did something that commanded Resuza's rapt attention. The monk took a blue sphere out of the folds of his cloak that appeared identical to the one she held. The monk paused, nodded as if he had just made an important decision, and then tossed the sphere into a raging fireplace. Resuza let out an audible cry of disbelief.

"What did you see?" asked Hill softly.

"The monk was holding a sphere like this one and tossed it into a fire!"

"Hmm," said Hill. He stared up at the ceiling and pursed his lips.

"What is it?" asked Resuza.

"I just remembered a bit of verse," replied Hill.

"Verse?"

"Yes," said Hill. "The verse that was inscribed on the statue of the Cyclops where Alfonso found the sphere. In the Straszydlo Forest."

"How did it go?" asked Resuza. "Can you remember?"

"I can," replied Hill. He then cleared his throat, closed his eyes, and recalled the ancient words:

This old sphere may be pried.
Many a clever person has tried.
Remember how the Cyclops died.
Through the ear and not the eye.

What exactly does the future hold?
Its many secrets remain untold.
Hidden in the burning hot and biting cold.
Is the key to a future foretold.

"What do you suppose it means?" asked Resuza.

"Well, the first stanza provides the clues needed to unlock the sphere from the statue," replied Hill. "And I suppose the second stanza also provides clues, perhaps clues to revealing its true power."

"Do you think that we are meant to toss the sphere into the fire, just like the monk did?" asked Resuza.

"And then perhaps toss it into 'the biting cold'?" asked Hill as he raised an eyebrow.

"Yes, that must be it!"

"Hmm," said Hill. "My main concern is that the sphere is our only effective weapon. It's a gamble. If we destroy it, we would be defenseless."

Resuza looked at the sphere. She burned with curiosity but had no interest in returning a broken weapon to Alfonso. After all, it was the Great Sleeper's personal weapon. "I don't think we should try," she said.

"I agree," said Hill. "There's no reason to do so, and we're certainly not desperate." He smiled tiredly. "Not yet."

CHAPTER 48

KIRIL'S RUSE

KIRIL STAGGERED down the narrow, snow-filled pathway. On both sides of the path loomed massive walls of razor hedges. He glanced backwards again and was relieved to see that no one was there.

It had been snowing for many hours and even though the maze was protected by branches overhead, quite a bit of snow had gotten through and accumulated in high drifts. Now at last the storm had eased, and in the hours before sunrise, a deep calm had fallen over the maze. It was a calm so complete and so enticing that Kiril was tempted to sit and rest. But he knew he couldn't. If he did so, it would only be a matter of time before he bled to death.

The puncture from the thorn was deep and bleeding steadily.

Kiril had knotted a cloth tightly around his hand to cover the wound, but even so, he was steadily losing blood. In what seemed like only minutes, the cloth had turned red. Under other circumstances, if he were able to visit a modern hospital, he could simply get an infusion of a clotting factor that would quickly stop the bleeding. There were other remedies as well, remedies that he'd been using for centuries. There were certain herbs—like bilberry, grape seed extract, scotch broom, stinging nettle, witch hazel, and yarrow—that could be used by hemophiliacs to help them make their blood congeal. But none of that was available. The only thing that would save him now was the green ash of the Founding Tree of Jasber.

There was also another matter. Kiril was fighting off the temptation to eat one of the red lotus berries that grew on the hedges. Of course, he had taken some Uralian nightshade with him—and this herb could be used to break one's addiction to lotus berries—but it was an unreliable remedy. Kiril had neither the time nor inclination to take chances.

As he walked onward, he felt near death. The fight at the gate had taken a serious toll. Still, he was disciplined enough to sop up the blood to ensure he wouldn't leave a trail. His fevered mind thought of the person who taught him everything he knew about the razor hedges—his father, Kemal Spratic.

As a young man, Kiril's father had served as a labyrinth sweeper. Being a labyrinth sweeper was a highly coveted position in Jasber. These were the elite, the hardy few tough enough to fight off snow snakes and clever enough to deal with any intruders who had found their way into the maze. Kemal had distinguished himself in his service as a sweeper and this seemed to prove to everyone, especially the elders of Jasber, that he was capable of running the Jasber Gate, which he ultimately went on to do.

At one time, when he was still a boy, Kiril himself had entertained the fantasy that he too would be a labyrinth sweeper. Throughout the early years of his childhood, Kiril begged his father to tell him stories about the labyrinth. Kemal Spratic was a serious man, but he loved his son and therefore each night at bedtime, he indulged Kiril's wishes and told stories about the two years that he had spent working in the labyrinth.

Kiril recalled one story in particular—an incident when Kemal had almost eaten a lotus berry near the end of his tour of duty in the labyrinth. Typically, a labyrinth sweeper served in this position for two years and, during this time, made a series of month-long journeys through the maze. At the end of each journey, the sweeper was allowed to return to Jasber for a short rest, and then he or she was deployed back into the maze for another month. This pace was grueling and it was made more punishing by the fact that sweepers always traveled alone. Sometimes the sweepers passed one another in the maze, but the maze was so vast that such encounters occurred rarely—perhaps once a day at most. If and when two sweepers encountered each other, it was customary for them to brandish their khopeshes at shoulder height and clash their weapons so forcefully that the clanging sound carried for miles. No words were ever exchanged. This ritual was also a safety measure. If an imposter entered the maze dressed as a sweeper and tried to talk or simply walk past another sweeper, that person would immediately be cut down.

In this particular story, as Kiril recalled it, his father was near the end of his month-long journey and he had not seen another sweeper in many days. A week earlier, he had battled a snow snake and, during this skirmish, Kemal had lost his bag of provisions. Interestingly enough, the snow snakes did not care for human meat. They preferred the various rodents that inhabited the hedges. However, they were starkly territorial and willing to kill anything that disturbed them. The snake that Kemal had fought and vanquished had also destroyed his entire bag of supplies with one gulp and now Kemal was close to starvation. He was stumbling home, one step at a time, but the situation was becoming worse. In a moment of exhaustion, Kemal sat down to rest and soon found himself staring at a cluster of lotus berries dangling just a few inches from his face. Immediately, his mouth began to water as he smelled the sweet, luscious scent of the berries. Then, before he even realized what he was doing, Kemal reached out, plucked a single berry, and placed it on the tip of his tongue.

The consequences of swallowing the berry would be dire: the berry induced week-long comas and was highly addictive. Eventually, of course, another labyrinth sweeper would come upon Kemal. Yet, even then, a sweeper would be compelled to do nothing. According to the ancient code of the labyrinth sweepers, it was strictly forbidden to wake another sweeper from his coma or help break an addiction to lotus berries. Either sweepers were strong enough to do this on their own or they were condemned to remain in a coma forever.

"So I was sitting there with the lotus berry on the tip of my tongue and every sense in my body urging me to eat it," Kemal was fond of saying to his son. "And what saved me was *you*, Kiril, the thought of you. You were just a boy, and so perfect in every way—"

Kiril's reminiscing was interrupted by the sound of approaching footsteps. He looked up and noticed that someone in a scarlet robe was approaching him head-on. It was a labyrinth sweeper. Kiril took a deep breath and reminded himself that he had prepared for this moment. Kiril was dressed in a scarlet robe too, and he carried a khopesh. He certainly looked the part of a sweeper. The labyrinth sweeper drew nearer and Kiril saw that he was an enormous man, perhaps seven feet tall, with broad shoulders. The khopesh that he carried was quite large, almost twice the size of Kiril's. The two of them were now just ten paces apart. Kiril brandished his khopesh. The enormous man did likewise. They pulled even. Kiril raised his weapon overhead and whipped it toward the enormous sweeper. There was a deafening clang. Kiril felt tremendous vibrations ripple through his hands and he almost dropped his khopesh. He remembered to keep walking. He took a step and then two more. The open wound in his hand throbbed painfully, and he knew the blood was flowing in a steady stream. He felt weaker by the minute. Still, he kept his discipline. He didn't look back, but he sensed that they were each continuing on their respective ways. His ruse had worked.

Kiril kept walking for another ten minutes before stopping to glance backwards. The path was clear. He stared up and saw that the storm had cleared and the moon shone through an opening in the branches. It was time.

Kiril reached into his robe and pulled out a thin slab of rosewood. It was the lid to the box that Alfonso had found in Alexandria. Kiril brushed a hand over the lid, almost lovingly, and examined it closely. It was blank. There were no markings on it of any kind. Then he held it up so that the moonlight shone on

409

the surface of the lid. Over a period of several seconds, the moonlight caused an intricate map to appear.

It was a map of the razor hedges and it showed thousands of turns and passageways. In addition, there were three distinct markings. The first was of a door at the southern perimeter, which quite clearly was the entranceway to the maze. The second was a large lake at the northern end of the maze, which was Kiril's final destination. The third was the symbol of an X at the center of the maze. The X was glowing very brightly, as if this was where Kiril was meant to go. This had to be the location of the Great Sleeper's cottage. It made perfect sense. Only a Great Sleeper would ever go to Alexandria, take a rosewood box like this one, and then enter the maze. The X had to mark the location of the cottage, the place where all Great Sleepers, like Leif, were supposed to go.

Once he oriented himself, committing his specific path to memory, Kiril considered his next step. Time was of the essence. He was bleeding and therefore couldn't risk further delays. But he would have to pass by Leif's cottage anyway. Why not pay his old enemy a little visit? The very thought warmed him, like a fire on a cold night or a swig of strong spirit in the biting cold.

Kiril shook his head. "Don't be a fool," he muttered. "Your only goal is the armory."

This was true; the real prize was the armory in Jasber. This is where the Jasberians kept their supply of green ash and the canisters of ether from the city's Founding Tree. Of course the ether was his ultimate goal, but the Jasberian ash would likely save his life, in addition to restarting the clock and giving him decades, perhaps centuries, of life. Clearly, he needed to get to the armory as soon as possible. It was the logical thing to do. Still, he could not remove Leif's memory from his head, just as he could not remove the scar from his face.

Suddenly, the wind gusted, rattling the branches and thorns of the razor hedges. Kiril glanced around nervously. He was alone. He placed the rosewood lid back under his robe and continued trudging through the maze.

CHAPTER 49

THE AGELING

JUST AS HE ENTERED the labyrinth, Alfonso tripped over a buried root and fell headlong into a snowdrift. He floundered, swallowed snow, and in a blind panic tried to stand up straight. He assumed Kiril was waiting for him, and Alfonso's only remaining weapon was a small dagger hidden in his left boot. A hand shoved him backwards and when the snow cleared from his eyes, Alfonso saw the barrel of a wooden club poised to strike his face.

"Move and I'll kill ya," growled the man standing above Alfonso.

Just then, Kõrgu bounded up to Alfonso and let out a playful yelp.

"Alfonso?" said the man.

"Yeah, it's me," replied Alfonso.

The club wavered, then retreated.

"For the love of Magrewski, what are you doin' in here?" asked Bilblox. "I thought for sure you was Kiril. Good thing I said somethin' first."

Alfonso struggled to his feet and brushed the snow away from his face. He looked about and saw that he was in the middle of a narrow, snow-filled path, bordered on both sides by walls of thorns. The walls rose eighty feet high, and at the top branches and leaves from either side met and crisscrossed, forming a thick canopy. Swirling flakes of snow angled their way through, but, for the most part, the walls and the ceiling of the labyrinth insulated them from the world outside. Not that this was especially reassuring. They were trapped here.

"Any signs of Kiril?" asked Alfonso.

"No, I tried to listen for him, but he'd already run away," replied Bilblox. "Then I think that lady came rushin' in here. She took off up the trail after Kiril. It was just a minute or so ago, and then you come in and I thought it was Kiril doublin' back."

Alfonso scanned his eyes over the snow. There were two sets of footprints—one small and the other large—and they both headed away from the gate, down the trail, and deeper into the labyrinth. Alfonso took a closer look at the footprints. The large tracks had to be Kiril's, but the smaller ones were too petite to be the tracks of the young woman they had seen climbing the cliff and battling Kiril. They looked like the tracks of a child.

It didn't make sense.

"Come on," said Alfonso. "We better get going. Kiril is wounded and weak. I think we can handle him."

413

After several minutes of fast walking, they saw a clearing ahead and slowed down to approach more cautiously. The path emptied into a large hexagonal space, with five other paths leading in other directions.

In the middle of the clearing stood a little girl. She was wrapped in a brown robe much too large for her and was shivering uncontrollably. It was the same type of brown robe both the old woman and the younger woman had been wearing. As Alfonso and Bilblox entered the clearing, the girl looked at them with a strange, detached curiosity, as if they were animals at the zoo.

"The man with the scar has escaped," she announced. "The wind has blown snow across his tracks."

Alfonso stared at her, dumbfounded. She was right—Kiril's tracks had suddenly disappeared. However, Alfonso was astonished because she spoke Dormian in the same exact accent with the same mannerisms and facial expressions as the older woman they had found in the rowboat.

"Who in tarnation is that?" exclaimed Bilblox. "That sounds like a little girl."

"It is," confirmed Alfonso.

"Does she live in the maze?" asked Bilblox.

Alfonso stared at the girl very closely. "Do I know you?" he asked in Dormian.

"Yes, of course," replied the little girl. "We met on the boat. You're the one who rescued me. Thank you."

"That's impossible," replied Alfonso. "I rescued an old woman from the boat."

"That was me," said the little girl. She stared at him with eyes that conveyed the utmost seriousness. "I'm an ageling."

414

Alfonso looked up sharply. He recalled Imad's directive to find the ageling, the one who could find his father.

"A what?" asked Bilblox.

"An ageling. I shift from being a child to an adult to an old woman," explained the girl. "Mostly it depends on what kind of mood I'm in, but the elders say eventually I'll be able to control it. For now, when I'm tired I tend to become old, and when I need to be fast and strong, I'm a young woman. However, I most prefer being eight years old, which is my true age."

Alfonso turned to Bilblox and asked, "Did you get that?"

"Yup," said Bilblox in astonishment. "Just when ya thought it couldn't get any crazier, we come across the old lady from the rowboat. I can't wait to see Jasber!"

He turned to the girl. "You're looking for Kiril, the man with the scar?"

"Yes," she replied. "I believe he went that way." She pointed off to a trail on the left.

"Ya sound like yer shiverin'," said Bilblox as he reached into his pack, pulled out a blanket, and offered it to the girl. "Put this on, and let's keep goin' in the direction ya think Kiril went. Meanwhile, we'll look for a place to rest and make a fire. Then ya can tell us what's goin' on. Besides, I'm gonna need to sit down soon. I feel a really bad headache comin' on."

§

As they walked silently through the maze, Alfonso marveled at the hedges that surrounded them. The vast thickets of branches were absolutely impenetrable and yet they never crossed over into the path. Indeed, the hedges were so well groomed that Alfonso felt as if he were in a rather nightmarish version of an English garden. Yet, oddly enough, none of the branches bore signs of being cut or shaped by a human hand. They appeared to be wild but orderly, as if they had simply decided to shape themselves into vertical blockades.

Alfonso, Bilblox, Kõrgu, and the girl kept walking. Deeper into the labyrinth, the wind died away, but still the snow drifted lightly to the ground. The silence was total, and there were no signs of Kiril.

They eventually stopped in an area where the narrow path became slightly wider. Alfonso began building a fire using some dried wood they had brought with them. He couldn't find any dead branches from the hedges, and finally he cut away a lone leaf. He dangled the leaf over the fire, but the leaf refused to burn. Instead, it simply glowed red, like a piece of metal that was heating up.

"We should conserve our wood," Alfonso remarked. "I don't think this hedge can be burned."

Bilblox was sitting on the ground with his head in his heads. He was moaning softly. This was very unusual. Alfonso had never—not even once—seen Bilblox display any signs of being in such pain.

"Bilblox," said Alfonso tenderly, "are you all right?"

"It's a bad one," whispered Bilblox. "A really bad one. Feels like someone's takin' an ice pick to my brain."

"Have your headaches been getting worse?" inquired Alfonso.

Bilblox nodded. "They don't last long, but every headache is worse than the one before," he replied hoarsely. "I don't know how much more of this I can take."

"Have some food," suggested Alfonso. "It'll make you feel better."

Alfonso took out a tin box wrapped in heavy cloth. He opened the lid and immediately began to salivate at the rich smells of leftover mutton, prepared by Second-Floor Man. There were also two loaves of heavily crusted sourdough bread. Alfonso put the tin over the fire to heat it up. As they waited for the food to warm, he dug into his backpack and checked the contents of the small box he had been carrying with him since Marseilles. The vials of Polyvalent Crotalid Antivenin were thankfully intact, although Alfonso's skin crawled every time he looked at them.

When the food was ready, Alfonso offered it to both Bilblox and the girl. The threesome ate silently, and afterward, everyone, including Bilblox, seemed to feel a bit better.

Alfonso cleaned off the dishes in the snow and then turned to the girl, who was sitting next to the fire, perched on her feet like a ragtag bird.

"What's your name?"

Alfonso was startled to see that the girl was now a teenager, roughly his age. She had put on six inches and her hair had lengthened from her shoulders down to her waist—all in the span of seconds.

"You're . . . you're . . ."

"About fourteen years old," answered the girl. "I must be feeling nervous. I always take on this age when I'm feeling this way. I hate it."

"I don't blame ya," said Bilblox weakly. "Bein' a teenager ain't exactly a picnic."

"What's your name?" Alfonso asked again.

"Marta," replied the girl.

"So tell us," said Alfonso, "how do you become an ageling?"

"Oh, there's really nothing to it," said Marta. "That's what happens when you rub the green ash into your eyes."

"Green ash," replied Alfonso matter-of-factly. He was doing his best to be casual. "So you're from Jasber?"

"Of course," said Marta. She looked surprised. "I'm the seer of Jasber."

She went on to explain how she had become a seer—how she'd rubbed the green ash into her eyes, entered a deep coma, and then returned to consciousness with the power of clairvoyance. She also described the vision she had earlier in the week, the vision in which Kiril set a fire in Jasber that burned much of the city and, ultimately, claimed her parents' lives. She explained that this vision had prompted her to flee Monastery Isle in the hopes of warning her parents but that her plan had failed and she ended up getting swept down the river and out into the Sea of Clouds.

"Marta," said Alfono finally. He reached out and touched her hand. "You know your way through this maze?"

"I think so," she slowly replied. "There is a grand loop that the sweepers always use. That's what they call it. It starts at the City Gate—you know, the gate into Jasber. Then it goes south, down to where we entered the maze. Then it heads north again, back toward the City Gate, and passes the Great Sleeper's cottage."

"Cottage!" exclaimed Alfonso. "What do you know about the cottage? That's where my dad might be!"

Marta gave an awkward look, and finally stammered, "I'm s-s-sorry, Alfonso . . ."

Alfonso went pale.

"Marta, ya gotta tell us, what do you know about his dad?" asked Bilblox.

"Well, honestly, not much," said Marta. "I mean, I think he must be Alfonso's father—they look so much alike."

"You've seen him?" asked Bilblox.

"No, I've never *actually* seen him," said Marta, rather nervously. "Everyone knows about him, of course, because he arrived with the Dormian bloom. I knew he was in his cottage. Everyone in Jasber knows that . . ."

"So how do ya know what he looks like?" asked Bilblox.

"Because I saw him in a vision," explained Marta.

"I don't understand," said Alfonso with a sigh of exasperation.

"Seers only have visions about the things we stare at," explained Marta. "That's why the monks positioned the chair so I was staring only at the Founding Tree. Anyway, when I saw Kiril climbing the cliff toward the razor hedges, I had a glimpse into Kiril's future." Her voice became quiet, so that Alfonso and Bilblox had to lean closer. "Kiril was watching . . . he was watching your father die in the snow."

"When? Where?" demanded Bilblox.

"I don't know when," said Marta defensively. "There was no clock. But it happened in the maze. There was blood on the snow and the smell of smoke in the air. Your father was right outside the cottage . . . I think."

Bilblox stood up at once and smothered the remains of the fire with his boot. "Let's get goin'," he said. "Maybe there's still time."

CHAPTER 50

THE SECRET OF THE SPHERE

AFTER HILL AND RESUZA had passed more than eighteen hours in the cave, the winter storm finally died down and it was time to leave. Hill was still very weak from his wound, and though he could stand to get more rest, they were almost out of food. All that remained was a dollop of honey. They needed to sail the catamaran back to the lighthouse.

Resuza glanced over at Hill. "You're right," he said. He had read her concern. "Shall we get going? A few days in the lighthouse will likely mend me up right quick. I think I'm stable enough to spend some time on the catamaran. Your makeshift bandages did the trick."

Resuza nodded. "With any luck we'll be back at the lighthouse in time for dinner," she said with forced cheer. "And then we can think about going back to these razor hedges and trying to find Alfonso and Bilblox."

After gathering up their belongings, they exited the cave and emerged into the glaring morning light. The skies had cleared and a gentle breeze was blowing. It took them several minutes to return to the small beach where they had left the catamaran. As they rounded the corner, Resuza saw the vessel and was happy to note that it had weathered the storm nicely. Her spirits lifted. She reached into her pocket and took out the sphere and decided to give it another toss.

However, at that moment, she got an uneasy feeling—the kind of feeling you get when you are being watched. She looked up and noticed a man standing on the deck of their catamaran, staring at them. He had appeared out of nowhere. Moments later, four other men climbed out of the cabin below. They were dressed entirely in furs and long, mangy beards swayed below their chins. Across their chests they wore belts of ammunition and each had a musket stuck into the belts.

Resuza's heart sank. It was highly unlikely that these people had boarded the catamaran with good intentions. Hill gripped her arm tightly. He had just seen them too.

One of the men stepped off the catamaran and onto the beach. He had a mane of fiery red hair that was only barely contained by a mud-colored woolen hat. The man whistled loudly and, an instant later, his four companions jumped down to the beach as well.

Resuza eyed Hill to gauge his reaction. He was gazing off into the distance. What was Hill looking at? Then she saw for herself. About a quarter mile off the shore, half concealed by a small iceberg, floated a long wooden barge.

"That must be their boat," remarked Hill.

"Who are they?" asked Resuza.

"Trouble," whispered Hill.

The five men walked quickly toward Resuza and Hill and stopped about twenty feet away. The man with the red beard shouted something in a foreign tongue, which Hill did not understand.

"Do you understand what he said?" asked Hill.

"I think so," said Resuza. "He says we have two choices. The first is that we go with them back to their boat."

"What's the second?"

"They kill us," replied Resuza.

"That doesn't sound like much of a choice," said Hill wearily. He eyed the men, all of whom were now pointing their muskets at them. "I think we better do as they say."

⊛

The man with the red beard positioned himself at the helm of the catamaran and steered it toward the wooden barge. Meanwhile, the other men kept their guns trained on Hill and Resuza. Resuza had moved the blue sphere into her pocket and she kept it at the ready, but it seemed downright suicidal to start a fight now. Painful as it was, they would have to wait for a more opportune moment to flee.

Once they reached the barge, the men ordered Hill and Resuza off the catamaran onto the barge itself, and then down a narrow set of stairs that led into the belly of the ship. Here, to their great dismay, Hill and Resuza found several hundred prisoners packed into a very small space. The hatch to the deck slammed shut behind them.

Hardly anyone looked up as Resuza and Hill entered. They all appeared sickly and malnourished. The prisoners were packed in so tightly that it was difficult to move about. There was a stench in the air so pungent that it made Resuza's nostrils burn. A grotesque man, more skeleton than human, sidled up to Resuza, who was standing in front of Hill.

"Scared?" he said with a terrible, rasping laugh. "Don't be too frightened, gorgeous. You'll be lookin' just as wretched as me and the other slaves soon enough."

"Slaves?" inquired Resuza.

"A few months ago, we were farmers," said the man. "And now we're all to be sold as slaves. Whaddya think you was on—a pleasure cruise? You'll make a pretty prize." He reached out a hand to touch her hair.

Hill sidled up alongside Resuza and pushed the man away.

"How long before we try to escape?" whispered Resuza.

Hill glanced around and shook his head grimly.

"First chance we get," replied Hill softly. "Though I'm not in fighting shape, it's a risk we'll have to take."

"We never should have surrendered ourselves," griped Resuza bitterly. "What were we thinking?"

"We were thinking that there is a time and a place to pick a fight or make a run for it," Hill replied. "And that wasn't it."

Resuza made no reply.

"Come on," said Hill. "There's a small stove in the corner. Let's go warm up."

Hill and Resuza pushed their way over to the corner where a thick-boned woman with gray hair and raw pink skin was warming up a pot of watery gruel.

"Mind if we warm up by the stove?" asked Resuza.

"Be my guest," said the woman. She spoke in a Uralic mountain dialect that Resuza understood. The woman took the pot off the stove and cradled it in her arms as if she were holding a great treasure. Then she opened the door to the stove and revealed a meager bed of burning coals. "Warm up while ya can, dearie," said the woman. "But don't be eyein' my pooridge cuz' I ain't sharin'."

Resuza and Hill huddled around the open door of the stove and greedily drew as close to the heat as they could. Together they stared blankly into the fire's embers. Slowly, without even fully thinking about it, Resuza reached into her pocket and took out the blue sphere. She eyed Hill.

Hill grimaced.

"I think the situation is officially desperate," said Resuza.

"It's our only weapon," whispered Hill.

"We don't know how to use the sphere," said Resuza. "Alfonso can control it much better than we can. He never should've given it to us! But now that we have it, and he's somewhere far away, it may help us in another way. After all, the monk threw it into the fire. What if it gives us an even greater weapon?"

With a sigh of resignation, Hill nodded.

Resuza looked around to see if anyone was watching them. There were no guards around and the slaves were all far too listless and deadened to pay them any mind. Resuza took the blue sphere and placed it directly into the coals of the fire. It turned purple and then red. Resuza glanced at Hill. "That should do it," whispered Hill. Resuza used her metal cup and discreetly prodded the sphere out of the fire and onto the floor near a mound of snow, which had been brought in to serve as drinking water for the prisoners. The sphere sizzled as it came in contact with the snow. Its glassy surface immediately cracked in several places and then rapidly dissolved into bluish colored sand. Sitting on the sand was a narrow five-inch-long cylinder of gleaming silver that, apparently, had been inside of the sphere itself. The cylinder tapered to a point at one end.

Resuza picked it up. "I've seen this before," she said softly.

Hill looked at her and then at the cylinder. "You're right," he whispered.

"It's one of the symbols of Jasber," said Resuza in an amazed voice. "We saw it on the rosewood lid and above the tunnel that leads to the Jasber Gate."

"Yes," said Hill. His eyes glimmered with excitement as he thought back to their conversation with Josephus weeks ago in Somnos. "I believe it's the Foreseeing Pen."

CHAPTER 51

A GLIMPSE OF SUMMER

DEEP WITHIN THE MAZE, a delicate layer of frost covered the thorns, while a thicker layer of snow covered the leaves of the hedges. It was bitterly cold, the kind of cold that causes tears to freeze within seconds and spit to crackle before it reaches the ground. Alfonso, Bilblox, and Marta trudged along through the maze, battling through snowdrifts and trying not to sweat from the exertion, because to sweat meant becoming even colder than they already were. They shivered down to their bones and feared going to sleep, because they might not wake up. Even Kõrgu, the massive wolf with her thick pelt of fur, shivered and whined. They were all exhausted and close to passing out.

It was late morning and they had been walking for eight

hours straight. They stood quietly at yet another intersection and looked at Marta, who leaned forward and stared directly down. Marta was scrutinizing the ground with the utmost concentration, never blinking or wiping away the occasional snowflake that landed on her cheek. She forgot about Alfonso and Bilblox and Kôrgu. She forgot about the maze, and her parents, and Jasber, and Dormia. She even forgot about herself and, as she did, she stopped feeling her limbs. The cold bite of the wind vanished, and gradually the snow on the ground began to thin and then melt away. The ground beneath her turned muddy and the air was warm. It was summer, late August to be exact. Marta was using her powers of foresight to see the ground as it would look in the future, roughly eight months from now.

It was very rare to see the maze without any snow or ice. This far north, and at this altitude, snow cover was more or less permanent, except for a short period each August. During this interval, no more than a few days and sometimes even less, the snow receded and the actual ground of the maze became visible. This is what Marta wanted to see, because beaten into the muddy earth was a faint but clear path, the result of countless generations of labyrinth sweepers following the grand loop that Marta had described to Bilblox and Alfonso. It was common knowledge that most sweepers followed a specific loop on their patrols through the maze. Although they often varied their route, this particular loop was the fastest and most direct to the key areas of the maze. Of course, the route itself was a closely kept secret. Because of the frequent snowfall, it was never visible to the naked eye except during the few days in August when the entire labyrinth thawed.

Marta studied the ground closely and saw the unmistakable

depression of a path in constant use. It continued straight and then, several hundred yards ahead, it turned left at an intersection. From here, she knew the path would twist and turn its way northward, all the way to the Great Sleeper's cottage and then on to the City Gate. And, at every intersection, Marta would have to stare at the ground and peer again into the future. For the most part, Marta could not will herself into having detailed visions of the future, like the one she'd had of Kiril burning Jasber Isle. She could, however, will herself into having very brief glimpses of the future, almost snapshots, which never lasted for more than a fraction of a second. Marta could control these flashes to a certain extent—even directing how far into the future she wanted to see—but the process exhausted her.

"It's straight ahead and then left at the first intersection," gasped Marta as she looked up from the ground. She was breathing heavily. She had already led them through four intersections, and she was getting quite tired. She also noticed her old and wrinkled hands, covered with liver spots and small, angry-red veins. They looked even older than before, and she noticed that they were shaking uncontrollably.

Alfonso shook his head. "You look even older than on the rowboat. I didn't think it was possible for you to get any older."

"Can you give me a hand?" croaked Marta. "I get very tired after I have my visions."

Kõrgu led Bilblox over to where Marta was standing. With great tenderness, Bilblox scooped Marta up and began walking forward with her in his arms. "Don't worry, er . . . ma'am," said Bilblox. "I can carry ya the whole way if need be."

"Thank you," gasped Marta.

They plodded onward through the snow in silence.

"Marta," said Alfonso finally, "in your vision, did you see my father actually dead?"

Marta paused. "He was lying on the ground, and he did not move," she replied.

"But that doesn't mean he was dead," replied Alfonso.

"No," said Marta. "But it's hard to imagine how he could have survived lying in the snow in that way, without moving."

"With any luck, we'll get there in time," said Bilblox.

"B-B-Beware," wheezed Marta, who now looked as if she were well over one hundred years old. "Beware of the snow snakes."

CHAPTER 52

THE GREAT SLEEPER'S COTTAGE

IT HAD BEEN MANY HOURS since Leif left the relative comfort of Zinedine's dirt cave. He knew that his survival depended on making it back to the cottage and finally he was close. In fact, he had almost made it to the cottage when he sensed that he was being followed. He could hear something long and heavy sliding through the snow. On several occasions, he glanced backwards, but each time he saw nothing. At times, he thought he saw powdery snowdrifts shifting, as if something was underneath them, but he couldn't be sure.

He suspected that it was a snow snake, the kind the sweepers had warned him about: up to a hundred feet long, as wide as a barrel, and fast. Lethal in every way. It appeared as if the snake was stalking him and it was only a matter of time before it struck. Somehow, he had to shake this creature. The cottage was nearby, and if he was correct, it was on the other side of the razor hedge he was currently facing.

It was time to do something he had only managed to do once before, something beyond hypnogogia. Like Alfonso, Leif could enter hypnogogia. At first, he had been content with just this ability. It had helped him many times along the trip to Jasber. And he continued to practice hypnogogia once he was banished to the cottage in the razor hedges, in the hopes that he would be able to escape. It was there, after studying the same Alexandria box as Alfonso, that he discovered that hypnogogia was not only an incredible ability to have, but it was also the doorway to the mastery of other skills. Of course, just to stay in hypnogogia was draining, so he had only scraped the surface of what he believed he could potentially do.

He was about to do something very dangerous, but there was no time for further practice. It would take all the remaining strength that he had. Leif inhaled a deep breath of cold air, pushed it down to the very bottom of his abdomen, and then exhaled slowly through his nostrils. A moment later, he was in hypnogogia. Quickly, he brought all of his attention to bear on a single molecule of oxygen and then he expanded his field of vision to see the billions of other molecules of oxygen shimmering around him. He extended out his arms and touched his index finger to a single molecule. Very gently, he brought his thumb next to the index finger so that both fingers were now touching the molecule. A split second later, he began spreading his two fingers apart. This action caused the molecule to widen. A hole appeared in the middle, as if the molecule had become a doughnut. It started to vibrate and glow with electricity. This spastic motion spread to the other oxygen molecules surrounding Leif, until the air around him crackled with energy.

Leif looked up and without a moment's hesitation walked directly into the razor hedges. Instead of being torn apart, as any normal person would have been, the thorns and branches expanded like the molecule, and Leif walked directly through the empty space in the middle. He emerged on the other side of the razor hedges and walked forward until he was several feet into open snow. Then he left hypnogogia and fell to his knees, overcome with exhaustion.

He had done it!

After taking a minute to collect himself, Leif looked up to see a welcome sight: a large clearing with a cottage in the middle of it. He smiled and rose to his feet. The sweepers had told him that the snakes would never dare attack the cottage. He'd be safe there. However, as he staggered toward the cottage, he saw there was just one problem. Standing in front of the porch was a man dressed in a fur coat. The man held a long sicklelike sword in one hand and a wide-brimmed hat in the other. Blood dripped steadily from a wound in his hand. His eyes were entirely white.

It was Kiril.

"I was just about to give up on you, dear friend," said Kiril calmly, as he put his hat onto his head. "I'm in a bit of a predicament myself, and I don't have a great deal of time. I was just about to leave, but my luck has changed, and here you are!"

"We need to get inside," gasped Leif. "There's a snake . . ."

Kiril nodded sympathetically.

"That was a very impressive little trick you just did," said Kiril in a lighthearted manner. "I've never seen anyone walk through a wall of razor hedges. I've heard that some Great Sleepers develop the powers to transvaporate, but I've never seen it." He looked coldly at Leif. "Though I'm the one bleeding to death, I must say, you look more exhausted than I do."

Leif nodded and gasped for air. He didn't have the strength to talk and instead kept moving toward the cabin. They were only feet away, and Leif eyed Kiril wearily.

Kiril tightened his grip on the hilt of his khopesh. Leif sensed what was about to happen and he dove to his right just as Kiril slashed at him with his blade. Leif landed heavily on the ground and moaned. He had narrowly missed the full force of Kiril's swipe, but the blade had grazed him and torn part of his shirt. Kiril quickly regained his composure and raised his sword to finish the job. At that moment, he sensed something large slithering behind him.

Instinctively, Kiril spun around. He didn't want to, with Leif finally at his mercy, but he knew he could not ignore whatever was behind him. He saw not one, but two monstrous snow snakes moving fast toward them. They were massive serpents, each about eighty feet long, with bodies as thick as tree trunks. They had sickly yellow eyes, gleaming white scales, and sharp fangs.

Kiril turned and ran, counting on the snakes to focus on Leif, who was obviously wounded and in no shape to defend himself. He was right. The two snakes circled around Leif and, finally, one of them sank its fangs into his neck. Leif screamed out in pain, jerked several times, and then went limp. The snakes then turned their attention to Kiril, who was about two hundred feet away.

Kiril glanced over his shoulder and realized he would not be able to outrun the snakes. He brandished his khopesh and began to twirl it with such speed that, from afar, the blade resembled a plane propellor. The snakes recoiled and appeared to be mesmerized by this display. They hissed and snapped, but they drew no closer. Eventually, they retreated back toward the cottage to collect Leif.

As the snakes turned toward his enemy, Kiril lowered the khopesh and leaned heavily against it. It was time to move. He turned and staggered back into the maze.

☙

Several hours later, Alfonso entered the clearing that surrounded the cottage, followed by Bilblox and Kõrgu. In his arms, Bilblox was carrying Marta, who now appeared to be seventy or perhaps eighty years old. Kõrgu saw the snow snakes first. She began to growl in a way that Bilbox had never heard before. The violence of her growl sent a shiver up his spine.

"What is it?" asked Bilblox.

"Two snow snakes," whispered Marta.

Alfonso looked at the snakes and knew the entire journey depended on his actions in the following minutes. Only through the powers of hypnogogia could anyone overcome these vicious beasts. What's more, everything about the current situation reminded him of his dream many weeks ago aboard the *Somnolenţă*, which meant that somewhere beyond the snakes lay his father, with puncture wounds in his neck.

He looked at Marta. "He's here, right? My dad is here."

She nodded.

"Stay put," Alfonso whispered. "I'll deal with the snakes."

The serpents had been circling the cottage probably for hours; their circular tracks were everywhere. They were in a foul mood and hissed at each other and glared at the dark cottage, where their prey was hiding.

Alfonso felt oddly calm as he approached the snakes. He spied a fluttering snowflake out of the corner of his eye, watched it shimmy and dance for a moment, and then eased his way into hypnogogia. It had begun to snow again.

Alfonso walked toward the cottage. Both snakes looked up, bared their fangs, and slithered toward him. Alfonso breathed deeply and felt the various currents of energy pulsing through the air around him. He suddenly felt light in his shoes, almost weightless. Alfonso leapt off the ground and jumped from snow particle to snow particle. Before a second passed, he was fifteen feet off the ground. Both serpents lunged up at him, but Alfonso danced through the air, nimbly avoiding their snapping jaws.

A slight wind blew. The snowflakes swirled and Alfonso swirled with them, spinning around in the air above the snakes, goading the serpents to attack again. Despite the situation, Alfonso couldn't help feeling elated as he rapidly gained confidence in the art of what he had come to think of as particle climbing. He had practiced this several times since opening the cloud door in Imad's antechamber. Alfonso discovered that he could climb the microscopic particles in the air, whether water, dust, or ice.

"What's goin' on?" demanded Bilblox, who was standing next to the entrance to the razor hedges. "Is the kid okay?"

"He's dancing in the sky," Marta whispered.

Alfonso continued to taunt the snakes for another few minutes until they were in a seething rage, snapping, hissing, and frothing venom. Alfonso then drifted over to the far end of the clearing, to a spot where the wind had formed an eddy of swirling snow. The serpents followed. At one point, one of them struck so close to Alfonso that its scales scraped Alfonso's feet. Alfonso landed on the ground. His back pressed against the razor hedges and he could feel the thorns puncture the outer layer of his winter parka. Both snakes sensed their moment of opportunity. They had their prey trapped. Alfonso roared at them. The snakes lunged. Just in the nick of time, Alfonso leapt into the swirling eddy of snow. He particle-climbed so rapidly that he appeared to be soaring upward. Meanwhile, both snakes lunged at the spot where Alfonso had been only a half-second before. They became tangled with each other, and gored themselves on the thousands of long, sharp thorns of the razor hedges. Their death screams were terrible to hear.

"What's happened?" demanded Bilblox. "I can't see a blasted thing. What in the name of Ivan Magrewski has happened?"

"The snakes are dead," replied Marta. "Now Alfonso is running to the cottage."

❧

The instant Alfonso's feet touched the ground, he sprinted for the door of the cottage. He opened it but saw nothing but darkness. After lighting a candle, Alfonso scanned the interior: it contained a small kitchen table, several bookcases along the wall, a scattering of stools and chairs, pots filled with potatoes, and a small bed wedged against the wall. It was piled high with musty blankets. Someone was lying on top of them, face-down. Alfonso approached, not daring to breathe.

"Dad?" he whispered.

Alfonso rolled the person over. It was a man, perhaps in his early fifties. A thick, knotted beard covered his face. Sweat ran freely down the exposed skin of his high cheekbones and forehead. He wore a heavy blue robe that looked as if it had not been washed in ages. Alfonso's legs gave out and he staggered and knelt against the bed. After all this time, there was no doubt in Alfonso's mind. It was his father.

"DAD!" Alfonso shouted. "DAD, WAKE UP!"

Leif Perplexon did not stir.

Alfonso ripped open Leif's blue robe and noticed his shirt and pants were drenched with sweat. Alfonso felt his father's neck and found a faint, unsteady pulse. Leif's forehead was boiling hot to the touch. His father's lips were swollen red and cracked. His legs and arms felt clammy. Turning back to Leif's neck, Alfonso found what he suspected to be the cause of his father's condition: two puncture wounds, about an inch apart, located midway down his father's neck. The skin around the punctures was tinged a gray-blue, exactly as his dream foretold.

Alfonso tore off his backpack and took out the box with the syringes that he had been dragging with him since Marseilles. His hands shook as if he were having a seizure. Dimly, he heard Bilblox's worried shouts.

Alfonso forced his exhausted, freezing hands to open the box, remove the protective wrapping from a syringe, and draw out the liquid from one of the bottles. He took his father's left arm and extended it toward him. He slapped the flat area between the forearm and the bicep. The yellow-white skin bloomed pink and a tiny vein popped up. Alfonso felt the vein with his index finger. Sweat ran freely down Alfonso's back. He focused his entire world on the tiny vein, took a deep breath, and plunged the needle into his father's arm. After the syringe emptied, he extracted the needle and did the same with the second one. When it was done, the empty needles clattered to the floor. Alfonso didn't notice. He stared at his father, waiting for a reaction.

There was nothing. Leif lay motionless on the bed, his yellow-white skin gleaming in the candlelight.

CHAPTER 53

THE FORESEEING PEN

IN THE HOLD OF THE SLAVE SHIP Resuza cradled the Foreseeing Pen in the palm of her hands. She hugged the wall and pretended to look out a rusty porthole. Hill peered over her shoulder to get a better look. The pen was made of two equal-size segments that fit seamlessly together. Resuza pulled the two segments apart and looked inside. It was empty: no cartridge, spring, or mechanism of any kind. Instead of a metal nib, like those used in fountain pens, the small tip of this pen was made of hollow glass and filled with a tiny amount of a milky orange liquid. On the other end, the top of the pen was crowned with an incredibly brilliant emerald. The following diagram was carved across the barrel of the pen, just below the emerald:

"Any idea what those symbols mean?" whispered Resuza.

Hill stroked his chin thoughtfully. "Oddly enough, I believe so," he replied. "They're astrological symbols."

"Really?"

"Yes," said Hill with a nod. "I used to spend a lot of time browsing in an occult shop in Chicago. The symbols represent the five classical elements. The top triangle represents fire and the bottom one is water. The triangle on the left is earth and the one on the right is air."

"What's the symbol in the center?" asked Resuza.

"That's the fifth symbol—ether," explained Hill. "Sometimes it's also known as quintessence and it is supposedly a magical property—the fabric of the cosmos and whatnot. In Dormia, they believe that the sap of the Founding Trees consists of ether. But the idea of ether exists in many cultures. The Hindus call it akasha. They believe that the knowledge of all human experience is recorded within something called the akashic records—and all of these records are encoded in every single drop of akasha."

"Do you suppose the pen has any other powers?" asked Resuza.

Hill motioned for Resuza to give him the pen. He took it from her and gently examined both segments. He then peered closely at the glass tip filled with the milky orange liquid.

"*Ether*," he whispered. "By Jove, I believe that's ether from a Founding Tree."

"That orange liquid?" Resuza asked.

Hill nodded. "I believe so," he replied. "Ether is rumored to be orange, and the symbol on the barrel clearly refers to it."

Resuza smiled cautiously. "We just need some sort of ink and we'll be able to put this pen to the test."

Hill furrowed his brow. He looked around, and his eyes settled on the stove and the tired clump of coals inside. He then returned his gaze to the pen. His fingers ran over the symbols of the five classical elements.

"I don't think the pen uses ink," replied Hill excitedly. "We use one of the classical elements, and right now, fire is available."

He approached the stove, opened the pen, and pointed the bottom segment of the pen at the burning coals. At first nothing happened, but when he drew nearer and the distance between the pen and the coals was no more than a few inches, a darting blue flame shot out of the stove and into the pen, lighting it as if it were a burner on a gas stove. Hill quickly fit the two pen segments together, capturing the flame inside. The pen looked and felt completely normal. No one would suspect that fire was nestled inside.

"Amazing!' said Resuza.

"Indeed," replied Hill as he handed the Foreseeing Pen back to Resuza, who immediately placed it deep within an inner pocket of her coat. "My dear girl, we took a chance by destroying that sphere, but I suspect our gamble has paid off. If this pen can manipulate the five basic elements of nature, we've got quite a weapon on our hands. Now we'll—"

Just then their conversation was interrupted by harsh shouts.

The red-haired man who had captured Hill and Resuza was standing on the stairway and addressing the prisoners.

"What's he saying?" asked Hill.

"He said we'll be getting off the boat in an hour and we'd better look strong and healthy."

"Why's that?"

"Because," explained Resuza, "we're about to be sold."

CHAPTER 54

FATHER AND SON

MANY HOURS PASSED before Leif regained consciousness. During that time, Alfonso never left his father's bedside. Although he was fairly certain that Leif could not understand him, he spent the time telling him about Judy and Pappy, World's End, and all the adventures that he had been through in the years since Leif had disappeared. At other times, he sat and stared intently at his dad, alternating between wild optimism and deep pessimism.

It was late morning the next day when Leif suddenly opened his eyes, sat up unsteadily in bed, and raised a thin, trembling hand to ward off the harsh sunlight. Alfonso didn't notice his dad wake up. He was asleep in a chair, after spending most of the night awake.

Leif stared at the young teenager sitting next to his bed. He tried to say something, but his throat was too dry. Slowly he raised one of his large hands to his face and rubbed it over his thick beard and then further up, over his high, pronounced cheekbones. Tears welled in his eyes and he felt faint.

"A-A—" Leif tried hoarsely to say Alfonso's name.

Alfonso stirred awake and for a second looked confused. Then he saw his father sitting in bed, only feet away, and he too began to cry. Leif motioned for Alfonso to sit next to him. Father and son sat on the bed, arms tightly clasped around each other. Alfonso buried his face in his dad's shoulder and started to shake with deep sobs. It was too much. After all these years, to see his dad alive was beyond overwhelming. Of course, Alfonso hoped that he'd find his dad, but to actually do it and see him living and breathing . . . Alfonso immediately thought of his mother. If only she were here to be part of this reunion.

"I thought you were gone," Alfonso sobbed. "Dad, I thought you were gone, y-you were dead."

"I know, son," whispered Leif. His voice was barely audible. He smiled for the first time in what felt like years. "Alfonso, my dear, dear boy. The light of my life—" His voice cracked again. "I can't believe how you've grown!"

They spent a few more minutes together and then Alfonso helped his father get out of bed. Soon, Leif met the other occupants of the cabin: a young girl, an enormous, hulking man with white eyes, and a large wolf that stood attentively at the man's side.

Alfonso introduced Leif to Marta, Bilblox, and Kõrgu. Leif took one look at Bilblox and said, "Magrewski longshoreman?"

Bilblox nodded proudly.

"I figured that," Leif replied with a smile. "You all look the same!"

Over food and hot tea, Alfonso and the others explained everything that had happened to them in the past few weeks. Leif listened intently.

"We're going home, Dad," concluded Alfonso, as he hugged his father again. "And I can't wait for you to see Hill and meet my friend Resuza. They're waiting for us at a lighthouse not far from here."

Leif smiled. "That no-account brother of mine!" he declared. "I can't believe he's become foreign minister of Somnos! Our father would have laughed at the very idea! I'm sure he's foreign minister mostly when asleep—that's when he tends to be a showoff! Well, we'll meet him soon enough, and we'll have a grand old time." He looked at Marta, who had been sitting there staring quietly at Leif the whole time. "But I understand we have to settle things here first, and pretty quickly too."

"Very quickly," insisted Marta. "We have to help my parents."

"You feel up to movin'?" asked Bilblox.

Leif nodded wearily, and his head drooped low between his bony shoulders. It was clear that he was still very weak. "I'll do my best to help," he said. "Any friends of Alfonso's are friends of mine."

"So how we gonna get into Jasber?" asked Bilblox.

"I only know of the gate that the sweepers use, which will be guarded," replied Marta. "They have orders to kill anyone they see who is not a sweeper, even a Great Sleeper. We wouldn't stand a chance there."

"That's true," replied Leif. "It's a terrible thing. A Great Sleeper risks his or her life to get them their Founding Tree, and how do they repay this gift? Leaving them to rot in this miserable cottage."

"So you don't know of any other way in?" Marta asked mournfully.

"I don't think so," replied Leif with a shake of his head. "Here, take a look."

He limped over to a corner of the cottage, opened an old wooden chest, and pulled out a large piece of parchment. It appeared to be a map of the labyrinth. Leif explained that he had copied this map from the lid of a rosewood box that he had found in Alexandria.

"I had that same box lid, but Josephus and then Kiril took it!" exclaimed Alfonso. "But I didn't see any map on it."

"That's because the map only appears when exposed to moonlight," explained Leif. He pointed out three landmarks on the map—the sweepers' entrance, a large lake, and an X at the center of the labyrinth. Leif explained that the X marked the spot where the cottage was located. Alfonso and Marta studied the map closely. The only writing of any kind on the map lay at the very bottom, where a set of Dormian hieroglyphs and the number 1109 were printed.

"What's that writing at the bottom?" asked Alfonso.

"It's probably the name of the person who made the map, and the year it was made," explained Marta.

"I assume that we're talking about the Dormian year 1109?" asked Leif.

"It would have to be," replied Alfonso.

"So I was meant to deliver my plant here to the cottage," said Leif. "That's what the *X* is all about, you see? The Great Sleeper arrives in Alexandria, gets the box with seeds, hatches the plant, and then delivers it to the spot marked *X*." He shook his head. "I can't believe the Jasberians are so paranoid." He looked slyly at Alfonso. "They'd get along well with Pappy."

"The Jasberians weren't always so fearful," interjected Marta.

"What do you mean?" asked Leif.

"Once upon a time the elders allowed Great Sleepers to enter Jasber," explained Marta. "There was even something called the Great Sleeper's Gate. But they closed it long ago."

"She's right," said Alfonso. "I read about it in the book from Josephus's study. Here, I can show you the passage."

Alfonso reached into his bag and pulled out the curious book titled *Un Destin Solitaire: Les Dormeurs Géant de Jasber*. He then flipped it open to the relevant page, read silently for a minute or so, and then offered a rough translation.

"It says the Great Sleeper's Gate was closed in the Dormian year 2021 and that both the labyrinth and the cottage were completed five years later, in the year 2026," explained Alfonso.

Leif furrowed his brow. "That's odd. It means that the map on the rosewood box is older than this cottage." He looked at Alfonso. "It's older by almost a thousand years!"

"Why does that matter?" asked Alfonso.

Leif and Bilblox both smiled.

"What yer old man is sayin'," said Bilblox, "is that the Jasberians had Great Sleepers coming to this *exact* spot long before there was ever a cottage here. So, Leif, what do ya reckon was here before the cottage?"

"I have a hunch," said Leif with a sudden grin. "I'd be willing to bet that the Jasberians simply built the cottage right over the place where the Great Sleeper's Gate once stood. It makes sense. It would be an easy fix for them. That way they wouldn't have to go back to Alexandria to change the map."

"So you're sayin' that the Great Sleeper's Gate is in the cottage?" asked Alfonso.

Leif nodded in a deliberate manner. He still looked weak and sickly, but his blue-gray eyes flashed with excitement. Alfonso smiled and fought back a sudden welling of emotion. It was a look he'd thought he would never see again.

"Come on," said Leif. "There is something I want to show you."

Leif led the way down a set of winding stone stairs that descended into the basement of the cottage. It was dark and gloomy, but Leif carried a lantern, and in the light of its flickering glow one thing was apparent: the basement was cavernous. Alfonso had assumed that a small cottage would have a small basement. Not so. The basement resembled a cave with its high ceiling and rough-hewn walls that looked as if they had been chiseled with pickaxes. The cave smelled dank and the air was alive with the sound of nesting bats. There was also a faint gurgling noise, as if a very small stream were running somewhere nearby.

"What is this place?" asked Bilblox. His voice echoed several times off the walls of the cave. "Doesn't seem like a basement."

"Strange, isn't it?" asked Leif as he limped onward. "Follow me—you'll want to see this."

They continued farther into the darkness of the cave and, as they walked, the sound of gurgling water grew louder. The floor glistened with dampness and soon they came to a place where several large piles of stones were stacked on either side of a tiny marble door built into the wall of the cave. The door had a small slot in the center almost like a mail slot, only thinner and longer. Tiny rivulets of water trickled from the cave through an opening at the bottom of the door, and then presumably downward into whatever lay beyond the door.

"I noticed that the water was trickling downward, so I spent eight solid months moving these stones," explained Leif. "Eventually I found this doorway. Imagine my disappointment when it was another dead end. I convinced myself it wasn't that big of a deal. Never in a million years would I have guessed that it might lead the way into Jasber."

"Does the door open?" asked Alfonso.

"Watch," replied Leif. Leif reached into the heavy blue robe he was wearing and pulled out a thin slab of wood. Alfonso recognized it immediately. It was the lid to the rosewood box. Leif took the wooden lid, inserted it into the slot in the center of the door, and then withdrew it. There was a click and then the door swung open.

They walked inside and saw why Leif had been so disappointed. A massive boulder about twenty feet into the passageway prevented anyone except for a small animal or water to pass through. "I've tried to push it forward, but it won't budge," explained Leif. "I also used my powers of hypnogogia and tried to walk through the boulder, but I've learned that stone is the most difficult matter to pass through, and this particular boulder was simply too thick. And so, unfortunately, I have no idea how to dislodge this hunk of rock."

"I know someone with the muscle to do it," said Alfonso with a smile.

Bilblox cleared his throat and stepped forward. He sniffed the air and walked straight toward the boulder, with Kõrgu at his side. For several minutes, he used his fingers to probe every inch of the boulder, although he concentrated his attention on the openings between the boulder and the passageway. He then placed his massive hands on the boulder, sucked in a huge breath of air, dropped into a squat, grunted fiercely, and heaved every iota of force that he could muster into the boulder. The boulder rocked forward ever so slightly.

"It'll move," said Bilblox confidently. "It'll take some work, but the water underfoot's been loosenin' it for a couple years. Alfonso, take a look along the sides and the bottom. Are there any rocks that I'm dislodgin'?"

The longshoreman continued to press against the boulder, forcing it to rock in place. Meanwhile, Alfonso scurried around and pulled out rocks that had been wedged between the boulder and the tunnel. As he did so, the boulder began to slide, inch by inch. Bilblox immediately seized upon this momentum and continued pushing, rocking the boulder back and forth, back and forth, back and forth, until a large chunk from the bottom of the boulder broke loose. This set free the massive hunk of stone and it began to roll down the passageway. The rolling boulder continued into the darkened tunnel for a number of seconds until they all heard the sound of a distant impact.

Marta ran down the passageway.

"Marta!" yelled Alfonso. "Come back!"

"It's okay," yelled Marta a few seconds later, her voice echoing in the dusty tunnel. "The boulder is broken into a hundred little pieces. It hit a wall where the passageway makes a turn. Let's go! We have to find my family!"

The sound of her footsteps receded as she ran deeper into the darkness.

CHAPTER 55

THE LAKE

BLOOD FLOWING FROM KIRIL'S CUTS dripped steadily to the ground and soaked much of his shirt and pants. It was hard to say how much blood he had lost, but far too much for comfort. It was only a matter of hours before he became too weak to carry on. Fortunately, he was almost at the lake.

As he plodded onward, Kiril allowed his thoughts to drift back to his father and his father's stories of the labyrinth. Kemal once told a story involving an ice-covered lake at the center of the maze. In his father's recounting of this story, it was strictly forbidden for any of the sweepers to walk onto the ice that covered the lake, though a handful of the sweepers did so anyway. These rebellious sweepers broke the rules, oddly enough, in order to go ice fishing. The lake was home to a number of sizeable Siberian arctic char, which when caught and roasted over a fire provided a delicious meal for a very hungry sweeper.

"If the sweepers are so hungry, why aren't they allowed to catch a fish in the lake?" Kiril had once asked his father, when he was seven or eight years old. "It doesn't seem fair."

"It is not a matter of fair or unfair," his father had replied. "Those were the rules and fairness had no bearing on them."

"Did you ever fish on the lake, Father?"

"Once," replied Kemal with a smile, as he ran his hand over his son's forehead. "I was a novice sweeper and I had eaten too much of my food too soon into my journey. I was hungry—hungrier than I'd ever been. So I used my khopesh to cut a hole into the ice and I fished for several hours until I had caught a handsome char. I was just pulling the fish out of the water when another sweeper appeared. He waited for me at the shore and then he took the fish from me."

"Why did he do that?" asked Kiril.

"For one thing, he was much bigger than I was, and he probably figured I wouldn't fight back," replied Kemal. "What's more, I was in no position to object, because I had broken the rules. Nothing was said, but the understanding was clear. I would hand over my fish and, in return, he would not report me."

"I still don't understand," said Kiril. "Why do the rules forbid you from catching fish?"

"Well," replied Kemal evasively, "I suppose it is because the lake has a very strong undertow."

"What's an undertow?"

"It's a strong current that can pull you under the water,"

explained Kemal. "Usually, only oceans have undertows, but the lake has a very strong undertow because it actually drains downward, deep into the earth. It makes the ice very unstable." He smiled at Kiril's furrowed brow. "Put all of this out of your mind. I did the wrong thing, and I accepted my punishment."

The young Kiril said nothing as he pondered what his father had said. Finally he spoke. "Father, if that sweeper had tried to take my fish," said Kiril, "I would have killed him. I would have hacked off his head with my khopesh."

"Now, now," said Kemal with a dismissive cluck of his tongue. "Such sentiments are not suitable for a boy of your age. You mustn't think such things. Now be a good boy and go and play."

⊛

As he stood at the edge of the frozen lake, Kiril was relieved not to find any trace of sweepers. The general feeling of emptiness at the lake was enhanced by the forlorn and almost ghostly nature of the surroundings. The lake was sizeable, at least a mile across in any given direction, and hemmed in on all sides by razor hedges. The openness of this space seemed to invite the wind, which blew with wicked ferocity and created miniature cyclones of snow that swirled and danced across the lake. The sun hung like a sullen orb on the edge of the horizon. Kiril was so weary he couldn't recall whether it was dusk or dawn.

He walked out onto the ice for one hundred paces before stopping. With the careful, overly focused air of someone who doubts his own strength, Kiril used his khopesh to cut a hole in the ice. He glanced behind and noticed the trail of his own blood. There was little time left. Kiril hurried back to shore and set to work building a fire. He used some kindling that he had stowed away under his robe and, after expending a great deal of effort, he nursed a small fire to life.

Kiril warmed his hands over the crackling flames and then set a small pot of water to boil over the fire's coals. The water warmed quickly and, as it began to boil, Kiril sprinkled herbs into the pot—first arrowroot, then goldenseal, and finally Dormian milk thistle. These were the key ingredients to sokÿvodee, an ancient elixir that, when taken in the proper proportions, allowed one to breathe underwater for a few minutes. When the concoction was finished brewing, Kiril drank it greedily. Seconds later, his body seized up, as if he were choking. He coughed violently and staggered to the spot where he had carved a hole in the ice. When he reached the hole, Kiril didn't even break his stride; he simply dove headfirst into the icy waters.

The current grabbed Kiril immediately and dragged him down toward the bottom of the lake. He sank quickly and, as he neared the bottom, he saw that the floor of the lake wasn't made of rock and dirt. It was made of ice. The miraculous thing—the image that Kiril would never forget for as long as he lived—was the ice glowing brightly, in the same cheery fashion as holiday lights in many of the cities he had visited. The ice-covered bottom reflected the lights of an entire city hidden beneath the lake. At long last, he had returned to Jasber.

CHAPTER 56

THE CITY OF JASBER

ALFONSO, LEIF, BILBLOX, AND KÕRGU ran down the darkened tunnel. Leif could run for no longer than a minute before needing to stop. Alfonso stayed behind with him, while Bilblox and Kõrgu raced ahead to catch Marta.

Leif needed several days of solid recuperation before setting out, but he understood that they had no time. He walked as quickly as he could, but the pain in his legs and side grew only sharper. He noticed Alfonso's worried look and shook his head.

"I'm all right," said Leif. "I don't think I can stand another encounter with Kiril, but I can keep walking." He paused and looked at Alfonso.

"Did you feel that?" he asked.

Alfonso looked strangely at him. "I did," he said. "It's like a small magnet, tugging at my insides."

"That's my Founding Tree," whispered Leif. "You probably felt that before, when you were in Somnos. The trees and the Great Sleepers have a close, almost symbiotic, relationship. Of course, you have the closest connection with the Founding Tree that you grew." He nodded with satisfaction. "We'll be in Jasber soon enough—I can feel it."

Eventually, the two caught up to the others.

"It's all right," said Bilblox. "I told Marta she has to stay with us. We're as eager as anyone to get t'Jasber, but Leif is in no condition to be runnin' around like a spring chicken."

Marta nodded and they continued single file through the crumbling tunnel. Marta chattered excitedly about her family. ". . . There are three of us kids and I'm in the middle and we all live on an island . . ."

"Wait a minute," said Bilblox suddenly. "We're still goin' down and we're goin' toward Jasber. Does that mean Jasber's underground?"

"Of course it is," replied Marta. She seemed annoyed that Bilblox had interrupted her.

"But how can that be?" pressed Bilblox. "How does the Foundin' Tree live underground without any sunlight? And how do ya live on an island underground?"

"There's plenty of light," said Marta. "The rays reflect down from the lake above the city, so we get plenty of indirect sunlight. Don't worry—it's a wonderful city! Much better than any other. You'll see."

The group continued down the tunnel for two hours or so

until they reached yet another roadblock, a pile of six or seven boulders that were far too heavy for any normal person to lift. Bilblox set to work immediately, heaving the stones aside, one at a time. "HURRY!" pleaded Marta, her face a mask of anguish and worry. "Please, Bilblox, *hurry.*"

Sweat poured down Bilblox's face. He ripped at the boulders and heaved them to the side. His muscles bulged and the pain from his exertions caused his arms to tremble. Finally, after a few minutes of backbreaking work, he opened up a passageway just large enough for them to fit through one by one. They entered an elegant chamber with elaborate tiles, carved stone leaves, and a domed ceiling, as if they were inside the top half of an egg. Despite its luxurious appearance, it appeared to be a seldom used storeroom. Several garden tools—rakes, hoes, and pickaxes—lay scattered on the floor. Burlap bags of soil were stacked against one wall. At the end of the chamber they saw a door made of a material they had never seen before. It was translucent, silky, but firm to the touch. Light filtered through from the other side.

Marta ran across the room and stopped hesitantly at the door. "We're here," she said in a soft voice. "This is a leaf from our Founding Tree." She pulled the leaf door to one side and they stepped through into a vast underground world.

They were standing inside an enormous cavern, and as Alfonso took in his surroundings, suddenly Jasber came into focus in his mind's eye. Alfonso always assumed that the city was situated on top of the cliff-sided island that jutted out of the Sea of the Clouds like a massive boulder, but in reality, a portion of this giant island was hollow inside and Jasber was situated inside this giant cavern, many miles across. It was an ingenious hiding place for an entire city.

Alfonso noticed that the ceiling of the cavern was made entirely of smooth, glacially hard ice, the kind that Eskimos call manirak. It glowed subtly, as if receiving the first rays of a polar sun. In all of his adventures, rarely had Alfonso been as dumbfounded as he was at that moment, when he realized that he was staring up at the bottom of a lake—a lake that sat directly above the city of Jasber. The floor of this lake and the ceiling above Jasber were one and the same, nothing more than ice. Alfonso had the sensation that he was visiting an aquarium because the ice, in effect, created a giant glass window that allowed everyone in Jasber to look up and see the aquatic world above them.

The air was cold and misty. The mist came from a raging waterfall that drained from the lake above and ran down one section of the cavern wall opposite them, about three miles distant. The waterfall crashed onto a pile of rocks, then spread out, covering the entire floor of the cavern, except for two rocky islands. The closer of the two islands was dominated by a palace with five tall, spindly towers, the tallest of which sparkled as if it were inlaid with thousands of diamonds.

The other island, the more distant of the two, had no buildings on it. This island's sole occupant was the Founding Tree of Jasber. There was no mistaking it. The bark of the tree was pale white, like that of a bald cypress, and its trunk rose up for half a mile before its branches emerged. Once they began, the branches were crowded together so closely that it was impossible to pick them out one by one. Large branches split multiple times into smaller ones, radiating outward like the shaggy mass of a bush. At first it appeared as if the tree had no leaves, but then Alfonso realized that there were billions of leaves, all of which were essentially transparent, like the door they had just passed through. The topmost branches and leaves touched the ice ceiling and merged with it, so that it looked as if the Founding Tree was actually helping prop up the ceiling.

At the moment, they were standing on a steeply banked slope covered in a plush carpet of fluorescent green moss. The moss exuded a soft light that made everything appear permanently bathed in an early evening light. Marta said it was znimber moss, the staple food in Jasber.

Alfonso looked at Leif. His father was staring intently at his tree.

"It looks fine," said Alfonso.

Leif said nothing. They kept walking at the fastest pace they dared. Meanwhile, Alfonso described the incredible world they had entered to Bilblox.

"Are you kiddin' me?" exclaimed Bilblox. "I'd do anythin' for just one—" At that moment, Kõrgu barked loudly. It was rare for her to do that, and it sounded like a warning.

"What's that for?" Alfonso asked.

"She smells smoke," replied Bilblox in a low voice. "I do too."

They continued down a faint path cut through the znimber moss and then descended along a series of curving steps carved into the stone walls of the cavern. The steps curved steeply alongside the cliff face. Soon they emerged onto the terraced heights above a stone bridge that spanned the river and led to a large island completely covered with tens of thousands of buildings. At long last, they had arrived at Jasber.

It was marvelous, a sight beyond the furthest limits of imagination. Red and yellow birds swirled in the updrafts of the buildings, and the entire city gave off an aura of peace and tranquility. The buildings were tall and slender, ranging from four stories to as many as thirty. They looked solid yet lightweight, and were elegantly constructed from wood and limestone and a darker material that was either metal or volcanic rock. Many buildings were crisscrossed with strips of copper and inlaid with glittering arches of glass and colorful precious stones. The buildings featured broad porches, gardens on every floor, shimmering curlicues of blue on the roofs that were probably swimming pools, and a medley of cupolas, towers, courtyards, and promontories. From the top of each building rose a thin metal sculpture that swayed gently in the wind. They were whimsical representations of fish and of trees and other types of plant life. Several narrow, dark blue canals cut their way through the island, bordered by larger gardens that were filled with many types of flowers and trees.

Despite seeing this incredible, wondrous city, Alfonso gasped in horror. He was staring at a section of the city, at the far end of the island, that was engulfed in a plume of flames and smoke. To make matters worse, the fire looked to be spreading. Buildings began to glow red and flames were jumping from rooftop to rooftop.

"We're too late," cried Marta. She was staring at a large building on the far corner of the island that had a green dome sticking up from each of its four corners. It was beginning to catch fire.

"The flames have already reached the city's armory—that's right next to my parents' house."

"Go on," Leif said to Alfonso. He was breathing very heavily and his face had turned a pale white. "I need to rest . . . I'm feeling very poorly . . . but I'll catch up."

"Kõrgu and I'll stay with yer old man," said Bilblox. "Go with Marta."

Marta took off down the steps toward the stone bridge that led to Jasber.

"Hurry," gasped Leif. "And for heaven's sake, be careful. We'll catch up as soon as we can."

Alfonso squeezed his father's hand and turned to run after Marta. Leif watched his son cross the bridge and disappear into the burning city.

CHAPTER 57

ALFONSO'S CHOICE

No one paid any attention to Alfonso and Marta as they raced through the streets of Jasber against the flow of panicked citizens. In the distance Alfonso heard a sizzling noise, the sort that occurs when fire and water meet, and he assumed that this was the sound of the firefighters trying to tame the blaze. He followed Marta as she ran through the hazy streets.

"Which way do we go?" gasped Alfonso. They had arrived at an intersection that was almost totally enveloped in a choking black smoke. "I don't see a way . . ."

"Stay away from there!" yelled a wild-eyed woman, whose blond hair was badly singed. She turned and pointed vaguely toward the direction of the armory. "Get away if you want to save yourself." The woman then turned and dashed toward the river.

"Follow me," said Marta. "I know the way even with my eyes closed. We are very close." She grabbed Alfonso's hand and led him toward the spot where the smoke was thickest. Alfonso resisted for a moment, but then acquiesced.

"Pull your shirt up over your mouth," commanded Marta. "Use it as a mask." Alfonso did this and followed Marta into the smoke. After thirty seconds or so, they emerged from the smoke cloud into a cobblestone town square. Here the smoke had given way to something else. It was steam. Their feet became wet, and they discovered that the entire square was covered in water. In the center of the square, three wooden cisterns had toppled to the ground and smashed open, allowing thousands of gallons of water to pour out and flood the square. The water had mostly extinguished the flames and, in so doing, had created billowing clouds of steam.

"Come," beckoned Marta.

Together they splashed their way across the square, darted down a narrow alleyway, and emerged onto a wide boulevard. On the other side of the boulevard sat a marble building with imposing outer walls and four green domes. It was Jasber's armory, the one they had seen from the bridge above the city. The two domes bordering the boulevard were on fire, as was the interior of the building. Even the marble walls were covered in black soot. The main gate, with its twenty-foot-tall intricately carved wooden doors, gaped open. Dozens of Jasberians dressed in scarlet cloaks were fleeing into the boulevard.

"The domes are collapsing!" yelled a man who stood by the gateway, helping people flee. "Everybody out!"

Alfonso glanced again at the nearest of the four domes. The wooden slats that made up the body of the dome had already burned off, leaving only a skeletal structure of several curved trusses. Flames were licking at the trusses, and it was only a matter of time before they also fell. As he stared at the dome, Alfonso sensed a movement out of the corner of his eye. A figure in a scarlet cloak stood on the roof of the complex. Something about the figure made Alfonso's heart thud with panic, but it was impossible to see any detail. Steam from the nearby square mingled with the smoke from the burning armory to produce a thick fog.

Alfonso focused on a burning ember that was wafting in the wind. A second later, he entered hypnogogia. He ignored the billions of particles streaming around him and trained his complete attention on the man in the scarlet cloak standing on the roof of the armory. It was Kiril.

"Alfonso!" yelled Marta. She tugged violently on Alfonso's sleeve. "That's my family!" Marta pointed toward the roof of a building directly opposite the armory. It was a five-story townhouse with fire visible on every floor. The only part of the townhouse not ablaze was the roof. Standing on the roof, huddled together in panic, was Marta's family: her father, mother, and two brothers.

She pulled on Alfonso's sleeve, screaming, "They're trapped, they're trapped!" It was true. They had nowhere to go. Their options were grim: either they would be swallowed up by the flames or they would jump.

"Do something!" screamed Marta. She was now sobbing hysterically. "They're going to die!"

Still in hypnogogia, Alfonso turned his attention to the steam coming from the nearby square. His eyes focused on the plumes of white vapor. The complexity of the billions of swirling water molecules was vast, dizzying, and even beautiful. He watched as the individual molecules morphed from liquid form into vapor, and he could feel minute surges of kinetic energy ripple through the air. It was easy to step onto individual particles of water that made up the vapor cloud. He rose effortlessly. The more Alfonso practiced particle climbing, the easier it became, especially in an environment filled with so much vapor. It was like floating up to the surface of a lake.

Alfonso drifted upward into the air. He glanced down and saw that the boulevard was filled with chaos. Jasberians fled every which way and clearly no one was in charge. He couldn't see Marta. Alfonso then looked toward the armory. He was at eye level with the roof.

Kiril was running toward the farthest dome, which appeared to be as yet untouched by the fire. He was running with a purpose. Nothing about him seemed to betray any panic. Clearly, this was all part of his plan. If Alfonso floated toward Kiril, he might reach him in less than a minute. He'd have a chance, especially in hypnogogia, of stopping him and making sure the Coe-Nyetz Tree was never grown and the cataclysm never came.

Alfonso glanced back at the townhouse where Marta's family was stranded. Already the edges of the roof were on fire. In minutes, the entire building would be consumed in flames, and Marta's family would perish. Still, if he chased after Kiril now, the roof would hold a little longer, wouldn't it? Would he have time to do both? As he hovered above the burning city of Jasber, Alfonso clenched his hands in frustration. There was no way around it—he had to make a terrible choice, and he had to make it now.

CHAPTER 58

INTO THE RIVER

Upon arriving at the city, Leif, Bilblox, and Kõrgu pushed their way toward the armory. The clearest route was along a stone boardwalk that ran parallel to the river. Along the edge of the boardwalk, a fence made of tightly wound leaves from the Founding Tree protected them from the river, since the current was fierce and the water frothed and swirled in violent surges. The boardwalk was packed with other Jasberians—mothers with their crying children, monks carrying their precious books, soldiers rushing to and fro, and terrified, yelping dogs scurrying underfoot. Smoke hung everywhere, fueling the panic and confusion.

Bilblox, of course, couldn't see any of this. He simply held on to Kõrgu's leash and followed along as best he could. Despite his lack of vision, however, Bilblox sensed the chaos around him and he also sensed that next to him, Leif's pace was becoming slower and more labored.

"Ya gotta take it easy," said Bilblox as they walked along. The noise around them was so loud that Bilblox had to yell to be heard. "Yer gonna kill yerself if ya keep goin' at this pace."

Leif was feeling increasingly weak. It was both dangerous and foolhardy for them to press on in this manner. Nonetheless, he shrugged off Bilblox's suggestions that they rest and instead limped onward.

"We must find Alfonso," gasped Leif. "He may need our help."

"Yer in no condition to help anyone," protested Bilblox.

Leif made no reply.

The two of them continued down the boardwalk until they reached a small harbor filled with several moored boats. Although the boats were already filled with people, others massed nearby in the vain hope of boarding them. The boardwalk continued across the harbor via a narrow wooden bridge that was packed with people fleeing the burning area, all pushing and shoving. About a hundred feet away from the bridge, Leif stopped and described the scene, and concluded that they too would have to cross the bridge.

"That's a bad idea," replied Bilblox. "Give yourself a rest."

"Once we cross that bridge, the armory is only a street away. I can see it," yelled Leif. "My son is there, and I won't stop for a rest!"

Leif pushed forward. Bilblox tightened his grip on Leif's shoulder and then cursed loudly.

"All right, all right!" said Bilblox. "Yer just as stubborn as yer son."

Several minutes later, the two of them were climbing the bridge and trying to scurry across it as quickly as possible. The bridge groaned under the weight of all the people. About halfway across, it belatedly occurred to Leif that the bridge was dangerously overloaded.

Leif glanced down. To his left was the harbor where the boats were moored and where people were gathered. To his right was the river. Leif kept walking as quickly as he could and Bilblox stumbled along behind him. Kõrgu began to whine as if she too were having second thoughts.

"Why is this bridge shakin'?" asked Bilblox.

"Too many people," yelled Leif. "We have to keep going!"

Moments later, Bilblox knew that something had gone horribly wrong when he felt the bridge lurch suddenly to the right. Everyone on the bridge let out a collective scream. Loud cracks could be heard from under their feet. Bilblox almost lost his footing, but at the last minute he grabbed the railing and kept his balance.

"What's wrong?" shouted Bilblox.

"The bridge is tipping into the river," yelled Leif. "It's buckling under the weight of all these people. The whole thing seems like it's going to tip into the river and take us with it unless we—"

Leif was interrupted as the bridge again gave a violent shudder. Another series of cracks echoed below them. Leif yelled something incomprehensible. Bilblox tightened his grip on Leif's shoulder, but it was too late. Leif simply slipped away. Bilblox could hear Leif yelling as he plummeted down. Seconds later he heard a splash. Leif had fallen into the river.

"LEIF!" yelled Bilblox.

He heard only hysterical shouts around him.

"LEIF! Are you all right?" yelled Bilblox.

Kõrgu began to bark frantically.

"Quiet now," commanded Bilblox. "Easy there."

Kõrgu went quiet. Bilblox strained his ears to hear everything he could. The bridge was eerily quiet. At the first warning signs, the Jasberians had begun to flee and now only Bilblox and a few stragglers stood in the middle of the bridge. Yet again, Bilblox felt a rage within his chest as his beefy hands curled together. *If only I could see, I'd know what to do,* he thought.

"Leif, are you there?" yelled Bilblox as loudly as he could.

"I'm okay," came a distant shout. "I'm holding . . . piece . . . wood."

"Can you swim to shore?" yelled Bilblox.

"Forget . . . me!" yelled Leif. "Get off the bridge!" A staccato of small cracking noises started nearby and began to engulf the entire bridge.

"Kõrgu, into the water!" Bilblox ordered. "Get Leif. HURRY!"

The massive wolf whined. Despite her master's command, it was hard to go against her instinct and leave his side. Bilblox knelt down and muzzled Kõrgu's ears. "Go now," he said. "Come on, Kõrgu. Rescue Leif."

Kõrgu barked loudly and jumped into the water. Immediately, she paddled toward Leif. Alfonso's father weakly grabbed Kõrgu's neck and they headed for the shore.

Crack! Crack!

The bridge shuddered. Seconds later, it swayed wildly, pitching Bilblox into the water, away from the relative safety of the harbor and into the raging current of the open river. He surfaced easily and began to tread water, hoping he'd hear a noise—any noise—that would tell him which way to swim.

CHAPTER 59

SLAVES

HILL AND RESUZA EMERGED from the hold of the slave ship and walked down the gangplank with the other prisoners. They had arrived at a settlement somewhere along the desolate shoreline of the Sea of Clouds. Dozens of circular domed tents, known as yurts, filled a rocky clearing. Beyond the clearing lay desolate scrubland. Horses were tied up to gnarled and bent pine trees. The smell of sizzling meat and smoke from domestic fires filled the air. Hill and Resuza ignored all of this. They were captivated by a long convoy sitting along the shoreline, made up of over a hundred sleds. Some contained prisoners, while others were empty. An ominous quiet hung over the settlement.

"What is this place?" asked Resuza as she and the other slaves lined up on the shore. She spoke in her native Uralic tongue and the man standing next to her grunted a terse reply.

"Slave camp," said the man. "This is where we get sold."

"Then what?" asked Resuza. "Where are we going?"

Their exchange was interrupted by the approach of several horsemen galloping toward them. The horsemen were dressed in leather armor covered with feathers, which made an eerily familiar flapping noise as the men approached.

"Oh *no*," whispered Resuza. She sounded like a young girl, and indeed Resuza felt that way, since the horror of her own family's destruction came back to her. The horsemen were Dragoonya.

Hill drew Resuza close to him. His thoughts drifted everywhere but kept returning to Nance, Alfonso, and his brother, whom he so desperately wanted to see again.

They stared blankly at the horsemen. Strangely, leading the group was a boy much smaller than the rest of the Dragoonya. He appeared to be about Alfonso's age and his eyes glowed in the sunlight. They were entirely white.

"That boy looks familiar," whispered Resuza.

Hill nodded.

The Dragoonya horsemen arrived in a flurry of billowing snow and pounding hooves. The boy who was leading them dismounted his horse and approached the group from the barge. Immediately, the slave traders knelt on the ground and bowed their heads. The slaves followed their cue, and all of them, including Hill and Resuza, knelt down and bowed their heads.

"Get up, vermin!" shouted the boy in Uralic.

The slaves and slave traders alike rose to their feet. The trader with the red beard, the one who seemed to be the leader, stepped forward and addressed the boy.

"Honored Master, we bring you one last group of slaves for the convoy," said the trader. "After you are through with them, they will die with little fuss."

"They look half dead," observed the boy.

"Dearest Master, they are in acceptable shape," insisted the red-haired trader. "We caught most of them within the week."

"Put them in the convoy," ordered the boy. "Give them bread and water, enough to sustain them but no more. It's seven days to Dargora and I want them alive when we get there."

"Did he say *Dargora?*" whispered Hill to Resuza.

Resuza nodded somberly.

The slave trader bowed with elaborate deference and then said, "It shall be so, Lord Nartam."

Resuza's knees buckled. Hill held her tight and prevented her from falling.

A short sinewy man with dark black hair, dressed in Dragoonya attire, approached Nartam.

"Konrad, any news of Kiril?" Nartam demanded.

Konrad bowed deeply. "No news, Lord Nartam, but I assure you that he will emerge soon enough. He promised."

"Indeed he did," replied Nartam. He turned and stalked back to his horse, followed by his Dragoonya henchmen. Amid a series of curses and blows, the slave traders began herding their prisoners into the sled cages. Meanwhile, the Dragoonya horsemen galloped away.

The slave traders, on edge from their encounter with the Dragoonya, savagely hit the prisoners as they forced them toward the cages. Some of the prisoners fell to the ground in abject fear. One or two tried to run but were mercilessly cut down.

Resuza and Hill shouldered their way into the middle of the group of prisoners to protect themselves.

"Nartam," whispered Resuza in astonishment. "How? He's just a boy."

Hill nodded. "It's what we feared," he said. "Of all people, Josephus was correct. After Firment gave us the news, he suspected that Nartam had ingested enough ash during his battle with Alfonso in the Founding Tree to become young again. It's incredible. He's now Alfonso's age."

Resuza stared at her adopted uncle. "You *knew!*" she whispered. "You knew all along!"

"Yes," Hill replied sadly. "It was Marcus Firment's greatest secret. The Wanderer said he had discovered Nartam at the head of a vast horde of Dragoonya, somewhere in the vicinity of the Sea of Clouds. Given the mood in Somnos, Firment's revelation would have panicked the entire city. Only Josephus, the Grand Vizier, and I knew. I'm sorry—we couldn't tell anyone. Not even you and Alfonso."

Resuza pursed her lips angrily, but said nothing. "Nartam can't discover us," she finally said.

"I know," replied Hill. "He'd do anything to learn about Jasber and Leif. And Alfonso." He paused. "And the Foreseeing Pen. Give it to me."

Resuza handed it over. "Are you going to use it now?"

"I'm not sure," replied Hill.

They maneuvered to the edge of the group of prisoners so that they were out of sight of the slave traders. Hill palmed the pen to hide it from view and pressed the emerald embedded in the top of the device. They heard a slight click. A second later, an incredibly thin streak of fire shot out of the tip. It struck a medium-size rock, scorched it, and cracked it in several pieces. A nearby prisoner gasped and pointed at the rock, though he was too addled to make the connection between the rock and Hill's actions. Hill quickly clicked the pen, and the flames disappeared.

"What are you doing?" Resuza whispered. "Use the fire to distract them. Burn all the scrubland!"

Hill shook his head and returned to the middle of the crowd of prisoners. They continued to march slowly toward the cages. Resuza looked at him questioningly.

"It's not the right time," he said. "We only have one shot at escaping and we don't know enough about the pen to use it well. We also may learn something about their plans. Why are they so desperate to find Kiril?"

Resuza slowly nodded. "My sister is in Dargora. Maybe we'll find her." They stared at each other and realized they had made their decision. In the future they'd look back on this fateful moment and wonder how things might've been different if they had made another choice.

The prisoners began entering the cages. Resuza and Hill were packed in one cage with a dozen other mute, sullen slaves. Hill dug inside his jacket and took out his Dormian passport, which indicated that he was the foreign minister of Somnos. With a deep breath, he tore up the passport into little pieces and scattered them in the snow beneath the cage. Once the convoy started, the paper would be trampled and destroyed.

That done, he looked at Resuza with a somber but determined expression. "We'll wait for the right time," he told her. "For the moment, though, our identities and the pen must remain hidden—even if it means becoming slaves."

CHAPTER 60

INTO THE FIRE

ALFONSO PARTICLE-CLIMBED toward Marta's family. When he was about twenty feet away, he shouted at them. They shrieked in fear when they saw a young teenager floating above them, surrounded by steam and smoke.

"I am a friend of Marta's," Alfonso yelled out in Dormian. "Let me help you!"

Before they had a chance to say anything, Alfonso swooped down and scooped up Marta's mother, a skinny, gray-haired woman who looked remarkably like her daughter. Alfonso had no time to explain himself further. The fire was already beginning to devour the roof of the townhouse and the heat was becoming unbearable. In his other arm, he grabbed Danyel, Marta's younger brother. They were terrified but luckily did not resist. Alfonso dropped them off next to Marta, and returned for her father and Stoven, her older brother.

Stoven reached up for Alfonso, but it was a different case for Marta's father, a burly, heavyset man. He shook his head when Alfonso tried to grab his hand. Understandably, he wasn't eager to grab hold of the outstretched arms of a skinny teenager who was somehow levitating in the air. Alfonso yelled for the man to grab hold. Flames were everywhere. The heat was now searing. The building was on the verge of collapsing. "Grab my hand!" screamed Alfonso.

"Papa, please!" yelled Stoven.

At last, Marta's father tentatively stretched his arms toward Alfonso, who grabbed them and turned to descend. At that moment, the entire building collapsed in a terrifying conflagration of flame and smoke and dust.

※

Once Marta's family was safe in the square, Alfonso—still in hypnogogia—began particle-climbing up toward the roof of the armory. When he arrived, he saw that all four of the armory's domes had now collapsed. The building's stone walls were still standing because they were flameproof, but the interior of the armory, which was furnished with a great deal of wood, was ablaze. The building's stone exterior was operating like a giant oven, cooking and burning its wooden interior.

It was into this hellish situation that Alfonso descended. He landed on a small support beam of the roof that was still intact, came out of hypnogogia to recharge, and then ran down a set of stone stairs that dropped into the armory itself. Here the air was dry and scorching hot.

As he ran through the top floor of the armory, Alfonso leapt over charred trusses, support beams, and blazing roof panels. He saw dozens of wooden cases that contained the armory's valuables: swords, shields, and helmets. He ignored all this and headed toward a prominent-looking doorway. Its bronze door gaped open and Alfonso sensed there was something special inside.

The doorway opened into a narrow room with high ceilings. The room's wooden walls, though on fire, were not destroyed. Rather, they blazed with a smooth blue flame. The stone floor gleamed like silver and it was hot to the touch, like a cast-iron skillet just taken off the flame. Alfonso could feel the heat softening the rubber soles of his shoes. Oddly, the room was devoid of smoke. Alfonso then saw a white-haired old man, dressed in a scarlet robe, who was kneeling in the middle of the room as if in prayer. Something about the man looked odd.

Alfonso approached and saw to his great horror that a knife was lodged in the man's back. Only the handle and an inch of the blade were visible. Alfonso rushed over to the man's side.

"We've got to get you out!" yelled Alfonso. "The building is about to collapse."

The old man looked up. Blood trickled from his mouth.

"It's too late," he wheezed. "T-Too late for me and too late for Jasber . . . The Gahno . . . He did this . . . He took *everything.*"

"Where did he go?" asked Alfonso.

The man groaned and leaned against Alfonso.

"I have to find him!" yelled Alfonso desperately.

"Too late," said the white-haired man. Tears streamed down

his face. "He took the ether, the ash, and he demanded the Foreseeing Pen, but thank heavens . . ." The man coughed violently. His eyes, which were terribly bloodshot, bulged outward. "Thank heavens we hid it away long, long ago."

He handed Alfonso a small leather envelope that had been hidden inside his robe.

"Take this and run," said the man. "Give it to the first monk you see. He'll know what to do with it."

"What is it?"

Bang! Bang! Bang!

The sound of several explosions echoed through the room. Smoke began to enter from the doorway. Alfonso's feet felt warm and he knew the floor was melting the soles of his shoes.

"It's the last of the green ash," said the man. "I hid it from the Gahno. Now run!" yelled the man. He screamed so violently that spittle flew into Alfonso's face.

Alfonso took the envelope and bolted back through the doorway and into the main room on the top floor. Here the heat was so strong that Alfonso feared that his skin was blistering. There was no way he could survive in the room for longer than a minute or two.

With one hand shielding his eyes, Alfonso spied a relatively unobstructed path across the room to the stone stairway that led back onto the roof. This was his escape route. He ran at full speed, leaping over burning debris as he went.

Alfonso was almost at the stairway when a large burning timber collapsed and fell directly in front of him, forcing him to leap recklessly into the air. He avoided the slab of wood but landed awkwardly on one foot and lost his balance and fell onto the steps. The leather envelope sprang loose from his hand and landed with a thud, causing a puff of green ash to billow out. Alfonso watched in disbelief and only after a few seconds did he think to cover his eyes.

But it was too late.

Green ash landed on Alfonso's face, and some of it dissolved in the moist film of his eyes. His heart rate slowed. His vision faded. His mind tumbled into darkness as he fell heavily onto the steps. In a matter of seconds, Alfonso transformed into a shriveled ninety-year-old man.

Not long after this, a young woman who appeared to be in her early twenties emerged from the smoke and flames. She was moving quickly, agilely, and with a great sense of purpose. The woman had red hair, green eyes, and a freckled face. She knelt down beside Alfonso's old, wizened body and felt his pulse. It was slow but steady. The young woman picked Alfonso up in her arms and, as best she could, ran through the burning debris toward the exit.

When the young woman emerged from the armory—and out into the safety of open air—she set the old man gently onto the ground. Just seconds later, she morphed into the form of a young girl. Several people noticed this phenomenon.

"Behold," cried an onlooker. "She's an ageling. It's Marta the Seer!"

The girl nodded curtly. She glanced down at Alfonso. He was deep in an ash-induced coma. "I'm no longer alone," Marta whispered into his ear. "We are both agelings now."

CHAPTER 61

AN UNLIKELY RESCUER

As THE WILD CURRENT of the river whisked Bilblox downstream, he struggled to keep his head above water. When he wasn't gasping for air, he was calling out in the dire hope that someone, anyone, might rescue him.

"HEY! Hallo!" Bilblox yelled. "HELP!"

No reply. Bilblox began to feel desperate. To make matters worse, he felt a new headache coming on, and somehow he sensed that this one would be the most excruciating one yet.

"Help!" he yelled.

A few seconds later, Bilblox felt a strong, sinewy hand grab under his arm and effortlessly pull him into a boat. Bilblox rubbed the water from his face.

"Thanks, buddy," gasped Bilblox. He instinctively shielded

his white eyes, conscious that whoever this Jasberian was, he or she would see them. "You really saved me!" exclaimed Bilblox.

The person in the boat laughed in a strangely familiar way.

"My good fellow," said the other person in the boat. "What's the matter with your eyes?"

"My eyes?" said Bilblox, cautiously. "Uh . . . er . . . What about them?"

"Oh, nothing in particular," replied the voice. "Just that they are entirely white."

Bilblox said nothing.

"Blind are you?"

"Yes," said Bilblox quietly. His headache was suddenly coming on strong and Bilblox felt as if someone were poking red-hot needles into his brain. Currents of pain radiated down his spine and he lost all feeling in his feet.

"And how would you like to see again?" asked the voice.

"What are ya talkin' about?" asked Bilblox weakly.

"Come now, don't you know who I am?"

Bilblox felt his legs weaken. It wasn't possible. After all that happened, he had been rescued by Kiril.

"No," whispered Bilblox. "NO!"

He lunged at Kiril with full force, his fists swinging wildly at the man they had pursued for so long. Kiril released the oars and wrapped his arms like a vise around Bilblox. They tumbled heavily to the bottom of the rowboat. Despite Bilblox's immense strength, Kiril had him in a hammerlock that was impossible to break.

"I may be about to drown, but so will you," muttered Bilblox.

"Not so," grunted Kiril. "You see, we're about to enter a whirlpool. It will knock us about, but ultimately we'll arrive at the Sea of Clouds. And, after that, I have a little rendezvous planned."

Bilblox struggled against Kiril's iron grip, but it was no use.

"My friend, I just took a pinch of Jasberian ash," remarked Kiril, as if they were sitting on a porch having a casual conversation. "At this point, I'm much, much stronger than you. Just relax. Soon we'll be through the whirlpool. Then, if you behave yourself, I may even offer you a pinch of ash to help ease your pain. You'd like that, wouldn't you?"

Bilblox stopped struggling. Water furiously churned around the boat. As the boat entered the whirlpool, it pitched downward and the stern rose almost perpendicular to the water. Kiril braced himself. As the boat plunged into the spiraling waters, he caught one last glimpse of his birthplace in flames.

EPILOGUE

IT WAS A BEAUTIFUL, sun-streaked morning in the Sea of Clouds. Clink woke up in the master's bedroom—a vast space on the top floor of the lighthouse occupied by a canopy bed, a thick bearskin carpet, and a bay window with a perfect view of the Ferramentum Archipelago. He heard a series of excited shouts and the sound of doors slamming from the floors below. Perhaps Misty had discovered Second-Floor Man's buttermilk and cheddar pancakes, complete with a dollop of wild blueberry preserves. Clink smiled. He climbed down from bed, put on a mink bathrobe twice as wide as he was, and opened the door. It was going to be another perfect day at the lighthouse.

Clink walked down the corridor and became aware of a slight

crick in his neck. He looked down at the vast array of gold and diamond-encrusted pendants hanging around his neck. Eventually, he'd probably have to wear less jewelry, but for the time being, he was determined to wear these baubles everywhere. He had spent his entire life trying to steal finery that was a fraction as valuable as this.

Misty appeared on the staircase, out of breath.

"Now seriously, dear cousin," said Clink jovially. "I know Second-Floor Man is skilled in the culinary arts, but you should pace yourself. There's an endless supply of top-notch food."

"So ya don' stop talkin' even when weighed down with half yer weight in gold?" said Misty with a sigh and a roll of her eyes. "Shut yer trap fer just a second 'n' listen! Colonel Treeknot—she's here! Half dead, a-course, but she's 'ere."

"Colonel Treeknot?" asked Clink. His heart raced. How could she possibly be alive? Clink ran downstairs behind Misty and found Nathalia Treeknot unconscious on the same couch they had laid Josephus on. Her eyes were swollen shut, and her skull shone through in several places, as if clumps of her hair had been yanked out. Her right leg was bent at an angle that meant it was broken in at least two, maybe three, places.

Second-Floor Man was tending to her. At the moment, he was gingerly feeling up and down her leg, trying to determine where the breaks had occurred.

He looked up at Clink and Misty.

"This is a friend of yours, Master Clink?" he asked.

"I'm not sure she's a friend," Clink carefully replied. "But we ought to help her."

Second-Floor Man nodded somberly. "This soldier has been

through terrible ordeals. It will take several months of recuperation, and it is unclear—perhaps unlikely—that she will walk again."

Nathalia moaned softly. Her head turned to the left and right, as if in her dreams she was still warding off attackers.

"How did she get here?" asked Clink.

"Jus' like us," replied Misty. "Somehow she found 'er way outta the Fault Roads and at the island picked up the same kinda rowboat and made 'er way 'ere. Poor thing. The things she musta seen. The boat washed up onshore, overturned, and First-Floor Man found 'er layin' there unconscious, 'er leg crushed by the boat."

"Well of course she will stay here," Clink replied magnanimously. "And when Alfonso, Hill, and the others return, Colonel Treeknot here will be able to provide them information about Kiril's plans. I'm sure she saw something that will help them."

"MASTER! MASTER!! MASTER CLEEENK!"

Third-Floor Lady suddenly began to yell in her loudest, most piercing voice.

"What now?" groaned Clink. The day had begun so beautifully and now there was excitement going on everywhere. Even though he was a pickpocket, he was not fond of excitement.

Clink and Misty rushed upstairs to find Third-Floor Lady in the alcove study, just off the staircase. She was looking through the tower's large spyglass, which could easily spot even tiny objects dozens of miles away.

"Whaddya see?" asked Misty.

"I am just walking by and then I decide to look for one minute only," explained Third-Floor Lady. "Then I point the spot-glass to the islands, the Ferramentum islands, and I see boat. Little boat made strangely."

"My catamaran!" yelled Clink excitedly. "I knew they'd come back! Let me see!"

He ran to the spyglass and peered out, barely daring to breathe. He adjusted the magnification and an object snapped into focus. It was a boat. Unfortunately, it was not the catamaran. The Dormian pickpocket groaned.

"What is it?" Misty demanded. "Is it them?"

"No," replied Clink in a most uncharacteristically sober voice. He stood up and let Misty look. Misty peered into the spyglass and gasped. It was a rowboat on the horizon, heading away from the lighthouse. Bilblox was at the oars, propelling the boat forward in a muscular, steady fashion. Sitting opposite him was Kiril, who was staring at the sun-flecked water and looking quite content.

THE END

Marta's Song: *There's More to Me*

Music and Lyrics by Celia Rose

gift I've been gi-ven could save our tree. I know I should stay here but there's

more out there for me. My spi - rit is wait-ing. It needs to be free.

There's more to me of this I'm sure. There's more to me.

I can do more than fad-ing here while wait-ing here for some one else to

see. There's more to life. There's more to me.

Verse 2

Every year since I was born
I've heard the story of a labyrinth of thorns
They say it protects us from strangers and thieves
But they've caged us in where no one enters and no one leaves
They've caged us in; where no one believes

To listen to the music recording, go to www.celiarosemusic.com.

These Great Sleepers Passed Through the Alexandria Crypt

As translated from the original Aramaic,
Russian, Hebrew, Latin, and Greek

BY FRANK KUJAWINSKI

Matthew Canna—southwest Mesopotamia
Isabel Chobor—Zululand
Ryan Kish—greater Hibernia
George Rusu—Byzantine Empire
Adara Bochanis—Romanian Village (Northeastern
   section)
Logan Miller—Polynesian Protectorate
Lauren Carroll—Gaul
Fiorabella—Roman Empire (North African section)
Alisala—Aztec Empire
Nikolas Gupta—Thebes
Brelan Zittelll—Longest Island (Greenland)
Leif Perplexon—United States of America

ACKNOWLEDGMENTS

We owe enormous debts of gratitude to so many. Let's start with our families . . .

Peter: I'd like to thank Nancy Celia Rose, Jo Kujawinski, Arlene Weinsier, Adele Prince, David, Charla, Lauren, and Brock Weinsier, Steven, Lauren, Ryan, and Gil Weinsier, Dan Kujawinski, Elizabeth Kujawinski-Behn, Mark Behn, and Alex Behn. And to Frank Kujawinski, Roland Francis Kujawinski, Tiana Kujawinski, and Clementine Kujawinski, in the soft breeze of summer, in the bite of winter, in the rain and snow and sleet and in the creak of a sleepless night, you are always with me.

Jake: First, to my two little sons, Sebastian and Lucian Halpern, as my own father once wrote: *You are the lights of my life.* You remind me of all that is good and wondrous in this world. To my wife, Kasia Lipska, I love you and admire the good work that you are doing as a doctor. To Greg Halpern and Witold Lipski, you are the best of brothers. Stephen Halpern, the archetype of a good father, thanks for always, always being there. To my mother, of course, this book is for you. And to Barbara Lipska, your indomitable spirit personified courage in the face of adversity. And, finally, thank you to Elizabeth Stanton, Mirek Gorski, and Paul Zuydhoek for your steadfast love and companionship.

Peter and Jake: The Dormia series owes no greater debt than to Svetlana Katz, our agent and greatest ally, as well as to Tina Bennett and Sally Willcox. Enormous thanks to our editor, Julia Richardson, to Jenn Taber, our publicist, and to Karen Walsh, Linda Magram, and Lisa DiSarro. For their work on the Dormia national anthem, "Marta's Song," and all other Dormian music, special thanks to the following exceptional musicians: Celia Rose, Chris Camilleri, Jessie Reagen Mann, and Jan Farrar-Royce.

Finally, we want to thank a number of people who have contributed to the success of the Dormia series. Thanks to our extraordinary intern Drew Shikoh. Also, over the past two years, we have visited more than two hundred schools and met tens of thousands of students.

Whatever success this book and series has, we truly owe it you: Tynley Baker, Chris Barlow, Heidi Bayreuther, Mary Benoit, Melissa Biehl, Jim Bowman, Cathy Buck, Teresa Carney, John Carrigan, Carol Chittenden, Kelly Conway, Christine Coombs, Linda Cordes, Beth Coyne, Susan Curtis, Jacquelin Devlin, Barb Diblasi, Brian Dillon, Melissa Donnarummo, Susan Dowdell, Eileen R. Doyle, Shannan Egli-Williams, Susan Esposito, Elias Estrada, Karen Everman, Gibson Fay-LeBlanc, Jeanne Fink, Mary Fosher, Diana Gehrt, Gwen Ginnochio, Natasha Goldberg, Nancy W. Goss, Janet Griffard, Jody Hartwig, Darlene Kenny Hayes, Marilyn Hersh, Deborah Hodge, Micki Holmes, Karen Howell, Rick Hribko, Sue Hurwitz, Peg Inserra, Judy Jones, Susan Kashmanian-Smith, Kevin Kay, Emily Kelsey, Meredyth Kezar, Jen Kirk, Marcia Klemp, Colette Klisky, Robyn Lacy, Bill Lataille, Wendy Leseman, Jane Lewis, Jessica Lewis, Robin Lewis, Sandy Lingo, Michael Lizardi, Kim Mach, Susan Mackay, Susan Martin, Mary-Beth Mason, Terry McCabe, Mary Kate Miglianti, Laureen Mody, Marybeth Molloy, Carol Napoli, Marion O'Shaughnessy, Andrea Owens, Susan Peets, Hava Preye, Scott Quasha, Mark Rabinowitz, Denise Rehder, Laura Rigney, Mary Jo Roberts, Kali Rohr, Randi Sawyer, Kalen Schloyer, Marie Schryver, Brian Sedey, Monica Selmont, Brenda Senseman, Drew Sieplinga, Diane Simpson, Becky Solan, Kathryn Spodick, Ron Stancil, Eileeen Sullivan, Sarah Tedesco, Jan Troy, Linn Virtue, Tamara Weinberg, Joan Welsh, Kimberly Yeo, and Virginia Young.